GRAND TOUR of Passion

Meg shivered with fear and pleasure as Piers pulled her closer, molding her thighs to his. He bunched her skirts and his hand slid under them to stroke her soft flesh. No one had ever touched her so—it was wrong, shameless—but so sweet! Flames danced up and down her skin wherever his gentle, exploring fingers glided. Meg moaned and clenched her teeth against the treacherous desires that were weakening her. "Piers, we . . . we have to be sensible."

"Do we?" His white teeth gleamed in the shadows as he smiled down at her, his eyes glazed with passion. "Sensible Meg. Aren't you tired of that role? You've been sensible for too long, my darling Meg. It's time to let me show you another world."

And Meg abandoned herself to this man who was taking her beyond the borders of all propriety . . . the man who had become her guide in a land of love where nothing was forbidden. . . .

Passage to Paradise

Kathleen Fraser

AN ONYX BOOK

NEW AMERICAN LIBRARY

SIGNET, SIGNET CLASSIC, MENTOR, ONYX, PLUME, MERIDIAN
and NAL BOOKS are published by NAL PENGUIN INC.,
1633 Broadway, New York, New York 10019

First Printing, November, 1987

1 2 3 4 5 6 7 8 9

PRINTED IN THE UNITED STATES OF AMERICA

One

Jacques Merlot, captain of the Ogowe River steamer *Brazza*, chewed on the stem of his pipe and gazed with ill-concealed impatience over the heads of the excited crowd on the pier. For ten long years he had been working for the Chargeurs Réunis, the French company that controlled river traffic in this remote corner of Central Africa. After all these years of taking the *Brazza* down the coast from Libreville, up the Ogowe River as far as the mission at Talagouga and back again to the coast, he would have sworn that nothing in Africa could surprise him.

He had grown so used to the soothing monotony of gray sky, yellow sand, and the black line of trees between them that he hardly noticed the scenery anymore, though he always kept an eye open for changes in the line of surf that might signal rocks under the water. And to him, the Mpongwe and Igalwa tribesmen who made up the bulk of his passengers were just another part of the scenery; he no longer noticed the brilliant contrast in colors provided by the bare-chested black men and their wives who were wrapped in lengths of gaudy Manchester trade cotton, with brass anklets gleaming on their legs and strings of red glass beads decorating the fetish bags around their necks. Staring over the crowd of men who pushed their way onto the steamer and squabbled for deck space, he puffed on his pipe and reflected that he'd give all ten years of colorful Africa for ten minutes in a little café he used to know in Montmartre, with a glass of something other than traders' gin to drink and a real white woman to sit on his lap, a woman with curly red hair to catch a man's eye and a bit of a figure to fill his hands, not like the slim fair-haired girl pushing her way through the crowd.

Fair-haired?

A *girl*?

The pipe clattered to the deck, showering shreds of burning tobacco on the passengers who squatted at Captain Jacques's feet, as his jaw slowly unhinged itself.

"*Nom d'un nom d'un nom*," he swore with less creativity than usual. "There's a white woman coming on board!"

"A female? That's debatable." Eight-Fingers Gaston, his mate, eyed the approaching figure more critically. "A missionary, I'd say. Skinny, plain, and twenty-five if she's a day. Psalm-singing all the way upriver, and scolding if a man takes a wee tot of spirit against the fever."

"Yes, but a *female* missionary. When was the last time you talked with a lady? Cheer up, Fingers. There's compensations for psalm-singing. Maybe she'll let you hold her hymnbook." Clapping his mate on the back, Captain Jacques pushed his way through the crowd of African tribesmen who squatted over every clear inch of the deck.

"Clear the way, you black bastards," he shouted amiably, not much caring whether they understood him or not. "Fingers, get below and clean out the passenger cabin! And tell that black poisoner of a cook to get his butt on shore and buy some of the governor's wine. Does he expect us to offer a lady trade gin?" With a kick here and a shove there, he made it to the narrow gangplank in time to lean over and offer a helping hand to the girl who was just uncertainly edging up the plank.

"I . . . oh, please, don't bother . . . that is . . . oh, thank you very much!" Meg Beaumont gasped in some confusion. She had at first instinctively recoiled from the grinning red-faced man who bent over the railing to offer her his hand; then, overbalancing on the narrow plank and catching one heel in the trailing hem of her skirt, she pitched forward into his arms in a most unladylike manner. Firm hands grasped her around the waist and lifted her bodily to the deck, where she stood still clutching her traveling bag and stammering embarrassed thanks.

"It's nothing, madame," said the red-faced man. "Permit me to introduce myself. I am Jacques Merlot, captain of this fine steamship."

Meg glanced around at blistered and peeling paint, the tattered remains of a striped canvas awning that had once covered the afterdeck, and a smokestack patched with riveted-on tin cans. Well, she couldn't complain that she hadn't been warned. The lieutenant governor of this tiny French colony had described the *Brazza* quite accurately while he was trying to dissuade her from continuing her journey to the interior.

"I am happy to meet you, Captain Merlot," she said, clutching her straw traveling bag with both hands. The two days she had spent in Libreville awaiting the arrival of the river steamer had taught her that Frenchmen were likely to kiss one's hand if one gave them half a chance. "My name is Beaumont—Meg Beaumont."

Something heaved under her instep and Meg jumped back with a squeak of surprise. She looked down and discovered that she was surrounded by black, half-naked bodies gleaming with sweat. One of the squatting men grinned at her and pulled his bruised hand out from under her foot, saying something in a soft voice that she couldn't quite catch.

"He is apologizing for having been in the way of your foot," Captain Merlot interpreted. While Meg was still blushing and stammering English apologies which clearly meant nothing to the man she'd stepped on, the captain went on to inform her that the *Brazza* was ready to depart as soon as her husband arrived on board.

"I . . . haven't got one," Meg said. The other thing she'd learned during her two days at Libreville was that absolutely everybody one met wanted to know where Madame's husband was. Not whether she had such an article—that was taken for granted—they simply assumed she had mislaid him temporarily.

Captain Merlot was no exception. "Oh, you are joining your husband upriver, then. He must be the new missionary at Lambarene? I had not realized he was a married man. That explains it. We see very few white women in this country, madame. Allow me to congratulate you on your courage and devotion. Your husband must be a very fortunate man indeed to have a wife who is not only beautiful but also brave."

After this bare-faced lie he made a successful grab for Meg's hand. There was a brief struggle while she clutched her traveling bag even more firmly, determined not to encourage such dubious Continental manners as hand-kissing; in the end Captain Merlot lifted both her hands and the traveling bag, bowed, and brushed his lips and frizzy beard over her tightly clenched fingers.

"I . . . I think I should like to go to my cabin now," Meg said faintly.

Captain Merlot kicked the three nearest deck passengers impartially and they wriggled out of the way, leaving a narrow path down which Meg threaded her way. She couldn't see any more of the deck than the path that opened before her and closed promptly behind her. Every inch of flat surface was covered with the deck passengers and their mats and cooking gear and sacks of food. Perhaps, she thought, that was just as well. If there were any large holes in the deck, she didn't want to know about them just now.

Monsieur Delaine, the lieutenant governor of Gabon, had already informed her that the *Brazza* was the only steamer presently making the run up the Ogowe River. The other steamer maintained by the Chargeurs Réunis, the *Fraternité*, had met with an unfortunate accident involving loose gunpowder and a monkey who had the run of the engine room; Meg's French was not sufficient for her to follow the exact details of the accident, but the conclusion was depressingly clear. The shattered hulk of the *Fraternité* was presently being used as a riverside clubhouse for the local government officials, and her interview with the lieutenant governor had taken place within ten feet of the gaping hole left by the explosion.

"If I might venture to make the suggestion,

Madame Beaumont, you could wait at the mission here in Libreville until the Chargeurs Réunis have sent out a refitted steamer," Monsieur Delaine had suggested. "It would be only a matter of a few months, and in any case there may be some difficulty in navigating the river at this time of year. We are in the dry season, you understand, and the sandbanks present some slight problems."

"The dry season?" Meg looked up at the heavy gray clouds that had been sending a placid drizzle down onto the deck of the *Fraternité* all morning.

"It is," said Monsieur Delaine, "a matter of comparatives. If you wait for the wet season, when the river is full, you will see what I mean."

"Thank you," Meg said, trying not to imagine what the wet season must be like, "but I'm afraid that is not an option. I must get to Lambarene as soon as possible."

Monsieur Delaine shrugged elegantly clad shoulders and ceased to press the point. "With Jacques Merlot in charge, you may go no further than the first sandbank in the Ogowe River. But at least you will be cool while you wait. This is our winter season."

Now, restraining the urge to mop up the trickle of sweat that ran down the back of her corset and soaked through to her white shirtwaist, Meg supposed that coolness also was a matter of comparatives. She had already discarded the close-woven dust cloak which had formed the first part of her tropical traveler's outfit, and she was beginning to think seriously of discarding the corset also as soon as she could find privacy in which to do so.

The long narrow cabin to which Captain Merlot escorted her was private indeed, being windowless, but it was also as stifling and hot as the wooden box which it resembled. Meg found that she lacked energy to unlace her corset, even had she been ready to abandon decorum to that extent. Dropping her straw case with a thump, she collapsed onto her bunk in an ungainly tangle of long limbs and floating strands of fair hair.

"Oh, bother, my hair's coming down again," she muttered. The silky fineness of her long straight hair had been a torment to her all her life, from the nursery days when Aunt Alice's maid had tried in vain to torture it into corkscrew curls. Now the locks of hair escaping from her bun stuck to the back of her neck and added one more niggling annoyance to the general heat and stuffiness.

Wedged between the end of the bunk and the cabin wall was a pile of wooden crates topped with a greenish, cracked mirror. Perched on the bunk, Meg peered into the mirror. It didn't reflect much beyond general outlines, but that was all right with her. All she ever used a mirror for was to see that her hair was straight and her collar smooth; she had long ago given looking hopefully into mirrors in search of some hint of developing beauty. She bit her lip, remembering the painful process of adjusting to reality that had begun when her father came home for good, ten years ago.

In her childhood Meg had scarcely known her father, the famous explorer Sir Digby Beaumont. Her mother had died when she was born and Sir Digby had promptly handed over the infant girl to the care of his only friends, the pair of absent-minded Orientalist scholars whom Meg had learned to call Aunt Alice and Uncle Henry. As he explained in one of his infrequent letters to Meg, a man who had just been entrusted with the leadership of the expedition in search of the lost Inca tombs could hardly be expected to waste his time burping a baby. Besides, Meg's courtesy aunt and uncle already had two sons, and Alice had always wanted a little girl.

Meg had scarcely minded the absence of the father she never knew. Growing up in Aunt Alice's helter-skelter household, playing nursery games with the two boys, and worshipping Harry, the elder, she had a happy childhood. Her only grief was that as she grew older, and her feelings for Harry matured, he still thought of her only as the little girl who trailed him and his brother at their games. When she was twelve he was a boastful schoolboy of fifteen; when she was a lanky schoolgirl of fifteen, he was a young man in the glory of his first year at Oxford, with no attention to spare for little Cousin Meg with her ink-stained fingers and torn stockings. She'd dreamed of the day when she would dazzle him with the glory of her coming-out party and her first grown-up dress, but Sir Digby's return to England had cut all those dreams off before they could mature.

In the summer when Meg was fifteen Sir Digby developed gout and heart trouble simultaneously, forcing his early retirement from the dangerous game of exploring strange jungles. Returning to England, he'd yanked Meg out of Aunt Alice's care to keep him company in the rambling old family mansion, way up in Yorkshire. The first time he caught Meg peering anxiously into a mirror, he'd told her bluntly that she was already as developed as she was ever going to get and that there was no point in making a guy of herself with laces and ribbons and such feminine fripperies. Looking at her wide-set gray eyes, long nose, and firm chin, Meg had regretfully agreed with her father's assessment.

"You'll never be pretty, so you might as well make yourself useful," Sir Digby had told her, and Meg had found little to quarrel with in that statement. Certainly she couldn't have been very useful to Aunt Alice and Uncle Henry, or they wouldn't have let her go like that, without a word of protest, without even writing to Sir Digby to see how she did! From that day forth she had put aside curly ringlets and lace-trimmed dresses in favor of a sensible bun and the plain sensible serge skirts in which she could run from housekeeping to working as her father's secretary whenever he shouted for her. Her only quiet rebellion was her secret dream that one day Harry would realize how much he missed her and would swoop down on Sir Digby's rambling country house to rescue her, like a knight freeing a maiden from a dragon.

But the knight never came, and gradually Meg found her father less of a dragon. She learned to deal calmly with his bouts of ill-temper, understanding that it must be hard for a man who'd been a world explorer to be forced by illness to settle in a remote country house. She learned more from his conversation than she'd ever picked up from the fashionable young ladies' finishing school Aunt Alice had sent her to; for lack of other companionship, she learned to love books, and even dared to dream wistfully of some day attending the new college for women at Girton.

Sir Digby's heart palpitations had developed into a full-fledged heart attack at the mention of this idea. Meg packed that dream, too, away, and concentrated on learning as much as she could from her work as her father's secretary. Transcribing his five-volume reminiscences had given her a copious if unconventional education, with considerably more information on Australian aborigines and Red Indian tribes than she would have acquired at Girton. And in any case, she didn't really need an education, for someday Harry would come for her . . .

By the time Meg truly believed that Harry had forgotten her, it was too late for her to break out of the circumscribed life Sir Digby's illness and his demands had created. Her only satisfaction was in the knowledge that her father needed her, and that everybody agreed she was doing the right thing by sacrificing her life to his needs.

She wondered, now, how her father was getting on with his new wife, the strong-minded Yorkshire woman who'd bullied him out of his heart palpitations and gout and into trading the rambling old family manor for a neat little bungalow by the sea. There had been no place for Meg in the little bungalow; and after ten years of energetically learning to make herself useful in whatever capacity Sir Digby required, it seemed that he had no further use for her. It was an uncommonly lonely feeling, not to be needed. . . .

"Stop that, now," Meg told herself, skewering her straw boater to the top of her bun with a determined stab of her hairpin. "There's no need to feel sorry for yourself, and anyway, it's not true. You *are* needed."

Her free hand stole to the black silk reticule that dangled from the waistband of her skirt, and within minutes she had forgotten Africa and heat and ramshackle boats, transported to another world as she read over the lines scrawled on a much-folded sheet of notepaper. When she'd first seen the letter, in England, it had carried her in fancy to the African jungle, dark and forbidding and mysterious . . . and exciting. Now that the jungle was just outside her cabin door, she read the letter again and imagined herself back in England, in the big shabby upstairs room that had been redefined from nursery to schoolroom to sitting room as Meg and the two boys grew up. She could almost hear the writer's voice; even the sight of his untidy careless scrawl made her feel like a girl again, ready to embark on one of the imaginative adventures that Harry's little brother dreamed up for the three of them to play at.

When Captain Merlot knocked at the cabin door to invite Meg up for dinner, he was pleased to see the lively sparkle in her eyes and the flush of excitement that brightened her pale cheeks. For a missionary, he told Fingers later, she wouldn't be half-bad-looking if one could get her out of those depressing white shirtwaists and black serge skirts, loosen her tight bun and her equally tight laces.

"Better not talk like that," Fingers advised. "She'll pray over you."

Captain Jacques took the warning to heart, and for the rest of the journey down the coast his conversation with Meg Beaumont was sorely constrained as he attempted to steer a perilous course between the natural gallantry of a Frenchman long denied the company of a white woman and the sober manners he supposed Madame Beaumont would expect of a man traveling with a missionary lady. The two English traders who also traveled on the *Brazza* adopted the same manner, and dinner-table conversations were remarkably stiff and formal until the Saturday night after their departure from Libreville.

The *Brazza* was anchored in the muddy shallows of Nazareth Bay, awaiting the tidal rush of water that should float the steamer over the bar and into the winding mangrove-lined channels of the Lower Ogowe. They always had to pause at this point and wait for the high tide; not infrequently the *Brazza* paused right atop a sandbank, tilting out of the water at an ignominious angle until the tide released her. Tonight, bearing in mind the sensibilities of his lady passenger, who might not be used to such small accidents, Captain Jacques had decided to anchor well out in the bay and wait for daylight as well as high water before proceeding. And as the next day was Sunday, Captain Jacques thought he might as well take credit for being an observing Christian. He might even keep the *Brazza* at anchor all day Sunday if it would please the lady; he had no fixed schedule to meet and no particular eagerness to end this journey with a white woman at his table, even if she was a missionary. Cap in hand, he approached Meg where she was leaning over the rail and inquired whether she would care to conduct Sunday services.

Meg had been staring in almost mesmerized fascination at the long monotonous line of the shore, which was broken by a tangle of mangroves where the channels of the Ogowe made their tortuous way out to sea. In the darkness the shore was one line of inky forest silhouetted against the brilliance of the night stars, while moonlight and natural phosphorescence combatted to add their own eerie brightness to the shimmering line of breakers. She was feeling for the first time that smallness which is said to afflict all of us under the stars, but which had never touched her spirit under the kindly familiar skies of England. All around her was this strange and almost terrible beauty, while before her was darkness, mystery—the African rain forest, the miles on miles of winding secret river channels. And at the end of her journey, the mystery that had brought her all this way upon discovering that there was still, in this world, one person who needed her.

From thinking of that one person, her thoughts naturally drifted on to Harry, who had never shown any signs of needing her at all. She had last seen Harry just before he left England for a Foreign Service posting in South America, and the brief, unsatisfactory visit he paid to his parents' house while she was visiting there had been enough to revive all her secret girlhood dreams. Twenty-eight now, and a rising young man in the service, Harry was still the golden god of her childhood.

Meg had been happy for the chance to be of service in getting his tropical kit together for him while he visited Aunt Alice and Uncle Henry, and she had been only a little dashed to find that he hardly noticed her in the midst of his flirtations with all the pretty neighborhood girls. Why shouldn't he take her for granted? She had always been good old dependable Meg, the loyal follower in their childhood games, the quiet little housekeeper for her father. After this trip, though, it would all be different. She would have shown the world that she could do something for herself—that she was truly a useful, worthwhile person. Then, when she came back, Harry would look at her with new eyes. . . .

When Captain Jacques touched Meg on the elbow with an apologetic cough, her daydream had just reached the point where Harry, instead of admiring her initiative or saying how useful she was, was gasping in stunned delight, "Why, Meg . . . Meg, you've grown beautiful! Meg, all these years I've been lacking something, and now I know what it was—you! Will you marry me, Meg?"

"Oh, yes, yes, I will, my darling!" Meg breathed out when Harry's imagined embrace turned into a real hand on her arm.

"Madame?"

Whirling, Meg looked into the puzzled brown eyes of Captain Jacques, illuminated by a beam of light from the open saloon door that fell directly across his face. Harry's vivid blue eyes and yellow curls faded back into dreamland, and she was grateful for the darkness that hid her blushes.

"I beg your pardon, Captain," she said. "I fear I did not quite hear what you were saying."

Captain Jacques repeated his request and Meg blinked in surprise. "Conduct services? Why ever would I want to do such a thing?"

"Most of your colleagues are insistent on Sabbath observations."

"Colleagues?"

Captain Jacques sighed, wondering if the English lady were perhaps a little simpleminded. One knew, of course, that the English were all mad—just look at that fellow in Lambarene, refusing to go home after he burned his factory down and was discharged from his trading firm, when any right-thinking man would have been only too happy to leave! But most of them could at least follow a straightforward conversation.

"At the mission in Lambarene," he explained patiently.

"Oh, is there a mission there? But I don't see what that has to do with me."

Light shone on Captain Jacques's muddled mind. "Madame is not a missionary?"

"Correct."

The captain took a deep breath and felt his stiffly correct posture relaxing into something more closely approximating his human shape. "Then Madame would not object if we were to steam over the bar at high tide tomorrow morning?"

"Madame would be delighted to proceed as soon as possible," Meg told him. "I am urgently needed in Lambarene." A worried frown creased her brow as she spoke. It had been weeks since the much-folded letter in her reticule had been written. Would she be in time? She didn't even know what disaster she was hurrying to avert—only that there was something terribly wrong in Lambarene.

Captain Jacques's brow furrowed. "But if your husband is not there yet, would it not be better to wait for him?"

Meg wondered briefly if the captain had been

dropped on his head as a child. One knew, of course, that all Frenchmen were mad—look at the queer stuff they ate, snails and garlic and all sorts of unwholesome things! But most of the French government officials in Libreville had at least been able to follow a simple conversation.

"I am not trying to meet my husband," Meg said slowly and clearly. "I am traveling alone."

Captain Jacques gave her a roguish smile and winked one eye slowly. "Ah, madame, now I understand. It is an affair of the heart. And the jealous husband—perhaps he follows? Never fear, madame. Captain Jacques will have you in Lambarene as quickly as steam and engines can get you there. And there is no other steamer serving the Ogowe River now, so Madame need not fear immediate pursuit."

Meg ground her teeth together in the way that had always caused Aunt Alice to shriek about wearing off the enamel. "It is *not* an affair of the heart. I am *not* meeting a lover."

The captain's repeated smiles and winks belied his token agreement. "Of course not. There are, after all, so many other pressing concerns that could draw a young English lady to this remote spot."

Somewhat belatedly Meg realized that she was going to have to come up with some sort of story to cover her insistence on getting to Lambarene. It wouldn't do to tell Captain Jacques the truth—not until she'd reached her destination and found out what was really going on. He seemed like a nice man, for a Frenchman, but she didn't have the right to trust anybody else with her suspicions.

Should she go along with his assumption that she was going to Lambarene to meet a husband or a lover? No, it would raise too many complications when they arrived at the town and no such person appeared. "As a matter of fact," she said loftily, "I'm going to . . . to . . ." A page from Volume Three of her father's reminiscences flashed before her eyes, all neatly copied out in her own smooth handwriting. "To investigate the primitive religious beliefs of the aboriginal tribes." The phrase had been used of some South American Indians with a nasty habit of poisoning their blowgun darts, but it might just as well apply to the friendly, peaceful black natives who were sleeping on the deck all around them.

Captain Jacques's grizzled eyebrows vanished under the peak of his blue wool hat. "To do *what*?"

"I'm going to study the natives," Meg said.

The captain waved one hand over the deck, covered as it was with sleeping bodies.

"What's wrong with these natives? Why must you go to Lambarene? Plenty of natives around Libreville, on the coast."

Meg could feel her brain working at top speed as she mentally flipped through page after page of Sir Digby Beaumont's reminiscences. What had been her father's excuse for the years he spent in remote and dangerous places?

"They have been spoiled by civilization. I want to go into the interior, to study the customs of the remote tribes untouched by European ways."

"The interior! Madame, that is no place for a white woman. Why, those murderous savages will smoke you over a cooking fire for a nice tasty addition to their larder. No, madame. You had much better stay on the nice quiet steamship. You can have a little cruise all the way up the river to Talagouga and then I'll take you back to Libreville, all safe and sound. Won't that be nice?" The captain gave Meg's hand a series of little reassuring pats that gradually lengthened until he was stroking halfway up her arm.

"I'm sorry, Captain Jacques." Meg leaned over the rail and waved one hand toward the shore, more to remove her hand from the captain's than to point out anything in the inky blackness of the forest before them. "I am dedicated to my research. And," she added, seeing a wonderful excuse for her next move opening up before her, "I mean to hire a guide. So you need have no concern about my safety. Now, if you will excuse me, I should like to retire to my cabin."

As she made her way across the deck to the short ladder, lifting her skirt and stepping over and between sleeping men, she heard the captain muttering to himself in French. From the first step of the ladder she turned and looked back. Captain Jacques was a dark, squat shape silhouetted against the purple sky, illuminated by the glow that came and went from his pipe bowl as he sucked furiously on the stem. "Guide!" he muttered. "*Nom d'un nom d'un nom*! What kind of guide will protect her from the cannibal Fans?"

Two

Once the delusion that she was a missionary had been gotten out of the way, Meg found that Captain Jacques, his mate Eight-Fingers Gaston, and the two English traders who were returning from leave all treated her with much less reserve. No longer afraid to take a drink or let a swear word escape in front of her, they invited her into the "lounge," consisting of an awning-shaded portion of deck with a few mildewed cushions for chairs, and passed the days of the *Brazza*'s upriver journey in competing to tell her stories about their lives in the bush. Meg listened with fascination tinged with foreboding, at the same time eagerly watching the panorama of the jungle unfolding before her.

They had steamed through Nazareth Bay at dawn on Sunday, a slow and anxious process marked by Captain Jacques's curses and the shouted reports of men standing at both sides of the boat taking soundings with long bamboo poles. With the exception of Captain Jacques and Gaston, the crew were all blacks—Kru-boys, the captain told her, recruited from Sierra Leone. They worked through the hottest weather for a pittance of the pay a white man would have required, met the captain's curses and insults with cheerful incomprehension, and taught Meg their own peculiar brand of Pidgin English as they shouted comments back and forth across the boat.

Once the anxious navigation of sandbars and mangrove roots was past, the river opened up into a smoothly rushing sheet of brown water walled in on either side with a forest of palm trees of various sorts. Meg thought her neck would break as she swiveled her head from side to side, trying to take in all the grandeur of the rain forest at once. The flashes of brilliant color against many shades of green—were they flowers or birds? Just as she decided that one particularly elegant arrangement of red flaring shapes must be a kind of climbing lily, the lily squawked and flew off to a higher tree, where it sat making ruffled noises at the steamer which had dared to disturb its peace. A little further up, there were white birds skimming low over the bronze surface of the river, and above them, swinging from the branch of a tree—yes, that was really a monkey!

"Now I *know* I'm in Africa," Meg said with deep satisfaction. She allowed the two English traders to persuade her to sit down on the afterdeck then, where she could watch the river rushing by in more comfort. Slowly she began to make out details among the confusing tangle of twisting water channels, massed stands of papyrus reeds, and the dark cliffs of the forest that walled them in on either side. Many of the highest trees were decorated with clusters of pinkish-brown young shoots, and others were covered with climbing vines bearing clusters of bright crimson berries or white and yellow flowers.

Curled up on a cushion under the protective shade of the tattered awning, Meg watched in delight while her companions endeavored to teach her the difference between coconut and oil palms, okume and mahogany and all the other trees of the rain forest. The traders' interest in botany not being of the greatest, the conversation soon rambled into topics of more immediate and personal interest, such as the night poor Grayson got drunk and tumbled into the water butt, the time Grayson lived on native chop for a week just to prove it could be done, the time . . .

"What's 'native chop'?" Meg asked, breaking into the rambling stream of reminiscences.

Mr. Cavanaugh, the gray-bearded trader who had the fund of 'Grayson' stories, paused to set his thoughts in order. "Manioc, ma'am. The staple food of all Africa."

"Cassava," put in the other trader, a slim pale-faced youth named Walters, whose hacking cough did not augur well for his chances of surviving another two years' tour of duty in the jungle.

"The natives call it fou-fou," added Eight-Fingers Gaston from his station beside the wheel, where he controlled the steering of the boat with one hand and gulped down glass after glass of trade gin with the other.

"The natives," said Cavanaugh, "call it agouma, m'vada, kank, fou-fou, and what you will. If a native offers you anything to eat, ma'am, don't bother to ask what he calls it. It'll be a grayish-white dough with the texture of library paste and the flavor of sour vinegar—*if* you're lucky—and it's the staff of life to them. I've known boys to run and lay a complaint with the French lieutenant governor because the poor devil of a trader who hired 'em has only plantains to feed 'em and they want their ration of cassava."

"Yes, and the lieutenant governor always rules against the trader," muttered young Walters. "Damned Frenchies! Excluding you, of course, Fingers. They don't want us English trading in their colony, and that's a fact. And what can we do about it, but smile and put up with whatever idiotic regulations they impose?"

"Grayson did something once," said Cavanaugh with a sly smile. He went on to recount a long, fantastic, and slightly obscene tale involving the trader Grayson, the French lieutenant governor, and a pig with digestive difficulties that had somehow been introduced into the lieutenant governor's immaculate house as material evidence in a court case between Grayson and the French trader François Chaillot.

"I am looking forward to meeting Mr. Grayson," Meg said at the end of the story. "He sounds like a very inventive man."

Cavanaugh gave an embarrassed cough and looked away. " 'Fraid that won't be possible, ma'am. He's dead now—fever."

"So's the old lieutenant governor," added Walters. "Fever. *He* went out the same year as my partner—but it was his own fault—he *would* sleep out on his veranda for the cool air. Night river air will kill a man sure as shooting, every time."

Cavanaugh nodded agreement. "If it's not the night air, the moonlight drives 'em crazy. Remember Volper—the fat Dutchman that went round the bend, holed up in his factory and held off the clerks with a shotgun loaded with old scrap iron, claiming they wanted to eat him?"

Walters shrugged. "Maybe they did. Volper

never did feed his people enough. You have to give 'em some fish along with the cassava, otherwise they get the protein craving. No, Volper was sane enough, just a little excitable."

"He's dead now, of course," said Cavanaugh to Meg.

"Fever?" she hazarded.

"Would have died of the fever, but the crocodiles got him first. See, he was so afraid of being eaten, he wouldn't come down from the top story of his factory. Crouched out on the veranda overhanging the river. Big fat man like that—the bamboo poles that held up the balcony couldn't support his weight, whole thing collapsed and down he went, right into the jaws of that old man-eater that used to prowl up around Talagouga. He got eaten, all right!" Cavanaugh's sharp crack of laughter made Meg jump. "But the brain fever already had ahold of him. There's not many white men last long out here, you see, ma'am. Walters and me, we're lucky ones, and that's because we eat right and live sensible. Glass of trade gin three times a day to burn off the mist fevers, sleep indoors, and never eat native chop. That's the way to do it."

Cavanaugh unfolded his long legs with a sigh of contentment and held his glass up to Fingers for another dash of the colorless spirit that all the men were drinking. "And," he added thoughtfully, "take your leave every couple of years. Stay too long on the river, a fellow can go bush-crazy even if the moonlight doesn't get him. Look at poor Damery."

"He that burned down his own factory?" Walters said with interest. "Is he still alive?"

Cavanaugh shrugged. "When I left three months

ago, he was doing his damnedest to drink himself to death. It's anybody's odds whether he's succeeded yet. I suppose we'll hear when we reach Lambarene. Maybe the poor devil's ready to go back to England by now. Hatton and Cookson fired him, of course, after that scandal with the black girls, and the factory burning was the last straw. He'd better go back. It's not good for a man to be out here with nothing to do."

"I don't think he can go back," said Walters. "Isn't he some sort of remittance man? Shipped out here in disgrace, family doesn't want him back, all that sort of thing?"

Cavanaugh gave another shrug and tossed off the last drops of his trade gin. "Then I suppose he'll die here, if he's not dead already. If the fever don't get him, the drink will." He frowned into his empty glass. "Bad show, though, don't you think? Englishman going downhill like that. Letting down the side, what? That's one chap you don't want to meet, Mrs. Beaumont, even if he is still alive. But you'll like the rest of the fellows. We'll have to have a dinner party to introduce you all round. Break out the good tinned food. D'you care for tinned pâté, Mrs. Beaumont? . . . Mrs. Beaumont?"

He looked around and discovered that Meg had slipped away to her cabin while he and Walters were discussing the sad case of Piers Damery. Cavanaugh hoped uneasily that he hadn't offended her. Young Damery's reputation was not really the sort of thing one ought to mention before a lady, but Mrs. Beaumont was such a good sport and so interested in his stories that he'd begun forgetting that she was an English lady. When they docked at Lambarene he'd invite her to a proper dinner party at his factory and try to show her that the bush traders weren't all a bunch of rough uncivilized rascals, the way the missionaries made them out to be.

On the morning when the *Brazza* steamed into Lambarene Meg was hanging over the rail as usual, imperiling herself and her insecurely anchored straw hat as she tried to take in every detail of the scene at once. To tell the truth, there was not that much to take in. On a hill above the river she could make out the outlines of three large square buildings, each surrounded by a fence some six to eight feet high. Between those buildings and the sandy bank where passengers were disembarking stood a handful of flimsy-looking huts with bark walls and bamboo posts. The red soil around the huts had been casually scratched up to support a straggling assortment of plants, and women in the ubiquitous bright-colored cotton wraps were carrying water from the river to the gardens in great clay jugs. Here, Meg noticed, they wore the wraps tied around the waist, instead of modestly hitched under their arms as the more citified women of Libreville had done.

And that was all there was. Meg could have laughed at her own stupidity in expecting some sort of a town. But where was she to stay? Her father would probably have marched into one of the native huts and taken it over in lordly style for his lodging; Meg knew she could not perform such an action with Sir Digby's assurance.

"Oh, never mind about that, ma'am," said Mr. Cavanaugh when Meg voiced her concern to him. "The Mission Évangélique, up at Kangwe, will put you up. That is . . . you aren't meeting your husband here?"

Meg shook her head. She had all but given up on explaining that she wasn't married; if it made people more comfortable to think that she was the sort of careless woman who would acquire a husband only to mislay him somewhere in the interior of Africa, that was their problem and not hers. Besides, until she had unraveled the mystery that had brought her to Lambarene, she felt it would be better to avoid all explanations entirely.

Avoiding Mr. Cavanaugh's eyes, she pretended deep interest in the dual stream of native passengers jostling up and down the gangplank. One European man stood out in the crowd, his white suit like a pale beacon amidst the Africans' glossy dark skins and color-splashed cotton wraps. Mr. Cavanaugh had mentioned an unemployed Englishman who lived in Lambarene; could this be the man? Meg leaned out over the rail, trying to catch a glimpse of his face as he mounted the gangplank. To her chagrin, he was looking down and minding his steps very carefully; all she could see was that he was dark-haired.

"Mr. Cavanaugh. That's not the man you mentioned to me, is it? The Englishman?" The stranger passed out of sight while Meg was still trying to indicate him without pointing rudely.

"Why?"

Meg wasn't quite ready to mention her plan of hiring the Englishman as a guide into the interior. Something told her Mr. Cavanaugh would disapprove. "Oh, no particular reason," she lied. "Only, I need to find—"

"A bath, a bed, a decent meal instead of the

unmentionable and unrecognizable substances served up by Captain Jacques?" said a voice that was certainly not English. She turned to see the dark-haired man she had watched smoothly insinuate himself between herself and Mr. Cavanaugh. He took her hand without waiting for an introduction.

"Oh, you're French," Meg exclaimed without thinking. "I'm so glad."

"I have always felicitated myself on the circumstance, though I fail to see why you should do the same."

Meg blushed. When would she learn to think before she spoke? "Oh. Well. It's just that . . . well, I need . . . It's complicated," she floundered unhappily.

"No matter. A beautiful young lady is not required to make sensible conversation; it is enough that you honor us with your presence. And no one could be coherent after a journey upriver on the *Brazza.*"

She had to look up to meet his eyes; that in itself was a new experience for Meg. So was the look she encountered there—at once warm and respectful, admiring and friendly. They were very dark eyes, flecked with amber specks the exact color of the bronze sheet of water flowing past the boat. His hair, too, was dark, and plastered close to his head as though he were in the habit of splashing it with water to restrain the unruly curls that were already breaking free again over a high forehead. And he was smiling at her as though they were old acquaintances.

Without knowing exactly why, she returned the smile. "You're a very perceptive man, sir."

"Not at all. I have myself suffered the miseries

of travel upon this mud scow, and understand precisely the degree of desire for a return to civilization which you must be feeling. But allow me to introduce myself." He lifted her hand to his lips briefly. She discovered that it was not necessarily unpleasant to have one's hand kissed by a Frenchman. "François Chaillot, local representative of Chaillot Père et Fils, the only French trading company in this outpost of French civilization. I trust you will not allow our national differences to interfere with our further acquaintance, Mademoiselle . . ."

"Beaumont," said Meg without thinking. "Meg Beaumont."

"*Meg*?" François Chaillot's dark brows drew together in a momentary frown of displeasure. "An awkward English name. How can a woman be beautiful, sensual, tempting—in short, how can she be a woman at all, with a name like Meg? I shall call you Marguerite," he announced, as if that settled the matter, "and you shall lunch at my factory on top of the hill there. You too, Cavanaugh, Walters. In my great generosity I allow you to partake of the joys of civilized conversation with this lovely woman."

Mr. Cavanaugh, who had been somewhat pushed into the background by François Chaillot's self-assured entry onto the scene, cleared his throat and pulled at his short gray beard. "Could hardly do otherwise, Chaillot," he said. "Would hardly be proper for Mrs. Beaumont to visit you without a chaperon."

The quick frown came and went on François Chaillot's darkly handsome face once again, fleeting as the ominous ripple of water over a concealed snag in the river. "Ah, yes. English manners—I had forgotten. But you are sadly unobservant, my friend. Mademoiselle wears no wedding ring. Only an Englishman," he said with a smile that almost removed the sting from his words, "could spend all this time on a tiny boat with a beautiful woman and fail to observe her hands."

Somewhat belatedly, Meg realized that François was still holding her hand. She flushed deeply and pulled back at the same instant when he released her fingers, only to cup one hand under her elbow and urge her toward the gangplank. Her murmured protests that she really ought to go up to—what was the place called, Kangwe?—and see about lodging for the night were brushed aside with the imperious statement that it was far too late for her to make the additional journey to the Mission Évangélique that afternoon.

"You will lodge with me tonight," he told her, "and tomorrow, when you have rested from the fatigues of your journey, we will discuss how I may best be of service to you hereafter. No, no"—he waved one hand to stop her incipient protest—" I insist. My honor as a French gentleman, the honor of France, demands no less courtesy toward a woman visiting our colony for the first time—and a young and lovely woman besides!"

Since she knew that was not true, Meg did not worry particularly about the danger that François Chaillot would try to flirt with her. He was just being polite—excessively polite—in a way that made it very difficult for her to refuse to go along with his plans.

Half an hour later, clean, refreshed from her tepid sponge bath, and wearing a fresh skirt and shirtwaist only slightly creased from the traveling bag, Meg joined François and the English traders on the spacious veranda that overhung the first story of Chaillot Père et Fils's place of business. If her first sight of Lambarene had disappointed her, her view of the comfortable way of life enjoyed by François Chaillot was rapidly reassuring her.

The walled compound had proved to contain three buildings, two small one-story sheds that were used for storage and this two-story house with bamboo walls and thatched roof. The bottom floor was set up as a shop, with barrels of nails, stacks of brass rods, and strings of glass beads gleaming in the shadows behind the counter, while lengths of gaily patterned cloth hung from rods overhead and swayed back and forth in the breeze. The second story, however, was almost palatial in its space and airiness, if somewhat empty. The room where Meg had washed herself and changed her clothes was furnished only with a pair of carved wooden stools and an enormous bed standing in the center of the floor and swathed with billowing white netting.

The sensuous look of that bed, and the knowledge (whispered to her, as a warning, by Cavanaugh on their march up the hill) that François Chaillot was unmarried, had given Meg some doubts about the propriety of accepting his hospitality; but she was reassured by the procession of African house servants who trooped in and out to carry water, bring up her bag, turn down the bed, and peep at the white woman. It wasn't, she thought defiantly, as if they would be literally *alone* in the house.

Besides, this was Africa, and one couldn't be expected to behave exactly as one would in London. Besides, she would feel uncommonly silly, refusing Monsieur Chaillot's kind offer of hospitality, just as though she thought herself the sort of beauty who would really tempt a man into ungentlemanly behavior! How he would laugh at her, to think she had taken his automatic French flattery seriously! No, he was very kind to offer her a place to stay for the night, and she would certainly not insult him by insisting on going on up the river to Kangwe.

Besides, whispered a voice inside her head, François Chaillot was the first gentleman she'd met in Africa who not only understood that she was unmarried but also seemed to consider her spinster state nothing out of the ordinary. Meg had begun to feel like a freak of nature; what was the harm in relaxing, if only for one afternoon and evening, in the company of somebody who made her feel like an acceptable human being again?

"What a lovely factory you have here, Monsieur Chaillot," she said when she joined the gentlemen on the wide veranda. She had learned from the traders' conversation on the way up the river that "factory," in Africa, meant not a manufacturing center full of machinery but a store full of cloth and copper, and she felt rather proud of herself for using the local language so casually and naturally.

" 'François,' I beg of you . . . *Marguerite*," murmured Monsieur Chaillot, managing somehow to bow, kiss her hand, and look up at her with those disturbing dark eyes all at once. Young Walters, who had jumped up to offer Meg his chair, was left standing in an awkward position while

François snapped his fingers and a servant scurried out with a light bamboo chaise on his head.

"You will find this more comfortable," said François, leading Meg to the chaise and seating himself at the foot of the bamboo seat, where he could continue to gaze into her eyes. "Allow me to offer you something to refresh you after the exertions of the journey." He snapped his fingers again; a black man dressed in dazzlingly white shirt and short trousers appeared and offered Meg a tray on which stood a glass of bright pink liquid. "My own compound of native fruit juices," François explained. "I think you will find it refreshingly different."

Walters sat down again, irritably scraping the legs of his chair across the matting which covered the veranda floor.

Meg tasted the strange drink and found it different indeed—sweet, tangy, with something that cooled her mouth at first and then made her feel warm at the back of her throat, so that she wanted another swallow and then another. Sipping the sweet drink gratefully, she found the steady pressure of François Chaillot's dark eyes unnerving, and so she looked out over the veranda railing instead of facing her host.

After a few seconds there was no need to pretend interest in the scene before her. On one side of the compound the forest rose up, dark with a hundred shades of dusky green and bright with as many varieties of strange new flowers. Near the ground she could just see shadowy, mysterious paths that wound in among the great trees.

To the other side she could look over the tops of the trees, as the ground fell away slightly. A rolling sea of green, immeasurable miles of unbroken forest, was bounded finally by the jagged edges of a mountain range set sharp and clear against the soft gray of the sky. The mountains were like a promise of something wonderful and exciting, the way life was supposed to be, a strong forceful line cutting across the monotonous gray clouds. Meg sipped her drink, hardly noticing the strange medley of tastes anymore, and longed for those mountains more intensely than she had ever wanted anything in her life.

More than she wanted Harry?

She felt as though the soft gray clouds were slowly soaking into her brain, making the inside of her head all woolly and confused. That was different . . . wasn't it? Harry was an unattainable dream. But the mountains could be reached.

Meg set her glass down on the table of split cane and watched in some surprise as the light table rocked back and forth. She had put the glass down harder than she meant to. Something seemed to be interfering with her judgment of distance; the mountains seemed closer, and the table farther away, than they actually were.

My goodness, she thought with a kind of pleased astonishment, I do believe I must be tipsy. Meg never drank alcohol, this being one of the habits—along with smoking, higher education, and riding bicycles—of which Sir Digby disapproved for women in his household. Consequently, she had had no means of recognizing the strange burning aftertaste of the drink François had given her. Now she wondered if that was what trade gin tasted like.

"François," she said aloud, "you're a very naughty man, giving a lady an alcoholic drink."

"Would you like another?" said François, calmly rescuing the rocking glass from the tilting tabletop.

"Yes," said Meg, surprising herself, "I believe I would." If this was what alcohol did to the system, she was all for it. She felt relaxed and calm and confident, all the things she had always wanted to be.

Even beautiful.

She returned François's smile and nodded occasionally while he continued a light conventional chatter, trying to ignore Mr. Cavanaugh's discouraging frown. What was there to frown about? Everything was wonderful. She'd only just arrived in Lambarene, and already she'd found a place to stay and this nice Frenchman who would help her with the next step of her project.

After Cavanaugh's and Walters' disparaging comments, Meg knew that she ought to wait until their departure before raising the subject of hiring a guide, but she was too impatient. They had already been sitting out on this veranda for what seemed like hours, and still there was no mention of the lunch François had promised, and she couldn't hope that they would go away until some time after lunch, and then François might have to go back to work or something. Besides, she wanted to get on with her project now, while she still felt able to conquer the world.

"François," she asked, interrupting his comments on the resemblance of the gray clouds to the soft gray eyes of a beautiful woman, "do you know a man called Piers Damery?"

François's dark eyes widened and he sat erect, carefully putting down his own glass on the straw matting that covered the veranda floor. Meg noticed that the liquid within the glass shook slightly as he put it down, and she was pleased to know she wasn't the only one whose sense of balance was affected by the drink. "Everyone in Lambarene knows Damery," he said, looking down at the trembling glass.

"Damned rascal," said Walters. "You wouldn't want to meet *him*, Mrs. Beaumont."

Cavanaugh cleared his throat. "Young fool, at any rate. But . . . not a fit topic of conversation before ladies? Apologize for bringing it up before, Mrs. Beaumont . . . beg you'll forgive me."

Meg favored all three men impartially with a brilliant smile. "I beg to disagree. You see, I require someone to guide me into the interior, and I think that Mr. Damery would serve my purposes quite well."

"Nonsense!" Cavanaugh exploded.

"Ridiculous!" said Walters at the same time. His thin, pale face was flushed red along the cheekbones, and he sat forward so suddenly that the bamboo legs of his chair gave a protesting squeak. "Mrs. Beaumont, you don't know what you're talking about. The man's an absolute rotter. If you *must* continue on into the interior, please let one of us—"

"But, gentlemen," said Meg reasonably, "you all have your duties to discharge here. You, Mr. Cavanaugh, and you, Mr. Walters, have already been absent from your factory for several months, and you told me on the way upriver how concerned you were that the natives you left in charge would have muddled your accounts. You could hardly justify another absence to your employers. As for Monsieur Chaillot, he has his own business to tend to. Now, I am sure there are any number of black gentlemen about who would be willing to guide me, but as I do not yet speak Mpongwe or Igalwa with any degree of fluency, I fear we might encounter some communication problems were I to set off alone with them."

"Unthinkable! Can't let a lady go off into the bush with a party of damned blacks." Cavanaugh tugged so fiercely at his short beard that Meg feared the gray bristles would come off in his hand.

"Thank you, Mr. Cavanaugh. I knew you'd agree with me." Meg smiled again at all three men. "You see that Mr. Damery, being at present unemployed, is the logical solution to my problem. Perhaps, after lunch, one of you would be so kind as to escort me to Mr. Damery's residence."

Walters was the first to reply to this reasonable request. "No, ma'am," he muttered, shaking his head. "You don't understand, Mrs. Beaumont . . . not the thing at all . . . can't introduce a lady to Damery."

"Perhaps I don't understand," said Meg, smiling again. Her lips were beginning to feel numb; perhaps, she thought, she had better not drink any more of this stuff François mixed. "Just what is Mr. Damery supposed to have done that is so terrible?"

Walters drew a deep breath. "To begin with," he said, "he's a remittance man. Don't know what he got up to in England, but I understand his family begged Hatton and Cookson to give him a job out here, just to keep him from making any more scandals at home. He had the factory upriver from here, at Talagouga, but apparently he misused the blacks something awful, until they revolted and burned the place down. Must've treated them like bloody slaves, begging your pardon, ma'am, for they never did anything like that, even to poor mad Volper the Dutchman."

"And afterward," said Cavanaugh, scowling fiercely at Meg, "there were certain accusations made against him. A matter of the native women being abused, some of 'em hardly more than children—forgive me if I don't say any more; but you *must* understand, ma'am, why you mustn't have anything to do with the fellow? No decent lady would."

"I thought you told me," said Meg, "that the colonial officials always took an African's word in any case against an Englishman's?"

Cavanaugh reddened and cast an agonized glance at his compatriot. "There may be some truth to that, ma'am," he admitted, "but why would any woman bring such stories, destroying her own reputation, unless they were true?"

"I don't know," said Meg thoughtfully, "but I'd like to talk to the women who brought the accusations."

"Can't do that," said Cavanaugh, wiping his brow with distant signs of relief. "They've all gone back to the bush by now. Can't blame 'em either—being forced into concubinage for young Damery's pleasure must not have given 'em much of a taste for English civilization."

François coughed apologetically. "I must confess, my friend, that there is something in what you say about our local government officials having a bias against the English. I don't, myself, feel that these stories about poor Damery were ever properly investigated. There might have been extenuating circumstances—"

"What about the girl he lashed with a rhinoceros-hide whip?" Walters interrupted. "Dammit, man, you saw the scars—we all did!"

François shrugged. "That poor mad creature? It may not have been an affair of passion—though, I admit, she was once quite lovely, before the beating. But perhaps he caught her stealing."

Meg was beginning to feel sick and dizzy, either from the stories or from her second glass of fruit juice and trade gin. Apparently no one questioned that Piers Damery had savagely mutilated a young girl—they were simply arguing about his reasons for doing so, as if that made any difference!

"In any case," François finished, spreading his hands, "I fear there is no question of your employing Piers Damery as a guide, my lovely Marguerite."

In her befuddled state it took Meg a moment to realize that he was addressing her. Her first impulse had been to look behind her for the beautiful woman who had inspired the warm look in François's eyes.

"Why not?" she asked bluntly. "You don't believe the stories about him."

François raised a protesting hand. "Not all the details of all the stories," he said softly, "but there is very often a grain of truth in such matters, much as it pains me to suppose such a thing about my dear friend Piers. However, the details of the past are not at issue here. What matters, Marguerite, is the present condition of the man—and Piers Damery," he said regretfully, "is a hopeless drunkard." He sighed. "I have tried to persuade him to go home. Surely his family would not refuse to take him in? I truly believe his only chance of recovery is a speedy return to England."

"It it that bad?" Meg asked.

"He is addicted to the bottle, suffers from hallucinations, and has not the strength to guide anyone ten steps into the interior—nor would I trust him, in his present state, to distinguish a dark jungle path from the gaping maw of a crocodile. The poor fellow mixes his dreams with his reality in a most disturbing way. I am afraid that his stay alone in that upriver factory began to unhinge his sanity, and the violent events of that night may have completed the work."

"Oh," said Meg rather faintly. "Oh, dear. I do see what you mean." This unexpected and unwelcome information certainly upset her brilliantly conceived plan to use Piers Damery as a guide.

Over the civilized lunch which François's cook had contrived from tinned foods and locally grown vegetables, Meg was careful to drink nothing but water and to talk nothing but trivialities. She needed time to rethink her plans, but François's dark eyes and his ceaseless flow of lightly flirtatious conversation gave her no chance to do so. Perhaps she should rest this afternoon—rest and think. After the months it had taken for the letter to reach her and for her to get to this remote spot, what would one day's delay matter?

It was a chance remark by Mr. Cavanaugh, as he took his leave after the meal, that decided her.

"I'm certainly glad you have given up this foolish project of scouting the interior, Mrs. Beaumont," he said, shaking hands with her like an English gentleman who disdained French fripperies and hand-kissing. "What was it—to study the natives or some such nonsense? You can find plenty of natives right here in Lambarene, and perhaps on Sunday Walters and I can take you for a little cruise on the river."

His casual assumption that she would give up her plans just because he disapproved set Meg's teeth on edge. Of course, Cavanaugh didn't know exactly what those plans were. How could he? She didn't know herself; she was moving one step at a time, blindly trusting that all that was needed here was courage and common sense. And the more she found out, the less likely that seemed. Still, she wasn't about to give up so easily. Rest this afternoon? Nonsense! By tomorrow morning François and the English traders would have come up with some plan to keep the silly English girl amused and out of trouble, something she couldn't refuse without giving offense—and then another day would pass, and another, and Lord knew when she would begin the task for which she had come to Africa.

"Given it up?" She smiled prettily at Mr. Cavanaugh. "Oh, no, indeed, I've done no such thing. I intend to visit Mr. Damery this afternoon and assess for myself his suitability as a guide."

"But . . . but . . . dammit, Mrs. Beaumont, we've all told you what kind of man Damery is! You wouldn't be safe with him!"

"Is there anyone else in Lambarene who is free to guide me?" Meg already knew the answer to that question; the lunchtime conversation had established that the only white men in Lambarene were these three traders and a missionary at the Mission Évangélique, and all of them were far too busy to take weeks off to escort a strange Englishwoman through the jungle.

"Well, no," Cavanaugh admitted reluctantly, "but you can't go with Damery."

Meg lifted her chin and looked down through her eyelashes at Cavanaugh. He was an inch or two shorter than she was, and for once in her life she was glad of her gawky, awkward height. "I will be the judge of that, Mr. Cavanaugh, when I have met the gentleman."

"You won't meet him," said Cavanaugh bluntly. "I know my duties by an English lady. I'm not going to take you to see him, and neither will Walters."

"If you won't escort me," said Meg sweetly, "I will simply have to find him for myself. I believe I have learned enough Pidgin English to inquire the way to Mr. Damery's house without your help."

Cavanaugh flushed and muttered something between his teeth. Meg couldn't quite understand the words, but they seemed to have to do with a strong desire to send all blithering, idiotic, interfering English girls back home where they belonged.

Meg sighed. She really hadn't wanted to alienate the English traders. She just seemed to have that effect on people. The headmistress of her boarding school used to look like that all the time, whenever she gave Meg one of her "little talks" on behavior. Really, Meg thought, Sir Digby was the only person she knew who could carry on a rational conversation without getting all emotional and frustrated. Perhaps that was why she had been able to put up with her father all these years.

Before Cavanaugh could rejoin battle, François Chaillot intervened. "But I am sure there is no need for these arguments," he said, taking Meg's arm and turning her slightly away from the English trader. "If you wish to visit my poor friend Damery, *ma chère* Marguerite, I will myself escort you to his house. Really, Cavanaugh, you misjudge poor Piers if you think he is a danger to anyone except himself. And you, Marguerite, may as well judge for yourself the truth of our assessment of this man."

Meg thanked François and apologized for taking him away from his factory for the afternoon.

"Do not regard it," he told her, smiling down at her through half-closed dark eyes. "Unlike our English friends, I have not been absent on leave for the past six months, and so can easily be spared for an afternoon. And it is no hardship to me to stroll through the forest with a pretty girl instead of standing behind a counter buying rubber and ivory from some great hulking Mpongwe warrior."

Shortly after the English traders departed for their own factory, François and Meg set out for Piers Damery's house. The gray clouds had burned off by midafternoon, to be replaced by a brilliant blue sky in which the golden orb of the sun struck down like hammer blows on a gong, raising steam from the moist earth and dazzling Meg's eyes. She was glad that she had insisted on bringing her sturdy old black umbrella on this trip. It might not be a very elegant lady's parasol, but it served to protect her head from the sun while they walked through the open area around the factory, and when they entered the forest she used it to whack away the creeping vines that reached out toward her on all sides. François watched her determined strides with some amusement.

"There's no need to hurry," he remarked. "It

is true that one cannot see Monsieur Damery's house from the compound, but the actual distance is not so great. It is only that this patch of rain forest intervenes."

François went on to explain that Piers had no lodging of his own, Hatton and Cookson having closed their trading operation in Gabon and sold the Lambarene factory when they discharged the mad Englishman who had made so much trouble for them here.

"Who bought the factory?" Meg asked. Somehow Lambarene did not seem like a place where the real-estate market would move quickly—if at all.

A shadow of embarrassment flickered across François's dark, even features. "As a matter of fact, I—that is, Chaillot Père et Fils, my firm—we took it off their hands. It was not my intention to profit from a comrade's misfortune, believe me!" he insisted. "Indeed, the Hatton and Cookson factory here is of very little use to me, being located, as you see, most inconveniently between the jungle and the bank of the Ogowe River. I have made use of the lower story of the building to keep some excess supplies of my own firm's, and Piers Damery is still living in the rooms above the storage area." He sighed. "Perhaps it is a foolish weakness on my part, for everyone agrees it would be better if he went back to England. But I feared that if I evicted him from the factory, he would go live in one of the native huts by the river, and that would cause a scandal of the most incredible kind. I am a weak man, Mademoiselle Beaumont."

"No," said Meg thoughtfully, looking at the play of light and shadow across François's handsome face as they pushed on through the rain forest. "I don't think it is weak to show kindness to a friend."

A number of questions occurred to her, such as why Piers Damery so obstinately refused to go home, and why François should think the Englishman would be welcome in the native huts if he had abused their women in the horrifying manner described to her. But somehow it did not seem the right time to bring up these matters. She fell silent and concentrated on watching her step in the tricky, vine-tangled paths of the forest.

Slowly, as they walked on in silence, the quiet grandeur of the forest began to seep into Meg's spirit, quieting her troubled thoughts. Perhaps it was not so hard after all to understand why Piers Damery refused to go back to England. When she had looked at it from the deck of the *Brazza*, the rain forest had seemed a dark forbidding place, frightening and even sinister with its tangle of creeping things and its mysteriously moving shadows. Now that she was actually in it, surrounded by the vast buttressed trees that pushed upward toward the sky like the columns of a cathedral, she began to see the strange hypnotic beauty of the forest. A hundred feet above her head, the boughs of the trees branched out and interlaced with one another to make a green canopy through which the fierce African sun was tamed to a cool shadowy light. From the branches hung vines, some thin as a lady's embroidery silk, some thick as her arm, tangled with one another as if some army of serpents had been arrested in mid-battle by a magic spell.

After a long time gazing about her in wonder, she lowered her eyes and met François's look with a slightly embarrassed smile. "Yes," he said before she could explain her fascination. "It is terrible . . . and wonderful."

"And beautiful," Meg murmured, but her companion demurred.

"Beauty," he said, "is the Champs-Élysées on a spring afternoon, or the Bois de Boulougne with the ladies in their carriages . . . or a beautiful woman." He reached out his hand to help Meg over a fallen log, giving her an intense dark-eyed look that said more clearly than words that she was to consider herself the object of his last statement.

The pressure of his hand aroused strange fluttering sensations in Meg's breast. As soon as she was over the log, she snatched her hand away and stepped out quickly, slashing right and left with the umbrella to clear her path. François Chaillot followed behind her, and she knew without looking around that he was smiling.

They were coming out of the depths of the rain forest now, into a region where the trees had been crudely girdled and where most of the bush vines lay in withered sections on the ground, hacked into pieces. Meg heard François muttering and simmering behind her, and slowed her steps so that he could catch up with her.

"What happened here?" she asked. After the quiet grandeur of the forest, the devastation of this section was doubly shocking, as though a destructive child had scribbled naughty words over one of the great paintings of the world.

"Waste!" François burt out. "The incredible, foolish wastefulness of the idiot *indigènes*. The difference between this section of bush and the rest of the forest, Marguerite, is that these vines had the misfortune to be rubber-bearing. When Chaillot Père et Fils was founded twenty years ago, all the forest around Lambarene was full of vines like these. But the *indigènes* were too lazy to collect the juice by making incisions in the living vines. They had to hack off sections as you see here, until the entire vine was destroyed—and since the plant propagates only from seed, once they have passed through an area with their hacking and chopping, the vines there are essentially destroyed. Now they must range ever farther afield, and we must pay more and more for the rubber they bring in, because it can only be collected from distant parts of the interior and passes through the hands of a dozen middlemen before it reaches us."

"It does seem rather a pity," Meg agreed. "Why don't you explain to them that it would be better not to kill the plants?"

Francois's harsh laugh resounded across the river, which they were approaching, startling a white heron into flapping upward in a few seconds of heavy-winged, ungainly flight. "Explain! My dear Marguerite, let you spend only one day trying to pound any understanding into those thick woolly heads, and then tell me how it is to be done. No, if they are to be reformed from their foolish ways, it is not teaching that is required, but methods of a nature inconceivably different—"

He broke off abruptly, and Meg saw that his high cheekbones were flushed dark with emotion. "Forgive me, Marguerite. I have been most unmannerly. You can have, of course, no great interest in these petty difficulties of a remote trading outpost. What a subject with which to entertain a pretty woman!" He laughed self-consciously. "I would endeavor to redeem myself in your eyes by making lighter conversation, but alas, our little stroll is almost at an end."

As he spoke, they rounded a bend in the path and a cleared space on the banks of the river opened before them. At the very edge of the river, with foundation poles set right into the bank and supporting a veranda that leaned out over the rushing sheet of brassy water, was the two-story structure of Hatton and Cookson's trading factory.

The air of dilapidation and neglect that surrounded the factory was in the strongest possible contrast to François Chaillot's neat establishment on the hill. The bamboo fence that surrounded the factory compound lay quite flat in several places, as though some large beast had trampled it down and nobody had bothered to repair the damage. And indeed, why should anyone? One of the small sheds within the compound had fallen quite down, and the other had a thatched roof that sagged dolorously inward to where a large black hole had rotted through the straw. The main building still stood, but it swayed drunkenly on its foundation posts as if to promise that its fall was soon to come, and already the impudent creeper vines of the forest, with their brilliant green leaves and clusters of scarlet berries, were twined around the supporting posts. Patches of grass and weeds, half-grown tree shoots, and red mounds of earth thrown up by some sort of insect littered the compound, eloquent witness to the neglect it had suffered since the firm of Hatton and Cookson closed its doors in Lambarene.

As they approached, a tall blond man with three days' frizz of unshaven beard on his chin stumbled out onto the veranda, chanting unintelligible words in a drunken monotone. He swayed back and forth, clutching at the veranda railing for balance. "Damn your interfering, Chaillot," he shouted, waving the bottle in his free hand, "get out of my compound!" On the last word the bottle went sailing over the compound in a glistening arc, sparkling with the reflected light of the sun, until it crashed at François's feet. Broken glass spattered the hem of Meg's plain sensible black serge skirt and a strong odor of alcoholic fumes arose from the puddle before François.

"*Mon Dieu*," Chaillot exclaimed, "that's brandy, not trade gin. I wonder where he got the stuff. Calm yourself, my friend," he called up to the unsteadily gesticulating figure on the veranda, "and moderate your language before the English *mademoiselle* here."

His warning was unnecessary. As soon as Piers Damery caught sight of the slender young woman emerging from the forest trail behind François Chaillot, his flow of curses came to an abrupt end. He stood quite still, gripping the veranda rail tightly, and stared at Meg as though he could not believe his eyes.

"No, she's not an apparition," François shouted up, laughing at Piers's look of amazement. "This time you are not dreaming, my friend." In an aside to Meg he muttered, "That is, assuming he sees you as you really are. Last time I called on poor Damery he complained most violently about the two dancing pink elephants I had brought with me. God knows what he thinks he is seeing now!"

Meg scarcely heard François's warning. All her attention was on the tall man who still bent over the veranda, staring at her with eyes of a piercing and unbelievable blue. It was hard to believe that he was only in his middle twenties. His face was worn with the marks of suffering, with dark hollows under the blue eyes, and his unshaven chin and wildly flying untrimmed yellow hair made him look like a derelict out of an East End doss house.

As she scanned his face, looking in vain for some softening expression, some hint of a smile that would make her feel he really was an English gentleman and pleased to see her, he removed his gripping hands from the veranda railing and stepped back. Moving stiffly, like a poorly jointed puppet, he made an awkward bow.

"My apologies, ma'am," he said in a quiet, slightly slurred voice that barely carried over the ceaseless hum of the flying insects that wheeled and darted about the compound. "I was not expecting . . . guests." His voice dropped still further on the last word, leaving Meg with the impression that he had started to say something else.

François took Meg's arm. "You have now seen him at his best," he told her in an undertone. "Shall we go?"

Meg shook off François's restraining hand. "By no means," she said. "I have a business proposition to put to you, Mr. Damery. May I come up?"

"A business proposition!" Piers Damery seemed to find this obscurely amusing. He laughed, hiccupped in the middle of the laugh, and began to cough. "All right, fair lady. You may join me in my castle—but not the Frenchman! No damned

Froggies in an Englishman's home!" He lifted a cracked but not unpleasant tenor voice in song. " 'Rule, Britannia . . . Britannia, rule the waves! Britons never, never, never, never . . .' "

Meg nodded to François. "It seems he is not so far gone that he cannot remember how to behave before a lady. I think I had better see him alone. Your presence seems to excite him."

François demurred, but Meg was firm. She intended to talk with Piers Damery, and it was clear that he would not talk business with her before François Chaillot. At last François reluctantly consented, with the proviso that he would return within an hour to guide her back to his compound. "Not," he said with a wry smile, "that I anticipate you will be in any danger of insult from that poor mad fellow. As you say, he seems to have retained some shreds of civilized behavior—and in any case, Marguerite, he would hardly attack so redoubtable an opponent as your black umbrella. No, if a private interview with him is necessary to convince you that he will be useless as a guide, I shall have to leave you to it—though I warn you, you will be wasting your time."

Before taking his leave, he touched Meg lightly on the arm and drew close to her. "Try, if you can, to persuade him to return to England," he murmured. "He won't listen to me—accuses me of having designs on this ramshackle factory, which in any case I now own! I would feel happier if I knew my poor friend was back in the bosom of his family, receiving the medical care which he so sorely needs."

"I will do my best to reconcile him to his family," Meg promised.

She stood in the neglected compound, watching François as he went down the forest path, until the last glimmer of his sparkling white shirt was hidden by the enclosing green of the jungle vines. Then, and only then, she took a firm grip on her black umbrella and mounted the rickety stairs to the top story of Piers Damery's factory, using the umbrella as a walking stick.

Three

The Englishman had vanished inside the two-room upper story of the factory by the time Meg reached the veranda. She followed him into the shady room that overlooked the veranda, wrinkling her nose involuntarily at the reek of alcoholic spirits.

At first sight the room itself seemed an appalling den of filth and clutter. Unwashed clothes and empty bottles littered the floor, while great spiderwebs swung from the bare rafters toward the one rickety table in the center of the room. There were ragged holes in the thatched roof, allowing the sunlight to spill in and illuminate the light coating of green mildew that covered rain-dampened walls and a pair of leather boots.

Damery was standing in the center of the room, one hand resting lightly on the table as though he could not quite give up that source of support. His face, behind the fuzz of blond beard, displayed nothing but courteous surprise at Meg's visit, but the pressure of his hand on the tabletop gave him away. The long elegant fingers were spread out on the tabletop, braced to take his weight, and the fingertips were white to the nails. Meg noted that those nails were clean and trimmed off squarely, and that his white shirt and trousers were actually quite clean except for a few spectacular splashes of red mud—hardly the standard of grooming one would expect of a drunken degenerate in the middle of the African rain forest.

But then, this man was no ordinary degenerate. He had been a gentleman once. Nothing brought that home to her more forcefully than the sight of his hands spread out on the tabletop, white with strain. Those long fingers should have been holding a book on a leather-topped library table, or guiding a prize hunter through its paces. Meg could visualize the man before her in the setting of a luxurious country house in England, urbane and civilized. What had brought him down to this level, to living the life of a drunken exile in this African backwater?

Damery was still staring at her with a stunned glassy look in his eyes, as though he couldn't believe what he saw. As though the sight of her was too painful for him to bear. That was something they'd have to get past before they could talk seriously. Raising her black umbrella, she poked Damery squarely in the middle of his chest. He sat down with a surprised "Ouf!" on the mildew-coated wooden chair behind him.

"Piers Damery, you're carrying on like a disgusting swine and I'm thoroughly ashamed of you," she told him, resting the tip of the umbrella against his chest. "Aunt Alice and Uncle Henry would be ashamed too, if they had any idea how you'd been behaving. Is this how a Damery reacts to misfortune?"

Piers grinned up at her. His blue eyes sparkled through the long fringe of untrimmed blond hair that fell down over his forehead. Despite her determination to keep strictly to business, Meg was swayed by his unquenchable charm. It must be his resemblance to Harry that made her long to brush the long hair away from his face. Would it feel as silky as it looked?

"No," Piers agreed cheerfully. "A Damery generally reacts to misfortune by marching into the middle of it and giving someone else a self-righteous lecture. Just like you're doing now—and you're only an adoptive Damery. How *are* you, Cousin Meg, and what the hell are you doing here?"

Meg fumbled in her reticule with her free hand and pulled out a creased, much-folded sheet of paper. "Recognize this?"

"Of course I don't recognize it," said Piers plaintively. "I can barely see it. If you'd quit poking me in the chest with that damned ferrule of yours, maybe I could get up and we could discuss this paper of yours in a civilized fashion."

And maybe it wouldn't be such a good idea to diminish the distance between them. Meg frowned slightly. Where had that thought come from? She'd known Piers from childhood; if her pulse was fluttering now, it was only with excitement at finding him alive and apparently well. It wasn't as though she were alone with Harry.

"Oh, sorry." Meg set her umbrella neatly in one corner and handed Piers the letter. The tips of her fingers brushed his and he snatched his hand away as if the brief contact had burned him. Why was he acting so jumpy?

He glanced down at the scrawled, almost illegible lines and his hand clenched, crushing the paper into a wad.

"My letter to Harry. How the devil did you get hold of it?"

Meg took the chair Piers had vacated, the only one in the room. She leaned one elbow on the dusty table and propped her chin on her fist, looking up at Piers with a slightly troubled frown on her face.

"It wasn't dishonorable," she told him. "At least, I don't think so. You see, I was staying with Aunt Alice and Uncle Henry when the letter came. Harry had just been posted to South America, and I had helped him get his tropical kit together."

"I'll just bet you did," said Piers. "Still acting as Harry's little slave, eh—just like when we were kids?"

"It wasn't like that," Meg defended herself. "He *needed* help. His last position was in Sweden, and he only had three weeks in England between postings, and of course he didn't have any of the things he needed for the tropics, and he had . . . a lot of people to visit and say good-by to." A lot of those people had been pretty, giggling little girls with petite hourglass figures. Remembering the way Harry had smiled down at girls like Isabel Hutchinson and Clementine Jervis, while he seemed to look right through her, gave Meg a tiny lump in her throat. Piers wasn't smiling at her, he was practically scowling, but even that was better than treating her as if she was invisible.

"Mmm." Piers nodded. "Yes, I'll just bet he needed your help—to polish his boots and run errands while he squired his girlfriends about. I'm disappointed in you, Megsie. I thought by now you'd have grown up enough to see through Harry."

"I don't know what you mean by that," Meg said sharply. "You trusted him enough to write when you needed help, didn't you? Now I suppose you're jealous because he's got a good career in the diplomatic service while you—" She stopped abruptly, wishing the words unsaid. Piers hadn't moved or spoken, yet she felt as though she had struck him across the face.

"While I've ruined myself yet again," Piers finished for her, but she felt that his thoughts were not really on the words. "Jealous," he repeated. "Yes. I might be that—though not of his career."

"Then of what?"

There was a pain behind Piers's wry smile that hurt her eyes. "If you don't know, then it doesn't matter. But I don't want to quarrel with you. Pax, Meg?"

"Pax," she agreed.

He turned the crumpled letter over and over in his hands. "From Sweden to South America, eh? I suppose it was sheer luck my letter reached him during his three weeks' leave. Maybe not such good luck, considering. I never would have thought he'd turn it over to you."

Meg swallowed and braced herself for the confession. "He didn't. It arrived the day after he left. I was making a parcel of things he'd forgotten, to send on after him, and Aunt Alice asked me to put your letter in with the rest of the things in the parcel. Only I happened to notice our secret sign on the envelope, and I thought . . ." She tried to swallow again, but her mouth seemed to have gone dry. In the comfortable, disorganized house in London it had seemed quite natural to open the letter, once she saw the curious design of crossed arrows that Piers had doodled in one corner. In their childhood games that symbol had meant "Secret and Urgent," and they'd scrawled it on every message they passed.

"You thought," Piers finished for her again, "that this time I might really have a secret-and-urgent message for Harry, and that it wouldn't bear waiting while the letter was forwarded halfway around the world to catch up with him."

Meg nodded and watched, mesmerized, as Piers tore the letter into shreds and let the fragments flutter to the torn straw matting on the floor. "Instead of which," he said with a sad smile, "you found only the maunderings of a drunken fool. I'm sorry you had to come all this way for nothing, Meg. It's a long trip to make, just to turn around and go right back."

He wasn't going to tear her limb from limb for opening his private mail. Meg let that thought sink in, and only now, when she felt safe, acknowledged that for a moment she'd been positively afraid of Piers. Which was ridiculous. He was only *Piers*, Harry's little brother who thought up all the adventures and then complained loudly when he didn't get to play the heroic parts, the boy of her own age with whom she'd squabbled and played games and thought up tricks to play on their long-suffering tutor.

But for a moment there, this lean, bronzed stranger with the lines of weariness on his face had seemed like a man, a strange and dangerous man at that. A man that no woman with any sense would visit alone in his lodgings; a man who could make any woman's pulses flutter, even when he was giving an excellent impression of a drunken derelict. Meg had never thought of Piers in such terms and she wished she could drive the thoughts away now.

Of course, after what he'd been through, Meg reminded herself, she should have expected him to have changed somewhat. But underneath, he was the same old Piers, schoolfellow and playmate. That thought gave her the courage to dispute his last and final-sounding statement.

"I . . . didn't think it was for nothing," she croaked.

"Oh, it is, Meg. It is." Piers dusted his hands and the last fragments of the shredded letter spiraled down through a dusty sunbeam.

"Your letter sounded rather serious." Meg twisted her hands together, feeling all the embarrassment that had attacked her when she first admitted to reading somebody else's mail. "It wasn't . . . I couldn't quite understand everything . . . but it sounded as though there had been some kind of scandal that made you lose your job. When the factory burned down. They were blaming you. You said you'd been unjustly accused and that you planned to stay on in Lambarene to try to discover what had really happened."

Piers was regarding her with an unnerving, steady blue gaze, head slightly cocked on one side and one fair eyebrow raised, as though he were listening to a child recount an amusing fantasy. "And *if* I said that, what has it to do with you?"

"You thought you might be in danger."

"I never wrote that!"

"N-no. But you asked Harry to settle your affairs if he didn't hear from you in three months, and to try to keep your parents from learning about the scandal. It certainly sounded as if you needed help," she concluded. "And . . . well, Papa had just remarried, you see, so he didn't need me anymore." The words sounded rather lonely and self-pitying—emotions Meg despised—so she moved on firmly. "So I came at once, naturally. Where do we start investigating?"

"There's nothing to investigate!" Piers wheeled away from the table and leaned against the wall beside the window opening, looking out over the sea of green trees and vines that had crept up to the very edge of the factory buildings in the months of neglect. He spoke again from there, his face hidden from Meg by one white-clad shoulder and an untidy mass of yellow hair falling down into his collar. "I was drunk when I wrote that letter. I don't know what I wrote—probably trying to soften the blow for the family—but it doesn't matter, Meg. All the accusations against me were absolutely true. And we'll leave it at that, because they're not the sort of stories a nice English girl should be hearing. You can't exonerate me. And nobody is going to investigate anything."

"Piers Damery!" Meg grabbed her black umbrella from the corner and prodded him between the shoulder blades. "How dare you lie to me like that?" Another sharp prod had the effect she wanted. Piers winced and turned around to grasp the tip of the umbrella and force it downward. The casual strength exerted in one twist of his hand startled her.

Now she could see his face, but he still refused to meet her eyes. She wasn't surprised. "For your information, I have already heard the lurid stories and I don't believe a word of them. Raping and beating native girls! It's not the kind of thing you'd do. You're wild and unrealiable and irresponsible and quite unbearably sarcastic sometimes, but you're not *vicious.*"

"*Merci du compliment,*" Piers said with a wince. "And remind me never to ask you for a testimonial to my character. What do you mean, wild?"

"Well," Meg said with a smile lifting the corners of her lips, "correct me if I'm wrong, but didn't you get sent down from Oxford for inviting some ladies of the evening to go swimming in the college fountain with you? As for irresponsible, what else would you call a man who dresses up his dog in a top hat and coat and brings it into the bank where he works to open an account for it?"

Piers shrugged. "I never did like that job."

"No," Meg agreed. "I can see that it wouldn't suit your temperament. I should have thought something like this would suit you much better. I certainly wouldn't have expected you to go in for wanton cruelty. Remember the day you bought the donkey from the circus-master on Brighton Pier because he was beating it so hard?"

Piers flushed. "The poor thing was nothing but skin and bones. Besides, it's not the same thing at all. I may not approve of cruelty to animals, but I can certainly see the appeal of beating women. Some women," he said, eyeing her with a glittering blue stare that made Meg almost apprehensive, "some women damn well ask for it. Either that, or they drive a man to drink. Dammit, Meg, will you go away and leave me to go to hell in my own way?"

Grabbing the open bottle that stood on the windowsill, he took a deep draft and wiped the back of his hand across his mouth with a contented sigh. "Nothing like a little brandy to drive away the blue devils. Now go away, Cousin Meg, there's a good girl. I'm not set up to entertain lady visitors. I didn't ask you out here. I don't want you here. I'm perfectly happy with my brandy and my giant green snakes."

"I thought they were dancing pink elephants. That's what François said."

Piers shrugged. "Kindly allow me to describe my own hallucinations. Today I feel like snakes. Hundreds and hundreds of snakes," he went on, grinning at Meg and waving the bottle about, "writhing and crawling about, just the way they do in the jungle. Hissing too, but mostly oozing about the room in great loops. Can't you see them?"

Meg almost could, so vivid was the description, and she was beginning to feel a little sick at the image of masses of writhing snakes. But something was not quite right with this picture of a man on the verge of delirium tremens—and she thought she knew what it was.

"Piers, I feel faint," she said, pushing herself up from the chair and taking a wobbling step toward him. "Would you give me a little of your brandy?"

Piers shook his head, still grinning through the fuzz of his beard. "Not good for nice English ladies. Go to the mission and have a cup of tea."

Meg stumbled forward another couple of steps, holding one hand to her head. Piers looked worried; he reached out his hand to support her.

Before he could stop her, Meg snatched the half-empty bottle out of his other hand and retreated to put the table between them. On her way she took a long swig out of the bottle.

"Ha! Colored water. I thought so. Damerys don't drink to excess—it's not one of the family failings. It's all an act, isn't it? Whom are you trying to fool, Piers?"

"You, among others," said Piers with the twisted smile that wrung her heart, "but I suppose I should have known better."

"You certainly should," said Meg, seating herself again and folding her hands together. "Now, Piers, I think you had better tell me what exactly is going on here. I have to understand what the problem is if I'm to help you."

Piers groaned and struck his brow theatrically. "Women! The only way you can help me, dear Cousin Meg, is to get yourself away from here as fast and as far as possible."

"The factory that burned down was somewhere up the river, wasn't it? Do you know who burned it? And don't tell me the story about you getting drunk and burning down your own factory, because we've already established that you've inherited the Damery aversion to alcohol. You can't even bring yourself to add a little brandy to the bottle—"

"To lend verisimilitude to an otherwise bald and unconvincing narrative."

Meg gave and involuntary laugh at the quotation from *The Mikado*. Piers had taken her to see the popular musical when it opened five years ago, when she visited the Damerys on one of her rare holidays from housekeeping for her father. That would have been just before he lost the job at the bank—or no, it was the job before that, the one as clerk-secretary for a politician friend of

Uncle Henry's. He lost that one, Meg recalled, for introducing several slightly off-color jokes into a speech he was supposed to be writing for the politician. The man had been too busy to read over the speech beforehand and had delivered the entire text, jokes and all, to the Church of England Ladies' Service Auxiliary at Stoke on Trent.

Meg's eyes misted over slightly as she recalled how young and carefree they'd both been. How had it all gone wrong? How had Piers's irrepressible high spirits brought him to this dead end in the tropics, while she turned into her father's depressed slave? Of the three of them, Harry was the only one who'd turned out all right in the end, she thought.

"Right," she said, wrenching her thoughts back to the unpromising present with an effort. "So who burned down the factory?"

Piers shrugged. "Damned if I know. Why do you think I'm lurching about here, drinking myself into an early grave, and otherwise making a blinking public nuisance of myself? I mean to find out what really happened, and to do that I need to stay in Africa. Without making anybody suspicious. And it seems to have worked. Nobody would suspect poor old Piers the drunk of secretly investigating a crime, would they?"

"So what have you found out?"

Piers looked embarrassed. "Well, actually, it's not that easy. Investigating. Especially if you've no idea where to start."

"You must have some idea," Meg persisted. "Or weren't you even there at the time?"

"Oh, I was there, all right. Dead drunk and reeking of brandy. Just ask anybody— No, Megsie, don't interrupt! That really is the truth. François found me, and he'd have no reason to lie—he's been the best friend a man could ask for all through these troubles. Maybe too good a friend, in fact. He keeps trying to rehabilitate me and send me home to England."

"Why don't you just tell him what you're really doing? If," Meg said carefully, "he's such a good friend and all that. He might be able to help you. He seems to know a lot about this area."

"He does," Piers agreed. "He also knows a lot of people in this area—and I don't know just who might be involved. I trust dear François's loyalty, but not his discretion—all Frenchmen talk too damn much."

"Unlike certain Englishmen," Meg said, "who can talk one's ear off without ever saying anything to the point. How did you come to be dead drunk and reeking of brandy while your factory burned down?"

"It's a long story. And a strange one. Sure you want to hear it?"

Meg nodded, hands tightly clasped in her lap. She felt she couldn't bear it if Piers sent her away now.

"Oh, all right." Piers folded himself down onto the floor, long limbs spread out before him, and leaned back against the wall. "It does seem a pity you should come all this way and not even know what's going on. It started about six months ago . . . after Gordon died suddenly. Quite suddenly. One night he was drinking with me, the next—gone." He stared past Meg, his blue eyes cloudy and unfocused.

"Fever?" Meg prompted as Piers seemed lost in his memories.

"Oh, did you know about Gordon?"

Meg sighed. "No. I've heard a few similar stories. Who was Gordon?"

"The other chap who worked for Hatton and Cookson. He was stationed up at Talagouga. After he went, I had to try to keep things going at both factories until they could send out another clerk from England. But there wasn't much business at Talagouga, so I stayed down here mostly and had an African clerk up there. Bright fellow—couldn't read or write, but he kept accounts on a kind of bead thing he had, and he could click up the numbers faster with that than I could with pen and paper. Anyway, things seemed to be going all right, until one evening when I was sitting out on the veranda there I heard someone singing in Mpongwe. Over and over again, same three notes, like a damn cricket chirping. I was about to shy a boot at the fellow and tell him to shut up; then I listened a little more carefully and understood the words."

"You know Mpongwe?" Meg exclaimed, forgetting her vow not to interrupt.

Piers shrugged. "I've been here a year and a half. Picked up a few scraps. Languages come easy to me—you know that—it's not as if I had to work at learning them. Regular work doesn't seem to be one of my talents."

Meg sighed and silently agreed. Unlike Harry, who had risen in the diplomatic service as much through his own steady application as through a judicious use of Uncle Henry's influence, Piers seemed destined to flit from scandal to scandal. Except, she reminded herself, for this last scandal, which was none of his making. But who, knowing Piers's past escapades, would ever believe it?

"What did the song say?" she asked.

"It was a warning. The words were, 'They are going to attack your factory at Talagouga tomorrow, they are going to attack your factory at Talagouga tomorrow . . .' "

Piers had taken the warning seriously enough to arm himself and set off upriver in the trading company's launch, accompanied by the three Kruboys who worked for him at Lambarene. At Talagouga they were attacked by masked men from a secret society.

"I know," said Meg, nodding wisely. "I heard about those secret societies from Mr. Cavanaugh. He said somebody tried to 'put Ikuku on him' to force him to raise the price he paid for rubber."

Piers scowled in her general direction, but without really seeing her. "You don't know anything about it. Ikuku is a perfectly respectable law society, in fact it's the main force for law and order here—ten times more effective than the few French government officials they have on the coast. Ikuku got after Cavanaugh because he was trying to make the natives take some kind of cheap American cloth for their rubber, instead of good Manchester cotton. These chaps that attacked us were Crocodile Society."

"Oh," said Meg in what she hoped was a suitably chastened tone. "Is that different? I mean . . . what exactly is the Crocodile Society?"

Piers's abstracted scowl frightened her not at all, but the way his blue eyes seemed to be looking right through her was something else. Despite the heat of the day, she felt a cold shiver down her spine, like a ghostly warning that she was about to meddle in matters no white person should try to understand.

"Nobody knows for sure. It's only started up in the last year, mostly along the Ogowe, and it's growing too fast and too strong for anybody to keep track of. There've been some murders. People tied in the river for the crocodiles to take. Of course the way they explain it here is that the leader of the society is a witch and has the power to change himself into a crocodile when it is time to take a victim."

"Then why don't they arrest the leader?"

"Because nobody knows who he is, stupid! The few people they've caught offering victims won't talk, and they manage to poison each other when they're taken to jail. *Will* you stop interrupting?"

Meg nodded and sat back docilely as Piers continued his rather gruesome story. The three Kru-boys had been killed in the attack, and Piers was taken prisoner. He expected to be killed at any moment, but instead the masked men tied his hands and thrust him into a tiny, hastily constructed hut which was full of smoke. Outside he could hear the factory burning. He thought he was going to burn up with it, and struggled to push his way out of the hut. He got his head out and saw a strange and terrifying sight, a naked man whose body was covered with fantastic patterns that glowed in the dark.

"I'd meant to try to get out through the hole I made in the hut, but I suppose I was a bit dizzy from the crack on the head I got during the fighting," Piers admitted, looking a bit sheepish. "Things started going round and round, and I couldn't be entirely sure I was seeing what I was seeing, if you follow me. So I just lay there with my head poking out of the hut, thinking it over quietly and enjoying the fresh air. The chap who glowed in the dark looked round and saw me and let out a yell, and then a couple of his friends came footing over with their whacking great spears. I thought I was done for! They shoved me back in the hut and plastered plantain leaves over the hole, and the smoke got worse and worse until I must have passed out. When I came to, I was in bed, in the Mission Évangélique across the river from my factory.

"Madame Fanchot—she's a widow, works at the mission—took care of me. My head was aching something awful, but there wasn't much else wrong except cuts and bruises. She told me François Chaillot had come upriver on the *Brazza.* He and Captain Jacques found me lying out on the sandbank, reeking of brandy and with empty bottles lying all about."

The factory was nothing but a pile of smoldering ashes. The natural assumption made by both François and Captain Jacques was that Piers had set his own factory on fire by accident and had been too drunk to do more than stumble to safety. When Piers protested this story and told them his confused memories of the fight before the fire, François only looked grave and advised him not to mention the matter. Piers didn't know why until, several days later, he returned to Lambarene to discover that several Mpongwe and Igalwa women were bringing charges against him for mistreating them. Two alternative stories about the fire had already circulated: one, that he had burned down his own factory in a drunken fit; the second, that the natives whom he had misused had revolted against his tyrannical rule and his enslavement of their women, burning down the factory and trying to kill Piers.

Meg nodded. "I heard both stories. It doesn't seem to have occurred to anybody that they can't *both* be true. I don't think your friends here reason very clearly, Piers."

He ran one hand through his long blond hair, pushing the dangling locks back from his forehead. "It doesn't matter," he said with a kind of weary impatience. "Whichever story Hatton and Cookson's chose to believe, it was bad enough to make them fire me and close down their trading operations here on the Ogowe." He looked up at Meg with a halfhearted attempt at a grin. "Which one do *you* believe?"

"Yours, of course," said Meg calmly. "You're not cruel and you've never lied to me. Now, if they said you'd done something incredibly silly and irresponsible, *that* I might believe."

Piers sagged back against the supporting wall with a hollow groan. "You do wonders for a chap's confidence, Meg. Didn't anybody ever tell you that you're supposed to gaze up at me with big wondering eyes and tell me how marvelous I am and that you have absolute faith in my ability to solve everything?"

"If I had absolute faith in your ability I wouldn't be here," Meg pointed out. "I thought you probably needed some help when I read your letter, and clearly I was right. Look at you! Six months since the factory burned down, and what have you done about investigating?"

"Dealing with the charges brought against me took a little time," Piers said rather indistinctly. "First I had to make sure I wasn't going to be jailed or deported."

"Don't grind your teeth, it's bad for the enamel."

"Fortunately, the lieutenant governor settled for dismissing me with a warning and forbidding me to trade in Gabon—not that I could anyway, since Hatton and Cookson quit shipping trade goods when they fired me."

"And what have you been doing since then?"

"Establishing a cover. Making sure nobody suspects me of staying around to investigate."

"I don't see why they should. You haven't done any investigating." Meg leaned forward, elbows propped on her knees, and began ticking off points on the fingers of her right hand. "Now, here's what we have to do, as I see it. First, find out if any other traders have been attacked."

"They haven't," said Piers. "At least, nothing serious. Cavanaugh and Walters had a little trouble last month, the natives didn't want to trade with them, but I think they were just suspicious over the rubber-price-fixing incident. And Chaillot's business is doing better than ever."

"Then the Crocodile Society isn't trying to stop all trade on the river," Meg concluded. "It's just you personally they don't like. So the first thing we have to do is find out what you did to offend them. Who around here belongs to the Crocodile Society that we can ask?"

Piers shook his head. "It's not the sort of thing they talk about. Besides, it doesn't seem to be centered here. All reports indicate the leader is somewhere upriver from Talagouga, up in the Fan country."

"I thought you said the people who attacked you were Mpongwe?" Meg had learned from the traders' talk that the different tribes of this region were as different as, say, French and English. The Mpongwe and Igalwa were peaceful and civilized—relatively, she added to herself, remembering the attack on Piers's factory. The Fan had a bad reputation for thievery, cannibalism, and various other unpleasant habits.

"The Crocodile Society," Piers explained, "unlike the law society, is pan-tribal. They're willing to terrorize and murder anybody from any tribe. That's one of the things that makes it so dangerous. Most of these native cults are confined to one tribe, and you can stamp them out be concentrating on the small area where the tribe lives. If this Crocodile Society gets going, it could spread across all of Africa."

Meg gave a decisive nod at the end of this explanation. "Then that's the second thing we've got to do. First, find out why the Crocodile Society is after you in particular, and then, stop what they're doing."

"You wouldn't," Piers inquired in carefully neutral tones, "care to add a few other minor tasks to that list, would you? Maybe we should also put the Russian anarchists out of business and find Jack the Ripper? How about world peace? An end to famine? A cure for influenza?"

Meg could feel herself flushing an unbecoming bright scarlet all the way up to the severely strained-back roots of fair hair at her forehead. Piers had always been able to cut her down to size with his sarcasm. The only way she knew to deal with it was to ignore him and plunge on as if he had not spoken.

"What time does the *Brazza* start up the river from here? It would be much simpler if we could take the steamer as far as Talagouga, don't you think? I realize that from there we'll probably have to hire a canoe and rowers."

"*We*," said Piers, "are not going anywhere. *You* are going back to England on the first boat that comes downriver, and I—"

"You," Meg snapped back in exact imitation of his tone, forgetting her resolve not to rise his bait, "will doubtless continue to sit on your rear end in Lambarene, giving a perfect imitation of a degenerate drunkard and waiting for the fever or the Crocodile Society to kill you so that you don't have to face your problems!"

"I will not, either," said Piers. "I was going to go upriver as soon as I got free of my legal difficulties, but I had the fever for two months. For your information, I was just getting ready to go back up to Talagouga when you showed up! Ask Captain Jacques if you don't believe me. I left a message at the dock asking him to take me on board as a passenger tomorrow morning. Now, of course, I'll have to stay and take care of you."

Meg told herself firmly that she was not going to descend to the kind of nursery squabbling that Piers seemed to be slipping into. "I don't see why you feel that way. The first boat back to the coast will be the *Brazza*, coming back down from Talagouga. She's the only steamer working the river right now. So what possible harm could it do if I just rode along with you as far as Talagouga?"

"It's not safe," Piers muttered, his blue eyes darting around in quick harassed glances as he avoided looking at Meg.

"*Please*, Piers?"

"No. It's too dangerous. You're a girl."

"There you go again!" Forgetting her good resolves once again, Meg jumped up, arms akimbo, and glared at Piers. She could feel her hair coming loose from its bun in damp sticky wisps, and the sensation only increased her irritation. Men didn't have to have long floating hair, and whalebone corsets that stabbed you when you tried to move, and chaperons and husbands and all sorts of unnecessary encumbrances. "You and Harry never let me have any of the adventures! Listen here, Piers Damery, I am tired of being the princess in the tower! I came all the way out to West Africa to help you slay this dragon, and you're not going to pack me off home like a naughty child!"

"Aren't I just!" Piers sounded, infuriatingly, more amused than angry. "Listen to yourself, Megsie. Do you think this is a nursery game? That's a real jungle out there, with real dangers, and I'm not dragging you along to get in my way and interfere with my plans. Now—"

One hand shot out and caught Meg's wrist as she swung her open palm at him. The other hand pressed down hard on her mouth. "Shh," he breathed in her ear. "Do you hear something?"

Now that they both were silent, Meg could hear what had alerted Piers: the stealthy rustle outside, under the veranda.

"Animals?" she whispered when he let go her.

"Maybe."

Moving with light, stealthy steps, Piers crossed the straw matting to the door and eased himself out onto the rickety stairs.

"Piers? *Mon ami*, are you feeling better? I have come to escort Mademoiselle Marguerite back to my factory. It is late and she ought not to stay longer."

François's cheerful voice, open and unsuspicious, floated up the stairwell. Piers looked over his shoulder at Meg and grinned. If he felt as foolish as she felt, Meg thought, it was a good thing François didn't know what wild suspicions had just floated through her mind. She had been all set to fend off an attack from sinister men in crocodile masks—and instead, it was only François, hinting that he might need to defend her virtue from Piers! A bubble of semihysterical laughter rose to her lips. If Francois only knew how ridiculous that thought was! Why, Piers was practically a brother to her! She might have forgotten that in the first shock of their meeting, but she was determined to keep it in mind from now on. They would both suffer needless embarrassment if she let Piers's resemblance to Harry trick her into acting as if she were attracted to him in that way.

"He's right, Miss Beaumont," Piers said formally, and Meg grasped that he wanted to preserve the secret of their relationship. Her heart lifted. Did this slight deception mean that he was admitting her into his plans after all? "It is almost dark. You had better return with Monsieur Chaillot."

Meg gave Piers the tips of her fingers in a cool, formal, English handshake as François mounted the stairs. The warmth of his hand threatened to overset her new resolutions, and she withdrew her own hand a little too hastily. Why did she feel so strangely short of breath whenever he looked at her or touched her? She would have to do better than this if they were to travel upriver together. "Yes, indeed, Mr. Damery. I have so enjoyed our little chat. If you will be so good as to call on me tomorrow, we can complete our business arrangements then."

The steps creaked; François took her elbow to guide her down. When she reached the ground she realized that it was late indeed. The sun was already low enough to cast long shadows across the clearing, and unless they hurried they would be caught by the swift tropical nightfall. Still, she couldn't refrain from casting one glance back up the stairs at Piers, a lonely figure half-hidden in shadow, his blond head bowed so that she could not see his face.

"You seem to have been a good influence on Damery," François remarked as they were making their way back through the devastated area of dead rubber vines. "I have not heard him sound so sober—or so much the gentleman—in a long time. But I do not like this talk of 'business arrangements,' Marguerite. Even if the poor fellow managed to pull himself together this evening, I fear he is no fit companion for a young lady journeying into the interior."

"Nothing is settled yet," Meg said evasively.

Which was perfectly true. She recalled, for instance, that Piers had not responded to her request that he visit her tomorrow. Could he be planning to leave early in the morning, to sneak off to Talagouga on the *Brazza* without her? It seemed all too likely. Well, two could play at that game. Piers might have a few surprises coming yet.

Four

As night drew to an end and the swift African dawn lit the sky with soft color, the sleeping jungle around Lambarene began to rustle with noise and movement. Monkeys chattered as they swung from tree to tree; the black-and-yellow wings of the weaverbirds flashed gaily as they began to squeak and fly from one ball-shaped nest to another; at the river, women collecting pails of water splashed in the swift-moving brown water and disturbed the fishing of a stork, who stalked indignantly off on his long stilts, taking care to keep well clear of a gnarled greenish-brown log that seemed to have beached itself on the sandbank. As the sun rose higher, warming the bank, the log opened its jaws, yawned, and lumbered halfway into the water, where it lay with one eye just above water, looking like a piece of driftwood and watching for any large and unwary food that might come near.

In the semideserted factory of Hatton and Cookson, with its tumbledown veranda leaning out directly over the riverbank, the beings who inhabit houses were also stirring and making their peculiar early-morning noises.

"For the last time, Meg, you're not going anywhere except back to England, and that's my final word! Understand?" Piers, barely awake and already very much harassed, pushed dangling locks of yellow hair out of his eyes and scowled at his troublesome morning visitor.

"I don't recall asking your opinion," Meg told him. She set down her traveling case and rubbed the small of her back with one hand. It had been a long and lonely walk through the forest that morning, and the traveling case in which all her clothes were packed had seemed uncommonly heavy before she reached the factory.

She'd gotten up before dawn to tiptoe out of François Chaillot's house, anticipating trouble from him as well as from Piers if either of them knew what she planned to do. Stopping by the pier to speak with Captain Jacques had delayed her so that it was almost light by the time she started down the path to Piers's factory, but the enveloping green shroud of the rain forest had turned the path into a dim tunnel down which she hurried almost blindly.

Noises overhead and all around her had added to her nervousness; not knowing the bush, she had taken a monkey's cautious explorations for the stalking of a panther, a swinging vine for a giant green snake. And then there was the real snake that had coiled affectionately around her wrist when she grabbed it for support, thinking it another hanging vine! Meg shivered and decided not to remember that particular incident. She was already heartily ashamed of her involuntary scream, particularly since the snake had seemed considerably more frightened than she was. The shock had caused her to increase her pace, with near-disastrous results. She'd stumbled several times, turned her ankle, torn her skirt, and bent one of the spokes of her trusty umbrella so that she doubted whether it would ever open again. But now she was here, anyway, with Piers under her eye where he couldn't get up to any nonsense without her.

"I can't let you go off alone," she told him now. "It's too dangerous."

The thought of Piers going off into the bush alone, possibly never to return, upset her more than she had anticipated. He couldn't disappear like that, not now when she'd just found him again! Their argument yesterday had made her feel alive and real again, not the shadowy "useful Meg" who served her father's needs or packed up Harry's tropical kit. And it had made her realize just how lonely she'd been in the years since she left the Damery household. Piers didn't look through her just because she wasn't pretty, or talk down to her just because she was a woman, or automatically flirt with her because she was the first white woman he'd seen for years. Granted, he was irritating and argumentative and sarcastic, but at least he made her feel like a person instead of a convenience. How could she give all that up?

"If it's dangerous for me," Piers riposted, "its twice as dangerous for you, and I'm not about to be saddled with a woman to take care of on a trip like this. You don't seem to understand, Meg, this isn't a pleasant little riverboat cruise. I may have to go deep into the bush. You can't tramp through miles of forest and live on native chop."

"I expect I'll quite like agouma," Meg told him. "I'm looking forward to tasting it." With each argument that Piers advanced, her determination to go with him increased. How could she give Piers up so soon after finding him? She looked at his angry face, blue eyes flashing dangerously, uncombed yellow hair sticking up on the back of his head, and felt a disabling wave of fondness that almost hurt her. She wanted to reach out and smooth his hair back, feel the roughness of his unshaven cheek against her palm . . .

Only to comfort him, of course. Meg told herself that while taking a firm grip on her bent umbrella to keep her hands from straying. All she felt for Piers, all she could possibly feel for him, was a sisterly fondness. After all, if he weren't practically her brother it wouldn't be proper for her to go off into the bush with him—and she was absolutely determined to do that.

"I'm going," she reiterated. "It's not fair. You men get to go all over the world having adventures and I've been stuck in England keeping house for Papa. This is my very first real adventure and I'm not going to let you stop me."

"It's not your adventure," Piers said irritably, "it's mine, and you're trying to horn in on it. Just like when you were a little girl, following Harry and me around and trying to play soldiers with us."

"Trying," Meg returned, stung, "*trying*? Ha! I was a better shot than either of you."

"With an india-rubber catapult! Meg, these people use real guns. This isn't a game anymore."

"Aha! So you admit there's something fishy going on upriver."

Piers ran a hand through his long yellow hair and sighed. He stared at Meg with a blend of frustration and desire. Damn the girl! What business did she have to come poking her long black umbrella in here, lecturing him like a schoolteacher, squabbling like a nursery brat, and looking so disturbingly grown up? She wasn't a kid any longer; even under that miserable black dress, even stiff and proper in the corset she doubtless insisted on wearing, his practiced eye could make out the lines of a disturbingly sensual female figure. If she let her hair out of that tight bun and discarded a few dozen petticoats, she would be lovely enough to disturb any man's concentration. Already she was playing hell with his; he needed to be thinking about canoes and supplies and the Crocodile Society, but when Meg was around he had to concentrate on willing away the tightening in his loins.

He could, of course, shock her by doing just what he longed to do—by taking her in his arms and kissing her until her hair floated loose about her shoulders and her breasts sprang to life under that whalebone cage and her lips burned against his. He could make her aware that she was a woman, and he was a man, and that it was pure folly for the two of them to go off together into the jungle.

He could shock her, upset her, and completely destroy the free-and-easy camaraderie that she offered him. But he could not bring himself to do that. He had to find some other way of dissuading Meg from this trip, something that wouldn't embarrass her with a display of feelings she couldn't reciprocate. Piers yanked again at his long untrimmed hair, hoping the pain in his scalp would distract him from the aching need in his groin. It didn't work worth a damn.

"Well?" Meg prodded. "You admit it?"

Piers had all but lost track of the nominal

subject of their argument. For a wild moment he thought she was challenging him to admit to the feelings of desire he had tried so hard to conceal from her. Then he remembered. Oh, yes. Something fishy going on up the river.

"Yes, of course I admit it. What do you mean by admit, anyway? I told you I thought somebody framed me, I told you I was going upriver to investigate it. But first I have to see you safely out of this mess. Now *will* you pack your things and go home like a good girl?"

Meg indicated the bulging straw traveling case, which she had set down behind her when she confronted Piers. "These are my things. I thought you might be planning to sneak away early without me. And Captain Jacques confirmed it. He's going to swing by here to pick up up, isn't he? So I won't notice you leaving from the pier. He can just as well take two extra passengers as one. I'm going with you."

Meg finished the speech by folding both hands over the hooked handle of her umbrella, fighting the strong urge to reach out and touch Piers's cheek and tell him it was going to be all right. She could imagine the strength of his jaw under her fingers, the slightly prickly warm surface of his cheek. Imagination ran riot, and in her mind he turned his head sideways to kiss the palm of her hand, as if he were the Harry of her dreams, the blond hero who both deserved and returned her affection. Without planning or willing it, she let go of the umbrella and brushed her fingers across his cheek.

"Women!" Piers ground out between his teeth. His face flushed dark red and he reached out for her, scowling. His broad, flexing hands clamped down on her shoulders and Meg was shaken back and forth until her own teeth rattled. "I have *had*," he announced between shakes, "just about *enough* . . . of your *interference* . . . in my affairs."

"They're my affairs too!" Meg shouted back at him. She could feel the loosening weight of her bun sliding back and forth; if he didn't let her go, it would come down entirely. "What happens to you is my business! You have *no right* to go and get yourself killed without me!"

"Who said anything about getting killed? Get this straight. I'm going up the river, and you're going home on the first boat if I have to *tie* you up and *throw* you *aboard*!" Meg's head snapped back and forth and she heard the rustling sigh as the hairpins holding her bun in place gave way and the weight of fine floating hair spilled down over her neck and ears.

"*Now* look what you've done! Damn you, Piers, will you let me go now?" She thought two hairpins had tinkled down onto the bare boards where the straw matting was worn through; another one was sticking at a cockeyed angle half in and half out of the mat. Where were the others? Still caught in her loose hair? What a ridiculous sight she must be, disheveled and with the darned shoulder seams of her dress about to give way under Piers's energetic shaking. Silly, childish tears blurred Meg's vision and she felt her cheeks burning. "Please, Piers, let me go. I have to . . . have to . . ."

The blaze of anger in Piers's bright blue eyes died out, to be replaced by a subtler warmth that was altogether unfamiliar to Meg. "No," he said—softly, compared with the uninhibited shouting of a moment earlier—"no, I don't think I will let you go . . . just yet."

His hands were firm and strong on her shoulders. Meg could only watch helplessly, uncomprehending, as his arms bent to draw her closer and closer to him. When their faces were inches apart he pressed his lips against hers, sliding one hand around to the back of her neck to hold her in his embrace.

There was no need for force. Meg's senses reeled under the warm, shockingly familiar onslaught of lips and tongue, the slight roughness of his unshaven cheek beneath her hand, and the subtle man-scent of his body. His arms were strong and tender at once, holding her and cradling her like a precious object that mustn't be allowed to get away, and the sweetness of his kiss was like music singing through her body. She responded without thinking, opening her mouth to his, leaning against his long body, and feeling the shivers of this new feeling run through her from toes to head. He groaned, burying his hands in the silky mass of hair that tumbled down her back, and pulled her closer against his hard, muscular chest. His kiss deepened, and became more demanding, and Meg felt herself weaken as a delicious fire spread through her body.

There were rustling noises that sounded as if they came from the straw matting beneath her feet. One corner of her brain shrieked, "Mice!" while another, older part of her commanded her to ignore the stealthy noises and concentrate on this new, alarming sensation that seemed to have replaced her blood with champagne and set up a choir of songbirds just outside the window.

The rustling noises grew louder and more insistent, and despite herself Meg found that the thought of mice running up her skirts was beginning to impair her ability to enjoy Piers's embrace. She turned her head to free herself and whispered, "Piers, darling . . ."

At the slightest push he released her, stepping back immediately and clasping his hands behind him. Meg felt disappointed first, then embarrassed as she saw how he refused to meet her eyes.

"I'm sorry, Meg," he said before she could tell him that she'd only pushed him away because she was worried about the mice in the matting. "I wasn't . . . I didn't mean . . ."

Humiliation dyed Meg's cheeks crimson and darkened her gray eyes to the exact color of the rain clouds that hung low over the Ogowe in the wet season. Piers saw the stormy look in her eyes, the sudden high color, and the way she tossed her head to push back the floating masses of unmanageable fair hair, and his heart turned over. This was his Meg, his best friend through childhood, and so much more besides. She'd grown into a thoroughly desirable woman, with the clouds of light hair framing her delicate heart-shaped face and with the long limbs to match his own, hidden beneath her clumsy serge skirts.

He'd thought yesterday that she might have had more of a chance with Harry if she'd quit straining her hair back into that tight and unbecoming bun and hiding her tall slim figure beneath ugly, bunchy skirts that made her look like somebody's housekeeper. He'd also thought that it was rather a pity nobody had ever taught her how to accentuate her delicate beauty instead of concealing it. Now he was shamefully glad of her ignorance. At last, with Harry on the other side of the world and Meg here, he might have his chance with her.

Except that he couldn't keep her with him. Even if she forgave him for the shameful way he'd lost control a moment ago, how could he guarantee that it wouldn't happen again? Piers groaned aloud, swayed by conflicting impulses that surprised him by their strength. How could he let Meg go, just when he'd made the startling discovery that his best friend had grown up into a lovely young woman? He was tempted by the thought of joining her on the long journey back to England, to take advantage of all the long moonlit nights on deck and the sweet-scented tropic breezes of Madeira. Perhaps there, with the constraining presence of the other passengers, he could manage to court her slowly enough to win her love without shocking her by the raw urgency of his desire.

But on the other hand, how could he go away and leave this scandal unresolved behind him? It would be running away; he'd be a man under a cloud forever, poor Piers Damery, whose family shipped him off to Africa and who couldn't even make a go of it out there.

Piers set his jaw. "Listen, Meg," he said, angrily fighting down those inner impulses that cried out to him to take her in his arms again and kiss her senseless. "I apologize. Please forgive me. It won't happen again. You have to understand . . ."

Meg saw the tight muscle jumping under his jaw, the angry look in his eyes, and thought she understood all too well. Men did these things on impulse, or so she'd been told; it had been a long time since Piers had seen a white woman, and for a moment he'd forgotten that she was only Cousin Meg, the long-legged tomboy he'd grown up with. Now he was afraid she'd taken his impulsive kiss too seriously, when the last thing he wanted was a romantic entanglement with his cousin. She would probably just die of humiliation if he went on and explained all that out loud in excruciating detail.

"It's all right," she said tonelessly. "You don't have to explain. I understand perfectly. Let's just forget it and say no more about it, shall we?"

"It's just," Piers said desperately, "that you're the only person who still believes in me, Meg. I can't risk losing that. I can't let you go upriver with me. It's too dangerous, it's going to be a rough trip, and I need somebody back home who'll be on my side if things don't work out—"

"If things don't work out," Meg snapped, "you probably won't need anybody. Ever again. And won't that make you happy!"

She folded her arms and turned away from him, fighting conflicting emotions which she herself did not fully understand. Why should she care if Piers wanted to kiss her, or didn't want to kiss her, or whatever? It wasn't as if it had been Harry holding her in his arms, then pushing her away. If Harry ever kissed her like that, Meg thought, she'd have nothing else to wish for on this earth. And if he pushed her away immediately afterward, as Piers had done—that didn't bear thinking about. She'd want to die.

Meg told herself that she didn't feel anywhere near that unhappy about Piers's rejection of her. How could she? It wouldn't make sense. She didn't *want* Piers to make love to her, only to take her upriver. Meg swallowed past a strange lump in her throat and blinked her eyes several times, trying to force back an irrational desire to cry. "It really doesn't matter," she said again. "I look on you as a brother, Piers. What else—"

"What's that?" Piers interrupted her rudely, and Meg spun around, surprised by his sharp urgent tone. His face was raised slightly and his long nose was twitching as he sniffed the air. "Do you smell smoke?"

Meg was about to say no, when a slight shift of the breeze brought an unmistakable pungent scent to her nostrils. She coughed and her eyes watered. All at once she remembered the furtive rustling noises that she had taken for mice in the straw. Could those sounds have been made by somebody moving below, in the storeroom?

"Piers, I might have heard someone down below a few minutes ago."

"We've got to get out of here." Piers grabbed Meg's wrist and yanked her toward the door. Just as they reached the doorway, the stairs went up in a blazing tower of flame. Piers jumped back, throwing himself in front of Meg; something hit her behind the knees as she stepped back, and she fell over her traveling case. Automatically her fingers closed around the well-worn handle and she half crawled, half-stumbled toward the veranda. Already, great greasy black clouds of smoke were billowing through the room, choking her and making her eyes smart.

Once on the veranda, she was able to stand up and gulp in wonderful fresh damp air rising straight from the bronze surface of the river. She looked down into the rushing current and her fingers froze to the veranda railing. There was no way to climb down from here, and already the flames were licking at the bamboo poles that supported the sagging balcony.

"Come *on.*" Piers tried to pry Meg's hand away from the railing. "We've got to get out of here. We'll have to jump!"

He had to shout to be heard over the roaring of the fire behind and below them. The factory was going up like straw in a dry summer, and the heat of the flames scorched the backs of Meg's legs through the muffling layers of skirt and petticoat and underpetticoat and knit stockings. Meg's knees shook and she was physically incapable of letting go of the railing. She had always been secretly afraid of heights, her worst nightmares had been dreams of falling, but no nightmare had approached the terror she felt at looking down at the swiftly rushing brown current below.

"I'd just as soon be burned as be eaten by crocodiles!"

"How do you feel about being blown up?"

"*What*?"

"François stores his extra gunpowder in barrels at the back of the storeroom. Once the fire gets that far—"

Piers didn't finish the sentence. He didn't need to. Meg's hand loosened its terrified grip on the railing without her volition. But she still couldn't move. Her legs wouldn't carry her over the rail and into the greasy swirling water below the house.

A horrible squawking noise rose over the roaring of the fire. Meg jumped convulsively and squeezed her eyes shut tightly, sure that the powder had just exploded.

But then why wasn't she dead? The squawking noise, like a giant chicken being tortured, recurred even closer. Meg opened her eyes again to see the rusty bulk of the *Brazza* steaming up the river. Captain Jacques was shouting frantic orders at the helmsman. They were close enough now that she could see the naked, sweating Kruboys who bent almost double to shovel more coal into the engine. The red glare of the engine fire echoed the flames that scorched her back.

Piers grasped the captain's intention before Meg did. "Jump!" he shouted in her ear. When she shook her head, he picked her up bodily by the waist and hurled her over the railing, as far out into the river as he could manage. Meg's skirts tangled around her legs and her loose hair whipped around her eyes. She held her breath, expecting the cold shock of the water. Instead she landed on something warm and yielding.

"Missy fit for jump far far?" A hand slapped her on the back and Meg was pulled upright by the African deck passengers who had cushioned her fall. A stabbing pain shot through her midsection. Had she broken a rib in the fall? A hasty exploration with the fingers of one hand convinced her that the damage was less serious. Two of the whalebone stays of her corset had snapped, and while the lower ends stabbed her in the side, the upper broken ends poked through her dress and probably ruined it beyond repair. Never mind! She leaned sideways, finding the position in which the broken stays hurt least, and breathed out a shaky laugh. Whalebone and serge could be replaced. People could not—and where was Piers?

"Look, Ma," shouted one of the other passengers, "sky him rain white people today!" As he spoke, two more thumps resounded on the deck. The first was Meg's traveling bag. The much-tried case of woven straw burst open on the deck, showering lacy white petticoats and embroidered corset covers on the fascinated passengers.

The second thump was Piers. He landed feet first, with a flat-footed thud that must have sent shock waves through his spine, but he didn't pause to recover his balance. "You all right, Megsie? Good show!" Then he was shouldering through the crowd, shouting at Captain Jacques to pull away quickly before the factory went up.

"Mid-channel!" Captain Jacques shouted at the steersman. When the response didn't come quickly enough to suit him, he grabbed the helm himself and pulled the *Brazza* around at right angles to the river current, dragging her ruthlessly across a shallow stretch and plowing right through some of the dead trees that had beached on the tip of a sandbank. There was a protesting screech from some deep part of the ship, but they made it over the sandbank with a crown of dead branches around the steamer's nose like a decoration of honor.

Meg stared back at the shore, where the brightness of the dawn sky was eclipsed by the roaring mass of golden flames that had been Piers's factory. As she watched, the flames seemed to explode outward from the center, sending clouds of black smoke roiling toward the heavens from an intolerably bright, red-hot center. The clap of sound made her ears ring; all around her she could see the deck passengers jabbering and waving their hands, but she couldn't hear what they were saying.

A friendly hand patted Meg on the back and she spun around to see Captain Jacques grinning at her and pointing to his own ears while he shook his head. She imitated his gestures, shook her own head vigorously, and was relieved to find her hearing slowly returning. The ringing noise was still there, but now she could also hear the clamor of the excited deck passengers, the twittering of the birds that had taken to the sky *en masse*, and the roaring of some jungle animal whose morning had been disturbed by the explosion.

Captain Jacques shoved a glass into her hand and Meg drained off the contents without asking what was in it. The clear liquid burned her throat and made her cough, but she felt better afterward. The trade gin lit a small fire in her stomach to offset the icy coldness of fear that had gripped her since she stood on the railing with fire behind her and water before her.

Piers came up behind her and put both arms around her waist. Meg leaned back against his body without speaking, feeling deeply contented to be there with him. She'd expected to be dead by now. In the reaction of escape, everything seemed more vivid and real to her—the bright vibrant colors that decked the walls of the rain forest, the strength of the muddy current divided on either side of the *Brazza*, the warm comfort of Piers close to her. The hardness of his body molded her to his shape, the warmth of his arms around her made her midsection quiver with strange feelings. She leaned her head against his shoulder and closed her eyes, feeling at once totally alive and totally passive to whatever might come next.

"Very good, my young friend," Captain Jacques told Piers. Meg jumped at the sound of his voice and unobtrusively moved away from Piers, blushing at the realization that she'd been practically embracing him in front of all these people!

"But one question," the captain went on, ignoring Meg's blushes. "Do you always leave town in such an *explosive* manner? Ha-ha-ha!" He threw his head back and roared with laughter. It was a fine bright day, nobody had been killed in the explosion, his beloved steamer was all right, and there was plenty of gin on board. Why were the two mad English people looking so strained and unhappy?

Five

The long narrow cabin that Meg had occupied on the way up to Lambarene was hers again for the remainder of the voyage. The *Brazza* had not been designed with the idea of catering to white women travelers, and there was only the one passenger cabin on board. Piers, as the traders had done on the way up, shared the crowded quarters occupied by Captain Jacques, his mate Gaston, and the green-stenciled boxes of trade gin.

The physical surroundings meant little to him; he was too restless to stay belowdecks for more than a few minutes at a time. He was grateful for the chance to shave and trim his hair and dress in Gaston's second-best land suit while one of the Kru-boys washed his own clothes. It was a relief to throw off the disguise of the scruffy, drunken degenerate, the image he'd been carefully building up so that no one in Lambarene would suspect he stayed in Africa for any reason besides his utter inability to face civilization again.

Now, he told himself, all disguises were at an end. He was finally on his way upriver, persuaded that the heart of the mystery lay there and not in the small European community at

Lambarene. There was no need to pretend incapacity any longer.

Deep in his heart he knew there was another reason for his sudden insistence on cleanliness. He couldn't bear to face Meg in his guise of a drunken bum. Even though she'd seen through the pretense immediately, something in him revolted at the thought of continuing to appear before her stinking and unshaven, his clothes reeking of the brandy he'd dumped over them.

Meg . . . Piers crossed his arms on the railing of the *Brazza's* afterdeck and folded his long body into a shape like a contorted question mark, staring unseeing at the panorama of African jungle life that drifted by. Twisted green shadows of the rain forest, chattering monkeys and a screeching parrot, a native village with women washing clothes in the river, and blue smoke of the cooking fires mingling with the intense blue of the sky, all passed before his eyes without making the slightest impression on his brain. All he could see was Meg as she'd looked up at him yesterday, her wide gray eyes like stormclouds, her lips full and hot from his angry kiss.

How lovely she'd been then, with her prim propriety disheveled, her calm assumptions shaken up! Piers cursed the clarity with which his mind insisted on repeating that kiss. The feel of her slender shoulders under his hands, the silky warmth of her mouth welcoming his. She had a sensual nature, little Meg, though she didn't know it yet. Give him a few days alone with her, and he'd wager he could make her forget his brother Harry ever existed.

Yes, gibed an independent corner of his recalcitrant mind. You with no right to speak to a decent woman, much less make love to one—you'll frighten her, shock her, take her by storm while she's too upset to understand what's going on. And then what?

Piers clenched his hands on the rusty top railing of the steamer. He had no right to think of Meg in that way. Even if she weren't still in love with Harry, there was no reason why she should settle for a man in his circumstances—and every reason why he should keep his hands off her. He would just have to think of her as the skinny little girl whom he and Harry had teased unmercifully as she joined in their childhood games.

Piers forced his mind back to those early years, before any of them had been shaken by the demands of adult life.

Memory temporarily erased his present surroundings and his present troubles. For all he knew or cared about his surroundings, he might have been back in England, where his golden-haired big brother led their trio in storming a fort or fighting Red Indians while the skinny, big-eyed Meg loaded their catapults, carried water, and insisted all too often on taking a shot at the enemy for herself.

At that time they'd seemed inseparable. How had they drifted apart so quickly? Meg, of course, had been taken away by her father to that remote Yorkshire mansion. Piers wondered if she knew that Sir Digby had discouraged them from writing to her, saying that letters would only upset her and make it difficult for her to settle into her new life. As far as he knew, his parents and Harry had obeyed the prohibition; he was the only one who'd occasionally scribbled a note to tell her about his escapades, and he hadn't been that regular a correspondent.

Then Harry, when he went away to college, had discovered fame and glory and ambition all in one term, or so it seemed. Suddenly the war games and pretenses had been put aside in favor of deadly earnest work, as he beat his brains out learning the languages that came so easily to Piers but not to him, as he spent his vacations visiting college friends whose parents had influence in the diplomatic service. Piers supposed the Foreign Office was Harry's natural home; he might not be as quick as Piers to pick up foreign languages and foreign ways, but he had the Damery charm in full measure, coupled with the hard-driving, competitive desire for success that kept him sternly pointed in the one direction.

But Lord, he'd become stuffy, with his single-minded insistence on work and advancement and getting ahead and making the right sort of friends! Piers almost laughed aloud to think how dismayed Harry had been when his little brother came up to Oxford, bright and irreverent and far more interested in pranks and beer than in tutorials and examinations. Piers knew he'd been a sad embarrassment to Harry, but he couldn't help it—there was something in him that couldn't resist tweaking the nose of stuffy Victorian morality. He'd always half-suspected that Harry was the one who'd turned him in for taking Shifty Kate and her girlfriends swimming in the college fountain, but he bore his brother no malice for it; Harry had his way to make, and he'd warned Piers often enough that he wasn't going to let family loyalty drag him into the cloud of scandal and incident and gossip that surrounded his young brother.

The thing he did hold against Harry was demonstrably none of his brother's fault: the fact that Meg's childhood crush on him had not gone away over the years. If anything, it was worse than ever. Piers scowled and shook a menacing fist over the railing at an incurious stork fishing from the sandbanks near shore. Why should Meg be content to spend her life packing up Harry's tropical kit and hoping for a casual smile from him? Dammit, she deserved better than that from life!

Like what? inquired the cynical voice at the back of his mind. Like a drifter, a lounger, a ne'er-do-well, a young man who couldn't settle to a steady job at home and drifted out to West Africa only to get into the worst scandal Gabon had seen since the end of the slave trade?

Piers straightened his long limbs, shot the cuffs of his borrowed shirt down toward his wrists with a practiced motion, and gave a firm nod to the collection of beached driftwood they were steaming past. One of the logs opened a broad eye and closed it again as the steamer disturbed the muddy back eddies of water around it.

All that was at an end, Piers promised himself. To be sure, he'd been most irresponsible with the series of jobs his long-suffering relatives found for him at home, but he'd done nothing to disgrace himself in their eyes—only to irritate his father beyond bearing. And the current scandal was none of his making. He would trace the problem to its roots upriver, force a confession from the leaders of the Crocodile Society, bring them to justice, exonerate his name, and go happily home to England with Meg, whom he would have wooed and won in his spare time while carrying out this adventurous program.

And, he promised himself, he meant to woo her—not to seduce her. Surely he had enough self-control left to keep him from taking advantage of a girl who hadn't the least idea what torments her full pouting lower lip and slender figure were putting him through. Surely he could keep his fingers from running through her silky hair, his hands from unbuttoning that tight blouse and unlacing the whalebone corset, his brute desires from overwhelming her gentle innocence. He'd be no kind of a man at all if he couldn't do that much for her.

Any other small projects? inquired his sardonic other voice. A few dragons to slay?

"By all means," said Piers. "Why not?"

But the first thing was to find Meg. His lips still tingled with the memory of her response to his first angry kiss. How seductive it was, that blend of innocence and unknowingly sensual response! What a lovely woman his long-legged, skinny friend had grown up into! It was too bad her heart was set on Harry, but as long as they were positively stuck with making the river journey from Lambarene to Talagouga together . . . well, Piers had never been one to let an opportunity go to waste. By the time they reached Talagouga, he resolved, he would at least have kissed Meg again—properly, and for long enough to find out if her response was just surprise, or if she could possibly care for him as a man. While he was upriver seeking out the leaders of the Crocodile Society, she could wait for him at the Mission Évangélique in Talagouga and think over which she wanted, a golden dream hero who hardly knew she existed or a real flesh-and-blood man who loved her right here and now. And by the time he came back triumphant, he'd be self-confident enough to sweep her right off her feet if she hadn't made the appropriate choice on her own.

Whistling under his breath, Piers set off to find Meg and carry out the first part of his program, without considering too deeply whether she was likely to comply with all parts of the plan.

He found her on a cushion in the shade of the awning above the afterdeck, holding a forgotten drink and watching the forest roll by as the *Brazza* tacked and veered upriver. They had to steer a tortuous course across the broad stream of the Ogowe to avoid all the sandbanks and snags and tempting fake channels that opened up among the trees; at one moment they were so close to the banks that bright green curling tendrils of vines hung down and brushed the top of the steamer, then a sudden change of course brought them into mid-channel with a gleaming bronze mirror dividing them from either shore. Meg sat on her heels and watched the quick changes in scenery and steering with rapt attention, so immersed in the mystery of the forest that she seemed quite unaware of Piers's approach behind her.

He dropped to one knee beside her and took the glass out of her fingers just before she spilled its contents all over the deck. As Meg jumped, her hand flew up, her arm hit the bottom of the glass Piers had just removed from her grasp, and pinkish liquid went spattering upward in a fountain that showered them both with lukewarm, sticky droplets.

"Oh . . . oh, my goodness, I'm so sorry," Meg stammered. It was just the sort of accident that used to send Sir Digby off into a fit of raving anger about being saddled with such a hopeless, awkward, regular Long Meg of a daughter. "Are you all right? Here, let me . . ." She scrubbed at the pink stain on Piers's sleeve with the first thing that came to hand, a fold of her own skirt.

"Oh, don't fuss, Meg. It was my fault for startling you." Piers set the now empty glass down in a corner behind him and patted her hand. The confident touch of his long bronzed fingers sent strange feelings through Meg, and she found herself suddenly afraid to meet his eyes. She wanted to jerk her hand free—no, she didn't, but she ought to—but then, it was only Piers, giving her a comforting brotherly caress, and how embarrassing it would be if she behaved as though she thought he was trying to flirt with her and then he thought he had to set her straight.

"I like your hair that way," Piers said. His voice was deeper and slower than she remembered. "Softer. Most becoming."

Meg's hands flew to her hair, desperately patting the loose strands back into place. "I wasn't trying to get myself up," she defended herself automatically. "It's just . . . well, I don't have enough hairpins left to do it up properly." After some frustrated wrestling with her two remaining hairpins and the floating masses of fine, fair, unmanageable hair, she had settled for braiding the locks at her temples into two slender plaits which could be drawn around to the back of her head, partially confining the crackling cloud that fell freely down her back to her waist. Sir Digby would have snorted and asked Meg if she thought she was trying to get herself up in Aesthetic Dress, like those silly women who followed the Pre-Raphaelites. And he would probably have followed up the query with some wounding comments on the folly of a tall, plain, awkward girl's doing anything to draw attention to her appearance.

Meg half-expected some comments from Piers, but instead he only lifted a lock of her pale, fine hair and spread it out over his fingers, where the individual strands glittered in the afternoon sunshine. "Most becoming," he murmured again. "Meg, you've grown up into a deuced lovely woman. Didn't anybody ever tell you that?" He lowered his lips to the smooth golden lock of hair spread over his hand.

For a moment Meg's heart thrilled within her. The words, the tone, the bright golden head bent before her, all might have come out of one of her daydreams of the day when Harry finally noticed her as a woman.

Then Piers raised his head, and she saw the bright demons dancing in his blue eyes, and she remembered that Harry was thousands of miles away. "Who'd have thought it," he said with a crooked smile, "little Meg with her ink-stained fingers and her catapult tucked into the top of one black stocking, turning into such a beauty!"

The mild teasing restored Meg's sense of perspective. This was just her old friend Piers, trying to make her feel comfortable about the slightly improper circumstances of their travel up the river. Traveling with a man she wasn't related to, with her one good dress already torn to shreds and her hair falling about her shoulders—yes, she might well have felt shy, if it had been anybody else but Piers. Even Harry would have been uncomfortable with such an unconventional situation, and that would have made her uncomfortable.

"Yes, indeed," she agreed cheerfully, twitching the lock of her hair out of Piers's fingers and pushing the heavy, shining mass back behind her shoulders, "I expect I'd better put my hair up when we reach Talagouga, or I'll drive the good gentlemen of the mission quite mad for my beauty! Perhaps one of the ladies there can lend me some hairpins."

Piers muttered something which Meg couldn't quite make out. It sounded as if he'd said, "I'll make damned sure she doesn't," but that was absurd. He must have said, "I'm sure she will," or something of that sort.

He was still kneeling by her side; the pose, with its suggestion of casual intimacy, made Meg feel slightly ill-at-ease. The foredeck of the *Brazza* was crowded with squatting and sleeping African passengers bound for their upriver villages, but this small section of afterdeck was reserved for the European members of the crew and the cabin passengers. On this stage of the trip, that meant just four people—herself, Piers, the captain, and his mate—and just now Captain Jacques and Gaston were fully occupied in swinging the steamer past one sandbank after another, as they navigated a particularly broad, shallow, and tricky part of the river. She and Piers were alone for all practical purposes; not, of course, that the concept disturbed her in the slightest! Heavens, after they hired canoes to take them upriver from Talagouga, it would be just the two of them in the bush with their native rowers, day after day after day! It was just . . . well, somehow she couldn't stop thinking about the moment when he had kissed her, just before the fire broke out.

"You know, Meg," Piers murmured, "until I saw you here, I'd almost forgotten how much fun we used to have together."

"Yes," Meg agreed. "You and I and Harry used to get up to all sorts of things, didn't we? What impossible children we must have been! I'm sure we drove Aunt Alice to despair many a time!"

"Mother never took her head out of an Oriental dictionary long enough to notice the uproar," Piers said dryly. "It was the tutors we drove to giving notice. But, Meg, we're not children anymore, and I still like being with you."

His hand rested on the deck beside her, less than an inch of space between them. Meg's skin tingled as she wondered how it would feel if he took her hand again. Then she wondered what was wrong with her, feeling this way about someone who was practically her brother! It must be his resemblance to Harry that was confusing her feelings.

"Oh, look," she exclaimed in pretended excitement. It was an excuse to raise her hand and point into the forest. "What is that lovely bird?"

Piers stared suspiciously at an unbroken green wall of trees and vines. "I don't see—" he began, but even as he spoke the steam sheered off into mid-channel and the forest receded to a dark green line in which nothing could be distinguished.

"What a pity," said Meg blandly, "it was really a most beautiful bird, with red and green tail feathers." She dropped both hands into her lap and folded them together. There, she told her hands severely, now don't get any ideas about brushing your fingers along Piers's wrist, or any other silly notions!

"You know, Piers," she said, striving for a light tone, "there is something we need to get straight if we're to travel together. About . . . what happened . . . just before the fire . . . you know?" She was finding it oddly hard to breathe.

Piers was looking at her with that crooked smile. "Yes. We do need to get that straight. And this is as good a time as any. At least we won't be interrupted by fires or callers or other natural disasters. Meg, I have to explain—"

"No, you don't," Meg said rapidly, before he could go on. "I understand *perfectly*."

Piers's eyes opened with a flash of blue, like the wings of a colorful forest bird startled into flight. "You do?"

"Yes, and I don't intend to make any more of the incident," Meg said. "I understand that men have these passing impulses, especially if they've been alone for a long time, and it didn't have anything to do with me personally."

"You feel quite sure of that, do you?" Piers leaned back against the wall behind them and dropped one long arm over Meg's shoulders.

Meg gave a hollow, unconvincing laugh. At least, it sounded quite false in her own ears; she would have to hope Piers was less perceptive. "Heavens, Piers, I'm not a silly girl of seventeen, expecting every man I meet to flirt with me! I know perfectly well I'm not the sort of girl you and Harry are attracted to."

"Let's just leave Harry out of this one conversation, shall we?"

"I only m-meant . . ." To her fury and dismay, Meg felt her wretched stammer coming back. She clamped her teeth down hard on her lower lip for a moment until she could go on calmly. "B-besides, it would be most improper if there were anything between us. I look on you as a brother, Piers, you know that."

"How reassuring!" His smooth, sarcastic tones were anything but brotherly.

"I just wanted to assure you," Meg said on a rush of her last breath, "that I certainly don't intend to make anything further of the incident."

"Don't you?" Piers's arm tightened around her shoulders, and he brought his face close to hers. She stared as if mesmerized into his bright blue eyes, noting every detail of his face, even the slight nicks where his razor had slipped along his jaw and the way the golden hairs of his eyebrows grew out in a spiraling curve. "What a pity. Because I," he said in a softly caressing voice that held her captive as much as the strength of his arm did, "I intend to make quite a lot more of it."

As his warm lips brushed hers, the world slipped and began to tilt gently sideways. Meg closed her eyes, giving in to the ecstatic rush of sensations that flooded her body, and tried to ignore the shrieking voice of protest in the back of her mind. This was wrong, all wrong—it wasn't what she had come to Africa for—and it was too piercingly sweet to deny. Her hands uncurled against Piers's chest and she could feel the beating of his heart through her open palms, and then through her soft breasts as her hands reached up around his neck and pulled him closer. His tongue parted her lips, skimming back and forth, teasing, then exploring the sweet cavern of her mouth slowly and deeply. Her mouth was liquid fire under his kiss and she felt a queer melting sensation in her bones.

A bone-jarring thud shook the decks of the steamer, and an elbow drove into Meg's midriff. She coughed, sputtered indignantly, and tried to shake Piers off her. He seemed to be trying to crawl into her skirt. The back of her neck was bent at a peculiar angle, and something was pulling her hair.

"S-sorry, Megsie." Piers raised himself above her on hands and knees. The slight tremor in his voice was due to laughter. As his weight came off her, she was able to push herself out of the corner into which she'd fallen. "I do pick my moments, don't I?"

"What happened?" Now that she was able to sit up, Meg realized that the deck was tilting sideways at a crazy angle. The steamer had stopped moving, and the shouts of the Kru-boys were followed by pounding feet and French curses around the helm.

"I rather think," said Piers, "that we've run aground on a sandbank."

Grasping the railing for support, he hauled himself to a more or less standing position and dusted off his clothes. "If you'll forgive me, I think I'd better see what I can do to help." Inching his way along the tip-tilted deck, he paused to look back at Meg with a flashing light of mischief in his blue eyes. "By the way, Megsie, have you ever considered: if you look on me as a brother, you must extend the same courtesy to dear old Harry." Chuckling at her widening eyes, he worked his way hand over hand along the railing toward the uptilted bows of the steamer.

After Captain Jacques had finished tearing at his hair, dancing up and down on the slanted deck, and announcing that they were stuck irretrievably until the rains brought high water to float the steamer off, the actual damage proved to be slight and easily repaired. One of the Kru-boys stripped to even less than his usual attire of ragged knee-breeches and red kerchief, and slipped overboard to examine the damage while his mates howled and beat the water with long sticks to discourage any crocodiles that might be in the vicinity. He came back on board and reported in Pidgin English that it should be possible to winch the boat free using a rope looped around one of the trees on the nearest shore.

Although Piers had said he was going to help, Meg noticed that he didn't take an active part in the rescue operations. While Captain Jacques and Eight-Fingers Gaston shouted orders at the sweating Kru-boys who hauled at the rope, he squatted on the deck and carried on a conversation in Mpongwe with one of the native passengers.

"Interesting point of view," he said finally, rising to his feet and making his way crabwise over the tilting deck to the place at the railing from which Meg was watching the rescue operations.

"It doesn't seem like the best of times to collect native lore," Meg teased him. "I suspect you were just trying to avoid getting your clothes wet and dirty." Captain Jacques and Gaston were now splashing around in two feet of muddy water, directing operations personally and with great vigor.

"Not a bit of it," said Piers with dignity. "I was carrying on with our investigation. You do remember why we are making this little jaunt upriver, don't you?"

Meg regarded his tall, white-clad form with sisterly exasperation. At least, she tried to keep it to that. The memory of that moment before the steamer went aground still had her breathing shaky and her hands damp. She felt as if part of herself had been left there in Piers's arms, as if she would not be whole again until he finished whatever it was he'd started to do. "Of course I remember the purpose of our journey."

And getting into meaningless entanglements with Piers was no part of that purpose. She had to remember that a kiss was just a casual entertainment to him, not the explosion of the senses that shook her whole universe. "But I don't happen to speak Mpongwe, Igalwa, Fan, and half a dozen other native dialects. Why don't you wipe those canary feathers off your face and tell me what you've discovered?"

"The gentleman in the top hat and Isabella-colored loincloth," said Piers, indicating the man with whom he had been talking, "expressed some surprise at the efforts the crew were making to keep away crocodiles while our friends were in the river. It seems he is convinced that crocodiles never eat people."

Meg knit her brows. "Really? I *am* surprised. Mr. Cavanaugh gave me to understand that they had carried away two women from Lambarene only this year, when they went down to get water from the river. The women, I mean, not the crocodiles."

"Of course they eat people. The important thing is why our friend believes otherwise. He says 'everybody' knows that some witches have the power to turn themselves into crocodiles when they hunger for human flesh, and that just now there is a very powerful crocodile witch among the upriver Fan, who has scared off all the other crocodile witches on the river. So, according to him, unless one happens to have annoyed this particular head witch, one is in no danger whatsoever from the crocodiles on the river."

Meg's fair brows almost met over the bridge of her nose. "I don't understand . . ."

"How they can believe such ridiculous things?"

"No," Meg said, "it doesn't sound any more complicated than the Trinity, and of course I believe that as a matter of faith, so I'm sure they can believe in men turning into crocodiles if they want to. The only difference is that the Trinity is true and this business of witches is false."

Piers snorted into his hand. "Er . . . quite so."

Meg regarded him suspiciously. "Piers! You haven't become an *atheist* as well as . . . as everything else?"

Piers shook his head. "No, Megsie. I was just struck by your way of putting it, that's all."

"What I was going to say," said Meg, "before I was so rudely interrupted, is that I don't understand what you could have done to annoy the head crocodile witch."

"Neither do I. But that's what I'm going upriver to find out."

"We," Meg corrected him. A wild triumphant

yell from the bows of the steamer drowned her out.

"What?"

A splash and a series of bumps heralded the success of the winching plan. The half-naked Kru-boys jumped back onto the steamer, yelling and shaking themselves so that water sprayed off their gleaming skin and onto the passengers. Captain Jacques and Gaston waded back aboard at a more sedate pace.

"You mean," Meg called over the shouts of victory and Captain Jacques's vociferous demands for a good head of steam from the engine room, "that's what *we* are going to find out."

But Piers was conferring with the captain on their chances of making it to the next village upriver without stopping to take on wood fuel, and the set of his squarely turned back suggested that he had no intention of hearing her correction.

Night fell over the Ogowe River as swiftly as dawn had come twelve hours before. One moment Meg was leaning over the railing of the *Brazza*, watching the lighted cooking fires and playing children in the riverside village where they had tied up for the night; the next, with no more warning than the harsh cry of a faraway bird, the white flowers that garlanded the river's rim folded their petals, and lavender shadows covered the village. A few heartbeats later, almost before the eyes had time to adjust, the river was swathed in soft velvety blackness in which the cooking fires onshore and the stars overhead shone out with piercing brightness.

A hand brushed Meg's arm and she jumped, letting out an involuntary little cry of surprise.

"Didn't mean to startle you," Piers apologized. "I've brought up your shawl. You shouldn't expose yourself to the night air—it brings on fevers."

Meg thought the well-known bad effects of the African night air might already have attacked her. She had been feeling quite normal a moment ago, but since Piers surprised her she felt waves of heat rising to her face and receding with equal rapidity, leaving her at once flushed and chilly.

Without waiting for her permission, Piers draped the light crocheted shawl over Meg's shoulders. His hands rested atop the shawl for a moment, holding her very lightly, yet it seemed to Meg that they weighed her down intolerably. She could neither speak nor move until he lifted his hands. Wouldn't he step back? Surely he must be through arranging the folds of the shawl now? Meg felt burning hot under the light cover.

As though he'd read her thoughts, Piers gave her shoulders a final pat and stepped to one side, joining her at the rail. For a while they leaned on the railing in companionable silence, listening to the quiet sounds of the rain forest settling to sleep, and Meg felt her equanimity returning. There was a sleepy clucking and whirring from the bark-sided hut near the water's edge. Hens, she wondered, or doves? She could ask Piers, but she felt reluctant to break their comfortable silence. Whichever the sound came from, it was a reassuringly domestic note and made her feel almost at home.

From high in the trees came a rustling noise, followed by the snapping of a branch and a chorus of agitated chittering. Meg pictured a monkey trusting his weight to a twig, nearly falling, and indignantly telling the world about it.

Farther away, out in midstream, the river rippled over a sandbank with a restful, sleepy gurgling sound. Splashing in the shallows told Meg that a long-legged bird was stalking to shore, regretfully giving up fishing for the night. In the distant depths of the forest a heavy, irregular drumming sound echoed through the night. She supposed it came from the famous "talking drums" that she'd read about in missionary reports.

All was exotic, yet somehow familiar and peaceful too. Meg felt, ridiculously, as though she had finally come home after years of wandering in strange and barren lands. Even if Piers hadn't wanted to prove his innocence, she thought, she would have been able to understand why he wanted to stay here. Once Africa got inside your soul, England must seem cold and lifeless by comparison.

She stole a glance at the man beside her, now visible only as a dark profile against the star-sprinkled sky. The firm chin and long nose, the hair already falling over his ears after that morning's hasty trim, all were as familiar to her as if she'd been looking at him for years instead of only two days. Meg's eyes lingered on the smooth line of his lips. Yes . . . Piers, too, was at once exotic and familiar. Which was he? The boy she'd played with, or the unhappy man who'd written that plea for help to his brother? Neither seemed to fit. Meg thought that somehow, in the long weeks between that anguished letter and her arrival, Piers must have found deep reserves or inner strength to draw on. She'd come to Africa thinking that she would bully him, for his own good, into doing whatever was necessary to clear his name and get his life back on track.

But the man she'd found here wasn't easy to bully, and he responded in unexpected ways. It seemed to Meg that she could still feel the insistent, angry pressure of Piers's lips on hers, the strength of his hands forcing her close to him while the assault on her senses melted her into acquiescence.

It wasn't anything she'd ever expected to feel for good old Piers. She'd imagined feeling that way if Harry ever took her in his arms . . .

No. No, she hadn't, Meg admitted honestly. She couldn't have imagined that anything could be so wonderful. And that was only *Piers's* kiss! If he could do that to her, what must it be like to be kissed by a man one loved and respected and looked up to, a man with purpose and ambition, like Harry Damery?

Meg longed to know. And with that longing, borne on the sweet flower-scented breeze that floated about them in the warm night, came a wicked, teasing thought. Harry Damery, after all, was several thousand miles away. And Piers was right here beside her. Wouldn't it be . . . well, *interesting* to find out what it would have been like if they hadn't been interrupted by the fire and the explosion? In fact, to take up where they had left off?

No such thing, Meg's better self said firmly. Piers doesn't think of you that way—he's done his best to explain that, poor man! And you certainly don't think of him as a lover! My goodness, how could you possibly get romantic about someone who used to copy your arithmetic lessons just before the tutor came in?

Meg glanced through her lashes at Piers and tried to superimpose her remembered image of an ink-stained schoolboy on the virile reality of the man beside her. It didn't work. Her eyes were trapped, lingering on his broad shoulders, on the tapering sweep down to narrow hips and long, muscular legs to which his white trousers clung in the heavy, damp air. This wasn't the schoolboy friend of her memory or the careless, irresponsible young man with whom she'd once enjoyed a few days' holiday in London. At some time when she wasn't looking, Piers had grown into a man, strong and masculine and commanding.

It isn't fair! cried Meg silently. They were both twenty-five, but the years that had made her feel old and faded had only gilded Piers with the African sun. Here she was already older than the laughing girls Harry Damery chose to squire around on his brief leave, only fit to spend the rest of her life being a sister to someone. The African adventure that had risen before her as a chance to give meaning to her life was no longer enough. She wanted something more, and her hands clenched and unclenched restlessly on the railing before her as she tried to discover what "more" a tall, plain woman, already past her first youth, could possibly hope for.

"What's the matter?" Piers asked softly. His hand covered hers for the briefest of moments, just long enough to send wild quivering thrills of fear and excitement through Meg's body; then he was leaning against the rail again, arms folded, staring at the small bright lights of the village fires.

Her fingers relaxed on the railing. That bolt of pleasure that transfixed her at Piers's touch might mean that she was a wicked, wanton girl, but at the moment Meg felt that was better than the image she'd been carrying so long of herself as the eternal spinster, the dried-up schoolteacher.

"Dried-up?" whispered the soft, moist evening breeze as it caressed her cheek and molded the heavy fabric of her skirt to her thighs.

"Faded?" quietly asked the white flowers at the river's edge, now visible only as blurs of lightness against the dark unknowable mass of the rain forest.

Meg laughed aloud, feeling a mad gaiety that had not possessed her since Sir Digby took her up to Yorkshire and she put her girlhood behind her. "Nothing's the matter, Piers," she told him. "I was thinking . . . stupid thoughts." She moved a little closer, feeling a renewed excitement when the edge of his white sleeve brushed her arm. The breeze from shore grew stronger, making Meg deliciously, dangerously aware of her body under the confining dark skirt and white shirtwaist. She had been forced to discard her corsets for lack of a piece of whalebone to repair the broken stay, but she had been unable, in the heat of the cabin, to make herself put on the red flannel petticoat that Aunt Alice had taught her was a lady's best protection against dangerous chills. The soft evening breeze, laden with the perfume of strange flowers and the green growing scent of the rain forest, pushed her lacy white petticoats against her thighs, made her feel how her uncorseted breasts nestled into the foaming whitework of her chemise.

"You are stupid," Piers agreed. "Take this

brother business, for instance. You do remember that we're not really related?" He paused, waiting for a reply that Meg felt unable to give. There was a heavy pulse beating at the base of her throat, and she couldn't seem to get enough air, no matter how deeply she breathed.

"Not at all related," Piers emphasized when she didn't speak. "In fact, I can't think of anybody I feel less related to than you, at this moment. So if that's a problem . . ."

"Why . . . would that be a problem?" Meg asked. The beating pulse had dropped to her chest, where it was pounding so hard that she was surprised Piers didn't notice. And her intake of air had narrowed to a thread, barely enough to keep her upright, not nearly enough for talking.

Piers turned his head and looked at her, his eyes two deep shadows in the glimmering oval of his face. "I don't know." His voice was low and husky, as though he too were having trouble breathing.

The river flowing past the boat rippled with a light, dancing rhythm in total contrast to the strength of its dark, irresistible current. Onshore, a woman lifted her voice in a slow, wailing chant that echoed through the darkness of the African night, evoking strange, dark images that stirred half-hidden in the shadows of Meg's thoughts.

She couldn't look at Piers anymore. His yellow head bending toward her, the outline of his body against the hot darkness of the night, were etched on her vision with a sharp clarity that almost hurt. With an effort of will, Meg wrenched her gaze from him and stared up at the sky.

The stars seemed to hang lower and shine brighter than they did in England, dancing lamps that swung from the deep velvety blue of the sky. She had the illusion that she could put up her fingers and capture one in her hand. Lower and lower the twinkling points of light danced before her, until the black line of the jungle cut them off. Deep and unknowable, that blackness stretched out before her, an unexplored territory that made her shiver with fear and anticipation.

"Cold?" Piers reached to pull up the shawl that had slipped to Meg's elbows, but his hand stopped just before his fingertips would have brushed against the knotted fringe. As though he were afraid of something; as though the touch would burn him. Meg waited in stillness, holding her breath, feeling that the next movement would make or break something new and infinitely precious. She fancied that she could feel the pressure of his hand through the quarter-inch of air that separated them; like waves of heat and sound, it beat against her skin.

Onshore, the African woman's wailing rose to a shuddering crescendo. She cried out sharply on a high note, three times, and silence fell.

"*Meg?*"

As though the woman's cry of release had freed him, Piers moved blindly forward. His fingertips just brushed against Meg's wrist where the tight cuff of her sleeve ended. She felt the touch with all her senses at once, a blinding fire that leapt through her body and ignited desires she hadn't even guessed at. She moved toward him and his hand closed around her wrist, holding her against the rail while his body covered hers and his mouth came down on hers with a desperate urgency she could not have fought if she wanted to.

But she didn't want to fight him. The same need was coursing through her blood, making her cling to Piers, knowing the long hard lines of his body through her dress and petticoats. Her lips tingled with his kiss and she returned the pressure without knowing what she did, opening her mouth under the demands he made, feeling herself on fire as he tasted her sweetness. Slowly his tongue traced the outlines of her full, soft lips, then slid past her teeth to sweep her mouth from corner to corner. His flavor was dark and heady; his cheek was rough under her palm, his arms were strong about her, and the culmination of all her girlish dreams was there in the dizzying intoxication of the moment.

His lips roamed Meg's face, placing soft kisses on her eyelids, nibbling gently on her ear. Then his mouth glided down the silky skin of her throat, pausing at the beating pulse at its base and igniting new fires of delight within her. He moved lower, half-kneeling to press his mouth on the tempting curves so inadequately confined by lacy chemise and white shirtwaist blouse. His mouth sought the taut peaks of her breasts through the thin fabric and the sharp pleasure of his touch made Meg feel as if her whole body was alight with ecstasy. Wonderingly, hardly knowing who or where she was, Meg caressed the golden head that was buried between her breasts.

"Oh, Harry . . ." she whispered.

Too late she caught the words, knew her mistake, wished them back. Piers's arms released her and he stood up, his face a palely glimmering oval against the darkness around them.

"Piers, no!" she cried, catching at his sleeve. "I didn't mean—"

Politely, gently, Piers shook himself free and stepped back. "Didn't you, Meg? Well, neither did I. It was a pleasant evening's amusement, but you'll excuse me if I draw the line at substituting for my absent brother."

Each word cut through her like a blow from one of the savage rhinoceros-hide whips the slave traders had once used. Meg felt as though she could easily sink down on the deck forever. But she didn't. She remained proudly erect, one hand behind her clutching the railing so tightly that the iron edges cut into her fingers, while Piers walked away from her without another word. When he was out of sight, she promised herself, she would go to her cabin and cry in decent privacy.

Six

As the *Brazza* approached Talagouga on the following day, the broad brassy sheet of the Ogowe narrowed to become a swiftly rushing stream bounded by high banks. The little steamer seemed to be physically huffing and puffing with the effort of fighting against the current, and Captain Jacques spent every minute at the wheel, the stem of an extinguished pipe clenched between his teeth, cursing under his breath in a rich mixture of French, Mpongwe, Fan, and West Coast Pidgin English.

The hills became steeper and steeper, their sides covered by masses of black weathered rock fringed by trees that clung to the bare rock by their tangled roots. The steamer was buffeted from side to side by the current as she entered a gloomy ravine where the water narrowed even further. As they rounded a bend, Meg saw the white houses of the Talagouga Mission planted on the steep hillside, seemingly in danger of tumbling straight into the river, while the deep channel was narrowed even more by a massive rocky island arising in midstream. A freak eddy of the current caught the *Brazza* and spun her sideways, lifting the stern wheel almost out of the water and threatening to dash the boat against the rock.

"Itala-ja-maguga!" Captain Jacques added a few descriptive phrases in gutter French, shook his fist at the rock, and wrenched the wheel hard around. A moment later the boat was resting in a placid side pool under the steep banks on the mission side of the river, moored to one of the great trees that grew horizontally out between boulders. Meg fancied that she could hear the *Brazza*'s overworked engines panting with relief.

"Itala-ja-maguga," Captain Jacques repeated. "Ascent on woe—that's what the natives call it. Some damned superstition that the spirits of the rock won't let boats or canoes pass this point. Nassau shortened the name to Talagouga when he built his mission here."

"Oh." Meg looked doubtfully upriver at the white froth that foamed around the base of the massive rocky island. "Er . . . *will* the spirits let anybody pass? I thought we nearly got killed just now." Only now, as she observed how the *Brazza* pulled against the mooring ropes that held her fast to the trees along the bank, did she realize that this seemingly placid stretch of water was in fact running as fast as the downriver reaches of the Ogowe. It was only by contrast with the rapids around the island that it had appeared quiet.

Captain Jacques took the pipe out of his mouth to wave it at the island. "Oh, that? Nothing. Happens every time. Takes a man of experience to know how to work the rapids. Besides, I don't go past this point," he added. "Neither will you, if you've got any sense. Have to take native canoes from here." He pointed over the side of the boat. Meg saw a long, narrow canoe, carved out of a single log with both ends worked to a sharp point, approaching the *Brazza.* A load of short, dark logs was lashed to a raft behind the canoe, and the half-naked rowers worked furiously with rhythmically swinging arms and grunted chants to keep the canoe and raft moving forward against the swiftly rushing current.

"She's not going any further than this," said a familiar voice behind her. Meg jumped, knocked Captain Jacques's pipe out of his hand, and reminded herself too late that she hadn't intended to betray any emotion when next she saw Piers. He had kept himself scrupulously out of her sight all morning, and she had gone from dreading their next meeting, to a slightly irritable anticipation of the meeting, to wondering if he would ever speak to her again.

As Piers continued his instructions to Captain Jacques, nodding in her direction but otherwise hardly acknowledging her presence, Meg began to wonder if he was in fact speaking to her. What he was saying—something to do with arrangements for picking them up again on the *Brazza*'s next journey upriver—made little impression on her; what mattered terribly was that he wouldn't even look at her while he said it.

While Piers and the captain talked, the load of wood was brought on board, swung over the side in bundles, and dropped on the deck by the singing Kru-boys. Deck passengers jostled along the railing, clutching their sleeping mats and baskets of food and shouting greetings to their friends ashore, while half a dozen smaller canoes darted to and from the steamer to take them ashore.

The deck passengers climbed down the sides

of the steamer, clutching at ropes and ledges with bare hands and feet. Some balanced loads on their heads, others threw their possessions into the canoes before starting the perilous descent. Meg watched them, swallowing uneasily and hoping that some other means of getting off the steamer would be available to her.

"Fine, fine," Captain Jacques agreed with Piers's last instructions. "I'll check with the mission each time I come upriver, to see if you're back yet. Just send a message if you're killed and eaten, all right, so I can stop checking?"

Piers grinned at this heartless request and promised to let the captain know by bush telegraph if he found himself in a Fan cooking pot.

"And the little lady?" the captain inquired. "She goes back with me?"

"No, I don't," Meg said, a shade too loudly. "I'm getting off here."

Piers nodded. "Yes, that would be best. She might not be safe in Lambarene."

"If you insist on talking *at* me instead of *to* me," Meg pointed out, "it's going to be very awkward trying to communicate when we're in the bush, miles and miles from any other Europeans."

Not waiting for Piers's response to this eminently reasonable comment, she dragged her traveling case toward the railing and prepared to tackle the difficult descent into the large canoe. As she hesitated at the railing, strong hands grasped her by the waist and lifted her over the rail.

"Hold my hands," Piers instructed. Grasping her wrists firmly, he lowered Meg over the side of the boat until she collapsed in a heap on the bottom of the big canoe. Almost as an afterthought, he tossed her traveling case over after her. It burst open when it hit the canoe, but this time Meg had prepared for this eventuality. Her remaining possessions were securely tied in a bundle inside the case. She caught the bundle and stuffed it back inside the overstrained case while Piers climbed down the side of the boat to join her.

"Are you speaking to me again?" Meg had had ample time that morning to think over her position. She had decided that it would be foolish to betray the slightest embarrassment over what had happened last night. After all, she hadn't asked Piers to kiss her. He hardly had any right to complain if he found out, in so doing, that she cared more for Harry than for him. And it wasn't any of his business anyway.

Now, as Piers surveyed her through slitted blue eyes, she felt a warm red flush creep up her face. "For the moment . . . yes. But you don't need to worry about any awkwardness in the bush. You're not coming with me. You can wait here in Talagouga until I come back."

Meg opened and shut her mouth several times while the rowers struck out for the rocky shore. She was still trying to think of the right thing to say when the canoe's tip bumped into the rocks of the shore and Piers scrambled out with disgusting agility, offering her a hand as she hesitated on her knees in the canoe. She grasped the proffered hand and jumped ashore, dragging her traveling case behind her. Piers turned and set off up the steep path without another word.

"I wish . . . you wouldn't . . . take it personally," Meg panted, following him, with one hand holding up her skirts in front so that she would pick up a minimum of African insects and red dirt on the way up to the mission. To their left, clinging to the steep slope of the hill, was a cluster of native huts where the Mpongwe rowers evidently lived. Dark-faced women and naked children ran out of the huts to watch the strangers pass. Meg marched on up the hill without turning her head. It was bad enough to quarrel with Piers again; she wasn't about to do it in front of a fascinated native audience.

"If you mean last night's little incident," Piers tossed back over his shoulder, "it means less than nothing to me."

"*Good.* Because that's what it means to me too."

"If you want to make a fool of yourself chasing after a fool like Harry, that's your problem."

"It's none of your business!" Meg riposted angrily. "Besides, I didn't ask you to kiss me."

Piers stopped at the top of the path and whirled around so abruptly that she almost bumped her nose into the second button of his shirt. "Didn't you?"

Meg tried to edge around him so that she could look him in the eye again instead of being forced by the slope of the path to stare at his shirtfront, but Piers's hands on her shoulders immobilized her.

"I d-don't know what you mean." She was out of breath; well, no wonder, after that climb up the steep hill.

"Don't you?" One of his hands lifted a lock of her pale-gold hair that had strayed out of its loose confinement. He twisted the lock of hair around his finger and gave a sharp tug. Meg barely repressed an indignant cry of surprise. "You mean you weren't in the mood to . . . experiment last night?"

His fingers moved caressingly down the pale silky length of the lock of hair he'd captured, brushing over her neck and shoulder. She felt dizzy, as if the path were swaying away under her feet.

"You had no idea what effect you might have on a man, standing there in the darkness and gazing pensively up at the stars?" His hand hovered inches above her breast, making Meg aware of how soft and vulnerable she felt without the protective armor of her corsets. Could Piers tell how her nipples had stiffened under the soft lacy cover of her chemise and the constraining fabric of her shirtwaist blouse? She wished he would take his hand away, or . . . or do something—she wouldn't let herself think what.

"You didn't have any sneaking little idea about using me to give you what you can't get from my self-centered big brother?" Now, at last, he moved his hand upward to cup her chin, forcing her to look up at him. The steep tilt of the path made her bend her head so far back that she was genuinely afraid of losing her balance; she swayed, trying to avoid the dangerous proximity of his mouth, and he caught her around the waist with his free hand. All he had to do was tighten his arm, and they would be locked together in an indecently public embrace.

"L-let me go, you bully!" Raising her skirts another inch, she stamped down hard on Piers's foot and followed the stamp with a well-aimed kick at his shin. Piers yelped and dropped her to clutch at his leg.

"I think you've lamed me for life. Haven't you outgrown nursery manners yet?"

"Have you?" Meg retorted.

His blue eyes flashed with amusement. "Dear girl, the breaches of manners for which I'm condemned are mostly things I never thought of in the nursery."

That wasn't worth the dignity of a reply. Nose in the air, Meg picked up her case and marched around Piers while he was still rubbing his bruised shin.

The path continued up a steep flight of steps to the mission house, which was raised above the ground in front by high poles. The back of the house was built right against the huge quartz boulders of the hillside.

Meg was still fuming at Piers as she started up the stairs, but her anger vanished when she saw the pale, careworn woman who waited for her at the door to the mission house. Clad in a simple black dress, with her hair twisted up in a careless knot that did nothing to show off its rich red-gold color, she was twisting her hands together and watching Meg's approach with anxious eyes.

"Is that man the new doctor?" she burst out in French as soon as Meg came within earshot. "Oh, please tell him to hurry! My husband is dreadfully sick, and he insists on getting out of bed to stop the sacrifice. Please, cannot M'sieu the doctor give him a draft to make him lie still and rest?"

In her halting schoolgirl French, Meg explained as best she could that she and Piers were only English visitors; they knew nothing of any new doctor. "But if I can help in any way, please tell me what to do," she added, feeling terribly awkward at her intrusion upon a house of sickness.

"Ah, yes, M'sieu Piers!" The Frenchwoman waved Meg's offer aside and a smile broke out over her tired face. "I should have recognized him at once, but there has been so much happening—and he looks older, *n'est-ce pas*?" Without waiting for a reply she hastened forward, both hands out to Piers, and looking ten years younger. "*Mon cher* Piers, how 'appy I am that you 'ave returned to us!" she announced in strongly accented English. She went on to ask what had happened with his firm, and whether they had yet discovered why those wicked savages had burned his factory down. Piers answered her, slipping into fluent and idiomatic French in the middle of his answer, and as they rattled on, Meg was left to guess the gist of their conversation from the few words she could catch and from the Frenchwoman's expressive gestures.

She pointed several times up the hill to where a pach of black was barely visible under new vegetation, and Meg guessed that this must be the site of the factory that had been burned down. Piers responded with a long face and an emphatic upward movement of his hands that conveyed, better than any words, the story of the fire and explosion in Lambarene. The Frenchwoman gave him a series of consoling little pats on the shoulder, reaching up on tiptoes to do so, and then pressed his hand in both her own.

Meg supposed she ought to be feeling glad that Piers had at least one friend besides herself. She tried very hard to superimpose a proper feeling of gratitude on her underlying sensations of fatigue, irritation, and awkwardness. The effort gave her a headache.

Presently the Frenchwoman came bustling back to her, towing Piers by one hand. "Please forgive me that I do not introduce myself," she apologized to Meg. "I am Madame Molinier, and it is my husband who is ill with the fever and therefore I do not think very clearly, but now Piers will make everything all right. Please, you will come inside?" She hurried ahead of them into the mission house.

Meg glanced at Piers and raised her eyebrows. "She seems to have a great deal of faith in you. Does she think you are a doctor?"

"She feels uneasy with her husband abed, and no other men in the house," Piers defended his hostess. "*Some* women do find a man useful for doing odd jobs here and there, you know."

"Do they indeed? I can't imagine why." Head high, Meg sailed into the mission house ahead of Piers. She followed Madame Molinier to a simple little guestroom whose bare board floor and walls were enlivened by gay little paintings of French scenes.

"These paintings were done by Madame Fanchot—Hélène," Madame Molinier explained. She looked sad, or rather, as though she felt she ought to look sad, mouth drawn down and eyes lowered. "Poor Hélène! Her husband died several months ago, but she is bearing his loss very bravely. You will meet Hélène soon."

"That will be very nice," said Meg without much interest in the poor old widowed lady. "Now, Madame Molinier, please do tell me how I can help you. I am very sorry to intrude on you at such a time."

Madame Molinier sighed and passed one hand over her brow. "Oh, the fever, that is not so very bad. Only Eugène must stay quiet for a day or so, or he will be very sick. That was how poor Hélène's husband died, getting up too soon after an attack. And now we have word that there is a sacrifice planned in the Fan village in the jungle, and he keeps insisting that he must get up and stop it—"

She broke off as a bell tinkled from a room across the hallway. "*J'arrive, Eugène!*" Patting her apron down, she flew across the hall to bend over her husband's bed.

Meg felt that she would be intruding if she followed Madame Molinier without invitation. Feeling a little bit lost and lonely, she wandered down the hall and found herself in a wide ceilingless room with a few battered pieces of furniture scattered about. Piers was standing at the far end of the room with his back to her, apparently examining a painting like the ones in the guestroom. A petite dark-haired girl rested one hand on his arm while she pointed out various features of the painting, chattering away in vivacious French.

Meg cleared her throat and the couple turned. "Ah . . . this is Meg," said Piers, looking distinctly annoyed. "My . . . er . . . She's traveling with me. This far," he added firmly. "Meg, this is Hélène Fanchot."

Meg realized that the dark-haired girl's gauzy black dress, cut close to her figure with an abundance of bows, beads, and ruching, could by a considerable stretch of the imagination be described as mourning. It could also, she thought, be described as the best possible garment for a small but voluptuous girl with glossy black hair and creamy skin. The clinging black cloth clearly outlined a generous figure squeezed into hourglass shape by, Meg surmised, excessively tight lacing. She painted her face, too—subtly, but the signs were there. But of course, men never noticed things like that. Piers probably thought the hussy was absolutely beautiful.

"How do you do, Madame Fanchot," she said, sticking out her hand. "I am happy to make your acquaintance."

Hélène Fanchot giggled, murmured a few words in broken English, looked up at Piers with an adoring gaze, giggled again, and switched to a rapid, idiomatic French that Meg could not begin to follow. She rather suspected that was the lady's intention.

Piers cleared his throat. "Hélène has kindly offered to take me on a tour of the mission grounds. She wishes to show me the improvements they have made since I was last here. Er . . . you'll be all right here? I suppose Madame Molinier will need you to help with the nursing and all that."

"I suppose so," Meg agreed.

When Piers and Hélène had vanished, she felt more lost than ever. She wandered around the large barren room, trying to take an interest in Hélène's paintings. To her eye they looked little better than the watercolor daubs produced by every English girl as an obligatory part of her finishing-school experience, but no doubt any bit of color was welcome to perk up the drab mission house. She wondered where Hélène got her painting supplies. She wondered how Hélène had arranged a mourning costume that looked as if it had come straight from the showroom of the Maison Rouff in Paris. She wondered how deeply one could feel the mourning if one paid so much attention to the exact placement of the jet beads that outlined the tight curves of one's black crepe bodice.

"Don't be catty, Meg," she admonished herself.

"Missy fit chop tea?" inquired a gentle voice behind her.

Meg whirled and saw a black man dressed in magenta pants and an orange flowered shirt standing a few feet behind her. The civilized effect of his clothing was offset by the triangular patterns of scars incised in both his cheeks, a limp piece of fur tucked into the back of his shorts and trailing down to his knees, and strings of bright red and blue trade beads knotted into his fuzzy hair. He was gripping a wooden tray in both hands. On a tray were a steaming teapot and a cracked mug with the handle broken off.

"I . . . yes, thank you," Meg said when she had recovered from the surprise. She wondered uneasily how long he had been standing there and how many of her thoughts she had muttered aloud. Oh, well, he probably only spoke Mpongwe and Pidgin English; he wouldn't have understood her.

That thought reminded Meg that although her French was awkward and her Mpongwe close to nonexistent, she had made some progress, while on the steamer, toward mastering the peculiar trade English used all over West Africa. She was not totally helpless. And since everybody else was busy, perhaps she could get his man to tell her more about this planned sacrifice that was upsetting Monsieur Molinier to the point he was willing to risk his health to stop it. Meg didn't think she'd be much help in the sickroom, but if she knew exactly what was going on, perhaps she could find some other way to make herself useful.

Seating herself on a worn horsehair sofa, she took the teapot and cup and poured out a thin stream of appallingly dark brownish fluid with tiny leaves floating in it. No doubt these French drank coffee and hadn't bothered to teach their servants the art of making a decent cup of tea, if they knew how to begin with, which was doubtful. Never mind, it was kind of this man to think of offering her the English beverage.

"No, don't go yet," she said hastily as the man turned to leave the room. He paused with an expression of courteous inquiry on his features. "I . . . er . . . what you name self?"

"I call Louis, missy."

Somehow Meg doubted that this tall black man with the beads knotted in his hair and the patterns of scars on his face had started life as Louis.

"When you lib for home, what you name?"

The reply had roughly seventeen syllables, starting with a noise like a rusty bicycle wheel under torture.

"I see. Well, er . . . Louis, s'pose you tell me what bad palaver humbug Monseer Molinier too much?"

This invitation to explain about the problem that was agitating Monsieur Molinier released a floodtide of pidgin eloquence. Squatting on the floor beside Meg's sofa, Louis explained with a wealth of gestures that the inhabitants of a Fan village some miles away had lately become very hostile to the French mission. For several years the missionaries had been trying to abolish the custom of sacrificing a few spare wives or slaves whenever a great man died. They had not been very successful, but then—Louis shrugged—who cared about a few women and slaves? Of course, he added quickly, *he* was a good Christian now and knew that human sacrifice was wrong, even if the victims were only women.

"So what's different about this time?" Meg inquired.

This sacrifice was not associated with a big funeral, it turned out. In the last year men from the interior had come to the village, spreading word of a new secret society, one headed by a very powerful spirit or witch—Louis wasn't sure which—who had the power to turn himself into a crocodile. None of the villagers were actually members of the Crocodile Society yet, but several of the people who were most outspoken against the new society had disappeared and it was believed the witch-crocodile had taken them. Already the Crocodile Society had begun directing every minute detail of village activity, from the way the men harvested rubber to the proper ceremonies before starting a monkey hunt. Monsieur Molinier had been preaching furiously against the cult, and the planned sacrifice was a way of striking back at the missionaries.

"Good God," Meg exclaimed, "you don't mean they've kidnapped a missionary! Or one of the mission servants?"

Louis shook his head. "No, missy. They fit for kill Cook's brother. Him no saved yet. And Cook no fit fix good chop ennyway," he added, evidently thinking that the cook's lack of ability in his profession made the planned sacrifice a little less reprehensible.

"I see," said Meg thoughtfully. "And when is this sacrifice to take place?"

"Sun he go down come up go down."

"Sunset tomorrow," Meg translated to herself. "And how far away is the Fan village, Louis?"

Louis couldn't tell her that, but by patient questioning Meg satisfied herself that the village was no more than an hour's walk from the mission. "Good! Then there's still time to stop the sacrifice. Can Cook show me the way to his village, do you think?"

Louis rolled his eyes upward. "Yes, missy, but you no go dere. Dey Fan no good men! Fan chop man!"

"We'll see about that." Meg stood up and looked around the room for her trusty black umbrella. Of course, she must have left it behind in the factory explosion at Lambarene. "Is there a trading factory there since Hatton and Cookson's burned down?"

The next half-hour was a whirlwind of activity in which Louis unwillingly participated. Madame Molinier, interrupted while spooning medicine down her husband's throat, rather absentmindedly gave Meg permission to take anything she needed from the mission store.

"I am afraid you will not find much that is useful to you," she apologized. "We do not carry hairpins, or ladies' clothing—although there is some of your Manchester cloth, if you could use that? Do you wish me to show you where everything is?"

"Thank you," said Meg, "I'll manage." She retreated hastily before Madame Molinier could ask just what she wanted from the store. It would probably be easier on the French lady's nerves if she continued to believe that Meg was only looking for some personal items.

"You go jungle with Cook, no midday chop," Louis protested a little later.

"You already told me Cook's chop be bad bad bad pass all," Meg retorted. Couldn't the Moliniers eat cold tinned food for one day in the interest of saving a human life? Why, if all went well, they'd even be back in plenty of time for the cook to prepare dinner. "Now, s'pose you no bring Cook, I make bad palaver pass all, you savvy?"

Louis nodded despondently and extracted the cook from the smoky outbuilding used for a kitchen, while Meg rooted through the supplies in the mission store and selected what she hoped would be a tempting assortment of trade goods.

Seven

Piers rather enjoyed Hélène Fanchot's attentions at first. Let Meg see, he thought, that *some* women appreciated a fellow without having to shut their eyes and pretend he was somebody else!

Hélène Fanchot certainly didn't shut her eyes. She kept both bright black orbs firmly fixed on Piers as she hung on his arm and whispered sweetly vivacious small talk to him. The "tour" of the mission took them only as far as the kitchen garden, where Hélène pleaded fatigue from the heat and sank down on a rustic seat under the tall trees that shaded the far end of the garden.

"I cannot run around in this heat the way you do." She pouted prettily. "You men forget that I am but a poor weak woman—and here I am in Africa without a man to take care of me!"

It did cross Piers's mind that Hélène had been the one to suggest the tour, but he forgot that when two sparkling tears glistened under her eyelashes. Patting Hélène's hand, he proffered some words of consolation from the untimely loss of her husband. Hélène leaned her head on his shoulder, murmuring that it was *so* good to have a man to lean on after all these lonely months; the strong musky scent of her perfume tickled Piers's nostrils; and before long Hélène was enthusiastically demonstrating that the loneliness had troubled her much more than the sad memory of her departed husband.

Piers found himself, quite irrationally, wishing that Meg could see him kissing Hélène Fanchot.

Why? he asked himself in between whispered compliments of the sort Hélène liked. "Darling, your hair is a glossy pool in which a man could drown." Wasn't there any pleasure in holding and kissing a voluptuous little armful like Hélène, besides the thought of scoring off his lanky friend Meg? "Your eyes are like the soft gray clouds in the rainy season."

"My eyes," Hélène pointed out, wriggling out of Piers's embrace, "are *black*."

"Of course they are," said Piers guiltily. "I can't imagine what I was thinking of." Somehow, even when he was kissing Hélène, his mind was full of stormy gray eyes and a cloud of pale gold hair; he kept remembering what it felt like to hold a tall, supple body in his arms, instead of Hélène's tiny, curvaceous form in its cage of artistically shaped whalebone corsets. He'd noticed instantly when Meg left off wearing her corsets on the boat, and mentally applauded the change, but he hadn't dared mention it.

Hélène pouted. "You were not thinking of *me* at all."

Piers set himself to convince her otherwise. It was a bit difficult, when his mind kept flashing images of Meg's slender waist and the surprising fullness of her breasts. Did she know, he wondered, how their weight caused betraying curves to be outlined in the front of her blouse? Did she guess how the sight made his palms itch to close over the tempting full globes? Surely not. No man had yet awakened her underlying sensuality. And he had no right to be the one.

Besides, she was only using him as a stand-in for his stuffy big brother. Piers concentrated on that thought, and on Hélène Fanchot, with such success that soon Hélène was giggling and protesting that he would be the ruin of her reputation. The only trouble was that he was slightly bored, even while he did and said all the right things.

"Darling Piers, not here," Hélène protested with a final voluptuous flounce that carried her half across his knees. "What will the servants think? Remember that I am a missionary. I must set an example for them." Her fingertips caressed his cheek, soft white little fingers with sharp nails that scored little lines across his face. "Tonight," she whispered in his ear, "if you are clever enough to find my room, who knows . . . ? I am only a weak woman, and you are so persuasive, my big strong Piers."

Suddenly Piers was disgusted as well as bored. He wanted to get away from her clinging musky perfume and her insinuating, wheedling voice. Hélène, he thought, was like one of those vines with the big white flowers that grew up the trees at the edge of the bush. Showy and sweet-smelling, but they got a strangehold on their supports, and before long the vine was flourishing gaily while the poor tree withered away from lack of sunshine.

He stood up so abruptly that Hélène had to scramble to her feet. "Piers, that is not kind!" she scolded.

"Mmm. We've been gone long enough. I should talk to Molinier about this affair of the sacrifice." Seeing Hélène's pouting lips and stormy eyes, Piers rephrased his decision to return to the mission house in terms that might be more acceptable to her. "I'm only thinking of your reputation," he lied. "We don't want to scandalize the good Madame and Monsieur Molinier, do we?"

Hélène giggled and tucked her arm under his arm as they started back to the mission house. "No, for I don't want any prying eyes on me tonight," she told Piers with an arch smile that for some reason made him feel slightly sick. Why should he hesitate to take what was so freely offered? He'd never hesitated before. . . . It was all Meg's fault; she'd upset him and made him so confused he didn't know what he was doing or what he wanted. Damn that girl! Why couldn't she stay out of his mind? Kissing Hélène Fanchot in the garden had done absolutely nothing to drive the memory of last night's kiss out of his head; instead it had had the opposite effect. The more he fondled Hélène's plump little body, the more he longed to feel Meg's suppleness against him again, the innocent sensuality of her lips and the sweet surprise with which she met his lovemaking.

The callousness with which she used him for practice, while dreaming of Harry—that was a better thing to remember, Piers told himself with savage anger and frustration.

When they reached the mission house, Piers found Madame Molinier looking distraught again and enlisting the help of the servants to hold Monsieur Molinier down. Feverish and not quite aware of his surroundings, he was tossing and turning in his bed and repeating that he must get up and go to the Fan village to stop the sacrifice. All Madame Molinier's ingenuity was required to keep him in bed, and she was looking distinctly frazzled from the hours of effort. Piers wondered why she hadn't enlisted Meg's help. Perhaps two women couldn't get along in a sickroom. Even Hélène was hanging back behind him, as though unwilling to invade the Moliniers' privacy.

"Melanie, where are my shoes?" Eugène Molinier demanded for the third time. Madame Molinier whisked his shoes out of sight under the bed and blocked his attempts to get up by advancing with a spoon and a medicine glass.

"Please, my love, you must rest," she cooed.

"*Tais-toi, Melanie*!" Eugène Molinier caught sight of Piers in the doorway and switched to English. "Ah, Monsieur Damery. Will you help me? I have to . . . have to . . ." His English failed him and he fell back against the bolster, muttering uneasily.

"Don't concern yourself, sir," Piers said, smiling and taking Monsieur Molinier's hand. He was shocked to feel how light and hot it was, like a dry leaf fluttering in the breeze. No wonder poor Madame Molinier was so distraught! "It is all taken care of. There will be no sacrifice."

"How . . . how is that possible?" Eugène Molinier demanded, raising himself on one elbow.

"It's . . . er . . . complicated. Won't you rest now? I'll explain it all tomorrow."

Piers went on producing soothing, vague reassurances while Madame Molinier hovered with the medicine glass. Finally Monsieur Molinier swallowed the spoonful of laudanum and fell into an uneasy slumber.

"How clever you are!" Madame Molinier exclaimed when her husband was asleep at last. She drew the mosquito curtains around his bed, swathing him in folds of white gauze, and tiptoed into the hall with Piers.

Piers rubbed his stiff shoulders. Now that the tension of dealing with Monsieur Molinier's fevered demands was over, he realized that he was tired and very hungry. They must have been in the sickroom for an hour or more, and he'd been wandering the mission grounds with Hélène for quite a while before that. He began to hope that Madame Molinier was not so worried about her husband as to forget about eating. A late lunch would be quite acceptable just now.

"How clever," Madame Molinier repeated. "I never thought of lying to him! But what shall we do tomorrow when he wakes up and finds out that the sacrifice is going on as planned?"

Piers hadn't thought that far ahead, his one thought being to soothe Monsieur Molinier out of his feverish determination to get up at once, but he saw now that he would have to follow through with his promises. "There's only one thing to do, isn't there?" he said, smiling down at Madame Molinier's care-worn face. "I shall have to go to the village and stop the sacrifice myself." Perhaps, though, it would be socially acceptable to sit down and have a bite to eat first. The ladies wouldn't want their brave rescuer to faint from hunger, would they?

"Oh, Piers, how brave you are!" Hélène Fanchot squeezed his free arm and looked at him admiringly. For a moment Piers really did feel strong and brave and infallible. There was nothing like Frenchwomen, he thought. Petite and adoring and unquestioning, they made a man able to perform deeds he'd never thought of. Now, that skinny, sarcastic Meg would probably have laughed at him and asked how he expected to stop a whole village of cannibal Fans from enjoying their planned evening's entertainment. Too bad she wasn't here to see how a real woman treated a man!

"That is wonderful, *mon cher* Piers," said Madame Molinier, "but how exactly do you propose to stop the sacrifice?"

Damn women! Piers thought. They were all alike, asking inconvenient questions and destroying a chap's confidence.

"Something will come to me when I get there," he said briefly. "Now, you two ladies just find me a decent gun and some ammunition, because I'm not going into Fan territory unarmed. And I need a guide. There must be somebody around here who knows the way to the village."

"Louis!" Madame Molinier called. "Louis, *viens ici*!"

When she explained Piers's requirements, the Mpongwe servant looked bewildered.

"Come, come," Madame Molinier scolded gently, "it is not so very difficult to find someone who will guide Monsieur to the village."

"No," said Louis, "but what for gemmum no go with missy?" He shrugged, obviously finding the ways of white people inscrutable, and turned to search out a gun and a guide for the white man with the yellow hair.

"Wait . . . wait a minute!" Piers caught Louis

by the shoulder and spun him around. "What you mean, go with missy? Where missy go?"

Louis shrugged. "Missy go for bush one time."

"She's run away. She's set off on her own. She's gone mad!" Piers yanked at his hair. "Women!"

Several minutes of questioning elicited Louis's understanding of the story: the white woman who came with Piers had gone mad and had vanished into the bush with the mission cook and her suitcase.

The bit about the mission cook reassured Piers. He feared Meg might have gone to the Fan village, but as far as he knew, all the mission servants were Mpongwes and Igalwas. They wouldn't be caught dead in a Fan village—or rather, that was the only way they could be caught there. But where else could Meg have gone?

He was still trying to convince himself she'd merely gone for a walk when one of the Mpongwe girls who worked at the mission arrived to inquire, "How I make Missy bed fit for sleep when all Missy cloes lib for bed?"

Piers dashed to the guest chamber and flung open the door. The neat, plain white bed was covered with a top-dressing of chemises, petticoats, corset covers, shirtwaists, combs, brushes, shoe hooks, and miscellaneous toilet articles whose use he could only guess at.

"Calm, Piers. Keep calm," he told himself. "Think out the sequence. There *is* a logical sequence of events here, you just have to figure it out." Clutching his head, he tried to think, tried to fight the irrational conviction that Meg was in terrible danger somewhere and needed his help—

and that it was all his fault for leaving her while he flirted with Hélène Fanchot.

"*Think*," he insisted again. "She emptied her suitcase onto the bed. Then she kidnapped the mission cook and set off into the bush with an empty suitcase. Possibility one, she's gone raving mad. Quite likely, the damn woman had to be insane or she wouldn't have wanted to come with me in the first place, but in that case I have no idea which way she went and no way to find her. So we'll consider possibility two, she's not crazy, she had some plan. All I have to figure out is what she was planning, go the same direction, find her before she gets killed by elephants or snakes or cannibals, and . . ." His fingers flexed suggestively, as though he were already wrapping them around Meg's slender neck. When he caught up with that damn girl, he would kill her! No, first he'd kiss her until her knees bent backward, nuzzle his face into those perversely tempting breasts so softly free under her blouse, run his hands up and down the long slender length of her back and the swelling curve of her hips and the long smooth thighs he'd only guessed at so far, revel in possession of all he'd so nearly lost forever . . . *Then* he would kill her. If she wasn't dead already. Which God couldn't do to him; it wouldn't be fair, to let him save her from fire and explosion only to lose her within a hundred feet of a peaceful mission station.

"And what," inquired Hélène Fanchot plaintively, "are we to do for lunch, if your friend has taken the cook with her? I do think he might have been considerate enough to wait until this afternoon."

"He was probably upset about his brother, poor fellow," Madame Molinier excused the cook. "I only hope he hasn't decided to go and be sacrificed in his brother's place."

"Yes," Hélène agreed, "it would be a pity to lose the only mission servant we've got who can light the big wooden range."

"What's that? Sacrificed?" Piers's head came up and he stared at the two women with a light flickering to life in his blue eyes. "I thought the sacrifice was in a Fan village. Aren't all your servants Mpongwes or Igalwas?"

"All but the cook," explained Madame Molinier.

"And I *was* nervous about that," put in Hélène, "given their habits in the wild." She tittered. "One wishes to inspect the meat he uses most carefully, *tu comprends*."

"But Jerome has worked out very well," said Madame Molinier, "except for his habit of wearing a monkey fur as a loincloth, which is most unsanitary in the kitchen. I for one have no wish to ingest monkey hairs in my soup!" A shadow of doubt crossed her face. "That is, until now. It is most unlike Jerome to go off without a word of warning like this! Hélène, do you think you could possibly . . ."

Hélène Fanchot raised her soft white hands in protest. "No. I have *never* understood the big range. We shall simply have to open a tin for lunch."

"Will you two females stop chattering about food!" Piers snapped. "Jerome must have taken Meg back to the Fan village. How can I catch up with them?" *Could* he catch up with them? Meg must have left while he and Hélène were touring the mission grounds—at least two hours ago, maybe three. How far away was this village?

Madame Molinier shook her head sadly and explained that none of the other servants would even consider guiding Piers to the Fan village. They were afraid of being kept for dinner. "Although I myself feel the rumors of cannibalism are greatly exaggerated," she said. "My dear Eugène has never actually seen them eating human flesh. Still, there is no denying that the Fan do have a very bad reputation among the other tribes. And they have been slow in coming to hear the good word of our blessed Lord. Jerome is—was—our only convert from the tribe."

By dint of patient questioning Piers got Madame Molinier and one of the Mpongwe servants to point out the direction in which they thought the Fan village lay. True, they pointed with equal firmness at two different paths, but, as Louis cheerfully observed, both paths started off in approximately the same direction—though, as he added with equal cheer, there was no telling where one of these meandering bush paths would end up.

Madame Molinier had brought the requested gun and ammunition. Adding a pocket compass and a machete to his gear, Piers strapped the hunting rifle over his back and set off alone down the narrower and less-well-trodden of the bush paths. He reasoned that since the Mpongwe and Igalwa who lived in the vicinity of the mission were afraid to go to the Fan village, any path that led there must be very little used.

The fringes of the bush around the mission were the usual tangle of scrubby, weedy plants growing over one another in a promiscuous free-for-all, each one attempting to cut off its neighbor's view of the sun and each sending at least one tendril across the path to trip unwary feet. After twenty paces or so the tall trees of the forest reasserted their rule, and Piers moved quickly and silently through the environment he had learned to love during his months on the Ogowe.

All around him, tall columns of tree trunks rose to a green canopy of interlaced branches and vines that formed an unbroken ceiling over the rain forest, covering the area below with dim greenish light. Gloomy though the forest was, here and there it was brightened by flowers that had dropped from the overhead canopy—great handfuls of orange and white and pink, hinting at the world of color and scent and light that swayed in the breezes far above him. Every once in a while, when a break in the dense canopy overhead allowed a patch of sunlight to reach the ground, a rubber vine would burst into brilliant flower, twining itself upward toward the light.

Piers found himself thinking of Meg as he glanced up at one of those bursts of glory. She was like that, a vine growing in shadow, flowering only now in her first freedom. Already, in the few days she'd been in Africa, he could see her spirit and body blossoming. Taking off her corsets had been an excellent start. If only she was still all right! She had to be. He had to get to her in time; then they could start over. This time he would be patient. He would give her time to get over her infatuation with Harry. He would prove his worthiness. Only let him find her!

The path meandered on, and Piers's impatience

actually slowed his passage as he tripped over vines and caught himself in impenetrable patches of brush that had looked like promising short-cuts. Finally he forced himself to relax and move slowly and cautiously, respecting the power of the bush. He knew he would actually get to the village sooner if he took the time to follow the path properly; but it was hard to be sensible when Meg had been missing for . . . How long was it now? Piers glanced at a ray of sun filtering through the dense tangle of vines overhead. Surely the angle of the sun couldn't be as low as he thought.

Still, it must have been three hours since she left, perhaps more. Could he have taken the wrong path? Piers moved on light feet through the dense rain forest, noting every crushed leaf or disturbed patch of mold that might indicate someone else had passed this way before him. His heart leapt up at the sight of a white thread dangling from a thorny branch that slanted low across the path. Could that have come from Meg's blouse? He couldn't be sure. Though most of the natives wore gaudily patterned Manchester-cotton prints, a few of them had white shirts handed down from some European master. But surely Meg's white shirtwaist was of finer, softer fabric than the native shirts? His fingers remembered the texture of the cloth under his hands, and the slender fragility of Meg under the blouse. But a single thread wasn't enough of a clue.

A few steps further on he spied a gleam of gold in the dimness of the forest. Reaching into the air, he felt a feather-light strand of hair brush his fingers, tugged and freed it from the bush rope that had captured it. That had to be Meg's! His eye fell on a discarded wreath of pink flowers draped over a fallen log that blocked the path ahead, and he knew no more doubt. She would have been braiding the flowers as she walked, along, then she would have had to put them down so that she could use both hands to clamber over the log. The picture was as clear in his mind's eye as if he'd seen her in person, skirts hiked up to reveal a slender black-stockinged ankle, jumping over the log with a vivacity that made her breasts sway under the torn shirtwaist. Why hadn't he been there? How could she go off like this without a word? Didn't she realize what a tempting picture she'd present to any man who happened to see her?

"Damned female!" Piers muttered between clenched teeth, rolling his eyes heavenward in exasperation. "Goes out for a walk in the bush without telling anyone, strolls along making herself a daisy chain—what does she think this is, a Sunday-school picnic?"

"There is a happy land," sang a cheerful cacophony of voices from somewhere ahead of him on the narrow path, "far, far away." The accents were thickly and distinctly African, the tune was no longer recognizable as such, but the words came through clearly to Piers. As he listened, a loud confident contralto was raised, carrying the last lines of the hymn along with a faint memory of the original melody. " 'Where saints in glory stand, bright, bright as day!' "

"Meg!" Piers leapt over the fallen log and ran down the path, reaching over his shoulder for the gun as he went. Already loaded, thank goodness. Now he had only to cock it and . . .

He burst around a bend in the path, holding the shotgun pointed before him in both hands, and stopped stock-still at the sight of Meg marching along before a dejected mission servant and three fierce-looking Fan gentlemen. Her hair was tumbling in a loose golden cloud around her face, the thin white shirtwaist blouse was soaked through and sticking to her body, and there was a long rip on the side of her muddy serge skirt. She looked absolutely beautiful to Piers.

The rush of relief turned to anger before he'd caught his breath. The three Fan warriors behind her might as easily have chosen to spear her through the heart as to follow her to the mission. From the appearance of them, they were total savages. Two of them wore only plaits of monkey fur around their waists, and had fantastic hairstyles of mud and beads and red-dyed palm fronds; the third was more conservatively dressed in a leopardskin skirt, with some long black tubular object pulled down over his wavy hair and falling over his shoulders behind. After a moment Piers recognized the strange thing as one of Meg's stockings.

All three of the Fans carried long spears ornamented with baroque curls and twists of jagged metal, broad-bladed knives stuck into their waistbands, and small throwing axes slung over their tattooed shoulders. Piers's blood ran cold at the thought of Meg casually trampling through the jungle with these savages. And this particular tribe had a nasty reputation for cooking and eating their enemies!

"Meg, are you out of your mind?" Piers demanded. "What the devil have you been playing at now?"

"Good afternoon, Piers. How nice that you brought a gun, now we won't have to sing anymore. But is it loaded? Didn't anybody ever tell you it's dangerous to run with a loaded gun?"

Piers slowly realized that the grinding sound he heard after Meg's greeting came from his own jaws. Slowly, moving very carefully lest he give in to the temptation to throw something, he lowered his gun. "Didn't anybody tell you," he riposted, "that it's dangerous to go traipsing off in the jungle by yourself?"

"But I wasn't by myself," Meg objected. "I had Cook to guide me. And . . . oh, I'm sorry, I should have introduced you!" She pulled one brawny Fan warrior forward by the wrist. "This is Kema—at least, that's as much of his name as I can pronounce—Cook's brother, you know, the one who was supposed to be given to the Crocodile God. And these two gentlemen kindly offered to escort us all home again, only we happened to meet a leopard on the way and nobody had brought any ammunition, so I thought we should sing."

"What good," Piers demanded, momentarily diverted, "what conceivable good did singing to the leopard do?"

Meg looked smug. "Well, the poor beast left, and I must say I don't blame it. You heard our singing—wouldn't you have left the neighborhood if something set up a noise like that?"

Piers mopped his sweating brow. "Now that you mention it, yes. I always did think you had the worst singing voice in the world, Meg, but that was before I heard an African choir in full voice. Why did you choose an English hymn to mutilate?"

"Because I don't know any French ones, obviously. Now, if you're quite through interrogating me over trifles, Piers, shall we go on back to the mission? We really shouldn't dilly-dally here until dark, you know."

"Dilly-dally." Piers ground his teeth again. "Dammit, Meg, do you have the faintest idea how much worry you've caused everyone at the mission?"

Meg raised one fair eyebrow. "Not too much, I'd say, if it took you this long to come looking for me. Did Madame Fanchot give you a nice tour of the mission?"

"Hélène Fanchot," said Piers between his teeth, "is not the point! The point is that you've been grossly inconsiderate and you could have been killed and I think I'll possibly kill you myself!" He raised his hands toward her shoulders, intending to shake her till her teeth rattled, and suddenly found three ocher-haired naked Africans between him and Meg.

"No hurt white ma!" thundered the tallest and fiercest of the three, the one Meg had introduced as Kema.

Meg smirked visibly as Piers lowered his hands and backed off. "All right," he said, controlling his anger with an effort. "I'll kill you later. Now, let's get back to the mission!"

Meg insisted that Piers precede her along the path. He understood why when they reached the log where she'd lost her wreath of flowers. Turning back to offer his hand, he caught a flash of white leg as she vaulted over without help, skirts pulled up almost to her knees. Her legs were absolutely bare under the black skirt and layers of white petticoats. Indecent. Piers felt sweat breaking out on his forehead as his imagination ran riot under those lacy flounces of white, conjuring up images of just how far up she was bare and how shapely those long legs might be. He clenched and unclenched his fists and turned away just in time to miss Meg's look of puzzlement at his scowl.

As they walked single file along the narrow path, Meg explained that she'd offered the Fan village elders an assortment of brass rods, cotton cloth, and glass beads from the mission store in exchange for Kema's life. Some bargaining had been required, but the visible and shining presence of the trade goods, together with the fact that the leaders of the Crocodile Society were far away in another village, had eventually swung the elders around to Meg's position.

"I did have to throw in a few extra things," Meg admitted with a sigh. "I didn't really regret parting with the stockings, but I did like that traveling case."

Piers began to understand the provocative glimpses of bare leg that he'd seen when she lifted her skirts to scramble over the log. "You didn't just discard the stockings because of heat?"

Meg gave him a disdainful look. "I'm not going to stop dressing like a lady just because the circumstances are a little difficult, Piers. The trade goods I brought weren't quite enough to buy Kema off with, so I had to barter with whatever else I could spare. I hadn't quite expected they would want my stockings, but I do see that they make quite unusual headdresses, and wearing them one at a time over the head certainly does solve the problem of what to do when one of a pair gets lost in the wash."

Piers had to laugh at the mental picture of a Fan warrior prinked out in his best leopardskin loincloth and Meg's second-best black stockings, and for a few minutes he almost forgot to be furious with her. Where the path widened for a few hundred yards they walked hand in hand, and when Meg expressed interest in a brightly colored flower that hung tantalizingly out of reach, Piers climbed up the tree to pluck it for her. He was a little ruffled, on reaching the ground, to find that while he was shinnying up the smooth ebony trunk, Kema had found a whole armful of identical flowers growing from a hollow log a few feet away.

"Never mind," said Meg with a saucy grin, "the exercise will do you good." She gathered the flowers into a bouquet and peeped over them at Piers. "Hard work and cold baths, my boy, will keep you safe from the Hélène Fanchots of this world."

"Aha! I knew you got yourself lost in the bush just to pry me away from Hélène. Admit it."

"You overrate yourself," Meg retorted, "and anyway, I wasn't lost. *I* knew where I was all along. Oh, look, isn't that an interesting knot?"

She knelt by the side of the path, dropping her armload of flowers to examine a rubber vine that was being milked by means of several small incisions cut along the length of its stem. Under each incision a small hollowed-out gourd was placed, and the milky juice dripped slowly into the gourd as they watched. The vine was lashed to each gourd by a smaller, thinner piece of bush rope arranged to a complicated knot, so that none of the liquid rubber should be lost.

"This must be what François Chaillot was talking about," Meg explained.

Piers nodded. "Yes, I remember he had some cockamamie theory about teaching the natives how to harvest rubber without killing the vines. Never had much success, though."

"Well, somebody's succeeding," Meg pointed out. "That will make François happy. Isn't it funny that they'd go to all that trouble with that complex knot, though? I mean, it is quite beautiful, but a simple square knot would have done just as well. This looks like something out of the back of the *Boys' Own Naval Manual.*"

Kema and his fellow tribesmen shuffled their feet. "You come now, white ma," said Kema uneasily. "Big rain him fall for sky soon soon pass all." His friends concurred. All three looked more gray than black in the deep shadows of the forest, and their hands seemed to be shaking slightly.

"I don't see any sign of a storm," Meg disputed, but she let the Fans hurry her on down the path. Their uneasiness was real enough, even if she couldn't see what had caused it.

Piers sniffed disapprovingly when they reached the cleared space around the mission house. The cook dragged his rescued brother off toward the smoky kitchen shed, while the other two Fans vanished silently into the jungle without a word of farewell. "Clear skies in all directions. You women are too nervous."

Meg gave him a withering look and stalked off toward the house, hoping for a cold bath such as the one she had sarcastically recommended to Piers. Couldn't he see that the Fans had wanted to get out of that section of rain forest, and hadn't wanted to tell them why? Let Piers make a show of bravery if he wanted to. She, for one, didn't want to even think about encountering something so fierce that it could turn three fierce Fan warriors an interesting shade of grayish-blue with purple tremors around the edges.

As it happened, though he couldn't have known it, Piers was wrong. Some very definite storm-clouds were gathering downriver, in the neighborhood of Lambarene.

Eight

François Chaillot was enjoying a midmorning social hour with the two English traders, Cavanaugh and Walters, when the hooting of a steamer from far downriver interrupted their pleasant gossip session about the latest misdeeds of that young rotter Damery.

"The *Brazza*? Back so soon?"

Cavanaugh tilted his graying head and listened carefully as another wailing hoot sounded over the brassy surface of the Ogowe. "No, my God, it's coming from downriver. Must be the new steamer at last!"

The three men piled out of Cavanaugh's sitting room with the unbridled enthusiasm of schoolboys on their first day of leave. A new steamer would have to have been sent out from Europe. Its arrival would mean mail, news, and possibly some interesting passengers.

"There she is now!" Walters climbed on top of an upended crate that had once carried bottles of trade gin and shaded his eyes, peering down the wide bronze stretch of water that rushed down past Lambarene to lose itself in the mangrove swamps of the coast. Just where the river curved around a wide stand of ebony trees, the sparkle of light reflecting off metal was barely visible.

"A new steamer," Cavanaugh exulted, and rubbed his hands together. "No more pigging it up and down the river on the *Brazza*. No more putting up with that damned Frog, Jacques Merlot, telling us if we don't like his steamer we're welcome to take another boat. Oh, sorry, Chaillot."

"No need to apologize," said François Chaillot with an imperturbable smile. "I am well aware of the opinion you English have of my people—even though it is we who have explored this mighty continent and opened it up for your 'nation of shopkeepers' to exploit."

A brief wrangle ensued about the respective merits of the Frenchman Brazza and the Englishman Stanley as explorers. Young Walters' excited cries, reporting on the progress of the new steamer, punctuated the argument without being deemed worthy of further attention from the participants. Only when he fell abruptly silent did they wheel around to stare in consternation at the ramshackle contraption inching its way up the river.

The gleam that they had seen came from a shiny new section of pipe in the midsection of the smokestack. It was obviously a recent replacement, for the rest of the smokestack was red with rust, leaked blue puffs of smoke at every joint, and tilted crazily back toward the stern of the boat.

The prevailing color of the woodwork was a muddy brown resulting from years of weathering, but here and there a flaking patch of paint showed that the original intention of the owners had been to make the boat a bilious green. All along the side nearest them, the deck railing had given up the struggle to stand upright; it sagged down to repose on the deck honeycombed with rotten patches, while the passengers squatting on the deck were in imminent danger of falling either overboard or through one of the casually patched holes.

As the steamer approached, it seemed to be listing more and more to port. "Good God Almighty," muttered Cavanaugh, "she'll heel over in a moment if the skipper don't take care!" Already the brown muddy waters of the Ogowe were lapping over onto the deck while the African passengers squealed and wriggled out of the way.

The nameless boat crept up to the pier at a steady, snaillike crawl and stopped by the simple expedient of bumping head-on into the pier. François threw his hands up in the air. "*Sacrebleu*! Is the captain mad? He will destroy my so beautiful pier!"

"Not much danger of that," said Cavanaugh dryly. "The pier is harder than the boat."

And so it proved. The steamer impaled herself on the forward braces of the pier, moving slowly and majestically up like a giant crocodile swallowing the long narrow pier. Water poured into the gaping, splintery hole and the African passengers dived into the water with shrieks of alarm, dog-paddling frantically toward shore. While they scrambled to safety, shaking themselves and showering muddy droplets of the Ogowe over the three traders, a little man in a blue coat resplendent with brass buttons jumped over the prow of the steamer and landed neatly on what was left of the pier. Behind him, the ship gurgled gently and began sinking into the brown water, held up now only by the end of the pier which she had swallowed.

"*That*," said Cavanaugh, "is not a new steamer!"

"So perceptive, my English colleagues," murmured François Chaillot. He held out one hand to the new arrival. "Felicitations on your . . . er . . . unique mode of arrival, my friend. Do tell me, how do you propose to remove that unsightly excrescence from the end of my pier?"

The little man shrugged and spread his open palms out. "She removes herself, M'sieur. And a good riddance to an old scow! It is a humiliation indescribable that I, Jean-Baptiste Marmont, descendant of a marshal of France, should be required to pilot such a *cochon* of a steamer. She may sink into the mud and be eaten by crocodiles for all of me. Bah! May the Chargeurs Réunis also sink into the mud with their entire penny-pinching board of directors—"

He broke off with an aggrieved grunt, observing that he had lost the attention of the French trader. François Chaillot was staring openmouthed at the slowly sinking outline of the nameless wreck. Over the railing came a tall, lithe man clad in immaculate white shirt and trousers, with the sun glinting off his yellow hair. The flash of his blue eyes, the distinctive outline of his high, slightly beaky nose and firm chin, were all familiar—and incredible—to François.

"Damery!" he ejaculated, clutching at Jean-Baptiste Marmont's coat sleeve for support. The tall man paused in mid-stride halfway down the pier. François's voice had carried clearly over the intervening space. "Why, yes, that is my name," he drawled, "but I don't believe I've had the pleasure, old chap."

"You're not Piers," said Cavanaugh, looking back and forth between François and the new arrival.

"Ever perceptive," murmured François. "But the resemblance is astonishing. Clean up Piers, shave him, and keep him sober for a week, and you might have something very like this gentleman."

The tall stranger's brow cleared and he strode briskly forward, one hand extended. "Do I gather that you are friends of my young brother's? Beg to introduce myself—pray forgive the informality. My name is Harry Damery. Was heading for South America when I got a change in posting. Needed to replace some chap on the Gold Coast, it seems. Took a tramp steamer across, had to change at Libreville, thought I'd just pop up the river and see how old Piers was getting on while I happened to be in the neighborhood. Famous good luck, running into you chaps. Friends of Piers's, are you?"

He looked from one silent, frowning face to another. "I say, how *is* old Piers getting on? Oh Lord, he hasn't been up to any more tricks like dressing up his dog to open a bank account, has he? He promised Mater *faithfully* he'd try to make a go of it this time . . ."

Harry Damery's voice trailed off and he glanced in perplexity at the two English traders. Cavanaugh tugged at his beard and stared at the stinking hulk in the river. "Well, you see . . ." Walters began. He stopped, coughed in embarrassment, and then was unable to stop coughing.

As usual, François Chaillot was the first of the traders to recover his social manner. "I am afraid that this time it is a matter more serious than the dressing of a dog, Monsieur Damery. And, perhaps, not to be discussed here. If you will do me the honor of coming to my factory for lunch, perhaps I can explain to you . . ."

He nodded and half-turned away, but Harry Damery stood his ground. "I should prefer, if you don't mind," he said, thrusting out his jaw, "to go first to my brother's factory. Can you tell me where it is?"

"That's just the trouble," exclaimed young Walters, unhappily recovered from his spasm of coughing, "it *isn't*—not anymore. He's gone and burned it down, just like the other one . . ."

He shriveled into silence under Cavanaugh's steely glare and ran one finger around a shirt collar grown suddenly too tight for him.

"The other one," Harry repeated the last words slowly. "And my brother—where is he?"

François Chaillot sighed and took the Englishman by the arm. "That too is a long story, and not one to be heard in the heat of the noonday sun. You will be so good as to accompany me?"

This time Harry made no protest, but turned up the hill toward the luxurious factory of Chaillot Père et Fils. The two English traders and the voluble little captain of the sunken steamer followed at a discreet distance, ignoring François's palpable hints that they might do better to lunch at the English factory while he personally broke the news of Piers's many misadventures to his brother.

Over a lunch of tinned ham and locally produced turtle-parrot soup, François tried to explain the present situation as it was understood in Lambarene. He glided delicately over the question of the first factory's burning and did not even mention the stories of Piers's abuse of the natives; when Walters hinted at these, Cavanaugh and Chaillot both stared him down. Harry could guess that something was being kept back from him, but he didn't press the issue; of more importance to him now was his brother's present situation.

That situation, as François explained it, seemed desperate enough. François was at pains to emphasize that they could not know all the facts in the case, but the story recounted by traders who had witnessed Piers's gradual dissolution over the months spoke for itself. After several months of existing on François's charity and trying to drink himself into an early grave, he had crowned his earlier folly by setting the Lambarene factory on fire and abducting a European girl who had come out here on some errand which Harry didn't quite understand.

"She seemed confused," François said, "and had some obsession with going into the interior." He heaved a sigh. "*Ma pauvre Marguerite*! I hope she may not have come to some harm in Piers's company. I did not think the poor wretch would be actually dangerous, you understand, or I should not have permitted her to call upon him."

"I don't understand." Harry frowned. "The explosion happened early in the morning—just at dawn, you said?"

François nodded solemnly. "It is a mercy that one of my own Mpongwe servants happened to be in the area and saw your brother's miraculous escape from the fire, otherwise we should have thought him dead. Miraculous indeed! The building went up like dry tinder, and with all the powder I had stored on the lower floor, one would not have expected any human being to survive—especially poor Piers, with his drink-sodden mind. Do not you English have a proverb that *le bon Dieu* smiles on children and idiots? Perhaps his protection also extends to drunkards."

"The girl escaped too, you said?" Harry prompted as he sat musing and looking over the veranda at the faraway ranges of the Sierra del Cristal.

"Yes. My servant saw Piers throw her over the balcony onto the steamer, which fortuitously happened to be passing. Then he jumped onto the *Brazza* himself."

"Well, if she was in his room at dawn," Harry said with his first glimmer of satisfaction, "she was probably no better than she should be, and I doubt very much that my brother can be said to have abducted her."

"There is, however, the matter of the fire. The second fire in a matter of some months." François gave Harry a sympathetic look. "I have no intention of pursuing the matter myself, you understand. The loss of the goods I had stored in the factory is of no importance, compared with the happiness of knowing my good friend Piers is still alive. However, I fear the French civil authorities have taken a different view of the matter. It was all I could do to persuade the lieutenant governor not to arrest poor Piers after the first . . . er . . . incidents. This time he is certain to be charged with arson and—I fear the governor will not take so lenient a view as you, Monsieur Damery—with abduction. After all," said François sententiously, "even a *fille de joie*—which I do *not* believe this Marguerite to have been—but even such a one is entitled to better treatment than being tossed onto the deck of a steamer and carried off into the interior of Africa."

Harry rested his chin on one clenched fist, pondering the Frenchman's words. This Chaillot seemed a good enough sort; he'd certainly tried to make every excuse for Piers's misdeeds. Piers didn't deserve such a good friend! Harry felt his indignation rising as he thought over the sorry tale that had been unfolded before him. What was the matter with Piers? He seemed to have progressed from casual mischief to deliberately doing everything he could to wreck his career—and Harry's.

"He might have considered my career, at least, if he had no thought of his own," Harry muttered while the traders tactfully left him to his thoughts. "Damn the boy! All my life I've had him hanging around my neck."

At Oxford, when he was cramming for a First, Piers had burst in upon his studies with a crowd of partying friends, and Harry had found himself forced to participate in the revels on pain of being summarily detrousered and dragged through the college fishpond. He still winced in memory of the dean's lecture on that occasion. The old gentleman seemed to have thought it was his duty, as the older and wiser member of the family, to restrain Piers's excesses—as though anybody had ever had the slightest restraining effect on him!

"Sir, I've pointed out the error of his ways to Piers on numerous occasions," he had told the dean.

Dean Ingraham sighed and polished his brass-rimmed spectacles. "I'm sure you have. Perhaps that is part of the problem."

"Sir?"

They parted in mutual incomprehension, and Harry only took a Second in his examinations. He still thought he would have managed a creditable First if he hadn't been distracted.

Then after he left college to become Sir Monteagle Stevins' private secretary, here must come Piers to London, having been sent down from Oxford for some prank the nature of which Harry preferred not to understand. It seemed to be connected with certain soi-disant "ladies" of a type he himself had never lowered himself to consort with.

"I'm sure you haven't, big brother." Piers grinned impudently when Harry permitted himself the merest passing reference to the unfortunate circumstances.

Thank heavens, Harry had been able to prevent the various pranks which cost Piers his various London jobs from coming to the ears of Sir Monteagle. Heaven only knew what the Undersecretary for Imports and Exports would have made of such a disreputable family connection as Piers! He certainly would never have recommended Harry for that distinguished post in Sweden which, Harry flattered himself, he had carried out with the dignity required of a member of Her Majesty's diplomatic service. Harry's last act before leaving for Sweden had been to use Lord Monteagle's influence—in a necessarily roundabout manner—to get Piers shipped off to this remote colony in equatorial Africa, where one hoped he could do no more harm.

Instead, it seemed he had only redoubled his efforts to drag the family name through the mud.

"Is there no end to this persecution?" Harry

raised his eyes to the heavens and then looked, more practically, at François Chaillot. "Tell me, Monseer . . . uh . . . Shallot. What is going to happen to Piers when the French authorities catch up with him?"

A sympathetic grimace crossed François's face. "I shall exert what influence I have, that much I promise you. But these are serious crimes with which he is charged. I fear he will be sentenced to spend some years in one of our penal colonies."

"A Damery in a French penal colony!" The disgrace was unthinkable. Why couldn't Piers have taken the gentlemanly way out and blown his own brains out, rather than embarking on this daredevil escapade into the interior of Africa?

"He may, of course, fail to return," François suggested. "There are many dangers awaiting a traveler into the interior, and my poor Piers is hardly in a fit condition to look after himself."

"That only makes it worse." Harry's jaw jutted forward and he stared over the balcony at the undulating expanse of green forest bounded by the blue line of the Sierra del Cristal. Despite François's hints at his brother's dissolute condition, Harry had no doubt of Piers's ability to reappear, laughing and ragged and unrepentant, whenever he chose to do so. But what of this girl whom he'd dragged off with him? Doubtless a hussy who deserved no consideration, but still, one couldn't leave a female to the mercies of the African jungle, with no better protection than his careless rakehell of a brother.

"If he comes back? To stand his trial? And brings the girl back?" he asked after lengthy contemplation of the possibilities.

François Chaillot shrugged and spread his hands. "The sentence might be reduced."

"A Damery in a French penal colony." Harry closed his eyes briefly. "The disgrace would kill our mother." As for his own career, he might consider that at an end—the diplomatic service would not look kindly on a young man with such a stain on the family honor.

"Pray do not distress yourself," said François kindly. "As I told you, there is every likelihood that he will not return. This misguided flight must have been prompted by his desire to evade payment for his crimes. To avoid justice he will have to go far inland, far beyond the last white settlements at Talagouga—and the survival rate of white men alone in the interior is not high. It is sad, I know, but perhaps it is the better solution for your family that he be allowed to . . . vanish."

"To die, you mean," Harry corrected. Some roughness in his throat made the words come out more harshly than he intended. He saw the Frenchman's brows shoot up in arcs that matched the upward movement of his shoulders. They didn't like saying things straight out, these Frenchies. Too bad. The fellow was proposing they abandon Piers to death by jungle fever, bad water, snakebite, cannibals, or any of the other dangers of the interior. Would it be better done if they wrapped the thing up in pretty words?

He shook his head. "No. Can't do that. Might be best," he conceded, feeling an unaccustomed pang at the thought that Piers might indeed have troubled him for the last time, "but you forget—there's a lady involved. Well, a woman," he corrected himself, still unwilling to give too much credit to this unknown Marguerite who visited men's rooms at dawn.

François shrugged again. "I do not forget, Monsieur Damery. But what can we do? It is in God's hands."

"Not yet," Harry corrected him. He stood up and stretched, feeling as if he were shaking off the cloying aftereffects of the rich meal and the heavy wine. The warm, damp air was heavy against his face; moving through it made him feel as if he were wading through water. But an Englishman didn't let little things like murderous country and inhospitable climate beat him. And it was time to show this Frog how a real English gentleman handled tragedy in the family.

"Not yet," he repeated, looking down on the French trader's smooth dark head with a grim smile. "I'm going after them. They can't have gone far yet."

"If you think to bring Piers back," François warned, "you may have some difficulty."

"Piers," said Harry with grim confidence, "will do what is best for the family. Once I've talked to him. And this woman must be rescued."

François jumped to his feet. "No, Monsieur Damery! I cannot permit this! You know nothing of our jungle, of life in the bush. You will die too, and how will this benefit Piers? Shall I be charged with writing to your mother the news that both her sons have disappeared into the jungle? On my honor as a Frenchman, I cannot allow you to do this thing!"

"Not your option," Harry pointed out.

After some argument, finding Harry immovable in his resolve to set out immediately after Piers, François proposed a compromise. Rather than see Harry set out alone, he would close down his factory and accompany him upriver.

"At least as far as Talagouga," he said. "There we may get news of our runaways, and you can decide what is best to do next."

Harry nodded, scarcely hearing the Frenchman's words. He knew already what had to be done. No matter how far Piers and the girl had fled, he would track them down. The girl would be brought back to civilization, and Piers . . .

Harry thought of the loaded pistol at the bottom of his valise. The last and only thing Piers could do for his family now was to save them the disgrace of a public trial and condemnation; the only thing Harry could do for Piers was to give him the opportunity of doing so in a swift and painless fashion. His death would close the books on this unhappy story of arson, rape, and abduction, and their parents need never know anything but that their younger son had died in Africa.

François was still jabbering away in his ear. Something about the necessity to wait for the return of the *Brazza*, the steamer Piers had taken upriver, since the wreck this morning left that the only boat currently operating on the river.

"Yes . . . yes, very well," Harry cut him off abruptly. "We'll leave as soon as the *Brazza* gets back. How long do we have to wait?"

"It should return any day now," François promised. "Until then, you will of course stay with me."

Some miles upriver, halfway between Talagouga and Lambarene, Captain Jacques Merlot paced the deck of the *Brazza* with a strange crabwise shuffle. His peculiar gait was necessitated by the fact that the steamer was tilted at a twenty-degree angle, her prow sticking nakedly atop the sandbank which had so nearly captured them on the upriver run.

"When the rains come she'll float off," his mate pointed out for the tenth time that morning.

"The rains! And when will the rains come?" Captain Jacques scowled up at the brassy sky.

Fingers sniffed the air and peered upriver. "Should be any day now. You know that as well as I."

"Aye," Captain Jacques growled, "and could be a month late, like they were last year."

Fingers shrugged and grinned. There could be worse fates than sitting on a sandbank for a month or so, with no work to do, and a plentiful supply of trade gin in the cases stacked in the forward cabin.

Nine

Once Monsieur Molinier woke to find that the sacrifice had indeed been stopped and that the proposed victim was safe in his own kitchen, his fever went down rapidly.

"I don't know how to thank you," Melanie Molinier said to Piers and Meg. "He will get well now, I think."

"I knew you would save the situation, *mon cher* Piers," cooed Hélène Fanchot, hanging on Piers's arm and batting her long lashes at him in a manner Meg, personally, thought quite uncalled-for. She snorted and stalked off to talk with Kema, leaving Piers to gaze into Hélène's melting black eyes if he wanted to. If he couldn't tell a designing widow when he met one, that was his problem. She for one had better things to do—like saving Piers's honor for him. Kema and the other two Fans might be able to tell her something useful about this Crocodile Society that was causing all the trouble.

Piers found her some time later, squatting on her heels in the kitchen and tasting the savory stew that the cook Jerome had produced from two stringy fowls and a handful of limp native greens. She was like a lamb in the middle of the dark room, with her flaxen hair floating about her shoulders and her face alight with interest.

For a moment, unreasonably, Piers resented everything about her. Why did she have to be so lively and interested in everything around her? He found her delight in Africa damnably seductive, compared to the languid boredom affected by most Europeans. Her attitude was almost as alluring as the graceful curve of her back above the narrow waistband on her dark skirt, as the line of her hips under the limp fabric. She must have discarded yet another petticoat—and that was a line of thought he'd best not pursue, Piers told himself, wiping his forehead. He glanced around the kitchen in search of something to take his mind off Meg's lingerie. Kema lounged in one corner, chewing on something dark and stringy that Piers preferred not to identify, and the other two Fans were playing a gambling game with a handful of smooth stones and some lines scraped in the dirt floor.

"Planning to dine with your new friends?" he inquired with a sarcastic lilt that made Meg flush up to her fair eyebrows. "Perhaps you feel more at home here than sitting in the dining room like a lady."

"The conversation," said Meg with dignity, rising to her feet in one fluid movement, "is certainly superior to what I was hearing indoors. I have learned several *very interesting* things from Kema and his friends."

"Such as?" Piers held the door open for her and Meg swept out of the dirt-floored shed with a gracious inclination of her head toward her new acquaintances.

"I don't suppose you would be interested," she

said loftily. "I can see that Hélène Fanchot's conversation must be much more stimulating than information about the Crocodile Society."

Piers, following meekly behind her, ducked his head lest she turn around and see his involuntary grin. So his Long Meg was jealous, was she! He began to think more kindly of the clinging, flirting ways of the little widow.

"Not," Meg added with unnecessary emphasis, "that I care what sort of trouble you get yourself in. It's nothing to me if you want to flirt with all the widows between here and Stanley Pool!"

"Unfortunately, most of 'em are fat and black," Piers said with feigned regret, "and I was never attracted to filed teeth. A lovely girl like Hélène Fanchot is like a cool spring of water in the wilderness."

Meg stalked ahead of him, wrapped in a nearly visible cloud of offended dignity, and Piers grinned all the way to the mission house.

Over a dinner of chicken stew, greens, and tinned snails opened by Madame Molinier as a special treat for her guests, Piers repented for teasing Meg by doing his best to turn Hélène Fanchot's flirtatious overtures into a general conversation between him and the three women. He succeeded only moderately well, but Meg noted his efforts and began to thaw as the meal progressed. Piers unobtrusively refilled her wineglass several times, blessed Jerome for the quantity of thirst-inducing hot peppers he had incorporated into the chicken stew, and began to hope that this evening might mark some further progress in his relationship with Meg. If she could be jealous over something as trivial as his flirtation with Hélène, he thought hopefully, she must not be entirely indifferent to him. All he had to do was to make her forget this schoolgirl infatuation with Harry. And he did, after all, have an unfair advantage in this particular contest. He was here, and Harry was thousands of miles away.

After dinner Piers steered Meg out onto the broad veranda that ran around three sides of the house. "Why don't we sit here and enjoy the cool breezes," he suggested, "and you can tell me all about the Fans and the Crocodile Society." He indicated a hammock of knotted sisal strung between two rafters and easily big enough to accommodate two people who were on reasonably good terms with one another.

"Hah. I thought you'd be friendlier when you realized I had some useful information." Meg sat down on a straight-backed wooden chair, arms folded, and Piers regretfully took the hammock by himself. Did she have any idea how enticing she was, with her face slightly flushed from the wine and her walk just slightly loosened by the alcohol? How the devil could a woman saunter across the veranda with that tantalizing sway of the hips, only to plunk herself down on the hardest possible chair and imitate a wooden image?

"Tell me about it," he suggested, lounging back with his arms clasped behind his head, "and then I can demonstrate my ability to be friendly without ulterior motives." Not concerning the Crocodile Society, anyway. Piers was uncomfortably aware that Meg might consider his other motives as less than pure, but that, he told himself, was her lookout. If a girl would go traipsing around Africa with no corset to hide her slim figure and her fair hair floating about her face like a cloud of gold, she ought to expect that a man would have a hard time keeping his hands off her. Anyway, he'd acted like a perfect gentleman ever since that morning, and what had it gotten him? Instead of being mad about his kissing her, she was mad about his kissing Hélène Fanchot. If he was to be in trouble anyway, it might as well be for something worthwhile.

"Kema knows quite a lot about the Crocodile Society," Meg told him. "Among other things, he said that a lot of young men with nothing better to do have made themselves into a sort of unofficial army for the Crocodile Society, and they'll do anything the leader says the Crocodile God wants. Kema was under some pressure to join them, and he wouldn't; that's why he was marked out for sacrifice."

"Why wouldn't he join?"

"Because," said Meg triumphantly, "he doesn't approve of the things the Crocodile God tells them to do—such as kidnapping women for the leader, and working regular hours, and *burning down people's huts*!"

Piers guffawed, but recovered himself quickly at Meg's indignant look. "Sorry, Megsie," he apologized, "I was just taken by the juxtaposition of regular work with other major crimes against society. I believe I could get to like this Kema fellow."

Meg sighed. "I *wish* you'd pay attention to the main point, Piers. We now have proof that the Crocodile Society has a sideline of arson."

"Legally speaking, Kema's statement does not constitute proof."

"But it might be enough to clear you with

Hatton and Cookson, and to convince the French authorities that there's no case against you."

It was Piers's turn to sigh. "I doubt it, Meg. Burning down native huts to terrorize people into joining a secret society is one thing. An unprovoked attack on a European trading factory is something else entirely. They'll ask me what their reason was for burning the factory, and that I still don't know."

"That," said Meg triumphantly, "is why we are going on up the river. To find the head of the Crocodile Society and *ask* him why he had the factory burned down."

"He might not want to tell us," Piers pointed out. "In fact, he might be deuced unfriendly about it."

"We'll ask very politely, and we'll keep our guns loaded. And we'll go with a full crew of armed rowers. I'm not *foolhardy*, Piers."

"That," muttered Piers, "is debatable. Fortunately, we don't have to put it to the test. Before you can question this mysterious chap, you have to find him—and there's an awful lot of jungle out there." Privately he had to admit Meg's plan made some sense. It might be the only way to clear his name. But they couldn't very well go off into the jungle from here with no clearer plan than questioning every Fan villager in the interior.

"I know where his village is." Meg's voice was quiet but smug.

"You do? Where?"

"Up the river, Kema says; beyond the rapids. He says there's a stream that joins the Ogowe past the third set of rapids, and the Crocodile Society leader has his headquarters in a village on the east bank of that stream, at the top of some tall cliffs."

Piers frowned at that description. "Meg, are you sure? There's no river like that on the maps."

"Not yet. But you told me yourself that the maps are far from complete. And the Sierra del Cristal mountains are that way. Couldn't this stream come from them?"

"By God!" Piers exclaimed, incautiously sitting bolt upright in the hammock. The net of sisal ropes heaved and almost dumped him over the side and he retained his place only by an undignified scramble. "You're right, of course. No one has ever established where the waters of the Sierra del Cristal drain. If they feed the Ogowe, that could explain why this river is great even in the dry season. We could discover a new river—a new land—a place no European has ever been before! We'll put this river on the maps!"

"And," Meg pointed out, "clear your name."

"That too." And then he'd be free to court Meg as he wanted to. None of this fencing and playing word games, Piers promised himself. Once he'd cleared himself of the accusations that had been brought against him, by God, he'd sweep her off her feet, kiss away her doubts and protests, and damned well make her forget Harry, that tin-soldier hero of her childhood!

And in the meantime, there were rapids to cross and unexplored rivers to discover. Rather a pity old Megsie couldn't come with him beyond this point, actually. Piers found it most stimulating to his imagination, trying to guess which article of her clothing would next fall victim to the hazards of African travel. Still, it was quite unacceptable—a female couldn't go traveling into the interior, and he could hardly guarantee his own safety in Fan country, let alone hers. Meg would just have to stay here in Talagouga with the missionary ladies, and someday soon he would come back to her with the solution to the mystery in one hand and a newly discovered river in the other, and she'd welcome him as a hero.

The picture of that joyful return was as intoxicating as the memory of Meg's slender white ankles. Elaborating on just how Meg would greet him in the future, Piers completely lost track of what she was saying right now. A sharp prod in the ribs brought him back to consciousness of the immediate present.

"You're not listening," Meg accused. "Piers, this is serious! We have to make our plans right away, before this old witch doctor, or whatever he is, hears that we're coming after him."

We?

Piers nodded and responded with noncommittal grunts while Meg blithely went on talking about the number of rowers they would need and whether they could be recruited from the Mpongwe village near the mission. She seemed to be assuming that they would continue traveling together. A sticky situation, Piers thought. How to handle it? He'd already had a taste of Meg's determination, and he didn't fancy the confrontation that would result when he told her that she couldn't accompany him any farther.

You'd think that by now she would understand how improper it would be. But for all her shock when he kissed her, she didn't seem to understand what being alone with her in the middle of Africa was doing to his self-control. She was still a child at heart, she thought that when he kissed her she could close her eyes and dream of Harry and everything would be all right and she'd always be safe.

Piers longed to show Meg exactly how far she was from being safe with him. They were alone out here on the veranda; would she stop him if he pulled her into the hammock, found out for himself whether she had donned a spare pair of stockings, explored the feel of those soft round breasts whose outlines had been tempting him ever since she left off her corsets? Could he burn away the memory of her dream lover with the reality of his kisses, the urgency of his body?

Piers felt sweat trickling down his back as the tantalizing images filled his mind. Clearly he didn't dare risk any sort of confrontation with Meg at all. He appeared to have less than no control where she was concerned. Perhaps the best thing would be not to argue with her tonight, but simply to slip away in the early morning before she was awake. Presented with a *fait accompli*, Meg would have no option but to settle down quietly at the mission and await his return.

"Piers," Meg said in exasperated tones of strained patience, "are you thinking about this voyage at all?"

"I certainly am," he assured her. That much was true, even if his thoughts weren't running along quite the same lines as Meg's.

"Well, then, how many rowers do you think we'll need? I thought one canoe would suffice for the two of us, but Madame Molinier seems to think nobody ever set out into the interior without a ridiculous quantity of tinned food and camp beds and mosquito nets and . . . oh, I don't know half what she told me to take, because she doesn't know the English words and my French vocabulary doesn't extend to provisioning a camping expedition. I really need your help, Piers."

"Don't worry about it. I'll take care of everything. Tomorrow," Piers promised. Meg's chatter about luggage only reinforced her certainty that he'd have to be made to allow a female to accompany him. Even a quite reasonable woman like Meg couldn't travel without an almighty fuss and six times as much baggage as anybody needed!

"But we should plan . . ." Meg protested.

Piers sat up in the hammock, more cautiously this time, and reached out a hand toward Meg. Her fingers brushed the back of his hand, glimmering white in the darkness, and the intense shock of pleasure that jolted through him made him withdraw hurriedly from what he had intended as a comforting pat. The longer he spent with Meg, the harder it was to control his baser impulses. It was probably, he thought grimly, a good thing she'd refused his hint that they could share the hammock. He was no longer sure that he could trust himself to court her slowly and gently; he wanted to pin her under him and kiss her until her lips melted under his and her hair fell loose in a spun-gold cloud and she couldn't see anything but him.

"Don't *worry*," he repeated thickly. His mouth was dry and the blood was thumping in his temples like the beat of a faraway drum in the bush. "I told you, I'll take care of everything. Tomorrow." Everything, he thought, including the white soft temptation of Meg, who thought she loved his brother . . . Meg, whom he couldn't ask to marry him until he'd cleared his name . . . Meg, who could drive him mad without even trying any of the flirtatious little tricks practiced by the Hélène Fanchots of this world. God help mankind if she ever discovered those tricks! But then she wouldn't be his sweet, straightforward Meg anymore.

It was almost more than he could bear, now, to think of leaving her here without a word. Would she hate him? Would she wait for him? He cursed the weakness that made him long for just one word to make him sure of her before he set off.

"Meg . . ."

"Yes?" She was sitting on the edge of that hideous home-carved wooden chair, tense and straight-backed as a young caryatid under the invisible load of *his* problems—a load he must not, could not permit her to shoulder any longer. The words he'd been about to say died on his tongue. There was no way he could get the reassurance he craved without giving her some hint of his plan to leave her here. And he didn't give much for his chances against Meg's stubbornness, if she guessed what he intended.

He had to say something; she was waiting. A dozen sentences flashed through his brain, all impossible, all discarded as soon as he thought of them. Meg, I love you. Wait for me. If I come back, will you marry me? Me, not Harry. You don't really love Harry. You don't know him. He's a pompous young ass and he wouldn't make you happy.

Piers groaned. There wasn't anything he could say, not now. He didn't dare let her know that she was going to have to stay in Talagouga, and he didn't have the right to ask her to marry him, and she still thought she was in love with Harry.

"Nothing," he said finally, and then, "The whole situation is bloody impossible!"

"What's impossible? Piers . . ." She stood up. "Piers, are you taking a fever?" Her fingers brushed across his forehead and he leapt from the hammock, every sense alive and receptive to her touch. He clenched both hands behind his back to keep himself from seizing her. "You're sweating. I knew we shouldn't have come outside. Everybody says the night air is dangerous."

"Meg, believe me," Piers said between his teeth, "I'm not feverish. I have a lot on my mind. Now, why don't you go to bed, like a good girl, and let me think?"

She stood very straight, hands clasped before her, a slim dark column wrapped in shadow. Only her face and hands and the loosely piled masses of her fair hair glimmered palely against the warm black night. "Well, if you're not sick, you are behaving very strangely. You asked me to come out here to talk and now all you do is groan and stare off into the distance."

"Piers! *Chéri*, where are you?" A door swung open, and a warm triangle of lamplight swept across the uneven wide planks of the veranda. Hélène Fanchot came out onto the veranda with hurried little steps that made her seem to be gliding under the smooth bell of her skirt. Piers sank back into the hammock, doubling up to hide the evidence of his arousal. Meg, bless her, was too innocent to know what the straining pressure at the front of his pants meant, but Hélène was likely to make some comment that would give him away.

Hélène stopped when she saw Meg, and her trilling, birdlike speech dropped into more normal tones. "Mademoiselle Marguerite! Alone out here with Piers? English customs," she clucked. "In France it is not at all *convenable* that an unmarried woman should have the *tête-à-tête* with a gentleman. Piers, I am so sorry to have kept you waiting."

"This is not France," Meg said. "This is Africa. And tomorrow I shall be traveling alone with Mr. Damery, whom I consider in the light of a brother. I was merely entertaining him until you arrived." She gave Hélène a freezing glance. "I am sure you will entertain him much better than I could. And of course, since you are so much older than I, and widowed, it will be quite proper for you to do so. Piers, I think that it would be only polite of you to offer Madame Fanchot your seat."

On the last word her hand shot out and she twitched the hammock sideways so dexterously that the entire unsteady contraption rolled over. "Wait a minute! Meg, you don't understand . . ." He was tilting sideways. Piers grabbed unavailingly at the ropes, felt his feet shooting up and the hammock rolling away from under him, and landed on the boards with a thump that knocked the breath out of him. By the time he'd recovered, Meg had stalked inside, Hélène was kneeling and cooing over his bruises, and he had lost all inclination to tell Meg that he and Hélène Fanchot had not had a prearranged assignation on the veranda.

Ten

Piers shivered and stamped his feet as he waited for the headman of the Mpongwe village to finish his discussion with the young men Piers had asked for as rowers. By English standards he supposed it was warm enough, but he had been living on the Ogowe long enough to feel quite as cold as the natives did in the predawn mist that rose from the river in creeping white coils. When he awoke before dawn, just as the sky was lightening, he'd been in too much of a hurry to get out of the mission house to think about what clothes he put on. Dressed in the light shirt and trousers he'd worn on the journey, his shoes in one hand, he'd tiptoed over the creaking boards of the hall and had made it out to the red path below the house without hearing a stir from Meg's room. The brisk walk down the hill to the collection of native huts that huddled on the riverbank had kept him warm enough, but now, standing still while the endless tribal palaver went on, he felt as if the chilly white mist were creeping into his very bones.

For want of anything better to do, he stared through the open door of the headman's house, directly in front of him. Like all the houses in the village, it was a simple square with corner posts of bamboo holding up horizontal slats of cane. The house was large enough to comprise several rooms, with a fenced compound in back stretching down to the riverbank, and in the dim interior of the front room Piers could make out the bright colors of English cloth and the gleam of metal cooking pots. Clearly the headman was wealthy by Mpongwe standards, and it was a good bet that much of his wealth came from hiring out teams of rowers to take mission visitors up and down the river. Why was he making such a palaver over Piers's simple request?

Finally the low-toned chattering ceased and the headman turned back to Piers with an apologetic smile on his wrinkled old face. "Sorry, massa. Him boy no good pass all, no fit go up Spirit River."

"Wass matta?" Piers asked, falling easily into the singsong pidgin that was the principal means of communication up and down the coast. Why were the rowers turning down this offer of work? They'd taken him up the Ogowe before, although only on short trips. And what was this "Spirit River" nonsense? "What this palava bout Spirit River? I want go upriver, him been upriver, why dis humbug?"

The headman shook his head. "Missy say you go so-so dis way, dat way." Kneeling on the ground, he sketched a crooked line running east and west, to represent the Ogowe, then a line branching off toward the north. He pointed at the second line and shook his head again, emphatically. "Spirit River. No good! No good! Dat no Mpongwe country, dat Fan country. Dem Fan chop man, no chop my boys."

Piers sighed. No one had ever actually proved

that the Fan were cannibals, but their reputation for eating human flesh added to the general aura of terror surrounding these fierce warrior tribesmen who had come out of the north only a few generations ago, according to the old song-tellers who carried tribal history in their heads. It was probably pointless to try to improve the Fan reputation at this late date. Besides, it might well be true that they ate men. They certainly weren't choosy about what else they ate.

"Fan no chop white man," he told the headman with more confidence than he felt. "I carry big gun, bang bang, scare dem Fan. I take care of you boys."

"Dem Fan, dey carry gun too," the headman pointed out.

Piers argued and harangued for several minutes more, offering a ridiculous amount of "dash" to the headman and promising to pay the rowers triple the usual rates, but nothing he said made the slightest visible impression.

"Dis be bad palaver," the headman said finally, making a chopping motion downward with the edge of one hand to indicate that the discussion was finished. "You stay here, massa. Itala-jagouga good place, spirit him finish here, all him bad spirit go up river to Spirit River. Dat place plenty bad bad pass all, and dem Fan dey bad too!"

Piers sighed and accepted defeat, if only temporarily. Perhaps when Eugène Molinier got well he would be able to talk some sense into these people, or perhaps Piers could go to a village farther upstream where they didn't know about his plans to explore this so-called "Spirit River." He could hire the rowers on the pretext of a short journey upstream, and once they were actually at the mouth of the feared river, perhaps a white man's example would give them the courage to overcome their superstitious fears of the place. After all, that was how Talagouga had been settled; the natives believed that Eugène Molinier had driven out a nest of bad spirits when he built the mission here.

It was just damned bad luck that Meg had told the natives here about their plans to go up this mysterious tributary to the Ogowe. If she hadn't . . . Piers pounded one fist against his palm, scowling so fearfully that the headmen took a cautious step backward. It was perfectly reasonable that Meg should have tried out her newly learned pidgin by interrogating the headman about this tributary river, but when exactly had she done so? She'd not been alone for a minute last night until she swept off to bed.

"When you talk white missy?" he demanded.

He could hardly believe the headman's explanation that Meg had already come down to the village, the night before, and had hired the four strongest rowers to take her up the river.

"So that's what she was doing when I thought she went to bed!" Piers had to chuckle. God bless Meg. Who'd ever have thought she would have the courage to come down to the native settlement after dark, all by herself, and negotiate to hire a canoe and rowers? No . . . that wasn't fair. It wasn't courage she lacked, only good sense. All the same, she couldn't be allowed to go on like this. It was unthinkable that he should take a white woman with him into the unknown upper reaches of the tributaries to the Ogowe. Besides . . .

"Wait a minute!" he said abruptly. "I thought you told me your chaps wouldn't go into Fan country."

"Of course they won't go by themselves, Piers," said a brisk, confident voice behind him. Piers whirled and saw Meg coming up the steep path that led to the river. The morning mist swirled in white wreaths around her skirt, but the reflection of the rising sun off the river behind her surrounded her carelessly piled fair hair with a golden glow that almost blinded him. Tall and slender and uncompromising in her black skirt and high-necked white shirtwaist, she marched up the slippery path as confidently as though her laced boots were treading the sidewalks of Kensington.

"Surely you've lived here long enough to know that Mpongwes are afraid of Fans," she went on as soon as she reached the top of the path where Piers and the headman stood. "I'm taking Kema and Michael and David with me."

"Michael," Piers repeated, uncomprehending. "David." He had the sensation that events were moving too fast for him, as though the mighty current of the Ogowe were sweeping him inexorably back downstream into the tangled miles of mangrove swamps that led to the sea. "Who the devil—?"

"Kema's Fan friends," Meg interrupted with just a trace of impatience in her voice. "I can't pronounce their tribal names, and anyway, I expect they'll convert to Christianity now that they're under a good influence, so I thought it would be simpler all around to give them good Christian names now. They aren't in any hurry to go back to their village, and once they saw the mission store they wanted some nice cloth to take back to their wives, so I've hired them for a yard of cotton print cloth a day—payable when we return. Kema says he has some friends up the Spirit River, so we won't have to worry about being attacked by other Fan villages. And then I've hired four Mpongwe boys to complete the crew."

"You need only six rowers for one of these canoes." It was a stupid, pointless remark, Piers knew, but it was also a piece of reality to which he could anchor himself as the tide of events swept past him: Meg had hired one more rower than she needed. She wasn't quite as perfect as she thought herself.

"I know *that*," said Meg, "but obviously, if you're going to mix Mpongwes and Fans on a voyage, the Mpongwes have to outnumber the Fans. Otherwise they're afraid of being killed and eaten, don't you see? By the way," she went on, sparing Piers the embarrassment of admitting he hadn't got that far in his reasoning, "I thought it might be better if we didn't discuss our real reason for going upriver, don't you think?"

She drew closer to Piers and lowered her voice. The fine, loose tendrils of her hair brushed his cheek and he could smell the subtle flowery perfume of her English soap as she murmured so that the headman shouldn't overhear her, "Mentioning the Crocodile Society seems to make these people nervous. So we're traders."

"Traders!"

"Yes," Meg said, "I've arranged with Madame Molinier to take some goods from the mission store on credit, as much as the canoe will hold. And I've explained to Kema and his friends that we want to go up this tributary river and open up trade with the Fan villages in the interior. They thought it was quite a good idea. Michael seems to feel that once he parades his new head-dress around the villages, it will become quite the rage and everyone will want one like it."

Piers deduced that Michael was the six-foot Fan who had followed Meg, wearing little but filed teeth, copper bracelets, and one of Meg's black stockings pulled down over his head. "Do you think you will have enough stockings to meet the demand?"

Meg brushed this petty quibble aside with a wave of her hand. "If not, I'll teach some of the girls to knit. Madame Molinier is letting me have some wool from her personal supplies, and you can make knitting needles out of some of the coils of wire we're taking along to trade."

Piers realized that he was in grave danger of seeming to accede to Meg's insane plan. She was moving along so briskly that she almost made it seem like a sensible venture—setting off into the African bush with her knitting needles and her black cotton stockings to trade with the cannibals!

'There's just two problems, Meg," he said with a grin. "I don't know how to knit, and you're not coming with me."

"What are you talking about?" Meg's voice rose and she stepped back from Piers, staring up into his face as if she couldn't believe what she heard.

"I'm sorry," he said gently. He felt like a dirty dog now, letting Meg think all this time that he was going to let her come on the expedition, just to keep from quarreling with her any earlier than he had to. But dammit, he defended himself, any reasonable woman would have seen by now that the idea of her coming along was quite impossible! Any normal girl would have been shocked into an immediate return to civilization by the heat and the insects and the dirt and the brooding loneliness of the bush that surrounded them. Not to mention his own behavior. "I should have told you earlier, Meg, I can't permit you to accompany me past Talagouga. It's too dangerous. You're going to wait here until I return."

Meg's chin was jutting out in a way that gave her a distinctly mulish look. "Seems to me we had this argument once before, in Lambarene, and I won that time."

"You won nothing," Piers retorted. "I threw you onto the steamer to save your life. We never finished our discussion. Now I'm finishing it. You can't go on, Meg, and that's final."

Folding his arms and staring up the hill at the mission house, Piers waited in some apprehension for her response after this flat announcement. He was not sure exactly what he feared. Screams of anger? Tears? Pouting and sulking? A cajoling attempt to make him change his mind? In Piers's experience, that was how girls usually reacted to being told they couldn't have something. But none of those reactions seemed typical of Meg, and he felt that he would have to think less of her, whichever she chose.

He stole a cautious glance at Meg and should have been relieved to see that instead of dissolving into tears and tantrums, she was smiling. But there was an unpleasant edge to her smile that made him, if anything, more nervous than he'd been before.

"All right, Piers," she said meekly, and his tense body sagged with momentary relief. He felt almost disappointed that she'd given in so easily—it wasn't what he'd expected of Meg. But then, neither were feminine tantrums.

"If you don't want to ride in my canoe," she went on, "you don't have to. Feel perfectly free to make up your own way upriver—if you can. If you change your mind, I'll be departing in half an hour. You should just have time to pack." She turned on her heel and began plodding up the path toward the mission house as if there was no more to say.

Piers sprang after Meg and caught her by the upper arm, whirling her around with a fierce jerk that sent her stumbling against his chest. He caught and held her there for a moment only, until she recovered her balance, but the momentary closeness of her slim uncorseted body was enough to distract him from his carefully reasoned arguments. "Meg, you can't go," he repeated helplessly. "I can't allow it."

Allow it? He couldn't even force his arms to relax and free her from this involuntary embrace. And Meg was making no move to free herself.

"Allow it?" She laughed up at him, standing passive in the circle of his arms. "You can't stop me, Piers. I'm free, white, and over twenty-one. I've hired a boat and rowers, and what's more, they're the only rowers you'll get to come into Fan country. Unless you want to go into Kema's village and recruit some Fans of your own?"

The taunt released Piers from his momentary paralysis, igniting the fires that had smoldered under his skin since Meg fell against him. His arms tightened, crushing her against him, and he bent his head to claim her smiling lips. The fire leapt from his mouth to hers—he could feel the instant when her cool unresponsive lips quickened against his, becoming warm and soft with promise, and the stiff unyielding body in his arms became pliable against him. Drinking in her moist, shuddering breath, he lost himself in the warm satin of her mouth, the feel of her round soft breasts pressing against his chest. Sweetness and danger roared through his veins and left him blind and deaf and insensate to everything except the sweetness of holding Meg against him as he'd been longing to do ever since she came to Africa.

A little gasp of pain broke from her lips and he realized that he'd been holding her cruelly tight. His arms slackened and she caught her breath as she moved away from him. The prim white blouse clung to her body now, outlining the lace ruffles of her chemise and the soft pliant curves under that, and one long fair curl had come loose to hang down over her shoulder in touching disarray.

Now, with returning sanity, Piers felt only dismay at what he'd done. What had happened to all his good intentions? Hold off . . . don't frighten her . . . court her slowly . . . above all, don't speak until you have a right to speak to her, until you've cleared your name and have something more to offer her than a share in your disgrace. Those were the words of wisdom he'd drummed into himself all through the lonely nights; and all his wisdom had vanished like the morning mists, burned off by the touch and the closeness of Meg as the rising sun had burned the last shreds of white mist off the river.

Anxiously he searched her face for some hint of the fear and repulsion he expected to find there. Her lips were bruised and swollen from the fierceness of his kiss. How she must despise him—a disgraced man, a failure, who could do no better than attack a girl whose heart was given elsewhere! What a fool he was! He knew that the way to treat Meg was to give her time to forget Harry, to win her affections slowly and gently, yet whenever he touched her all his sensible plans went up in the blaze of desire he felt for her.

But he read no hatred in her wide, dreamy gray eyes. She was looking up at him with a cloudy unfocused gaze, and her reddened lips moved slowly without sound, as though she were trying to make sense of what had just happened to them.

"I'm . . . sorry, Meg," he said huskily. "I shouldn't have done that—I had no right. Forgive me?"

It seemed an eternity before she spoke, and then her voice was soft and unsure, not the brisk confident tones she had used earlier. "As an argument for keeping me from going upriver with you," she said, "it seems to lack something."

"I should think that would have convinced you if nothing else would. Don't you see how improper it would be for the two of us to go off together?"

Meg's laugh was a low husky chuckle, worlds away from Hélène Fanchot's birdlike trill, and infinitely more intoxicating to Piers. "Darling Piers. Isn't it a little late to insist on strict propriety? And are you really trying to frighten me out of going upriver by pretending that you might attack me as soon as we got out of sight of the mission? Don't be ridiculous. You're like my brother. I can remember when we used to have our bath together."

"We were *three years old.* It's different now, Meg. You're a grown woman, and I'm . . . I'm . . ." He clenched his fists.

"Still acting like a three-year-old in a tantrum, because somebody else has the toys you want," Meg finished, the mocking smile back on her face. "Don't be childish, Piers. Admit it—you're just jealous because I thought of hiring the Fans as rowers before you did." She turned away from him and started back up the path to the mission house.

"You can't go!" Piers shouted at her slim, erect back.

Meg plodded steadily on, every line of her body expressing determination to ignore him. He shook his fist at her and then returned to the village. Since the damned girl wouldn't see reason, there was only one way to stop her. He would pay the Mpongwe rowers she'd hired double or triple whatever she'd offered, and promise to get them a Fan escort. He'd hire every able-bodied man in the village if he had to, if it was the only way to protect Meg from herself.

The path to the mission house wound back and forth up the steeply sloping hill, with several hairpin turns. Around one of these turns, hidden from the village by a red mound of clay and from the mission by a stand of trees at the edge of the garden, Meg dropped to her knees under one of the trees and buried her face in her shaking hands. Thank heaven she'd gotten away from Piers without betraying herself. Why had he kissed her like that? To try to embarrass or frighten her out of going on? It couldn't have been out of desire for her—his own stumbling apology had made that clear, anyway, yesterday it had been perfectly obvious that he found Hélène Fanchot more attractive than he did her.

And with good reason, too, thought Meg bleakly. Any man would rather have a pretty, little, vivacious, fashionable *slut* like the widow Fanchot, than a tall, awkward beanpole of a girl who couldn't say two words without getting into an argument, or move two steps without tripping over her own feet. It was a good thing, too, else it really would be improper for her and Piers to go off together in the bush. There was no reason for her to feel so grim about it.

And no reason, either, to be so embarrassed over her own reaction to Piers's kiss. It was probably because he looked so much like Harry—that was why her body kept responding so disgracefully to him, even though her mind told her it was only good old ne'er-do-well Piers holding her. Fortunately, he didn't seem to have noticed how disgracefully she lost control of herself whenever he touched her. Probably he kissed girls all the time, Meg thought, calling forth her most scathing sarcasm in an effort to regain control over her feelings. Scores of girls . . . hundreds of girls . . . girls all over three continents and two hemispheres had probably been kissed by Piers Damery. What to her had been an intoxicating delight beyond her wildest imaginings was probably no more than a casual exchange of compliments to a man like Piers.

If Harry ever kissed her, she would probably see at once that it was quite different and much nicer to be kissed by a man you loved and respected. Though, Meg had to admit, she couldn't honestly imagine anything much pleasanter—on a purely physical level, of course—than what had just passed between her and Piers on the river path.

Dwelling on those purely physical sensations was not a good idea either. The mere memory of them made her face flush and her heart beat faster. Meg, folded her hands in her lap and made mental lists of the trade goods she would need to take from the mission store, until she felt that her equanimity was quite restored. Then, and only then, she rose to her feet and set off up the path with long determined strides. There was no time to be lost if she and Piers were to depart before the heat of the midday sun made travel impossible.

She had no doubt that he would come around to her way of thinking before the canoe was packed. What else was there for him to do? Meg chuckled with internal satisfaction at the thought of how neatly she had arranged matters. How much easier it was to deal with people when you had a little confidence in yourself! Stopping Kema's sacrifice had been her first adventure, hiring her own rowers had been the second. Now she was inviting Piers to join her instead of begging him to take her along. Made all the difference in the world.

And there was absolutely no need to dwell too much on the incident on the river path. They would both do much better to go on as if it had never happened.

Eleven

Meg leaned cautiously back against the mound of sleeping mats in the middle of the canoe, taking care not to move too quickly. She had already discovered that the long hollowed-out logs which the Mpongwe used for river travel were sensitive to the least motion of the passengers; an unwary dart to one side to admire a brightly colored flower, or to the other side to watch the current swirling around a vicious-looking rock in midstream, set the canoe rocking so violently that M'bo, the head rower, who stood in the bows of the canoe, called back, "Please to sit down, ah!"

They had made a late departure, three full hours after daybreak, loaded down with far more baggage than Meg personally thought necessary. Her canoe was piled high with sleeping mats and mosquito nets, while she sat on a great tin box full of the Manchester printed cotton cloth that she hoped to use for trade goods. Her personal possessions had been reduced to the change of underwear and her spare skirt, a brush and comb, and a bottle of quinine for fever; all were neatly stowed in a tin box at her feet. Behind her, six pairs of rowers stood paddling in unison, while Kema steered from the stern. Ahead of them was a second canoe, containing Piers, the food supplies, and the other two Fans, along with ten Mpongwe rowers.

It seemed to Meg that one canoe alone contained more than they really needed to take on a short expedition. They were posing as traders, after all; couldn't they stop at native villages along the way, sleep in their huts, and eat the local food supplemented by the fish they would catch in the river? But Piers, once he grudgingly agreed to "permit" her to go along, had taken over the planning of the expedition in an odiously high-handed manner. At least two canoes would be necessary, he decreed—one to carry the sleeping supplies and trade goods, one for his ammunition and the provisions he insisted on taking. What was more, he insisted on doubling the normal complement of rowers in each canoe, saying that they had no way of knowing how bad the rapids would be on this Spirit River.

"We'll get more information if we sleep and eat in the villages," Meg had protested as Piers recklessly mortgaged more and more of her credit for tins of beef and dried milk and ham, strings of sausages and loaves of bread, candles and sugar and a small packet of tea.

"We'll get sick, too," Piers had told her, ruthlessly adding another mosquito net and two cushions to the mounting pile of things to go in the lead canoe. "Meg, just take my word for it. You won't like native chop."

"How do you know?" she muttered mutinously. "I've never tried it." She suspected that all this extra baggage was Piers's way of demonstrating how much trouble it was to take a woman along.

Surely he wouldn't have set off by himself with all these supplies!

Ignoring her, Piers frowned at the tiny package of tea. "Wish we had more, but Melanie says this is all she can spare."

"Go make eyes at Hélène Fanchot," Meg suggested. "I'm sure she would be happy to give you the keys to the storeroom."

Piers only chuckled, and Meg settled herself atop the pile of bedding with folded arms, resolving not to say another word about all the unnecessary trouble and expense he was going to. She would just have to demonstrate to him that she was as hardy as any man he might have traveled with. She vowed not to complain of heat or fatigue, to pronounce any smoky and mosquito-ridden hut they were offered a delightful lodging, to eat whatever their hosts were having for dinner while Piers dined in lonely splendor on tea and tinned meat.

Now, four hours into their journey, she had not the slightest urge to complain about anything. The rowers, experienced in the ways of the river, kept the two canoes close to shore, where the current was relatively slow and the great trees arching overhead shaded them. The sun was at its zenith and the sparkling light reflected off the center of the river dazzled Meg's eyes whenever she chanced to look that way, but here in the shadows it was deliciously cool and almost as dark as at evening. Behind her, the rowers set up a melodious, rhythmic chant that relaxed her tired brain and made her feel as though she could almost sleep right here on the water. The relatively slow pace of the canoe gave her a chance to look at and marvel over the exotic beauty of the rain forest as they passed, and when she grew bored with watching the scenery she had only to call to M'bo and their canoe shot ahead so that she could converse with Piers.

"What are they singing?" she called to Piers on one of those occasions when the river broadened and their canoes could move abreast through the wide reaches of the shallows. "Can you understand them?"

Piers chuckled and obligingly translated. " 'The white men are heavy, the white men's baggage is heavy. We toil all day for a mouthful of plantains so that the white men can sit at their ease.' "

"Oh!" Meg abandoned her comfortable lounging posture on the bedding to sit bolt upright.

Piers went on translating. " 'What does the black man need? A little manioc and a little tobacco. What does the white man need? Too many things to say in a song, O my brothers.' "

"It wasn't *my* idea to bring all this unnecessary baggage," Meg reminded him.

"Oh, don't worry about it," said Piers. "They're only hinting that we should dash them a little something besides their rations and the cloth—some tobacco would do nicely."

"I didn't bring any tobacco."

"I did," said Piers with a smug smile.

Meg was rather relieved when M'bo shouted warning of a nasty stretch of fast water ahead and her canoe was forced to drop back behind Piers's again. Shortly thereafter the roaring of the water made even shouted conversation impossible.

The river had broadened after Talagouga, but now it was growing more narrow with each splash of the paddles that propelled them forward. The banks rose precipitously to become the foothills of the mountains Meg had admired from Lambarene, shutting off all but a narrow strip of sky, and great black rocks dotted the banks under a fringe of fallen trees. More such rocks nosed up in the riverbed, poking their menacing black snouts out of the water and setting the brown current foaming around them. The noonday sun shone down on these rocks, illuminating the splashing particles of water so that they seemed to be surrounded by a rainbow haze. For several minutes Meg was so entranced by the beauty of the scene that she hardly realized how much faster the current was flowing or how the powerful pull of the water tugged the canoe against the rower's best efforts.

A shout from ahead alerted her to the growing danger. Piers's canoe was just entering on a narrow stretch of water, guarded on either side by the great black boulders. The swift current, forced between and over the rocks, seized on the canoe and tossed it up and down like a matchstick. Meg had to grasp the sides of her own canoe to keep from being tossed overboard as they neared the rapids, but all her attention was bent on the shining blond head that she could just see amid the spraying water ahead of them. A corkscrew pitch and toss of the canoe jerked Piers's head rower off his feet. He tumbled into the bottom of the boat with a doleful cry. Why wasn't he up again? Was he hurt? The other rowers could never steer through the rapids without a man in the bow to guide them.

There was a brief pause as the rowers missed their stroke and the canoe lost headway. The river currents tugged at the stern; in a moment, if they didn't recover their speed, the canoe would be whirling around and around downstream until it smashed into the waiting black rocks. In that pause, Piers leapt up and took the paddle from the hand of the fallen rower. He was shouting something, a rhythmic cadence to keep the rowers at their work; Meg could just make out the strong tones of his voice through the burbling roar of the rapids. He made his way forward to the bow and took up the head rower's vacated position, using his long leaf-shaped paddle to fend off rocks while he called an unceasing flow of directions back to the rowers.

With agonizing slowness the canoe crept forward, seeming to gain no more than an inch at a time against the sucking, tugging current between the boulders. But they were making it through. Meg watched Piers's powerful shoulders straining against the current, his body clearly outlined through the water-soaked shirt. The hunting rifle that he wore strapped to his back swayed with each motion of his arms. She prayed silently, urgently, her lower lip caught between her teeth to keep her from crying out. Only when Piers had conned the canoe out of the dangerous stretch did she relax—and then, with a shudder, she realized that her own canoe had still to go through those rapids.

Past the rapids there was slack water again, and then a twist in the river carried Piers's canoe out of sight. Meg fought down an irrational feeling of panic that gripped her when his fair head disappeared behind the tangle of rocks and vines and fallen trees that jutted out into the river. Somehow, as long as she could see Piers ahead, she had felt safe without realizing it. Now she knew that she was soaked through to the skin with the spray from the river, and that the dreadful bobbing whirlpools of the rapids lay between them. She gripped the sides of the canoe so hard that her hands turned white with strain, and as the rowers took up their paddles she prayed not to disgrace herself by crying out or fainting or, worse, being sick.

Before they had moved out of the slack water there was a shout from the bank. Meg's head jerked up and she saw Piers clinging to a tree, leaning out almost over the river as he shouted directions in Mpongwe to the rowers. M'bo laughed and raised a hand in acknowledgment. "We go by bank," he told Meg over his shoulder, "no fast water."

But how was that possible? As the canoe moved forward, Meg saw clearly that at the place where the point of tree-covered rocks jutted out, where Piers was standing, the black rocks and the spraying water between them came well up to the shore. There simply was no more slack water for them to row through. Even now the canoe was pitching and tossing as the first rush of water from the rapids struck it.

"Stand up, Meg!" Piers yelled through his cupped hands.

Her knees wouldn't obey her; her hands wouldn't let go of the sides of the canoe. She crouched, paralyzed, under the deafening spray of cold river water.

"Now!"

Somehow, she never knew how, she was up on one knee, then had both feet braced against the rolling of the canoe. The overhanging trees grazed her hair and she flinched back.

"Jump for bank, sah!" yelled M'bo, stooping in the bow to duck under the tree branches.

Meg made a wild despairing leap and felt her hands scrabbling at the rock wall that faced them. The fingers of her left hand closed over a thorny vine and she felt a tearing pain in her palm, but she hung on for dear life, afraid to seek another handhold as the canoe glided out from beneath her. A steely grip caught her right wrist as she felt for a handhold in the sheer rock, and she felt herself being tugged up over the projecting rock face and into a nest of dead branches. Her shoulder flamed out in protest; then her kicking feet found a crevice in the rock and she took some of her own weight, pushed upward and got one knee over the rock, let go of the thorny vine, and reached for Piers. He hauled her the last few inches and she sagged down in the midst of the branches, feeling more fond of this prickly nest than she had ever felt of the softest feather bed.

"Are you all right, Meg?"

She tried to answer him; to her horror, only a silly light-headed giggle came out. Below them, the canoe's crew had made it safely to land, and miraculously, the canoe had not capsized. Clinging to trees and vines, they were hauling it around the point by means of a short chain fastened to the bow.

"I wondered what that chain was for," Meg remarked. "V-very practical." Her voice was wobbling ridiculously, and she felt oddly short of breath, as though something had used up all the air and left her trying to breathe in a vacuum.

She looked up at Piers's worried blue eyes and giggled again.

"Oh, God," Piers muttered, "she must have cracked her head. Concussion—her wits are wandering."

"You never would agree I had any wits before," Meg said. "I think our relationship is improving." She stood up on shaky legs and pushed tangles of wet hair out of her eyes. "Bother, I think I lost my last good hairpin in the rapids. Well, I'm glad that's over."

"It's not," Piers said shortly. "According to M'bo, that's the first of three rapids we've got to pass today."

They had to do that two more times! Meg drew breath to protest. She was bruised from head to foot and soaked to the skin, and the mere thought of getting back in a canoe made her legs start trembling again. Surely they could make camp on the shore and go on tomorrow, when they were rested?

Now, why was Piers watching her like that, with a gleam of triumph in the dancing blue lights of his eyes? Just before she voiced her protest, Meg realized that she was playing into his hands. All he wanted was some evidence that she really couldn't stand the hardships of the journey. If she were foolish enough to complain now, when they were only a few hours away from Talagouga, he'd try to bully her into going back to stay at the Mission Évangélique while he went on alone and hogged all the adventure. It wouldn't work, of course. Meg had no intention of being sent back like a naughty child. But neither did she have the energy to get into another shouting argument with Piers . . . particularly if they really had two more sets of rapids to pass that day.

She drew another deep breath and folded her hands so that he wouldn't see how they trembled. "Then we'd better get on, hadn't we? It wouldn't be very pleasant to have to do this in the dark."

She thought there was a look of unwilling respect in Piers's eyes as he offered her his arm to help her down the steep far side of the point and back into the canoe. "Thank you," Meg said, "I can manage on my own."

She did fine until, halfway down the bank, her wet boot sole slipped over a smooth wet boulder. She threw herself backward, missed the branch she was reaching for, and went slithering ignominiously down the bank to land in a welter of skirts and broken branches at the muddy edge of the water.

Piers guffawed, and after a moment Meg forced herself to laugh too. "It's a good thing it was me and not you that slipped," she said, rising to her feet with as much dignity as the situation permitted.

"Why so?"

Meg pointed at the sharp ends of broken branches and the curling, thorny vines on which she had landed. "That stuff would have ripped right through your trousers. Whereas I was nicely protected by good thick skirts and several petticoats. Men's clothes," she said with a sniff, lifting her skirts to step daintily into the canoe, "are so impractical!"

The next few miles of the journey were enlivened by the comforting sense of having had the last word. Meg did long to know how soon they would encounter the next rapids, but she didn't dare to ask M'bo for fear that Piers would hear and start teasing her about being afraid.

Night overtook them before they reached the next set of rapids. The strong current in this narrow section of the river slowed their progress, tugging at the canoe and forcing the rowers to work hard for every inch of forward progress. Piers was forced to call a halt when the long shadows of the mountains on the north bank streaked across the brassy, turbulent expanse of river. A brief conference with M'bo elicited the information that he had two uncles who had married into the village they could just see around the next bend.

"We'll spend the night there," Piers decreed.

Meg drew a long shaky breath. She was relieved beyond words not to have to face the rapids again that night, but not for anything would she have admitted as much to Piers. "If you say so," she agreed, head bent demurely, "but I thought you were in a hurry to reach the Spirit River."

Piers's golden eyebrows met in a momentary scowl. "I am. But we can't navigate at night. You wouldn't understand."

"I'm sure you know best," Meg agreed. She raised her eyes just in time to catch a suspicious flash of blue between Piers's suddenly narrowed lids. She began to suspect she had overdone her pose of meek acquiescence. She was sure of it when they reached the village.

The huts were set some distance back from the riverbank, rather than clinging to the steep bank as the village near the mission had done. M'bo shouted to warn the villagers of their arrival, and before the canoes were tied up, a horde of excited friends and relatives had arrived to welcome M'bo and ask about every detail of his current assignment. They guided Piers and Meg along a well-trodden path that led to a cluster of squarish reed houses in a clearing of hard-packed red dirt. At once the women of the village redoubled their preparations for the evening meal, setting pots of water over the fire and bringing out their stores of dried agouma. M'bo explained that his relatives would be honored to share their meal with the white visitors.

"Excellent," said Piers blandly. "M'bo, please tell your relatives that an unfortunate stomach weakness makes it impossible for me to eat anything except certain specially prepared foods which I have brought for myself, but that my traveling companion is very fond of agouma and will be honored to share their feast." He grinned at Meg. "You did say that you could live on native chop. Now's your chance."

Meg looked doubtfully at the dirty, grease-rimmed calabashes in which a grayish, sour-smelling paste was being prepared.

"Wouldn't do to insult our hosts," Piers added with a sarcastic smile while M'bo was translating his excuses.

Meg had picked up enough words of the Mpongwe dialect by this time to understand that M'bo's translation explained Piers's refusal to join in the feast by mention of stomach devils and bowel spirits, with a strong hint that the devils would be likely to attack anybody who ate with the white man or even watched him eating. The explanation brought forth sympathetic smiles and understanding pats for the poor afflicted white man.

Piers strolled off to the spacious hut in the center of the village that had been allocated to their use, leaving Meg to maintain her company manners with a mixture of Pidgin English, a few words of Mpongwe, and a copious use of signs and smiles. The smiling goodwill of the women who brought her food made up for any difficulties in communication, but Meg found their constant poking and prodding and fingering of her dress and hair a sore trial.

Her first bite of the grayish paste in the calabash presented her with another trial. It seemed compounded of a mixture of flavors, in which sour milk and red pepper predominated, with hints of very old fish and other things about which she dared not think. The texture was very like the library paste which it resembled, and she thought she never would get the sticky mass down her throat without gagging. Just in time M'bo offered her another calabash full of some doubtful liquid. Meg gulped it down without thinking, intent only on washing down the mouthful of glutinous paste.

The women were squatting around her in a semicircle, their brass anklets and oiled braids glistening in the firelight, watching to see how the stranger would like their food. Meg forced herself to give a broad smile of appreciation. "Good pass all," she said, hoping the message would be enough.

It wasn't. They were going to stay and watch till she finished the stuff. Groaning inwardly, Meg dipped into the calabash and ate the rest of the agouma as quickly as possible, washing it down with copious drafts of the weakly alcoholic, soapy drink M'bo had offered her.

Her display of appetite had the opposite effect of what she had intended. When she was nearly through with the sour paste, two of the women went to the men's circle and returned carrying an enormous bowl made of a hollowed-out log and full to the brim with freshly made agouma.

"No!" Meg exclaimed involuntarily, and turned to M'bo for help. In halting Pidgin English she asked him if he couldn't conjure up a few stomach devils for her too.

Meg rather thought that M'bo explained that white women were weak and sickly and could barely eat enough to keep a bird alive, but that they didn't need more food than that because they did no work. Certainly part of his speech was accompanied by a pantomime of her lounging against the cushions as they rowed upstream, then sitting bolt upright with alarm and finally jumping for the bank at the point by the rapids. The women laughed heartily at this recital, but at least they didn't press any more food on her.

Just to make sure that everybody understood that dinnertime was over, Meg asked M'bo if he would go to the canoes and bring out one of her boxes of trade goods. When he came back, she unrolled a length of bright cotton with red and yellow flowers on a blue background. Even in the firelight the colors glowed like jewels, and the effect in the brilliant equatorial sunlight would be positively blinding. The women crowded near, fingering the cloth and exclaiming over its beauty, while Meg asked if they had any rubber or ivory to trade. For trade purposes she found that her few words of Mpongwe and Pidgin English served quite well; the basic vocabulary of cloth and rubber and money was known all up and down the river, wherever traders had traveled in the past.

The business seemed to be going quite well, with the women bringing out balls of rubber and Meg testing each one for lumps of wood or pebbles in the middle, when a tall elderly Mpongwe rose from his place by the men's fire and strode over. Meg had been surreptitiously admiring his costume for some time. He was by far the most gorgeously dressed of the villagers, sporting a raveled satin loincloth with long ends that trailed on the ground, at least twenty strings of beads mixed with leopards' teeth and brass bells, and a tall battered silk hat to crown his gloriously mud-plastered hair.

"Headman of village," M'bo murmured as he approached. He waggled his head and rolled his eyes at Meg. She nodded to show that she appreciated his warning to treat this important man with all due respect.

Pushing the women aside, the headman planted himself in front of Meg and barked out a question in which she caught only the English words "Hatton and Cookson."

He must be asking if she were connected with that trading firm, she thought. She nodded vigorously and was astonished to see a dark scowl on the man's face. He addressed a few words to the women and shooed them away with vigorous flapping gestures. When he and Meg were alone, he scooped up the rubber balls and departed, kicking the length of flowered cloth contemptuously back toward her.

"Well!" Meg breathed. She picked up the cloth, automatically shaking the dust out of it, and turned to M'bo. "And just what was that about? What made him so angry?"

M'bo didn't know any more than she did, but he thought the headman had been frightened rather than angry. In any case they had no time to discuss it further. The men had gathered around the big hut that had been allocated to the visitors and were shouting for Piers to come out. Meg hurried toward the hut, still idiotically clutching the flowered cloth to her breast, and tried to push past the ring of Mpongwe men. The headman was haranguing Piers, whose blond head was bent in an attitude of courteous incomprehension; she couldn't see any more than that over the heads of the crowd.

M'bo whispered to her that it was nothing to be frightened about; the headman was telling Piers that he would have to move, that was all. He could not continue to occupy a hut in the center of the village. There was a danger of arousing the anger of some very bad spirits who lived in the neighborhood.

Meg felt her spine sagging with relief as it became clear that the crowd was not going to explode into violence. They merely escorted Meg and Piers out to the very edge of the village, to a tiny dilapidated hut where there was barely room to spread their sleeping mats. The villagers were polite but watchful, making sure that the foreigners left no contaminating trace of their presence in the big guest hut.

Twelve

A "bush light," a stick holding a big bubble of resinous gum, had been ignited in the men's fire and given to Piers so that he could see his way to their new quarters. Meg looked around the shabby little hut with dismay. The floor was trampled and muddy, as though some large animal had visited there recently, and she rather thought that a better light would show other signs of the animal's visit. One wall and half the roof were almost gone; the vines that laced the canes together had rotted away, leaving great gaps through which rain and wind could pour. And over the whole hut hung an indefinable musty scent, as of a place long disused and never cleaned.

Suppressing her dismay, Meg turned to Piers with an attempt at a bright smile. "It might be a bit crowded for the two of us, don't you think? I'll sleep outside—I really don't mind," she volunteered, trying to sound noble rather than eager.

Piers lowered the bush light and regarded her with a sardonic expression in his blue eyes. "There'll be no need for such a sacrifice," he told her. "The headman made it quite clear to me that we were both to stay exactly where he told us. Here," he added unnecessarily, gesturing with the hand that held the bush light. The sudden motion made the light sputter down and then flare up with an outpouring of greasy smoke that did nothing to improve the atmosphere in the tiny hut. Meg retreated outside, coughing and holding her length of cotton over her mouth and nose, while Piers and M'bo spread out sleeping mats and draped a length of mosquito netting between the two mats for a gesture of propriety.

"I suppose I'd better apologize for all this," Piers said when he rejoined Meg. "I don't know if you noticed, but M'bo embroidered somewhat on my excuses for not eating with the villagers. Some story about stomach devils. They must have decided it wasn't safe to let a man with strange devils in his stomach sleep in the village. I wish I knew why they waited until I was in the middle of dinner before getting upset, though," he added with his first show of feeling. "They hustled me out of there so fast I didn't even get a chance to finish my tin of deviled ham."

"Deviled ham." A tiny sigh of longing escaped Meg. "Was it good?"

"Top-hole." Piers grinned. "How was your dinner?"

"Don't ask. You might awaken my stomach devils . . . All right, Piers! I admit it. You were right to bring your own food, and if I abase myself humbly before you will you let me have dinner with you tomorrow night?"

"No need for that. I admire a woman who can admit when she's wrong. Just go for a little walk with me, and tomorrow you shall feast on potted breast of turkey." Piers took Meg's elbow and gently guided her away from the village, down the well-trodden path that led to the riverbank. Even in the darkness the smooth reddish earth gleamed in contrast to the tangle of vegetation on either side, so that they had no trouble finding their way down to the river. The lazy slap and gurgle of the slack water against a sandbank warned them when they were drawing close, even before a break in the vine-tangled trees showed them the starlit glimmer of water. Behind them, the sounds of the feasting villagers blended in with the small noises of the African bush, and the village fires were no more than a ruddy glow against the sky.

"I'm glad we came down here," Meg said. Now that they were well out of earshot of the village, she felt for the first time since their landing that she could talk freely to Piers.

"So am I," Piers murmured. The pressure of his hand on her elbow increased slightly. It didn't hurt; why did she feel as if flames were shooting up her arm? She tried to still her ragged breathing, to concentrate on what she had to tell him.

"Listen, Piers. I don't think it was your stomach devils that upset them."

'No? Then it must have been something else. Look, the moon is rising. In a few minutes it will make a silver bridge across the river."

"Piers, please! This is important." But wasn't the shivery feeling that possessed her at his touch equally important? She was vibrantly aware of the light pressure of each finger; she knew when he breathed and when his hand slid half an inch up her arm. The backs of his fingers brushed the sensitive underside of her breast and an almost painful thrill shot through her body. Wasn't this as important as solving the mystery?

No. Not to Piers. He was merely reacting automatically to moonlight and a girl's presence; he'd as good as told her so, many times. If his feelings for her went any deeper than that, wouldn't he have said so by now? Besides, Meg told herself, she didn't care for Piers in that way either. It was just that she wasn't used to a man's attentions, had no training in how to resist the siren sweetness that stirred in her blood. If Harry were here she would quickly see the difference between the two men, the difference between her mere sensual attraction to Piers and the respectful love she felt for Harry. Since Harry was on the other side of the world, she would just have to control her unruly feelings without that help.

As Piers's hand slid even farther up her arm, drawing her close to his body, Meg jerked away. Embarrassment made her clumsy; the abrupt movement made her as if she were pushing him away from her. He looked hurt. Probably he wasn't used to a girl who didn't fall into his arms at the first attempt. Well, it would be good for him to encounter one, for a change.

Drawing a deep breath to steady herself, Meg told Piers how the natives' attitude had changed when she claimed to be associated with Hatton and Cookson. She was gratified to see that as Piers understood her story, he gave her his full attention for once. The only trouble now was that her deep breathing wasn't having the desired affect. Every time she looked at Piers, she felt light-headed and short of breath, as though he were using up all the air around them. She fixed her eyes firmly on the glow of the rising moon behind the trees and waited for his response to her story.

"And M'bo said they were frightened . . . but I'll lay bail they weren't frightened of me personally," Piers mused. "Everything went fine until you mentioned Hatton and Cookson, you say? Now, why should they be afraid of a perfectly respectable English trading firm?"

Meg shook her head. "I don't know. But it might have something to do with your trouble . . . mightn't it? What if whoever framed you wasn't striking at you personally, but at Hatton and Cookson's through you?"

"What if, indeed." Piers stared out over the river. The moon glowed orange through the trees on the opposite bank, and the lazy ripples and gurgles of the river currents were the loudest sound in the night. The heavy moist air pressed down on them with a gentle weight that made every movement languorous and slow.

Meg felt intensely uncomfortable, she didn't know why; it was as though the silence of the bush around them were about to be broken by the cry of a hunting cat or the screech of its prey. As though something must happen to break the soft silence of the night. "It doesn't really get us much farther, does it?"

"It's another piece of evidence . . . look, the moon is making a bridge for us. I told you it would happen." The paling orb of the moon had risen above the treetops while they were wrapped in their silent thoughts, and now a shimmering line of silver danced across the broad reach of the water before them.

The bushes between them and the water's edge impeded Meg's view. She moved a little closer to Piers, her eyes fixed on the silvery track, and her shoulder brushed against his.

The involuntary touch, after her conscious efforts at avoiding him, took her by surprise, and a thrill of pleasure ran through her. She felt weak and vulnerable, unable any longer to conceal the trembling desire that his masculine presence awoke within her. She swayed toward Piers and he caught her in his arms, kissing her hungrily. His mouth moved possessively over hers and she responded to his urgency without shame or fear, knowing only the joy of the touch she had been avoiding for so long. Shamelessly she pressed her lips against his, matching the thrust of his tongue with her own. When he would have released her, she put her hands on his shoulders, thrilling at the feel of that strong masculine body under her palms, and clasped him to her without thinking of the consequences. Her hands slid lower to explore the curves and planes of his back. A stifled moan broke from his lips and his hands dug into her flesh, pressing her against him as if he wanted to become one with her here on the banks of the river.

"Meg, you're wonderful," he murmured between kisses. "Always were . . . best pal a man could have . . ." He laughed. "No. I didn't mean that. Not just that. But the way you took those rapids without flinching . . . And tonight . . . Sour manioc for supper, and spiders in the hut, and I haven't heard a word of complaint out of you yet. You're as game as a boy could be, and so much more than a boy." His hand moving over the uncorseted curves of her body gave emphasis to his words, setting her on fire beneath the muffling layers of skirt and cotton petticoat and flannel petticoat and linen drawers, camisole and ruffled corset cover and fichu and all the other stupid, unnecessary layers of cloth that lay between them.

One broad hand slipped under her blouse and explored the firm, high breasts half-exposed by her low-cut lacy camisole. Meg felt close to fainting as his calloused thumb moved in gentle circles over her skin, teasing her nipples into taut hard buds. How could his casual touch turn her knees to water and her will to the faint whisper of a faraway wind? She didn't know; she only knew that she was losing all her hard-won sensible attitudes, and she felt lighter than air as they slipped away from her. Just now, nothing mattered but the sensual rapture Piers was awakening in her, this sweet drunkenness that made her feel as though she were waltzing in the wind.

Meg shivered with fear and pleasure together as Piers's free hand cupped her buttocks and pulled her closer, molding her thighs to his. He bunched her skirts and slid under them to stroke and knead her soft flesh. No one had ever touched her so—it was wrong, shameless . . . but so sweet! Flames danced up and down her skin wherever his gentle, exploring fingers glided. Meg moaned and clenched her teeth against the treacherous desires that were weakening her. "Piers, we . . . we have to be sensible."

"Do we?" His white teeth gleamed briefly in the shadows as he smiled down at her, his eyes glared with passion, "Sensible Meg. Aren't you tired of that role? You've been sensible for too long, my darling Meg. It's time to let me show you another world."

Meg gave up the unequal struggle. Half of herself and all of Piers joined to urge these new delights upon her. With a little sob of pleasure she gave herself up to the hard hands that held her so tenderly, the warm velvety lips whose pressure awakened her body to new wellsprings of delight. Her blouse was half-open now, and Piers was tenderly caressing her bare skin, fingers cupping her soft breasts, one thumb brushing rhythmically back and forth across the nipple until she could hardly bear the intense pleasure. His lips clung briefly to hers, then drifted downward to her throat, then down again, tracing a path of trembling delight over her flesh. Then his mouth was at her breast, insistently tugging at its delectable rosy peak.

She felt a melting heat between her thighs even before he touched her there. His lips and hands were still caressing her body with agonizing slowness, and she knew instinctively that she needed him to release the taut knots of desire that were building within her. She arched upward under his hand, sighing with pleasure, and a new shaft of pure delight shot through the center of her being.

She moaned her pleasure aloud, clasping him to her, even while her tardy mind cried: *But this is Piers . . . the wrong brother!*

It was far too late for that warning.

Piers was trembling with his own unreleased desire when he freed her, disheveled and breathing raggedly, and she raised shaking hands to push the fine sprays of golden hair back from her face. Her cheeks burned now at the thought of the liberties she'd permitted. How could she have been so shameless? And the worst thing was, she would let him do it again. Anytime.

She looked half-fearfully at Piers's shadowed face. What did he think of a woman who . . .

well, who behaved as she'd just done? Did he scorn her? Did he find her laughable?

The answer was not long in coming.

"Meg, you're wonderful," Piers repeated. "I never knew a woman could be a friend as well as . . . Meg, I wasn't going to say anything yet. I know it's too soon, I don't have the right, not while I'm in disgrace. But I can't do without you, Meg. I love you."

"Love . . . me?" Meg had so often imagined hearing those words from a tall, handsome man whose blond hair gleamed in the moonlight. For a moment the fact that she'd dreamed of Harry, not Piers, escaped her; it had been so long since she'd ever really expected to hear words of love in real life. People didn't love her, not plain, gawky, useful Meg. At worst they didn't quite see her, at best they valued her for the services she could perform—keeping house for her father, packing Harry's tropical kit, finding a Fan guide to take her and Piers upriver. On this journey Meg had discovered herself to be brave and competent and resourceful—but all those things together didn't add up to love. You couldn't earn love that way; that was the bitter lesson her father's indifference had taught her, rubbed in by the way Harry had forgotten her as soon as she was out of the family circle.

No, it was impossible that Piers could mean what he said. He was grateful for her help on this journey, grateful because she was the one person left who believed in him; it would be a dirty trick to hold him to what he said when his gratitude, and his natural habits of flirting with the nearest girl, lured him into overestimating his feelings. Ruthlessly Meg dampened the glowing spark of joy that had sprung up inside her, quite unreasonably, when Piers kissed her; the spark that had become a leaping flame when he said the words she'd dreamed of hearing someday from Harry.

"No. I mean, Piers, you don't have to . . . I mean . . ." There was an unexpected tightening in her throat. For a moment Meg couldn't find the words to explain to Piers that he couldn't mean it, that nobody ever loved her and she didn't expect it, and in that moment Piers fatally misinterpreted her hesitation. His arms slackened and he released her, putting her away from him very gently as though he was afraid she, or he, might break when they separated.

"I know, I know." Piers turned away from Meg and affected great interest in the moonlit ripples of the river. "You're in love with Harry. Always have been. I can't blame you. After all, he's a fine, solid, upstanding citizen—hasn't made a hash out of his life the way I've done. But there it is. I've always cared for you, Meg, but you never could see me behind Harry's golden glow. Who could? It's all right, Meg," he said, still in that carefully gentle voice that broke her heart. "I'm just telling you how I feel. I don't expect you to do anything about it."

In love with Harry. Meg tried to collect her scattered thoughts. It was true, of course. Harry had always been her ideal, the benevolent older brother, the golden demigod of the young man, the career diplomat forging his own path with his inimitable self-assurance. As Piers said, who wouldn't be in love with him?

Dreams of the day when Harry would see her as a woman had helped to keep Meg's spirits up through the long dreary years of keeping house and transcribing notes for her father in their cold Yorkshire mansion. And if those dreams had faded a little by the time her father's surprising remarriage had released her, one visit to the Damerys had been sufficient to rekindle all her old feelings for Harry. Of course he still didn't see her; he treated her as a convenience, but it didn't hurt her feelings. She had learned in her years with Sir Digby to expect nothing better. Besides, it was a privilege to help Harry in any way she could, from penning his notes of acceptance to the social engagements to which he was invited to collecting and packing his kit for tropical service.

"Don't look so *worried*, Meg!" Piers's voice came explosively out of the shadows, closer than she'd realized, and she became aware that she had been frowning into the silver path of the moon. "This needn't affect our expedition. You're the best damned friend a man ever had, and the best traveling companion—I have to admit that now—you're game, Megsie, and you won't let yourself be thrown by a little trifle like some wastrel's falling in love with you."

"Don't call yourself a wastrel, Piers!" Meg said, more sharply than she'd intended. "You were framed, and we're going to find out who did it and why. I won't have you slouching round despising yourself and giving up without a fight—not when I've come all the way from England to help you. I won't allow it!"

Piers's chuckle reassured her. He was beginning to sound more like his old self; the dreary, defeated note was leaving his voice. "Still my best friend, Meg," he said, with a little catch in his voice. "All right. We'll go on, and . . . don't worry, will you? You may not have seen much to justify it, but I swear to you I've never forced my attentions upon an unwilling woman. I'll keep my hands off you from now on, and we'll go on as we started, as good friends."

Good friends? A fortnight ago that would have been all Meg wanted from Piers, the opportunity to share his adventure as his friend and companion. Now the prospect seemed unutterably bleak, and her schoolgirl dreams of Harry were as fragile and false as Christmas tinsel against the shining reality of the moonlight that made Piers's blond head sparkle with flashes of silver fire. Harry was at the other side of the world, and dreaming of him had been a way to keep herself sane in the loneliness of her father's household. Had it ever been anything more? Meg didn't know. All she knew was that she could no longer hold on to a wish and a dream and a desperate attempt to conjure up Harry's face in her mind, not with the warm breathing reality of Piers and his incredible confession of love.

With a catch in her own breath, Meg admitted it to herself: she didn't want to go on as Piers's good friend, his courtesy cousin. More than anything else, she longed for him to take her in his arms again, to kiss her in that hungry, desperate, demanding way that made her ache with longing down to her very bones. But he had withdrawn completely from her now. He was leaning against a tree at the edge of the path, arms folded, staring moodily out over the water. They might as well have been separated by the width of the Atlantic Ocean as by those two feet of distance,

Meg thought despairingly, for she'd never have the courage to close the space between them.

And just why not? jeered a voice in her head. You thought you were so brave, coming out to Africa by yourself, facing fires and rapids, forcing Piers to take you along. But when there's a real test of your courage, you're just a gawky schoolgirl without two words to say for yourself.

"I'm not in love with Harry anymore, Piers," she said, stepping out in front of his tree and forcing him to look at her, rather than at the river. "I don't think I ever was. That was a schoolgirl's dream—a way of playing at being in love."

"Girls may play at such things," said Piers. "I wouldn't know. I've never been in love before."

"Neither had I." Meg moved closer, brushing against him. "Now I know the difference." Her cheeks were burning; thank goodness it was too dark for Piers to see how she blushed! Would he never take her hints? "Piers, I . . . I'm not a little girl anymore."

"I . . . noticed that . . . some time ago," Piers agreed in a husky whisper. His hands had dropped to his sides; Meg was standing so close that the ruffled front of her white shirtwaist touched his chest with the rise and fall of her breathing. His hand brushed hers, seized upon her long fingers and held them in a loose clasp that sent quivering thrills of pleasure along her palm. "Let's . . . go back to the hut."

"Yes . . ." Meg felt a tiny, traitorous quiver of fear mixed with the pleasure of Piers's firm, strong fingers enfolding her own. It was all right, she told herself. This was Piers. He would never do anything to hurt her. They loved each other. Whatever was to happen now, it was right.

Hand in hand, bemused as if one of the thick night mists that swirled around the river had closed around them, they wandered slowly back down the path of beaten red clay. Meg's senses were achingly alive to every sound, scent, and motion of the tropical night: the rustling and slight tug on her skirts where briars reached out to hold her back, the sleepy cries of birds settling for the night deep within the rain forest, the cloying sweet scent of some white lilylike flowers that covered a dead tree stump just before their hut.

Just as they reached the flower-covered stump, the moonlight gleamed on a masked form with a headdress of tall, dancing feathers. Piers's hand closed about her wrist with a warning squeeze, but Meg had already stopped behind the tree. They watched in silence as the witch doctor circled the hut twice and then vanished into the darkness.

Even the sight of that fantastically beplumed and beaded figure slipping away from the vicinity of the hut did nothing to disturb Meg's sensual haze. If the local witch doctor wanted to invoke some extra fetish to protect the village from the white people and their attendant demons, she didn't object. She was only happy that they had been moved to this little hut on the outskirts of the village, where distance and fear alike would protect them from the prying eyes of the Mpongwe villagers.

She stooped to go through the low door opening of the hut before Piers, thinking that they would have to drape some more netting or sheets over the opening for privacy. Once inside, she stood straight, took an unwary breath, and almost gagged as a smell of putrefying flesh hit her nostrils. Choking, she stumbled outside again and pushed Piers away from the hut.

"Don't ... go in there," she said in a gasp. Tears were streaming from her eyes and she found it difficult to talk, but few breaths of the sweet night air helped to settle her quivering stomach.

"What's the matter?"

Meg took a deep breath and folded her hands over her midriff to stop them shaking. "You know that animal that made a mess in there earlier? I think it's gone back in there to die."

Piers stuck his head in at the door opening and came back looking somewhat shaken himself. "Whatever that is, it didn't die just this evening. Where's that bush light? I'll have to have a look round inside." Taking several deep breaths, he clamped his lips shut and reentered the hut, holding the extinguished torch in one hand. There was a scrape of matches, a spurt of blue flame, and then the resinous torch flared up with a gout of orange fire. Meg heard Piers tossing their bedding around and saw the bush light moving from wall to wall, the flame clearly visible through the many chinks in the dilapidated hut.

After a few moments he came out holding a small leather bag in his free hand. Meg recoiled in disgust at the smell. "Is that it? Quick, throw it away."

"Not so fast," Piers contradicted her. "This wasn't in the hut when we left—the witch doctor must have left it just now. It could be an important clue." He held his torch close to the bag and frowned over the complicated knot that held it shut. "The trouble is, I have to make sure of tying it the same way when I put it back, or they'll know I was fooling with it."

Meg held her nose and inspected the knot. "Dat's easy," she said, "Id's de sabe—" Frustrated, she retreated to a distance from which she could talk normally. "I've seen that knot before. Around those rubber vines near Talagouga—remember?"

Piers shook his head. "All these fetish knots look alike to me."

"That's because you don't do needlework," said Meg. "I don't know why nobody bothers to teach men some really useful skills. *I* could retie that bag in a jiffy. Well? Are you going to open it, or just stand there fondling it all night?"

"I can think of better things to fondle," said Piers. The torchlight set golden sparks dancing in his blue eyes as he spoke, and rimmed his head with gold. Meg backed away another step, feeling suddenly shy and unsure of herself. If she'd been able to see Piers clearly by the river, she thought, she'd never have had the courage to approach him so brazenly. He was dauntingly masculine, blazing bright in the torchlight, gay and confident and sure of himself. Everything she'd painted Harry in her imagination, Piers was in reality. How could she have chased a dream for so long, ignoring what lay under her hand?

"Hold this," Piers ordered her, thrusting out the flaming bush light. Meg took the torch and stood with one hand over her mouth and nose as Piers fumbled with the knotted vine that tied the bag shut. It fell loose at last and he shook out the contents of the fetish bag onto the palm of his hand.

"My God!" With a swing of his arm, he threw the black and decomposing bits of meat far out into the bush before Meg had gotten more than a glimpse of them. "How utterly foul. I'm not keeping a thing like that around, and I don't care if it offends the locals." The bag followed its contents, dropping without a sound into the inky blackness of the bush.

"What was it?" Now that the putrefying smell was fading away, Meg found her curiosity reviving.

Piers took the torch from her and upended it on the ground. The flaming ball of resin sizzled against the earth for a moment and then went out, leaving a thin spiral of smoke drifting upward to cleanse the air where they had been standing. "You don't want to know."

Meg suspected he was right, but some instinct made her stand her ground. Friends, he had said, and companions. If she had to lose that comradeship because they were also in love . . . No, it didn't bear thinking about. "We're in this together," she insisted, "and if you can touch it, I can surely stand to hear about it."

"Fingers," Piers said. "Human fingers. A big toe. An ear. Something that might have been an eyeball, but I couldn't tell, the decomposition was so—"

One hand over her mouth, retching, Meg fled to the path. It was several minutes before she recovered herself and returned to the hut, where she was thankful to see that Piers had dragged their bedding outside and draped the mosquito nets over two bushes, one on either side of the path. She didn't think she could have slept in the malodorous little hut that night.

The enchanted, loving, sensual spell of the evening had been effectually broken by Piers's discovery. Meg was grateful to see that he'd set up the sleeping mats a foot or so apart, with separate draperies of mosquito netting covering each one. She crawled under her netting and loosened her clothing slightly in the darkness, reminding herself to wake up before dawn so that she could make herself decent again before anybody was stirring.

When she stretched out on the mat, all the aches and bruises of the day awoke to trouble her. And there was something else that nagged at her mind and wouldn't let her sleep, something about that horrid fetish bag. . . . Suddenly she knew what it was.

"Piers?"

A sleepy grumble answered her.

"Piers, these people are Mpongwe."

"Very . . . mmm . . . perceptive."

"They're not cannibals."

"And a jolly good thing for us, seeing how popular we are in these parts."

"Yes, but listen, Piers. If they're not cannibals, if they bury their dead properly, what are they doing with a fetish bag containing human parts? Doesn't that sound more like something you'd expect to find in a Fan village?"

"By God!" Piers was fully awake now. "You're right, Megsie. And the Crocodile Society seems to be centered in Fan territory, on the Spirit River."

"And I saw those knots on the rubber vines in Talagouga, and the Fans were afraid to talk about them. Just as the people here are afraid of us. It all fits together somehow—" A gigantic yawn interrupted Meg's words and set her reasoning all awry. "If I could just figure out what it all means!" She'd almost had it a minute ago; now her clues were scattering again into a mass of unrelated facts.

Piers lifted the mosquito netting and squeezed her shoulder—a brief, comradely, unerotic squeeze, "Damned if I don't think you will figure it out, Megsie. You're the brains of this outfit. Smartest thing I ever did, bringing you along. . . . Meg? You there?"

Soft, even breathing was his only answer. Sleep had claimed Meg in the very midst of her detective work.

Thirteen

A sound of shouting brought Piers instantly from drowsy half-slumber to full wakefulness. As he shoved his shirt down into his pants and buckled his belt, he noted that the sky was lighter toward the east and that the white morning mists from the river were wreathing and coiling about their sleeping place. The mist right here was so thick that even Meg, under her mosquito netting, was only visible to him as a shapeless lump of bedding and mats.

"Meg?" He spoke softly, not wishing to alarm her. If those shouts meant trouble in the village, they had best dress and be on their way as quickly as possible, before the villagers decided to associate the trouble with the white visitors. "Meg!"

She wasn't answering. Piers stuck one hand under the netting to shake her awake and felt only tumbled sheets beneath his exploring fingers.

"Meg!" He jumped up and drew on his boots, too agitated even to shake them out for scorpions. She'd disappeared while he was sleeping, and those shouts . . . But the noise didn't seem to be coming from the direction of the village. The mist confused sounds and directions, but it sounded as if the disturbance was at the river. Seizing the loaded gun that he always laid by his bedside at night, Piers turned on his heel and hurried down the path of packed red clay. His boots slipped on the dew-wet path and drops of sweat fell from his forehead as he ran. What trouble had that damned girl gotten into *now*?

By the time he reached the river, the sun had already cleared the tops of the trees, burning off the white coils of mist and streaking the muddy water with sheets of golden light. A crowd of Mpongwe villagers and his own rowers were gathered above the steep slide of red clay that served the village for a canoe landing, pointing and shouting at something in the water. Piers shouldered through the crowd to see for himself what had caused the excitement.

The noises of the awakening forest made a subtle counterpoint to the shouts that had disturbed him—the harsh cries of parrots in the trees, the chatter of monkeys, and an irregular splashing that he'd taken for the sound of the native women getting water in the shallows. Now he saw the slender dark line of a Mpongwe canoe sliding across the golden water, a hollowed-out tree trunk that curved to long sharp points at bow and stern. The splashing came from a single rower—a slender girl whose loose fair hair made a silver-gilt cloud above her simple white blouse. She plied her paddle with great energy but little skill, first on one side of the canoe and then on the other, while the boat wavered uncertainly against the slow current in the shallows.

On either side of the river, the sleeping forest slowly came to life without paying much attention to this new phenomenon in their midst. Tall birds stalked delicately among the shallows, monkeys swung from the trees overhead, and on a sandbank far downstream, an ancient giant crocodile crawled lazily out to enjoy the first rays of the morning sun. Only Meg's energetic, unskilled paddling and the unsteady rocking of her canoe disturbed the peaceful balance of life along the great river.

"Oh, my God," Piers breathed. He turned furiously to M'bo, who was standing beside him. "Why the devil did you let her have a canoe? She'll be drowned!"

The head rower shrugged and indicated that it was none of his business if crazy white women wanted to drown themselves. Besides, he added, the white missy should be safe enough as long as she stayed in slack water.

"Well, that's true enough," Piers allowed. He relaxed slightly as the canoe approached the narrow landing place, a naked slide of slippery red mud. He could see Meg clearly now, kneeling in the center of the canoe, with her hair coming loose and sticking to her face as she labored over the paddle with intense concentration. She needed to steer a little to the right if she was to stop at the landing place, Piers thought. Ah, now she had it—no, there went the canoe wavering out toward the middle of the river again . . . Damn the girl! If she didn't turn in at the landing place, he'd have to pull her up the steep rocky face of the bank farther up.

"Meg! Hi, Meg!" he shouted. "Turn this way!"

Meg glanced up and her severe expression of concentration was transformed into a blaze of light as she recognized Piers. "Piers! Look, I'm learning to manage a canoe!"

"I see that," Piers called. "Now come back! You can't take her into swift water!"

Meg cupped one hand to her ear and Piers danced up and down on the riverbank, almost choking on his rage and fear. "You can hear me perfectly well! Now, come back, dammit!"

"Eh?"

In her inattention, Meg had ceased paddling, and the slow current in the shallows was carrying the canoe inexorably down toward the landing place. She smiled, waved at Piers, grabbed the paddle, and gave two or three vigorous strokes just before she would have drifted into the safety of the red mud slide. The canoe shot forward and to the left, toward the center of the river. Piers watched in helpless horror as the strong current of the main stream grabbed the canoe's head and spun it out into midstream like a chip of wood, bouncing Meg from side to side. The canoe spun around and around several times despite Meg's frantic paddling; then the current dragged it down the river stern-first until it crashed into a fallen tree that had lodged across the river, its branches resting on the broad sandbank where the old crocodile was sunning himself. With a chill of horror Piers saw the beast raise one eyelid and lazily open his gaping jaws as if to receive the bounty sent him by the river.

Piers shouldered his gun and aimed into the flash of orange that was the crocodile's open mouth. He had time to get off just one shot before the canoe swept between him and the beast, and he could not see whether he had hit the crocodile. Before he could move to get a better view, the canoe collided with the broad tree trunk that lay athwart the stream. The pointed stern went down with a splintering noise, the bow of the canoe tossed up into midair, and Meg disappeared from view. The last thing he was conscious of seeing was the muddy brown water closing over her bright head.

Piers threw the gun down and had his shirt and shoes off before he was aware of what he was doing. He plunged down the bank toward the foaming brown current, his eyes glued to the spot near the tree trunk where Meg had disappeared. She might have been knocked out in the collision, might have been swept downstream—no, that was unthinkable. He had to find her. Couldn't waste time on trying to shoot the crocodile again. Had to get Meg out of the water first.

Something was restraining him, hampering his attempt to dive into the river. He chopped down hard with the edge of his palm on the black hand that had seized his arm, drove his elbow backward into the midriff of the man on the other side, and heard a grunt of pain as he recoiled. But there were more hands fastening on him now, too many, and as he went down under the cumulative pressure, he heard voices shouting in his ears—something about not interfering with a sacrifice to the Crocodile God. . . .

Half-smothering under the weight of a dozen brawny Mpongwe men, Piers struggled to free himself and shouted for help. Pounding feet and piercing Fan war cries signaled the approach of Kema and his friends. But they went straight past him, toward the river. There were three splashes in quick succession, then gasps of amazement from the men holding him down. The entangling arms and hands fell away, the bodies across his legs and torso lifted their weight, and Piers regained his feet to see the three fierce Fan warriors dancing and splashing in the shallows around a very muddy, soaking-wet girl whose prim black skirt was ripped from waist to hemline and whose hair dripped over her face in naiad's streamers.

"Meg!" Piers wanted to kill her. The Fans were chanting a song of triumph now, something about the white woman whose devils were stronger than the Crocodile God, while Kema banged out an accompaniment on the overturned canoe that floated peacefully in the shallows. Behind them, a group of Mpongwe villagers heaved something long and green that they had snared in a net of bush ropes. It took Piers a moment to recognize their trophy as the corpse of the giant crocodile.

Meg was laughing as Michael and David hoisted her up on their shoulders and carried her to shore. Laughing! What did she think this was, a Sunday-school treat? She didn't look much like a Sunday-school teacher now, with her blouse practically transparent from the water that plastered it to her figure. He could count the ruffles of lace on her chemise. Worse, he could clearly see the dark outline of her nipples and the full curves of her breasts, and so could every naked savage on the riverbank.

Piers met her at the bank, his lips compressed to a thin line and his eyes shooting blue sparks. At a nod from him the two Fans put Meg down, so that she had to stand on her own shaky legs before him. He was pleased to see the laughter dying from Meg's face as she looked up at him. By God, she ought to be scared! With her hair darkened by the water and clinging close to her head, her eyes impossibly wide and dark as gray stormclouds, her full sensuous lips denying the meekness of her pose, she was unbearably seductive. And the need to keep his hands off her only increased Piers's anger.

"If you ever—*ever*—pull a fool trick like that again," he said, speaking slowly and distinctly to control the quiver in his voice, "I shall beat you until you wish you had died in the river! Whatever possessed you to make a show of yourself for these savages? Do you like having every Mpongwe in the village gawking at your body through those wet clothes?"

Two bright spots of color burned in Meg's cheeks, and she thrust her lower lip out in a little-girl pout that made him want to kiss the stubbornness out of her mouth. "If I were a man you wouldn't complain about a little thing like my getting a ducking in the river."

"If you were a man," Piers retorted, "you wouldn't look so indecently exposed right now. Besides, that's not the point. Do you realize the danger you were in? How dare you risk your life like that! You could have been killed!"

Meg's chin set in the firm lines that meant she didn't intend to hear a word he said. "Yes, I thought so myself a couple of times," she said cockily, "but it's all right now, I know how to steer. Didn't you see the way I righted the canoe and brought her back after we had that lucky collision with the tree?"

"All right now?" Piers echoed. "All *right* now! You . . . you . . ." He found himself, to his fury, momentarily speechless.

"Don't gobble like a turkey cock, Piers," Meg advised him. "We have to set an example of dignity and civilized behavior for these people."

It was the last straw. As she climbed past him up the slippery red mud bank, Piers seized her by the shoulders and swung her around to face him again. He felt her wince of pain as his fingers bit into her shoulders, and knew a moment's obscure satisfaction at having gotten that much reaction from her. "You . . . damned . . . little . . . fool," he ground out between his teeth, giving her a good shake with each word. "I forbid you ever to go off without telling me again! Do . . . you . . . understand?"

Meg's teeth were rattling in her head with the force of his shakes, and she knew there would be bruises on her shoulders tomorrow where he was gripping her so hard, but she was rapidly growing too angry to care for such small physical matters. It was intolerable to have him so close to her, so angry, and half-naked to boot. Every shake came within an inch of bringing her up against his bare chest; the crisply curling triangle of golden hair that arrowed down from his chest to the waistband of his pants mesmerized her, and the sheer blinding force of his fury emanated outward from him in waves of heat that left her trembling from head to foot. Her own anger was her only refuge. "Don't you d-dare t-talk to me like that, you brute!" she shouted at the top of her voice. "And let me go!"

There was a low growling sound behind and to each side of him. Piers glanced around and saw that Michael and David had moved in close on either side of him. Michael had pulled a broad jagged blade out of the palm-fiber sheath that hung from his leopardskin belt, and David was reaching into the knots of his oiled hair for a long slender shaft tipped with a barbed iron hook. Kema was not visible, but a repetition of the growling noise behind him gave Piers a clue as to his whereabouts. The skin on the back of his neck prickled as he imagined what nasty weapon Kema was drawing from his clanking assortment of spears and jagged battleaxes.

"I think," Meg said more quietly, "they are afraid you'll hurt me, Piers. . . . It might be a good idea if you let me go."

Piers released Meg's shoulders and stepped back a half-pace, afraid of treading on Kema. He raised his open hands in a pacific gesture and the Fans also stepped back. Experimentally, he reached for Meg again. Kema snarled behind him and Michael balanced his broad notched knife on the palm of one hand with a hopeful smile. Piers let his hands fall.

"The Fans," Meg said with a sniff, "appear to be gentlemen. They don't approve of hurting women, and they have some notion of gratitude—unlike certain other parties I could name."

"And just what am I supposed to be grateful for?" shouted Piers, tried to the limits of his endurance by Meg's disdainful smile. "The privilege of watching you try to throw yourself to the crocodiles?"

Meg winced at his angry shout, and Piers couldn't resist a quick glance around to see if the Fans objected to his shouting at Meg also. All seemed to be well; they had backed off and sheathed their weapons, though they were watching Piers as if to warn him not to try anything violent.

"All right," he told Meg, fighting to regain his self-control. "Just this once I won't beat you—richly though you deserve it. But I want you to understand just exactly what kind of an idiot you've been. Isn't it enough that I have to drag a female along on this expedition, without having you do your best to go and get yourself killed whenever I'm not looking? From now on you follow orders, or I'm going to pack you up and send you back to Talagouga under guard."

It was an empty threat, and the twinkle in Meg's wide gray eyes showed that she knew it as well as he did. The damned Fans weren't going to let him send Meg anywhere she didn't want to go. If he didn't reestablish his moral superiority, and quickly, she would be trying to take command of this whole expedition—and God only knew what her next mad adventure would be! A sick chill settled in the pit of his belly as he relived the moment when her fair head had disappeared beneath the muddy brown waters of the Ogowe.

"From now on," he repeated harshly, trying desperately to pound some sense into Meg's head with words, since he couldn't do it any other way, "from now on you will obey me absolutely."

"You never told me not to take a canoe out on my own," Meg pointed out.

"I never told you not to put beans in your ears either! Now, listen here, young Meg . . ."

As Piers seemed determined to go on lecturing her *ad infinitum,* Meg stopped trying to get him to calm down and listen to reason. Besides, she wasn't feeling very calm herself anymore. She'd just accomplished a considerable feat, taking a long Mpongwe canoe out single-handed and learning how to steer it with one paddle. If Piers were at all fair-minded, he'd admit that was a tricky thing to do, managing one of those long slender canoes in the rushing current of the Ogowe narrows, and what's more, it was a skill that might well come in handy on their trip! She'd imagined him praising her initiative—instead he was lecturing her like a small child that couldn't be let out to cross the street by itself!

What was more, Meg thought as the lecture continued, he wasn't being at all fair with these continued complaints about the burden of taking a female along on "his" expedition. Had she asked for special treatment? Had she slowed them down in any way? She had not. Last night he'd praised her for being a good companion, for enduring the dangers of the rapids and the exhausting crossing of the point without a word of complaint. What had gone wrong since then?

Only one thing had changed that Meg could think of. That was their confession of mutual love last night. Suddenly, since she'd acquiesced to Piers's embraces and even kissed him back, he was treating her like a painted fashion doll to be set on a pedestal and ignored. What had happened to all his fine words about finding a woman who could be both his friend and his love? Ha! All his "love" meant was that he thought he owned her and could tell her what to do, just like her father. She hadn't come all the way out to tropical Africa for this!

There was no point in trying to interrupt him before he'd had his say. Meg had learned that much about managing men in her years of coddling Sir Digby and his temperament. But she hadn't expected to have to apply the knowledge to Piers—*Piers*, of all people! Fuming inwardly, she waited until he'd repeated everything he had to say at least three times. "Are you quite through?" she inquired coldly when at last he paused for breath.

"I think that covers the main points." Piers's chest was heaving as if he'd run through the jungle to get to her, and his bare shoulders glistened in the morning sunlight. Meg clenched her hands at her sides, willing herself not to give in to the sheer animal attraction of the man. Hadn't she learned last night how deadly that could be? One single moment of weakness, and suddenly she wasn't a person to Piers anymore, with the right to make her own decisions and run her own risks. She was a toy. She'd thought to gain a lover; instead she'd lost her best friend in the world. There was a stabbing ache deep in her chest at that thought, and tears prickled behind her eyes, but she would not let them fall.

"Good. Because I think you've said quite enough." For a moment the pain in her chest almost choked Meg so that she could not go on.

"You're sorry?" Piers looked wary, yet hopeful. Anger flared in Meg, consuming the pain that she knew she would feel later. How dare he think she would apologize to him for a minor error in judgment like getting swept down the river in a fast current?

"I certainly am." She bit off the words one by one, afraid to let all her wounded feelings show. "Not for taking the canoe out—no. But for believing you last night. For thinking you could still be my friend if I let you make love to me."

"What the devil does that have to do with it?" Piers raked his open fingers through his hair until it stood out around his head like a spiky halo. His blue eyes glared at her and the sun shone off the golden stubble on his unshaven chin and Meg wanted to collapse against his chest and be held while she admitted just how scared she'd been when the canoe went down. But that easy path was closed to her forever now.

"Everything," she answered his question crisply. "Your whole reaction this morning just proves to me that you can't mix love and friendship, and we should never have tried. I'm just grateful I found out before I went too far! The best thing that ever happened to me was finding that fetish bag last night. It stopped me before I made a fatal mistake. I should have known better than to trust you—damn you, Piers, I thought you were my friend, but you're not, you're just another bully of a *man*. You . . . "

The tears wouldn't be stopped anymore. She turned away from him, covering her eyes with the back of one muddy hand.

"Of course I'm a man! What did you think I was, a bloody eunuch? Now, you listen here, my girl, you've got a few things to learn about men and women. You—"

Meg started away convulsively from the touch of his hand on her shoulder. "Don't you dare touch me, you . . . you oversexed brute!" Sobbing aloud, she ran up the path toward the village, longing for nothing so much as to hide herself from Piers and from all the villagers' curious eyes.

By the time Meg reached the hut where they had spent the night, she had calmed down somewhat. The heat of the day was drying her clothes on her body and as she walked more slowly she realized that part of her anger had been due to the discomfort and humiliation of her position—standing there on the riverbank, with her clothes and hair dripping a puddle of muddy Ogowe water around her, while Piers lectured her like a naughty child!

Meg yanked a comb through her damp, tangled locks until they were reduced to some sort of order. Her skirt was a wreck, with that long rip showing a froth of white petticoat every time she moved, but she couldn't face going into the dilapidated little hut to change in privacy. In the daylight it looked even worse than it had by torchlight; she felt sure there were spiders inside. Besides, there was precious little privacy to be gained inside a building whose rotted palm-frond mats left half of one side and most of the roof open to any curious gaze.

Meg rooted through her reticule, looking for some way to repair her appearance, and longed for the tin box of trade goods with its lengths of cotton and fine wire. She didn't have the moral courage to go down to the riverbank where the boxes were stored. Never mind, she could improvise. Her two remaining hairpins would not suffice to put her hair up in a decent bun, but they worked well enough as improvised pins to cobble her skit together. After some thought she unraveled a length of black thread from the ripped hem and bound her front hair in two long braids. At least that would keep the fine waving locks out of her face. As for her back hair, it would just have to hang down in an undisciplined mass until it dried; maybe then she would be able to braid it tightly and coil it up somehow.

The success of her improvisation put Meg in a better frame of mind, confident once again that she could conquer any challenge the African bush had to offer. Except, perhaps, for the problem of Piers. . . . Her lower lip began to tremble until she clamped down on it with two firm white teeth. Better not to think about Piers. They were in this thing together, and they would have to work out some semblance of civilized behavior. Last night's momentary madness would simply have to be forgotten.

Meg told herself that she had all but forgotten it already.

The tantalizing smell of frying fish crept over the tall bushes that shielded the hut from the main body of the village. Meg sniffed the air appreciatively and decided that it was definitely time to resume peaceful relations with Piers. She wasn't about to choke down another calabash of agouma, or fou-fou, or whatever they called the foul stuff, while he gorged himself on fresh-caught fish for breakfast!

Meg set forth with a determined stride, following her nose toward the delicious aroma. Curiously, the smells seemed to be coming from the village rather than from the riverbank. Had Piers managed to reestablish good relations with the villagers already?

Halfway to the village, Meg encountered a deputation of Mpongwe women in faded cotton petticoats, their bare breasts gleaming red with a mixture of oil and powdered bark, their ears adorned with broad copper and brass rings. Smiling and bowing, they beckoned her toward the village, indicating in sign language that they would be honored to have her join them for breakfast.

With a concealed sigh Meg accepted the invitation, trying not to show her regret for the tantalizing fried fish. "Oh, well," she told herself, "better a bowl of agouma where peace is than a fresh fish and hatred thereof." Not that she and

Piers hated each other, of course, but she told herself vaguely that it was the principle of the thing.

As they rounded the last curve in the path before the village, an amazing sight met Meg's eyes. The long double row of houses, each with its dirt-floored veranda facing the "street," held a smiling, happy crowd of women busy with their cooking tasks. At the end of the row, where the guesthouse stood, Piers was seated upon a three-legged stool while the men of the village directed his attention to an array of delicacies laid out on plantain leaves or in shallow carved gourds. The women escorting Meg urged her to take a similar seat beside Piers.

"Our stock seems to have gone up here," she muttered out of the corner of her mouth as she sat down. "What did you do?"

Piers shrugged and spread his hands, pretending ignorance, but she caught his glance toward the corner where a group of hunters was engaged in slitting open the massive old crocodile Piers had killed with one shot. So that was it! No doubt the villagers were grateful to him for ridding them of the old predator.

They had no further opportunity to talk, as the headman of the village launched into a long and flowery speech of thanks which M'bo translated for Meg's benefit into Pidgin English. To her surprise, the speech seemed to be directed at her more than at Piers. The burden of his remarks was that the white woman had proved that her spirit was greater than that of the witch who used the crocodile as his tool, possibly even greater than that of the Crocodile God himself, and they wanted her to stay and protect the village henceforth.

"You mean, they want Piers to stay," Meg corrected M'bo at this point. "He's the one who shot the crocodile." Naturally they had been impressed by the accuracy of his rifle; it was a vast improvement on the battered old muzzle-loading guns carried by the tribesmen, loaded with an assortment of scrap iron and fetish charms.

M'bo repeated that Piers was free to go; it was Meg they wanted to keep in the village, and this feast was in her honor.

Piers gave her a nasty grin. "There's some merit to the suggestion. At least I wouldn't have to worry about you for the rest of the trip."

"Piers, don't be ridiculous!" Meg said, more sharply than she intended. "I can't stay here. It's out of the question. M'bo, why do they want me to stay? *I* didn't kill the crocodile."

M'bo sighed, rolled his eyes heavenward until only the whites showed, and begged the headman's indulgence while he educated the white woman, who had a strong devil but was appallingly ignorant of the workings of the spirit world. Crocodiles, he explained patiently, did not kill people. They only served as the familiars of witches, dragging the people away and delivering their bodies to the witches who used human parts to make their most powerful fetish medicines. That Piers had shot this particular crocodile would no doubt inconvenience the witch, but it was much more important that Meg had escaped the trap laid for her, proving the superior quality of her protective spirits.

"That's ridiculous," Meg exclaimed. She turned to Piers. "Can't you convince them?"

"Why should I? I think it's an elegant solution to our problem. You've made it quite clear that you don't want to have anything to do with me. Fine. Why don't you stay here like a good little girl and protect our hosts from witches, while I finish this little job on the Spirit River?"

"Men!" Meg propped her chin on her clenched fists, her elbows in her lap, and glowered past the headman at the circle of hunters surrounding the dead crocodile. Something gleaming caught her eye and with a smothered exclamation of surprise she jumped up and threaded her way among the spread-out dishes of the feast. The stench of blood and the buzzing of flies around the eviscerated corpse of the crocodile made her falter, but she pinched her nose shut with one hand and picked up the gleaming object she had seen at the end of the stick.

"Look here," she said, marching back to the headman but addressing herself to M'bo as interpreter. "This came out of the crocodile. You still say crocodile no chop man, how he chop this, savvy?"

"This" was a woman's brass anklet, still warm from the crocodile's stomach, pitiful witness to one of the many victims the old beast had doubtless claimed from the riverside villages.

M'bo shrugged and explained patiently that the witch who used this particular crocodile doubtless found it good policy to reward him with a few trinkets from the victims' bodies from time to time.

"Oh, I give up!" Meg dropped the stick and threw up her hands in disgust. "These people are perfectly crazy! And what's more, they have an answer for everything! If I argue with him anymore, I'll start thinking what he says makes sense!"

"I can sympathize," said Piers unexpectedly.

Meg shot him a suspicious glance. "You can?"

"Certainly. Talking with you," he explained, "often gives me the same feeling. Now, will you sit down and eat? The food's getting cold while you and M'bo argue theology."

Meg had been putting off her second encounter with native chop, but now that she looked closely at the array of dishes spread out before them, she began to feel more optimistic about the breakfast. The inevitable agouma was there, bowls and calabashes full of the sour grayish-white paste, but spread out on plantain leaves and nestled in tightly woven palm-leaf baskets were a number of more appetizing-looking delicacies. She saw tiny fish fried in cornmeal, a stew of okra and squash in reddish sauce, a basket of small reddish grapelike fruits, and a bowl of rice topped with a rich chocolate-colored sauce. Each dish in turn was picked up, briefly held under Piers's nose, then ceremoniously passed to Meg for her

"Women eating before men?" she queried Piers. These manners ran contrary to everything she'd heard about the lowly status of women in Africa.

Piers wore a disgusted, long-suffering look. "If you remember, I'm supposed to have stomach devils. I can't eat any of this stuff. They're just holding it up so I can enjoy the smells." His stomach gave a long rumble on the last words and Meg giggled most indelicately.

"What a pity," she teased him. "Perhaps I can persuade them to let you have a little agouma . . . seeing that I'm so powerful in the spirit world."

"You," warned Piers, "could still be left in this village to protect them from witch-crocodiles."

Meg burned her fingers on the fried fish and got rice all over her lap while trying to dip balls of rice into the sauce in the approved two-finger technique shown her by the women, but she didn't care; it was a delicious meal, and as soon as they got upriver and out of sight of the village she could change into her spare skirt and blouse and wash these things. By talking very fast whenever a calabash of agouma was presented to her she managed to avoid taking more than a token mouthful of the slippery paste, and even that went down better when coated with the peppery red sauce from the vegetable stew. Over the last of the meal she persuaded M'bo to explain to the villagers that she could not stay with them because she was going on up to the Spirit River to conquer the Crocodile God in his home. The headman looked sad at this news but stated that if anybody could conquer the Crocodile God, it would be a person with strong personal devils like Meg.

"I have to agree with the part about strong personal devils," Piers muttered.

Meg tossed her head and tried to ignore his snide comments. She almost regretted the end of the feast. Now she and Piers would have to set off again, and they were still barely on speaking terms. Indeed, every time she remembered her abandon on the previous night, she felt blushes creeping down her throat to stain the white skin under her ruffled chemise. And she was about to set off into the jungle alone with this man! She must be crazy.

But how dreadfully humiliating it would be to

back down at this point and agree to stay in the Mpongwe village! No, she couldn't do that. Besides, heaven only knew what sort of a mess Piers would get himself into without her advice and guidance. They'd just have to go on as if nothing had ever happened between them. Nothing really had happened anyway, she thought, feeling almost grateful to the village witch doctor with his disgusting fetish bag full of human fingers and toes.

Meg found her determination to go on normally strained to the limit when she and Piers took their departure. The closer she got to actually setting off up the river with him, the harder she found it to suppress memories of their impassioned embraces last night. Those long tanned hands, now competently lifting supplies into the lead canoe, had roved over her body with impudent familiarity; the chiseled lips, now compressed in irritation whenever he glanced at her, had pressed fiery kisses on her own mouth. Whatever she chose to pretend for Piers's sake, Meg knew that her body would never forget those shameful, abandoned, betraying moments.

In an effort to fight her memories, Meg became even more cold and remote toward Piers than she wanted to be. When he put one hand under her elbow to help her into the canoe, she shook off his touch, alarmed by the fiery excitement that coursed through her veins.

"All right, my lady," he muttered. "I wasn't going to defile your virgin purity. Get into the damn canoe by yourself."

Meg managed the awkward step with her head high, afraid to look at Piers for fear he'd see her feelings written on her face. Her dignified retreat was fatally marred when the canoe slid away under her foot and she had to jump in, hitting the bottom of the log with a thump. A ripping sound warned her that the hairpins holding her skirt together had given way at the last minute. Piers guffawed heartily as she pulled herself up to a sitting position with both hands on the edges of the canoe.

"Don't worry about me," Meg said with freezing politeness. "You've made it perfectly clear you don't want to be encumbered with my company."

"My apologies." Piers made a sweeping bow before climbing into his own canoe. "I suppose a real gentleman, like your *beau idéal* Harry, would never dream of mentioning to a lady that she'd just left half her skirt in the river."

That ripping sound! Meg leaned over the side of the canoe and hauled in the dripping remnants of the back half of her skirt. "Thank you, Piers," she said belatedly. "I'm sorry I was rude."

But Piers had already gone ahead in the lead canoe. Meg wrung out her skirt over the side and reflected that Harry probably wouldn't have humiliated her by mentioning such a personal matter, but on the other hand it would have been very inconvenient to lose half of her skirt because of his delicacy. There was no denying that in certain circumstances Piers's lack of delicacy was just what one needed. And where did that leave them? Meg glowered at the back of his blond head as the canoes shoved off. Damn the man! Couldn't he stay obnoxious for long enough to simplify her feelings?

Many miles downstream, at Lambarene, another upriver expedition was setting off with an equal amount of tension. Tired of waiting for the rains to float his ship off the sandbank, Captain Jacques had eventually winched the *Brazza* free in a desperate maneuver that did some damage to engines and smokestack but allowed him to make it as far as Lambarene on half-power. Once there, he had refused to take off up the river again until the native blacksmiths had done what they could to repair his damaged engines. The more Harry and François tried to persuade him to hurry the repairs, the more meticulously he examined his engines and the more minor fixes he required done. Language difficulties had eventually defeated Harry, but François and Captain Jacques had gotten into a shouting match that lasted half of one hot steamy day. Eventually Jacques had declared that he would rather take off with possibly damaged engines than listen to more of that pipsqueak Chaillot's puerile curses. He informed Harry that the *Brazza* was at his service to take him up to Talagouga whenever he wished to leave. There was just one stipulation: he wasn't having François Chaillot on board. Harry would have to go alone if he wanted to go.

"It's not safe," François protested in vain. "You don't know the territory. You'll get lost."

"I've only to follow Piers."

"And that pistol in your pocket, *mon ami*? What is that for?"

Harry gave François an impenetrably bland look. "After all the warnings you have given me, I am surprised that you should question my carrying a firearm when I set off into the bush."

"A dueling pistol won't do you much good against a charging elephant."

"I think it will serve adequately for the most dangerous game I shall have to face."

Jaw set in firm lines, blue eyes blank, Harry Damery strode on board the damaged *Brazza* while François watched, helpless to prevent this last act of the tragedy from being played out. What would happen when Harry Damery met his erring brother? He swore under his breath as the steamer slipped out of sight. There was no way to predict or control the consequences of such a meeting. He *must* catch up with the young fools before it was too late.

Calling for one of his servants to ready a swift canoe for a journey to the coast, François wrote a note to the lieutenant governor of the colony. In the letter he requested a gunboat and an escort of soldiers so that he could go upriver and restore order by arresting that madman Piers Damery before the boy's brother killed him.

Fourteen

As if to punish Meg, Piers insisted on going straight on up the river without a pause. The rowers sweated and sang their plaintive chants, Meg sat in the middle of the second canoe and dripped river water, and she almost welcomed the next set of rapids when the bubbling water and low black rocks appeared before them. If they were forced to leap for the bank again, she thought, she would insist on staying on land long enough to unpack and put on her spare skirt, and Piers could jolly well put up with the delay!

Unfortunately, this particular section of the river offered no opportunity to portage the canoes past the worst of the rapids. On either side sheer black cliffs rose to forbidding heights, and the river ran through the narrow gully between the cliffs with the fury of the string of unbroken horses, foaming and leaping and hissing around the rocks that reared their menacing heads on every side.

Piers held his canoe back while Meg's crept up beside it. "What do you think, Meg?"

Her heart leapt that he was consulting her. At least she hadn't lost his friendship, whatever else might have been lost in that moment of madness last night. Or—a chill doubt crept into her mind—was he only waiting for an excuse to send her back downriver?

"I'm game," she replied, hoping that he wouldn't see how her hands were trembling.

There was a blue flash of amusement from under Piers's thick golden eyebrows. "*Are* you? Well, I'm not so sure I am. These are only the second rapids, remember. If the next ones are worse yet, it's no wonder nobody's ever explored the Spirit River."

M'bo and Kema consulted between their respective canoes, shouting opinions back and forth in a mixture of Mpongwe, Fan, and trade English. At length M'bo reported that Kema said the rapids ahead were comparatively easy to cross. He had been up as far as the mouth of the Spirit River many times and there was nothing as bad as this later on. M'bo himself wouldn't know; he had more sense than to go into bad devil-ridden places like the Spirit River, but doubtless the Fans and the peculiar devils of the white people would protect them all.

"We'll try it," Piers decided. He glanced at Meg. "If you're still willing?"

She nodded, not trusting her voice, and at a word of command from Piers both sets of rowers set to work with all their strength, trying to make enough headway to steer through the treacherous stretches of fast water.

In some ways it wasn't as bad as the rapids the day before had been, if only because the two canoes followed one another so closely that Meg didn't have time to think. Kneeling in the center of the canoe, she used the broken half of an old paddle to help the rowers fend off from one rock after another. Rainbow spray hit her in the face, the shouts of the lead rower mingled with the roaring of the water, her shoulders ached from the constant and unaccustomed effort, and there was no time to look beyond the very next hazard ahead of them. Then, just as she thought she must collapse in the bottom of the canoe, they were through and into a relatively quiet stretch of water. The river still ran fast and high between the black cliffs, but at least here they had only the current to battle; no rocks raised themselves from the streambed like water monsters lurking to devour the frail canoes.

"Whew!" Piers passed the back of one hand across his forehead, brushing away the sweaty yellow locks that hung down over his eyes, and turned to grin encouragement at Meg. They rounded a slight bend in the river while he was still looking back at her. Beyond his turned head, Meg saw with horror an onrushing wall of white water, splitting on either side of a monstrous black crag that reared up in the very center of the river. She gave an inarticulate cry of alarm that was all but drowned out by the sound of the rushing water. Piers spun around and grabbed a paddle; her last sight before the water engulfed them both was of his broad shoulders working against the current, the thin fabric of his white shirt plastered to his body by the viciously spraying water.

Noise, roaring, and cold surrounded her, and something wet smacked her in the face. Meg closed her eyes involuntarily for a moment. A grinding jolt tore through the right side of the canoe and water poured over her head. Surely her last moment had come! She waited numbly for the canoe to overturn and spill her into the river. Instead there was the warmth of sun on her face, the sound of jokes being shouted across the river by the rowers in the two canoes. Slowly Meg opened her eyes on a peaceful scene. Somehow, she had no idea how, they had made it past the black crag. Once again the river ran straight and smooth, and Piers was grinning as if the entire show had been nothing but an amusement-park ride.

"Meg?" he asked anxiously.

She took a deep, welcome breath of the damp air. "I'm fine. Let's go on."

"First," Piers said, "I want to have a little talk with your Fan friend about his notion of 'easy water.' "

Before he'd finished the sentence the now-familiar roaring of rapids drowned him out. Both sets of rowers groaned and bent to their paddles as the water around them began to boil with suppressed fury. Meg peered upstream but could see nothing to account for the sudden treacherous changes in the current. She could feel how the water tugged capriciously at the canoe, forcing it now this way, now that, and always threatening to spin it around like a chip in a millstream. But the surface of the river around them was smooth and unbroken except where the water bubbled up in strange ruffling patterns.

"Oh, it's all right, this one isn't so—"

Meg swallowed the end of her sentence as the canoe jolted upward like a bucking horse. There was a sharp crack, and pain shot through her knee. The rowers gave shrill cries of alarm as the canoe tipped backward and to the right. Meg saw the lead rower throw himself out of the canoe, hands and feet outstretched. The push of his feet shoved the canoe still farther to the right, spilling out tin boxes and bundles behind her as the rushing water poured over the sides. She leaned as far as she could to the left to trim the canoe. Obligingly, it wallowed over that way and gave one last heave that tipped her out into the water. Cold, muddy, metallic-tasting river water filled her mouth and nose, dragged at her skirts, and carried her along the bottom. Arms flailing, she tried to force her way to the top of the stream, but she was helpless against the merciless current that forced her down. Her thrashing limbs were bruised against rocks and her lungs were burning with the need for air. Her last conscious thought was: The rocks were all underwater—that's why we didn't see them.

It seemed an extraordinarily brilliant piece of reasoning, but she had no time to congratulate herself on it. The violent pull of the current cracked her head against a boulder and the world exploded in a shower of pain-filled stars.

The world was black shot through with long jagged streaks of red. Meg waved a protesting hand to drive away the shooting red darts. They made her head hurt so! And she couldn't breathe. She gulped in air and the red streaks darted in among her ribs, lancing her with cruel little jolts of pain. She tried to hold very still, to keep them from tormenting her, but an uncontrollable fit of coughing seized her. Then there was water, a torrent of it, spilling out of her mouth and nose, and her brain began to function again. She was lying facedown on the riverbank. The sun was burning down on her shoulders and legs, and her chest hurt. Everything hurt.

It had required a long painful process of reasoning to establish these few facts, and now that she had them, it seemed as though she might be entitled to rest for a while. It would be so comfortable to go to sleep right here on the sandy bank. But there was something wrong . . . something she had to do . . .

"Piers!" Meg's body jerked convulsively and she scrambled to her hands and knees. A wave of dizziness swept her and she stayed crouching there for a moment, fighting the weakness that urged her to lie down again.

Where was Piers? She stared out over the tossing brown waves of the river. The green wall of vegetation on the other side of the river seemed to stare back at her with blank insolence. Canoes, rowers, luggage had all been swallowed up without a trace. And Piers? If he had been alive, he would have found her. Meg felt irrationally certain of that. He must have drowned in the rapids. The stabbing pain of that loss was succeeded by a chill, heavy despair that sank to the pit of her stomach like the cold weight of river water she had swallowed.

She was totally alone in the wilderness.

Meg felt a bubble of panic rising inside her. She put the back of her hand against her mouth to hold back the scream that wanted to rip free. The rain forest towered around her, dark, incomprehensible, mysterious, menacing. The flowers and birds that had seemed so beautiful this morning now took on leering, contorted shapes. The flowers could be poisonous; the birds would laugh at her and fly away. Without guides or supplies or a canoe, she had no hope of survival.

Not that it mattered very much. Nothing mattered anymore. Piers was dead, dead because of this foolhardy expedition that she had egged him on to make. If she—busybody, interfering Meg Beaumont—hadn't come out here with her her meddling propensity for setting things straight, Piers might eventually have gone back to England. Aunt Alice and Uncle Henry might have been a little disappointed in him, but they would have forgiven him as they always did. Piers might have been hurt at being "forgiven" for things he never did, and his unknown enemy might have got off scot-free, but what did that matter? He would have been alive to stroll down Piccadilly, to annoy Harry with his practical jokes, to tease Meg. His natural ebullience and joy in life would have reasserted themselves eventually.

Meg remembered all that shining vitality that was wrapped up in the six feet of bone and muscle and quicksilver grace called Piers Damery. Impossible to think of all that lying dead and inert at the bottom of the Ogowe River, enshrouded in a cloak of river mud! Even with the evidence before her, the silence of the jungle and the terrifying ordeal which she'd survived only by a miracle, Meg couldn't believe that Piers had been snuffed out of existence so easily and quickly as that. The sun was still high overhead; it wasn't noon yet. She couldn't have been knocked out for more than a few minutes. How could everything have changed so quickly? It should have taken more than a trick current in the river, a submerged rock, and a moment's inattention to destroy all that strength and life.

"Then why am I believing it?" she said aloud. The sound of her own voice, coming harshly out of a throat raw with coughing, echoed strangely in her ears before it was swallowed up by the muffling folds of vines and trees and bushes all around her. All the same, the sound of good plain English words gave her new confidence.

"I *won't* believe it," Meg repeated, squeezing her eyes shut to stop the tears that threatened to contradict her. "Piers isn't dead—he can't be dead."

In that case, why hadn't he come to find her? Perhaps he had been knocked unconscious, as she had been. He might still be unconscious, needing her help. There was no reason why he shouldn't have been washed up on the bank somewhere, just as she had been. No reason at all, Meg told herself, resolutely denying the negative brooding silence of the bush.

The place where she had been washed ashore was a long, sloping golden sandbank that rose gently from the water's edge to the shadowy green pillars of the trees in the rain forest. Meg knelt at the edge of the bank and rinsed off her face and shoulders in the swift-flowing water, discovering as she did so that her skin was covered with a network of small scratches. Some freak of the current that tumbled her among the rocks in the rapids had stripped off her shirtwaist and the torn remnants of her skirt, leaving her incongruously clad in a torn lacy chemise, three white petticoats with flounces to the knee, and her black button-up boots. The sun was already burning her shoulders, and Meg hunted in vain for some remnant of her clothes with which to cover herself before concluding that she would just have to take care to walk in the shadow of the trees as much as possible. She broke a stick from one of the inevitable dead trees that trailed down the bank and into the water and stood irresolutely on the sandbank, scanning the impenetrable jungle on both sides of the river and trying to decide where to begin her search for Piers.

Clearly she had been swept some distance downstream, but how far? This stretch of the river looked just like a hundred other sections that they'd passed through since leaving Talagouga the previous morning: close-growing green trees on either side, woven together by a tangling mass of flowered vines, and the river between them shining in the sun like an arrow of bronze.

Eventually Meg decided that she must somehow have been swept down past the second set of rapids, the first they had encountered that morning, but must have stopped somewhere short of the Mpongwe village and the terrifying rapids below the village. If she had passed the village, surely someone would have noticed her and set off to rescue her, and in any case she didn't believe that anyone could survive being dragged unconscious past the first rapids and around that sharp point where the river bent almost back on itself like a hairpin.

Very well. No one could survive that first set of rapids. Piers was alive—she clung to that as an article of faith, for without Piers she didn't have the will to do anything, even to try to save herself—therefore he had been cast up onshore somewhere before the village and the rapids, probably somewhere upstream of where she was standing.

"It's not," Meg said aloud, "a very strong syllogism." But it was all she had to go on, and she was pleased to find that her voice was steadier than it had been a moment ago. Grasping the stick firmly in her right hand, she set off into the forest on a path parallel with the river, prodding the bush ahead of her for snakes with every step she took.

It proved impossible to stay within the shelter of the trees for long. There was no path along here, and after a dozen steps Meg had lost the outermost flounce of her petticoat to a nest of thorny vines covered with poisonous-looking dark red fruits. She had to scramble along the rocks that lined the riverbank, bruising her fingers and in imminent peril of slipping into the water at every step. When the cliffs rose too steep for her to clamber along them, she fought her way through the bush again, swatting at the thorny vines and watching for a break that would let her get back close to the river.

Every few steps she paused and called Piers's name, until her throat grew too sore and parched to allow her to shout any longer. She looked longingly at the brown water rushing past her. Piers had warned her most strictly against drinking any of the river water before it had been boiled and filtered. But surely, after the quantities she'd swallowed already, it could make no difference? . . . Meg found herself irrationally unwilling to break a single one of the rules Piers had laid down for their survival.

"Don't drink the river water," she whispered to herself. "Watch for snakes dropping down from above. Never shoot except to kill—a wounded animal is dangerous. Shake out your boots every morning to dislodge insects and snakes." The last two pieces of advice did not seem too immediately applicable. She had no gun and no intention of doing anything except cowering behind a tree if any large animal presented itself. As for shaking out her boots, she doubted that she would ever take them off again. If she did, she would certainly lack the resolution to put them on over swollen, blistered feet.

As she struggled on through the bush, the temptation to sit down for a moment, to take off her boots and bathe her feet in the river, to gulp down great cool drafts of the muddy water, became almost overpowering. All that kept her going was the fear that once she gave in to any of those desires, she would never get up again. She began to bargain with herself as she stumbled along through the tall colonnades of slender trees, picking her way among vines and thorny bushes. Far below her the river sparkled in the afternoon sunlight, at the foot of a sheer black cliff that she could not have scaled even if she had decided to give up.

"Just go on till the next break in the cliffs," she told herself. "Then you can go down to the river and rest." And when a cracked canyon of sliding shale opened a way down to the river, she decided that ten minutes sitting in the shade of the trees would rest her quite as well as a scramble down to the water. And those ten minutes could be put off until she got around the next bend . . . no, until she reached that big tree with the curious mottled vine hanging down from it. . .

When the mottled vine flicked a bright red tongue at her and hauled itself up into the lower branches of the tree with a slithering noise, Meg was too tired and hot and thirsty to feel any alarm. Her determination to search for Piers had been reduced to a childlike certainty that she would find him at the end of her travels; she no longer bothered to search the infrequent sandbanks and rocks that broke the smooth line of the cliffs along the river's edge. All she could do was crash through the bush, vaguely trying to keep the river somewhere on her left, and slowly being forced farther and farther away from the water by the inexorable rise of the rocky cliffs.

The sound of some large body thrusting forward among the bushes to her left brought a cold chill of alertness flooding through her body. For a moment she stood quite still, trying to convince herself that she had heard only the echo of her own movements. Her heart thudded irregularly and a parrot screeched overhead, then departed in an irritated flap of scarlet and green. Just as she was beginning to breathe normally, the crashing noise recurred somewhere ahead of her, and Meg found reserves of energy she hadn't known she possessed until that moment. One frantic leap and her hands closed around the lowest branch of a nearby tree. Her booted feet kicked against the smooth trunk, feeling unavailingly for some purchase, while her arms felt as if they would come out of their sockets.

The beast made some inarticulate noise. It must be quite close now, Meg thought despairingly, and even as she gave one more heave upward, something closed about her ankle and yanked her out of her safe perch. Meg closed her eyes and gave herself up for lost, praying it would be quick.

"Goddammit, Meg, don't you dare faint on me!" an exasperated and thoroughly human voice swore at her. "As if I hadn't gone through enough today! I certainly can't carry you back to camp on my shoulders!"

Meg opened her eyes and saw Piers's scratched, sunburned face bending over her. One eye was almost closed by a swollen scratch that ran diagonally across his cheek, his hair was darkened by sweat to golden-brown strings, and his shirt was in tatters. She had never seen anything so beautiful in all her life.

"And what the devil were you doing in that tree?" he demanded irritably.

"I . . . thought you were . . . a wild animal." Meg giggled feebly at the look of horror on Piers's face. "Don't take offense, you do rather look the part," she defended herself in the cracked whisper that her voice had been reduced to.

"What happened to your voice?" Before she could answer, Piers had figured it out for himself. He pulled a flask out of his hip pocket and held it to Meg's lips.

How like Piers to come up with cool, fresh water in the wilderness! Meg took a long, grateful swallow and spluttered indignantly as something like a bolt of lightening coursed down her throat. "That's not water!"

"I mixed a little brandy with it," Piers admitted unrepentantly. "Restorative, and all that."

"A little . . . !" Words failed Meg, but she felt new strength coursing through her limbs. She sat up and realized for the first time that she was leaning in a circle of Piers's arm. The comforting strength of his shoulder supported her. She reached for the flask. That first swallow had done no more than take off the fierce edge of her thirst.

"Like it?"

"It's absolutely foul," Meg said. "Give me some more."

"All right, but take it slow. You can make yourself sick by drinking too fast . . . That's enough." He took the flask from her hands before she'd more than begun to drink. Meg gave a protesting whimper but found that a second gulp of the brandy-laced water had left her feeling much better. She was no longer so ragingly thirsty, and the aches and pains in her body seemed to have subsided behind a fuzzy warm haze of contentment. She snuggled against the comfortable bulwark of Piers's arm and let her head fall onto his shoulder.

"I thought you were dead," she murmured.

Piers gave a cracked laugh. "Oh, it takes more than a spill out of a canoe to kill me. I went out like a Mpongwe rower, hands and feet out to grab anything I could find. I got hold of a tree at the side of the rapids, and the rest of the crew distributed themselves over rocks and branches on both sides of the river. It took quite a while before we'd got everybody together again."

He paused. "Everybody except you. . . ." His blue eyes darkened as he relived the memory of those moments when, half-drowned, battered by the river and the rocks, he'd grasped that Meg was not among those saved. He had been, he thought, quite mad for a little while then; he couldn't remember much except trying to kill M'bo, who'd held him back from plunging into the rapids when all he wanted was to follow Meg.

"Saved my rifle and the brandy," he said, shaking his head to wipe away that memory. "Rest of our supplies are at the bottom of the river. Unless M'bo and the others have fished anything up by now. I . . . left them at it and came on to look for you. They said you must be drowned. I kept thinking we'd find you on the next rock, round the next bend." He stopped short, biting off the words as if the memory caused him intolerable pain. Meg looked up at his face and saw for the first time the white lines of exhaustion beneath his tan.

"Did it matter so much to you?" she asked. "You didn't want me along anyway."

"Dammit, Meg, try not to be more stupid than you can help!" Piers exploded. "Of course it mattered. I love you, you idiot!"

Meg couldn't repress another giggle. "It sounds like it."

"What does it take to convince you?" His arm tightened around her shoulders, his free hand lifted her chin, and his face hovered so close to hers that she could see the golden prickles of his incipient beard, the lines of strain at the corners of his eyes and the intense deep blue of those eyes . . . a blue she could drown in . . .

His mouth came down on hers with a suppressed fury that swept Meg away quite as thoroughly, and as irrevocably, as the rapids had done. Only this time she wasn't fighting it. Her arms went around Piers's neck of their own accord and she pulled him close to her, reveling in the warm living bone and muscle and beating heart that she felt next to her own body.

"Oh God, Meg," Piers groaned, trying to draw back. "I can't . . . I thought you were gone . . . Meg, I need you."

"And I need you," Meg whispered, hiding her face in the tattered sleeve of his shirt, shocked at her own temerity. But it was true. She no longer had the strength to withstand the tide of love that rose inexorably within her at every touch of Piers's long, lean body. The dreadful hour she had passed thinking she'd never feel those strong knowing hands on her again, never see the laughter in his blue eyes, had robbed her of modesty and sense alike. Nothing now mattered but to be as close to Piers as she could get, to share with him everything that she had and knew and was, until they were truly one.

His lips caressed her temples, her ears, and then her jawline. With one finger he lifted her chin and turned her to face him; then his mouth ravaged hers with deep, searing kisses. The straps of her chemise he slid down over her shoulders, his tanned fingers pushing the torn lacy ruffles down until her breasts lay free above a froth of mud-stained white lace. She caught her breath with her sheer delight of the sensations he evoked with the gentle touch of one finger, stroking around and around the creamy swell of her breast until the taut peak ached with longing for his hand. Her whole body was filled with those circles of pleasure, radiating outward from the slow caressing spiral that moved inward with tortuous leisure.

His other arm was beneath her shoulders, holding her tightly against the quivering joy that might otherwise have torn her apart. "Just lie back and let me love you, my darling," Piers murmured. His voice was low and husky and intoxicatingly sensual, each syllable sending new thrills of anticipation through her. "Meg, my Meg, you're mine now, nobody will ever take you from me. . . ."

The words didn't matter; all that mattered was the aching need deep inside her that built to a climax as his strong, sure hands moved with infinite gentleness over her white flesh. Lazily he stroked and kneaded the globes of her breasts, expertly exciting them. Meg was drowning in a sea of lace ruffles and crimson ribbons, unable to breathe for the sweetness of Piers's caresses awakening her to delights she'd never imagined. When he bent his head so that she could no longer see his face with that sweet, grave, loving look, she murmured in protest; then his lips brushed the taut peak that his hands had left untouched, and her world exploded in bright suns of ecstasy. She cried out and felt her body arching under his mouth, wanting nothing more than to prolong the moment—no, for if it lasted any longer she would surely die of pleasure—but it wasn't under her control any longer. Nothing was. All her being was driven by the sweet insistent pressure of his lips tormenting that one place that he had roused to such desire, the trembling heat that radiated through her breast from his kiss.

When at last he raised his head, Meg was as limp in his arms as though he had just plucked her out of the raging river tide, exhausted and contented. Even the lights dancing in his blue eyes could not rouse her to respond with more than a sleepy, contented smile.

"Now, Meg my darling, now just try to pretend you don't want me to love you!" Piers commanded with a smile that lit up his face.

"I can't," Meg murmured. "That was . . . I didn't know it was like that, Piers." She felt embarrassed again now that the sensual tide had receded, conscious of her half-naked condition and the forward way she'd practically thrown herself into his arms. There must, she thought, have been rather more brandy and less water in that flask of Piers's than she realized.

His confident smile faded, to be replaced by a look almost of consternation. At all costs she had to keep that hurt, bewildered look from his eyes.

"I don't regret it, Piers," she assured him, praying that he wouldn't notice her involuntary blushes. "I love you, I wanted you to teach me about love."

"Yes, well . . ." Piers looked off into the bush and Meg followed his gaze. She saw nothing but the green columns of vine-wrapped trees surrounding them. "Meg, there's a little more to it than that."

Well, of course there was. There were little matters like lifelong commitment, and shared joys and sorrows, and—Meg found herself blushing again—children. But she'd already known about that—she'd thought that was all there was to love. This strident, insistent joy that made her feel drunken and exalted at the same time—that was the part Piers had taught her, the part she'd never have guessed at. "Oh, I know all that," Meg told him. "But it's not important."

Piers's smile returned. "Maybe not to you, not yet, but it's damned important to a man, Meg darling. And I'll make it matter to you, too. Any man who doesn't is a fool or a brute."

Meg was puzzled by this last statement. In her experience, it was women who cared about the household, and children, and all the serious matters of life that came after a declaration of love. Men tended to brush off all that as unimportant, to treat a woman as something they could buy and put in a box and look at when it pleased them. But she hadn't time to ask Piers for an elucidation, for his hands were sliding down over her body with those agonizingly slow smooth caressing strokes, moving with impudent freedom under the tossed flounces of her petticoats, and she caught her breath at the revelation that he could make those fires begin under her skin wherever he touched her. His kisses fell on the soft underside of one elbow and wandered down the smooth white skin of her taut midriff, and then his fingers were tracing bright curves of desire under her petticoats and everything fell away before him, lacy flounces and white cotton and any barrier but her own quickened breathing as he knelt over her.

A smothered laugh and the abrupt cessation of those intoxicating movements startled her. He was tugging at her feet. "Any way you like, Meg darling, but *not* with your boots on!" His deft fingers untied the knotted laces and eased the boots off her tired feet even as she protested.

"I'll never get them on again! How will I walk upstream to the canoes—?"

"*Must* you think of walking at a time like this?"

A time like what? Meg wanted to ask, but his mouth hungrily devoured hers before she could speak, and then she could not speak for other reasons, including a floodtide of new sensations that made her previous feelings seem like the gentle English rain compared with an African river in full spate. The weight of his body pressed down on her, not heavy, but powerful and demanding, and in some dim corner of what passed for a brain she understood that he had taken off his own clothes, for she could feel the warmth of his bare skin against hers everywhere. His hands were everywhere too, gliding over the skin of her shoulders exploring the lines of her collarbones, tormenting the enticing rounded flesh of her breasts. His light, sure caress made her want only more and more, and a strange unfamiliar warmth was building between her thighs where he hadn't touched her at all. It almost hurt, the sweet intense pleasure of his caresses and the warm tight knot there, and when he knelt over her she was beyond anything but wanting that knot untied.

She was unprepared for the pain that shot through her body as he entered her. She cried out in surprise and tried to get away from him, but his hands were firm upon her shoulders and the long weight of his body held her down beneath him and his lips traced soothing incantations against the white skin of her breast. "It won't hurt anymore, Meg, I promise. Darling Meg, trust me now, just let me love you."

Love? This sharp hurt, tearing into her body? She wriggled indignantly in his grasp, but her resistance only seated him more firmly in her as he began to move with long slow strokes. He was right, it didn't hurt anymore. In fact, the rhythmic movements of his hips were releasing that tight knot of longing within her, smoothing her out and opening her up to something so bright that it made all that had gone before seem like children's games.

Moaning, Meg wrapped her legs around him, pulling him deeper inside her. Instinctively she moved her hips in time with his, rising on wave after wave of molten pleasure. Her eyes opened wide, cloudy and unseeing, as she tried to understand this new thing that was happening to her. Her body arched of its own accord, wanting to be even closer to Piers, and she heard her own breathing coming thick and fast like his. She clung to him, wordless, as they exploded together into some far place where nothing mattered except the clinging together of their two bodies, the attempt to achieve an impossible oneness for a brief moment.

In the peaceful aftermath, as they lay entangled together among the torn white flounces of Meg's petticoats, Piers raised his head and laughed at the slow look of wonder in her eyes. "I told you there was more to it, didn't I?" he teased.

"Mmm." Meg stretched languorously, feeling the smooth contentment that oozed through her limbs like something palpable, as if the sun that speckled through the treetops had been converted to warm sweet wine. "When's the next lesson?" Her eyes traveled the length of Piers's nude body, lingering on certain details she'd never really noticed before, like the sprinkling of golden hairs on his back and thighs, the long white scar on the back of one leg from some old injury, the smooth muscular curve of his hips.

"*Not* this afternoon. We've got some distance to travel to get back upstream to the camp where I left the rowers. And we've got to get you cleaned up first. There's a sandy inlet upstream where you can wash and rinse out those clothes."

"Mmm?" Meg rolled over and pillowed her head in her arms. "I've had all the water I want for one day, thank you. I think . . ." She was slipping away into the haze of warm contentment that had surrounded her ever since she found Piers again. "Think I'll take a little nap," she murmured, already feeling the comfortable darkness of sleep enfolding her.

A stinging slap cracked against her bottom and jerked Meg out of her drowsy haze. "What was that for?" She rolled over and sat up, careful to keep her weight on the side Piers hadn't hit.

"To wake you up." Piers grinned. "Come on, Meg. We can't sleep here. Have to go back to camp. Besides," he added thoughtfully, "I like it when you sit up fast like that. It makes your breasts quiver most enticingly. If I weren't a stern, sober, duty-oriented individual, you might even tempt me into another frolic."

Meg blushed scarlet and caught up one of her discarded petticoats to hold in front of her. "I . . . tempt you! Piers," she said as severely as she could manage under the circumstances, "have you no shame?"

"Not much. And for a little while, you hadn't either. Most interesting reaction to danger and excitement. I must spill you out in another set of rapids sometime and see if it works again—"

He broke off, laughing, to dodge the overripe fruit Meg found on the ground and hurled at him. "Not that stuff. It's poisonous. Try these, if you want to throw something," he recommended, tossing a spray of scarlet berries into her lap. "Better yet, come down to the river and I'll give you a chance to duck me." Seizing Meg's wrist, he pulled her down to the sandy inlet he'd promised, where a narrow creek split the forbidding black cliffs on either side to join with the main stream of the Ogowe. No crocodiles frequented this swift-running stream, and they were able to wash themselves and their clothes in the clear water before dressing again for the weary trek upriver.

Meg's boots, as she had predicted, refused to

go on again over her blistered feet. Piers contrived something with lengths of bark and bush rope, most ungainly-looking footgear, like small canoes, but Meg was grateful for the protection the bundles of bark gave her feet. "Just don't make a habit of requesting new shoes every day after we're married," he warned her.

"Are we going to be married?" Piers had already set off upstream; Meg, wading awkwardly in his wake, asked the question of his broad shoulders. His wet shirt, just washed in the creek, stuck to his back between the shoulder-blades and outlined the smooth flow of muscles under the thin white cotton.

"It's customary," Piers flung back over his shoulder.

"Yes . . ." Meg tried not to feel despondent. Of course, they would be married. She had assumed that when she went into his embrace. But it would be nice if he sounded a little more pleased about it, not so matter-of-fact.

"What's the matter now?" Piers looked back with a crooked grin. "Has it occurred to you that you could have a baby? Don't you want to give little Aloysius Adonis a name?"

"Not a name like that!"

"Digby Dionysius?"

As they climbed on across cliffs and stones, Piers's suggestions for names grew ever more outrageous and Meg giggled so much that she temporarily forgot small matters like fatigue, blisters, sunburn, and Piers's grim tone when he informed her that they were going to be married. Only when the sound of African voices raised in a plaintive missionary hymn warned her that they were approaching the rowers' camp did she come briefly to her senses.

"Piers! Stop!" Balanced on a slippery black rock, one foot almost in the water, she had to shriek over the rushing water and the tuneless hymn to get his attention.

He turned on his heel and came splashing back through the shallows, holding on to an exposed tree root to keep his balance on the slippery rocks. "What's the matter? Can't you make it to the next rock?" He held out his free arm. "Jump. I'll catch you."

"It's not that. I can't go in front of the rowers like this." Meg looked down at the expanse of sun-flushed skin exposed by her scanty costume. The white flounces of her petticoat, the foamy lace that trimmed her chemise, the thin muslin of her embroidered corset cover, were all plastered to her body by the river spray that kept them continually damp. From breast to shins she was covered only by the thin fabric that molded itself quite indecently to the natural curves of her body, and above and below that, she wasn't covered at all.

"Dear, you always look lovely to me," Piers offered in the dutiful tones of a henpecked husband. Splashing forward to the base of Meg's rock, he curved his arm about her waist and pulled her toward him. Meg held on to a tree root of her own and resisted the tug.

"I'm not decent!" she wailed. "I can't go around in my underwear!"

"In case you hadn't noticed, the Mpongwe don't have the concept of underwear. You're still wearing at least three layers of cloth, which is two more than the best-dressed Mpongwe lady ever wears and three more than sported by the fashionable Fan. They'll just think it's a pretty white dress. Now, will you quit fussing and come on? I'm hungry." Piers gave a sudden yank and Meg felt her improvised bark shoes slipping off the rock. She fell forward, arms flailing about his neck, and Piers hoisted her over his shoulder with a satisfied grunt.

Fifteen

The rowers greeted Piers and Meg with pleasure but with no sign of surprise. "I brought her back!" Piers announced, dramatically depositing Meg with a flourish between two cooking fires.

M'bo muttered the Mpongwe equivalent of "Of course," and went on to discuss what was clearly a more important matter: how did Piers want their lunch prepared?

Piers settled that question with a few emphatic gestures and retired with Meg to a fallen tree where she could sit well out of the smoke of the cooking fires. "I don't understand it," he muttered, pacing restlessly back and forth between Meg and the two groups of rowers. "They're acting as casually as if they fished white women out of the trackless jungle every day of their lives."

Meg smoothed the damp but fast-drying folds of her topmost petticoat. "Perhaps," she suggested, "they think a woman whose spirit can conquer the crocodile has nothing to fear from a few miles of rapids and rain forest."

Piers glanced at her with an amused glint in his eye. "Or perhaps they know that I never fail in anything I do."

"Oh, yeah?" Meg retorted inelegantly. "What

about getting sent down from Oxford, and the job at the bank, and—"

"Anything I really want," Piers cut her off with a lordly wave of his hand. His expression softened as he looked at Meg, perched on the log with the sun sending golden glints through her damp hair and imparting a soft glow to the expanses of formerly white skin exposed by her low-cut chemise. "Of course, I don't recall ever wanting anything so much as you . . ." he mused in a low voice that sent trembling shivers of excitement down Meg's spine. The way he was looking at her made her feel as if they were making love again, right here with the Fan and Mpongwe rowers squatting around their cooking fires, not ten feet away! The feelings aroused by the memory of their earlier loving were too strong for her to handle. She felt her own blushes creeping over her neck and bosom, coloring her sun-flushed skin even further.

"What about clearing your name?" she asked quickly—too quickly. "I mean, we're going to accomplish that too."

Piers's jaw set in determined lines that made him look years older and harder than the laughing lover who'd taken her in the forest. "Yes. I'll do that." He paused as if to make sure she would attach appropriate weight to what he said next. "But you're more important to me than solving this little mystery, Meg. Nearly losing you in the rapids this morning has taught me a lesson. Thank God it didn't come too late! We'll start back to Talagouga after we eat. Going downstream, we should go quite a bit faster. We'll reach the mission by sunset. I'll stay overnight and set off again in the morning."

There was a stern yet wary look in his eye as he finished the statement. What was he so worried about? Meg thought he was skirting around something he was afraid to state right out loud. And it was pretty clear what that something was.

"If you think we need to return to Talagouga for supplies, that's all right," she said slowly. "But there's something I don't like about the way you're using pronouns, Piers. *We* go back to Talagouga? *You* set out again in the morning?"

Piers folded his arms and stared down at her. "You heard me. You're not to risk yourself anymore. I forbid it."

"Oh, indeed?" Meg jumped to her feet, finding it impossible to shout satisfactorily while crouched on a log. "And just what gives you the right to pronounce on my actions? Since when do I ask you for permission every time I take a deep breath?" She clenched her fists and longed for her trusty black umbrella. A few cracks over the head from that steel-framed device were just what Piers needed to beat some sense into him.

"Since we're getting married, that's since when!" Piers shouted back. He grabbed her by the shoulders and shook her until her drying hair flew about her face in damp golden tangles. "As my wife, I expect you to accept my judgment. Starting *now*. You're going back to Talagouga, and that's final."

Meg twisted in Piers's grasp, trying unavailingly to break free. "Ohh," she breathed, shaking with rage. "You impossible man! That's totally unfair! Who hired the rowers? Who figured out how to get them to go into Fan country? You're not taking over my expedition just because you're a *man*, not this time, Piers Damery!"

Piers held her firmly, no longer shaking her, just waiting until she ran out of breath. "No," he said when she paused at last. "Because a man protects his wife. That's why."

"I don't recall asking you for protection," Meg spat back at him. "Oh, I should never . . . should never have let you—"

"You liked it well enough at the time. In fact, I think it was as much your idea as mine."

Tried beyond endurance, Meg twisted to get free again and aimed a vicious kick at Piers's shins. The flimsy bark shoe he'd improvised for her collapsed with the force of the blow and her toes felt as if they'd been broken. She clenched her teeth to keep from crying out. "I should never have let you take my boots off!"

"Next time," Piers said, "remind me to search you for weapons as well. If you'd still been wearing those clodhoppers, I'd have a broken leg, you little vixen. Now, will you calm down or do I have to put you across my knee and teach you some manners?"

"You and what six other men?" Meg gasped. She turned her head from side to side. "Kema! Michael! Aren't you going to tell this bully to lay off?"

Her Fan friends were still squatting lazily around their fire, grinning at the scene of the two white people quarreling. Michael volunteered a long statement which Kema translated into passable West Coast pidgin.

"You his wife now, sah! He beat you small-small, all right. No big stick, no blood, no beat pass all too much. He good man."

Piers gave Meg a brilliant smile of triumph. "Local custom is no longer on your side, my fair lady. The Fans seem to have assimilated the idea that you are my woman, even if it's taking you a little while to catch on. And according to their customs, I am entitled to beat my wife as long as I don't draw blood. So you'd better watch your mouth—and your feet—or you'll be paddling back to Talagouga with a sore bottom to add to your other ills."

"Consider the engagement at an end!" Meg retorted. "I'm no man's property, Piers Damery."

Piers hands released her and he stepped back. "You don't mean that, I hope."

His voice was quiet and level and frightened Meg more than if he'd continued shouting at her. Did she mean it? She hadn't had time to sort out her own feelings. The golden dream of Harry Damery had transmuted into the reality of Piers Damery. And she wasn't even sure, right now, that she liked Piers. But the thought of never seeing him again left her feeling cold and empty inside.

"Oh, what can I do?" she wailed. "If we're engaged, you're going to make me go back to Talagouga and wait while you go upriver, and maybe I'll never see you again! If we aren't engaged—"

"Then I will guarantee not to trouble you again," Piers said. He had backed up to lean against a tree at the edge of the riverbank, hands shoved into his pockets, yellow head cocked at a jaunty angle. The apparent relaxation of his pose belied the extreme tension evident in his low-pitched voice and the steady gaze of his blue eyes. "Well, Meg? You have to decide what you want sometime—and stick with it. I thought you'd made your decision a while ago. If you've changed your mind, you'd best tell me now."

Meg wished he would shout, argue, grab her and shake her again, throw her over his shoulder and carry her off into the bush. Anything but this tense, quiet waiting. What did Piers want? He'd been so quick to seize on her first hint of opposition to the idea of marrying him. Perhaps he'd openly proposed to her because he felt obliged, after what had passed between them earlier. In fact, he hadn't even proposed to her—he'd just taken their marriage as a settled decision and set off upriver without waiting to hear from her. Wasn't that how a man would treat an unpleasant duty, rather than a longed-for consummation of his wishes?

"What do you want, Piers?"

He didn't move from his post by the tree. "I thought I had made that tolerably clear by now."

Meg took one dragging step toward him, then another, horribly conscious that they were being watched by all the rowers. She told herself that it didn't matter. All that mattered was that she had to feel Piers's arms around her again, had to feel the kisses that swept her away and made her know how much he wanted her. If only he would kiss her again, then she would be sure he really wanted her, that he wasn't regretting those moments of abandon in the jungle. She felt sure she would be able to read the truth in his lips, though his voice was giving her no clue.

The distance between them suddenly seemed like a matter of miles, not feet and inches. Couldn't he make this any easier for her? Meg reached out one hand toward Piers, feeling it physically impossible to take another step without some encouragement from him.

The impasse was broken by an excited babble from the large circle of Mpongwe rowers. Piers's head whipped around as though whatever they were saying had captured all his attention, Meg tried to follow the conversation, but her few words of Mpongwe were totally inadequate to disentangle the threads of a dozen agitated voices all speaking at once. She caught the word for "wife," and then, in pidgin, "Bad palaver! Bad palaver!"

That was M'bo speaking, the lead rower who towered above the rest. He must be saying something about Piers and herself. But why was he shaking his open hand before a young rower who crouched before him, grinning apologetically and nodding his head to each of M'bo's exclamations?

The lead rower finished his short harangue by stabbing two fingers emphatically at the young man. The other man scrambled to his feet and hurled what was obviously an insult at M'bo, who turned his back and came over to Piers and Meg without bothering to listen to the young man's continued jabber.

"What happened?" Meg demanded of Piers as M'bo stalked toward him.

"M'bo pointed two fingers at him."

"I *saw* that."

"Means he's a twin. He isn't, of course, or he'd have been killed at birth. It's the worst insult you can give in Mpongwe."

Meg stored that information away for future use as M'bo explained just why he was so angry at the young rower. It seemed that M'nika had just now confessed that last year he had been involved in a "bad-wife palaver" with the village downstream where they had all spent the night. He had been nervous of being recognized when they landed there, but as the night wore on and nobody made a hostile move, he grew more and more confident. Toward dawn, when all the villagers were asleep, he had sneaked into a hut and renewed his affectionate relations with the headman's number-five wife, a sprightly young thing from his own native village. When they left that morning she had been unhappy to see him go, crying openly and hinting that she might confess everything to her husband.

"Oh, my God." Piers rubbed one hand across his forehead. "That's torn it. We'll have to wait until dark and sneak past the village. If she has told her husband, they'll be lying in wait to avenge his honor."

"Please, ah," M'bo insisted, addressing his remarks to a point in air midway between Piers and Meg. "I think more better we go *now*." He pointed upstream, away from the village.

"Out of the question," Piers shook his head. "We almost got killed in those rapids the first time, M'bo, or have you forgotten already? Some bad spirit live for them water, no let us pass."

M'bo riposted that the only bad spirit involved was the bad steering of Kema, that dirty Fan whom they were inexplicably using as a guide. Now that he, M'bo, knew what to expect from the submerged rocks that made the rapids so dangerous, he guaranteed to get them through safely. In any case, they had the white woman with the very strong personal devils with them, and she had already demonstrated her ability to conquer the spirits of the river. But M'bo wasn't too sure that any of them could overcome the spirits that haunted a party of angry villagers armed with guns.

"He's got a point there," Piers muttered. "Not that most of these chaps could hit the side of a barn with their antiquated muzzle-loaders, but that doesn't do much good when they stand ten feet away from you and spray you with miscellaneous scrap iron and fetish charms. If the wounds don't kill you, the infection will."

"It sounds a charming prospect," Meg agreed. "Perhaps we'd better go on?"

Piers frowned. "It means trusting M'bo and Kema to get us through the rapids. They didn't do so well last time. I don't know . . ."

He bowed his head in thought. A deafening bang resounded in the woods behind them and something whizzed into the tree trunk just behind where Piers's head had been a moment ago. Meg stared at the object in disbelief. It appeared to be a jagged shard of cast iron, almost half an inch broad at the base and three inches long, and it quivered slightly with the force that had buried its point in the tree trunk.

"Now I know." Piers grabbed Meg's hand and pulled her, slipping and sliding, down the steep bank to where the canoes were beached. "Everybody into the canoes!"

The rowers scrambled after them, falling down the bank in tangles of naked black limbs, and piled helter-skelter into the canoes before Piers had quite got the second canoe into the water. A solitary figure, daubed with ocher mud and ornamented with a tall knotted headdress, remained at the top of the bank while all the others were throwing themselves into the canoes. Kema chanted a defiant war song and raised his bow, calmly sending arrow after arrow into the mass of green vines that shielded the attackers from his view.

"Kema!" Piers bellowed. "Get the hell out of that!"

Kema shot the last arrow out of his ornamented leather quiver and came down the bank in two bounds to seat himself in the canoe where Piers and Meg awaited him. The other canoe was already out in midstream, the rowers paddling with all their might toward the rapids that lurked just around the corner.

There was no time to think or debate. As soon as Kema left off firing, the Mpongwe villagers attacked with high, shrill yells. Bits of iron, pebbles, and scraps of copper wire rattled against the sides of the canoe as they pulled away from the shore.

"Shooting low," Piers breathed. "But they won't put a hole through this wood. Get down!" His hand caught Meg by the nape of the neck and ruthlessly forced her down into the bottom of the canoe. Crouched there, she could see nothing but the rhythmic sweep of the paddles. The splashing as they hit the fast current in the center of the stream was punctuated by explosions and war cries from the bank. Suddenly one gun went off with a booming crack, much louder than anything they'd heard before, and a scream of pain tore through the other noises.

Piers gave a grim chuckle. "One of those guns exploded in a man's hand. Happens from time to time. They *will* stuff too much powder down the barrel, and then put in God knows what for bullets, and after a while the guns just can't take the abuse. Poor bastard! He won't use that hand again." As he spoke, he let go of Meg to raise his own rifle to his shoulder. The crack of gunfire deafened her and made her squeeze her eyes shut; when she looked again, one of the pursuing canoes had spun around out of control, while the occupants tried to haul a man back on board.

"Oh, good shot!"

"Unfortunately," said Piers between his teeth, "it was also my only shot. My ammunition is at the bottom of the river with the rest of our supplies."

Kema laughed. "Maybe old guns not so bad bad pass all, huh?" He pointed at the still fully functional, albeit old-fashioned guns that were being trained on them from the pursuing canoes.

"All very true, my Fan friend," said Piers. "At the moment, one of those old muzzle-loaders I was making fun of would be a hell of a lot more useful than this improved modern hunting rifle. At least I might be able to find powder and scrap iron for an old flintlock. This thing is useless until we get to a trading factory. But may I remind you that you're out of arrows too? Our options are rapidly diminishing."

"Please, sah, what mean di-min-ich . . . ?" Kema struggled over the unfamiliar word.

"It means we'd all better row like hell!"

Meg sat up and looked for something she could use as a paddle. The canoes were nearly empty after the disastrous wreck earlier, and half the rowers were using their hands and feet in lieu of better paddles.

"Dammit, Meg, get down!"

"We're out of range. And if I'm to be drowned again, I want to see what's happening to me this time."

The noise of the rapids cut off all further conversation. M'bo, in the canoe ahead, steered a tortuous course through the submerged rocks that had overturned them before, and Meg knelt in the bows and shouted back warnings as they scraped perilously close to one boulder or another. The rowers without paddles fended the rocks off with bare hands and feet that soon were streaked with blood from the constant scrapes they endured; those with paddles worked with all their strength, shoulders straining and sweat running down their foreheads, to maintain headway against the capricious swift-running current. Meg had only brief glimpses to spare for Piers and the rowers, and then they were in a thicker patch of rocks than they'd encountered before and then she had to concentrate completely on peering through foamy brown water. Was that a rock? No, a shadow. That one would get them for sure. . . . Past the danger, but the whirlpool ahead meant new traps underwater . . .

When they reached smooth water again, she was so dazed from the noise and the constant strain that she couldn't relax for a few minutes. She stared at the smooth brown current, wondering dully what kind of rock formation left no warning trace at all on the surface.

"We'll beach the canoes up there," Piers called. "We all need a rest." Meg looked back, saw him pointing at a sandy spit of land ahead, and slowly began to realize that the immediate danger was over. The attacking villagers had evidently decided not to follow them through the rapids, and she couldn't blame them. Given a moment to reflect, she might have decided to stay and be killed by the war party rather than drown in the rapids.

But they hadn't drowned! They'd made it through! Meg felt a bubbling exhilaration spread through her veins. How pleasant it was to be alive, especially when one hadn't planned on it! She looked at the sunshine above them, listened to the cries of birds in the jungle, felt the cool ripple of the water with new appreciation. When they reached the sand, she hopped out and helped Piers and the rowers haul the two canoes out of the water.

Piers watched Meg's lively movements with a deep appreciation of his own. Halfway through the rapids he had decided that Meg was too dangerous for any sane man to fool with and that if he had any sense he would let the broken engagement stay that way. How had he wound up here, risking death from rocks and water and crazy Mpongwe marksmen? He couldn't exactly retrace the steps now, and it didn't matter. The real point was that a man in Meg's orbit found himself doing all sorts of suicidal things that would never have happened if she hadn't come around to stir him up. And he'd wanted to marry her! He must have been crazy.

Now, safe on the far side of those sickening reaches of white water, he was beginning to remember why he'd wanted Meg so badly. Any of the girls he'd known in England would have been limp with exhaustion or enjoying a fit of hysterics after going through just half what Meg had experienced that day. Instead she looked like a young Valkyrie, drenched by spray, exhilarated by their brush with death, her lacy undergarments clinging to the surprisingly generous curves she'd been concealing under all those clothes, her hair, darkened by water to the color of a golden snake, coiling down her back. "Might as well admit it," Piers muttered to himself. "I'm still crazy."

"What's crazy?" inquired Meg, who'd heard only the last word.

"Uh . . . coming back down this river would be crazy," Piers improvised. "I don't particularly want to meet our downstream friends again, do you? Perhaps we'd better go back some other way."

Meg looked blankly at the foaming brown reaches of the Ogowe, at the wall of green that enclosed them on either side, and at the steep rocky hills rising to the north. "What other way?"

Piers glanced around the same scenery and felt a familiar wanderlust stirring within him. "I don't know. There's got to be something. Nobody's ever mapped all the rivers that feed into the Ogowe."

"Of course!" Meg's eyes sparkled and she dropped down on the sand at his feet to draw maps in the damp sand. "We have to go up the Spirit River anyway, don't we? We could begin by tracing it to its source, then we could work back overland through the Sierra del Cristal. Get more supplies at the first trading factory, then go back inland and map all the mountain streams and figure out where they go. We might even find unclaimed territory for England! In a few years . . ." She stopped suddenly and bit her lip. "I forgot. You don't want me along, do you?"

Piers lifted Meg to her feet. "Stand here."

"Why?"

"Because I can't kiss you properly when you're

squatting in the sand." Taking her in his arms, he devoted several minutes to a convincing demonstration of just how badly he wanted her. When Meg broke away, flushed and breathless, he kept her close to him and held her chin so that she had to meet his eyes. "That's how I want you," he told her. "Every minute of every day for the rest of my life, that's all! It's just that I don't like to see you in danger. So . . ." He paused for a moment until he could say the next words with the conviction they deserved. "We'll go back to England. I'll get a proper job, in a shop or something. And we'll be married. Is that clear?"

"And just how long," Meg inquired sweetly, "do you think you could stand clerking behind a counter or adding up accounts in some musty bank ledgers?"

"If it's necessary, I can do it."

"I think with that much willpower you could also brace yourself for the horrible sight of me in Africa." Meg slipped her arm around Piers's waist. "Because I don't like to see you bored. Which you would be, you know, if you came back to England and took a dull ordinary job, or let your family talk you into another 'respectable' position as somebody's secretary. And I'd be horribly bored too. And then we'd fight, and you'd probably beat me and draw blood, and then I'd be entitled to a Fan divorce, only we'd have to come back to Africa to get a Fan judge, so maybe it would be simpler if we stayed here in the first place."

Holding her breath, she waited for Piers's reaction to this mild teasing. If he continued to insist that as his wife she must be cosseted, protected from any sort of danger—or any *fun* . . .

Meg swallowed and tried to face the thought of a future without any of the freedom and adventure she'd tasted for the first time on this journey.

Piers frowned as he stared out over the river. "Has anybody ever told you that you're a very stubborn woman?"

"Your mother says I'm a nice helpful girl and such a comfort to have around the house."

"My mother obviously doesn't know you very well." Piers shrugged himself free of Meg's arm and took a few steps forward, to where the slack water lapped gently at the golden edge of the sandbank. "So we're going to stay in Africa and become great explorers, are we?"

Meg's heart leapt. "Please, Piers?"

"In that case," he said, still not looking at her, "you'd better reinstate the engagement."

"What?"

"You jilted me, remember? Just before we were attacked. I'm not going to go off up the Ogowe River with a shameless hussy who isn't even planning to marry her traveling companion."

Sixteen

Piers still had his doubts about the wisdom of going on without any of the supplies he had so laboriously assembled. On the other hand, as Meg pointed out, the extra ammunition for his rifle had been among those supplies; without that (or even with it, in her private opinion), she questioned the wisdom of returning down the Ogowe while their friends downstream were still excited. In fact, it might be a good idea to make some more distance up the river while the daylight lasted.

"Oh, all right, I do see your point," Piers grumbled. "Although I'm beginning to wonder if you didn't engineer the whole incident just to make sure I couldn't send you back to Talagouga."

Meg giggled. "I wish I were that smart."

"And I wish they hadn't attacked before we got lunch," said Piers, rubbing his flat stomach with a wistful expression.

"What was lunch, anyway? I thought all our supplies got lost in the river."

"They did. Kema shot a couple of monkeys. He was roasting one and stewing the other with mango-nut sauce."

Meg clamped her lips shut and forced back the queasy feeling that threatened her. "Sounds delicious. What a pity I missed this gourmet meal. Cheer up. Kema says there's a Fan village with some friends of his a little way up the Spirit River. If we start now, we can get there by sunset. They'll probably give us some delicious agouma."

"Yeah," Piers muttered, "with eyeball of explorer for a garnish." But he called to the rowers and they resumed their journey. This time Piers insisted that Meg stay in the same canoe with him. "I want to diminish your chances of getting lost," he said sternly. "Every time I take my eyes off you, you disappear."

Only a little way past the sandy strip where they had beached the canoes, the familiar sound of water roaring through a narrow gap reached their ears.

"Kema," Piers called, "are there more rapids ahead?"

"No, sah! No, sah! Him Spirit River."

"Well, that's good," said Piers. "I was beginning to think we'd never . . . Good Lord! We're not going up that damn thing!"

Between two massive black cliffs on the left bank of the river, a gray-green, foaming torrent shot out to mingle its cold mountain waters with the broader stream of the Ogowe. It looked like the rapids they'd barely survived, magnified tenfold and far more intimidating.

"No fear, sah!" Kema cried. "No fear! This small-small water, easy water."

With a dexterous twitch of his paddle he guided the long canoe straight into the greenish current. The rowers' paddles bent under the new strain and Kema yelled encouragement in every language he knew. Slowly the canoe crept ahead, defeating the steady pull of the current inch by inch, until the channel widened and the force of the Spirit River diminished accordingly.

"No rocks," Piers said. He wiped his forehead with one hand and pulled Meg closer to him with his other arm around her waist. "But I wouldn't call it 'easy water' exactly. . . . No wonder the place hasn't been explored."

The rowers pulled steadily now, chanting above the noise of the water, and they moved on through a deep, narrow channel into a new world. The steep black cliffs that rose on either side cut off most of the sunshine they had felt on the Ogowe, the green vines hanging down like a curtain filtered what light remained into a green sea, and the noise of the rushing water drowned out the small sounds of the jungle and made it seem as though they were moving through a paradise of solitude.

"It's beautiful!" Meg breathed, looking around her with shining eyes. "Even more lovely than the Ogowe. The Garden of Eden must have been like this—peaceful and serene and unspoiled. It's almost a pity to intrude upon these simple, primitive people." She trailed one hand over the side of the canoe, reveling in the fresh, cool feel of the water. "This stream must come from the melting snows of the Sierra del Cristal."

A whistling noise, high as a dragonfly's buzz, cut through the deep undertone of the rushing water, and Meg felt a stinging vibration in the palm of her hand. She snatched her hand off the side of the canoe and stared in shock at a slender arrow that had embedded itself in the canoe, landing in the space between where her thumb and forefinger had rested.

"I think more bettah we stop now, sah," Kema said.

"This is getting old," Piers grumbled. "Doesn't anybody around here extend a friendly welcome to visitors? Oh, never mind, never mind, I know the answer to that. But where the devil are we going to stop?"

While he was grumbling, Kema deftly steered the canoe right into one of the curtains of overhanging vines that covered the cliff face. The vines parted before the pointed prow of the canoe and revealed a narrow natural cleft in the rock, leaving just enough space to tie up their two canoes with the three that were already there. A thick length of dead vines tangled together hung down against the rock face at the point of the cleft.

While the Mpongwe rowers were making the canoes fast, Kema cupped his hands and shouted something up toward the top of the cliff. No response came, but neither did any more arrows.

"I thought you had friends here," Piers said silkily.

Kema gave a rather sickly smile. "If no friends, we be dead now." He pursed his lips and made a whistling noise uncannily reminiscent of the sound the arrow had made in its flight.

Piers winced. "All right. I take the point. Er ... you're not expecting us to climb up that thing, are you?"

Kema shrugged and scrambled nimbly up the length of knotted vines. Meg stared at the swaying bush rope in horror, realizing that the knots came at more or less regular intervals and that the irregular holes in the cliff face had been chipped out by human agency. This was the Fan version of a ladder!

"If Kema gets to the top and his 'friends' don't throw him over," Piers said in an undertone, "you'd better go next, so I can keep an eye on you."

Meg shook her head. "Uh-uh. Your turn next."

"Ladies first."

"A gentleman never follows a lady up a ladder."

"I already know what's under your skirts." Piers leered and cupped her bottom with one hand. The caress sent a shiver of pleasure through Meg, warming her to the point where she almost felt she could conquer the fear that threatened to paralyze her. "And I'm no gentleman."

"I thought that was my line." The "ladder" had stopped swaying now; Kema seemed to have reached the top of the cliff without incident. Meg tried to swallow, discovered that her mouth seemed full of cotton, and reached for the knotted vines with trembling hands. Her palms were damp and the living green vines she first touched were slippery under her hands. She reached in more firmly, getting a grip on the dry gray vines underneath, and felt marginally more confident. If she took this slowly and very, very carefully, perhaps it would be . . .

Strong warm hands slid under her buttocks and boosted her into the air. Meg kicked out, felt the vines under her feet, grabbed upward without thinking, and found herself dangling several feet off the ground. "Damn you, Piers," she gasped, "I wasn't ready!"

She dared not look down to deliver the stricture. The only way to go was upward; climbing down, even the few feet that she'd been made to travel, was beyond her. Meg set her teeth and began to climb.

It wasn't, she found, quite as bad as it had seemed when she watched Kema's ascent. The thick tangle of vines provided plenty of hand- and footholds, and Piers held the "ladder" steady at the bottom so that it didn't sway around with her weight. She progressed upward at a steady pace and didn't make the mistake of looking down until she was almost within reach of the clifftop.

And it was a mistake. At this distance, Piers was reduced to a bright dot where a chance shaft of sunlight fell on his uplifted face. Beyond him, the Mpongwe rowers were backing away, parting the curtain of vines to reveal the rushing green depths of the water. If she fell now . . .

A vision of her unprotected body bouncing off the cliff face a dozen times and finally sinking into the cold green water held Meg paralyzed on the cliff face, teeth chattering and palms sweating. She could feel her grip on the knotted vines loosening as her tired fingers slowly lost strength, but there was nothing she could do about it. She was doomed to slide slowly off the cliff, to fall slowly, slowly through infinite space until she spattered into nothing against the rocks . . .

Strong dark hands gripped her wrists and yanked her upward, breaking her hold on the vines with a single sharp tug. Meg felt the edge of the cliff under her breasts, then her stomach; legs kicking wildly, she rolled over and fell gratefully on the ground. The two men who'd reached over to haul her up left her there, panting like a landed fish, and returned to their discussion with Kema.

Meg had an uncomfortable feeling that this

discussion was not going as well as might be hoped. There were about twenty forest Fans standing around the top of the ladder, all of them armed with ancient muzzle-loading guns and several of them fondling the handles of their broad shovel-shaped knives. Their faces were grim and Kema's repeated calls for Ndeme, his friend in the village, produced no response.

While Meg gathered her breath, Michael came nimbly up the ladder, followed by Piers and then by David. The two Fans strolled casually to Kema and stood at his back, while Piers seated himself cross-legged on the ground beside Meg. She noticed that he was careful to move slowly and to show his empty hands at all times.

"M'bo and the rest of the Mpongwe decided to stay below," he muttered out of the side of his mouth. "Can't say that I blame them, really. Try not to look so worried—it may make them nervous."

"I *am* worried," Meg whispered back. "What happens next?"

Piers shrugged. "Depending on whether Kema finds Ndeme, we'll either have dinner or be dinner. If it comes to the latter, you'll have to see how quickly you can get back down the cliff. Don't worry—I'll cover your retreat."

Nothing about this plan was calculated to reassure Meg. Fortunately, it proved to be unnecessary. As the men surrounding Kema raised their voices, a fresh party of Fans joined the meeting. The leader of this group was a strong, handsome man in his middle years, attractively dressed in a twist of grayish cloth around his thighs and a bunch of leopard tails hung over one shoulder. Kema rushed forward with his hands outstretched, calling joyfully, "Ndeme, Ndeme!"

Ndeme grunted pleasantly and raised his own hands to touch Kema's, and all at once the mood of the crowd switched from threatening to jovial. Two of the warriors who'd been standing on either side of Kema slipped their knives back into the plaited grass-fiber sheaths, slapped Kema on the back, and offered open raised hands to Michael and David. Two more advanced on Piers and Meg and beckoned them toward the path with unmistakable gestures.

"We're in," Piers muttered. He rose in a single fluid motion, held up his own hands, and said cheerfully, "*Mboloani.*"

"*An, an,*" the Fans replied, and the whole party set off for the village, which proved to be only a short march from the cliffs.

The village consisted of two rows of bark huts, neatly aligned to form a single street with a larger hut at the end of the path. The organization of the huts was the only sign of any interest in neatness and cleanliness. The "street" was muddy, trampled by innumerable feet, and turned into a quagmire in which the puddles from yesterday's rain soaked up the blood running from a pile of offal and the scales from numerous half-eaten fish. As they marched down the filthy path, Meg saw a naked girl dart forward to scoop up some water from one of the larger puddles in a calabash. She carried her water back to a hollowed-out-log trough where the women were pounding cassava and flung it in to add to the sour paste. Meg swallowed hard and tried to look at other things. She had a sinking feeling that they were likely to be offered some of that cassava paste before the day was over.

They were ceremonially escorted to the smoky

palaver house at the far end of the street, where they sat on plaited mats and listened, or pretended to listen, to interminable speeches of welcome. Meg's attention wandered and she passed the time in investigating the interior of the house. The shape of the building, with its thatched roof overhanging a shady veranda on two sides, was like those in the Mpongwe village, but the interior decorations were quite different. A startling array of weapons decorated the walls, ranging from fantastically jagged and hooked battleaxes to baskets full of spiked bamboo splints. Between the displays of weapons hung ponderous shields of elephant hide, square in shape and painted with jagged lines of ocher and white.

Raised voices and sharp tones jerked her back to the speeches of the welcoming committee. Welcoming? That seemed no longer to be the tenor of the discussion. Kema was backing away from the village elders while a gentleman dressed in black rags and painted with soot harangued him. Without understanding Fan, Meg could tell that Kema was begging the other to wait a minute, please, they could get this little matter straightened out if he would only be patient. The dark-clad elder finally nodded and stepped back a pace while Kema squatted to confer with Piers and Meg.

"Bad-debt palaver," was what his wordy, agitated explanation came down to. It seemed that Kema had taken a large piece of ivory from the sooty gentleman on his last time in the village, promising to return with a beautiful English-made coat in payment. Now the elder wanted his coat; he also wanted to discuss all the previous times on which Kema and Kema's family had failed to meet their obligations. Old debts of Kema's mother's brother and then the elder's third wife's donkey were being raked over the coals; Meg couldn't follow all the details, but she gathered that Kema and the elder had a long and complicated history.

"Did you explain that we lost all our trade goods in the river?"

Kema shrugged and indicated that the elder wanted immediate payment.

"Well, that's ridiculous!" Meg exploded. "Obviously you can't pay him. You don't have anything. Look, just tell him that we'll give him a draft on your trading company, and he can pick out his own trade goods . . ."

Kema shook his head and looked very sad. He repeated that the gentleman wanted immediate payment.

"I think," Piers interpreted, "that the creditor means to foreclose on Kema's estate. Meaning Kema. They want to smoke our guide."

Meg swallowed. "They're really cannibals?"

"I don't know, but I think they really want to kill Kema. And I wouldn't eat any meat they may offer you at dinner—assuming we're still the guests of honor and not the main course. Safer to stick to the cassava."

Meg decided it would be kinder not to tell Piers what she'd observed of the Fan methods of cassava preparation. Besides, they had more immediate problems to worry about. "Offer them credit at a Hatton and Cookson trading post for the amount of the debt," she repeated to Kema. "Wouldn't he rather have a nice selection of cloth and beads than your head?"

Kema didn't seem too sure of this, but he translated the offer anyway. When he got to the words "Hatton and Cookson," a sort of shudder ran through the assembled elders and they drew back another pace.

"Good idea!" Piers whispered jubilantly to Meg. "Obviously they respect the English, even in this remote jungle village."

Meg wasn't too sure that "respect" was the right term for the reaction they were seeing. The movements of the elders had brought them within easy reach of the weapons with which the far wall of the palaver hut was decorated.

While the elders stood apart muttering in low tones, a young man who had been standing as a guard at the door of the hut pushed through the crowd to plant himself directly in front of Meg and Piers. To Meg's surprise, the old men made no move to reprove this insolence.

The young guard leaned on his spear and stared down at them in silence. Meg had time to observe that his shoulders were freshly tattooed in a pattern of complicated knotwork surmounted by a picture of a crocodile. She also noticed some rusty brown stains on the serrated edge of his spear blade, which was planted almost between her feet.

"You English traders? Hatton and Cookson?"

Piers opened his mouth to reply and Meg pinched him viciously on the thigh. "You crocodile witch?" she riposted.

The village elders turned a curious ashy-blue tinge and backed even farther away, laying hands on some of the weapons on the wall. Meg decided to abandon that line of questioning. Quickly, before Piers recovered from his shock and started talking, she explained that they were not English at all, but French, friends of the missionaries at Talagouga. She invited Kema to confirm the connection, and noticed a distinct slackening of tension when he did so.

"No trade?" the young guard persisted.

Meg shook her head vigorously. For the first time she felt grateful that all their trade goods were reposing in steel boxes on the bottom of the Ogowe.

"Good!" He turned away and grunted a few words at the elders, who stood aside respectfully to let him pass.

After a little more debate Meg succeeded in buying Kema's freedom for the price of her boots, Piers's watch (somewhat the worse for its repeated immersions in the river), and a lock of her own golden hair. The last item seemed to please the elders immoderately; they made quite a ceremony of slicing it off with a broad leaf-shaped knife, while Meg held her breath against the stink of partially cured leopardskins which formed such an important part of most Fan costumes.

"I wish I knew why they're so interested in your hair," Piers murmured.

Meg tossed her head and flashed him a smile. "Maybe they think it's pretty. Don't you?" What a time for her first flirtation, in a stinking palaver hut surrounded by cannibals! But she felt excited and successful and able to do anything. She'd saved the debt palaver, and the insolent young guard had given her a clue to the next phase of this mystery. If only she could be alone with Piers to talk it over, and . . .

Honesty forced Meg to admit that once she and Piers were alone again, talking wouldn't be the only thing on her mind. She blushed at the vivid images that filled her memory. Piers reached out to caress her remaining locks of fine fair hair, and she shivered with the memory of those broad tanned hands moving over her body, uncovering all the secrets of delight that had been hidden even from her, laying aside layers of lace and muslin and respectability to make her part of him.

"I think your hair is . . . quite beautiful," said Piers with a catch in his voice. "Do we have to go through with this ceremonial dinner?"

Meg's stomach gave an indelicate rumble at the mention of food. Even sour cassava paste would taste good, if she could keep her mind off the gory details of a Fan kitchen. Piers laughed and tugged at a lock of her hair, the way he'd done to tease her when she was a schoolgirl. "All right. I never starve my women . . . of anything they need."

The last words were spoken in a soft insinuating whisper that made Meg feel as though she had just stepped off a stair that she hadn't known was there—falling through space, weightless and fearless.

But first there was dinner to get through. Seated on log benches on opposite sides of a plaited grass mat, Meg and Piers ate balls of sticky cassava paste, boiled yams, and a stew of meat which Piers assured her in an undertone was only monkey. Meg couldn't remember another time in her life when she would have been relieved to know that she was eating monkey stew, but tonight it didn't seem to matter. She wasn't tasting anything anyway. Gazing into Piers's deep blue eyes, watching the flames of the cooking fire illuminate his sharp profile, she dipped two fingers into the calabash of sticky cassava paste and swallowed balls of the stuff without even gagging. All she could think about was Piers; all she could feel was a floating euphoria that they had survived all the dangers of the day.

Finally the feasting and speech-making came to an end and Meg and Piers were escorted to the palaver hut, where piles of grass mats had been unrolled to provide sleeping quarters for them. The hut was nice and solid and there was a good thick mat suspended before the one doorway, and Kema had announced his intentions of sleeping outside by the fire. Meg felt no compunction about disrobing in the darkness of the hut, no shyness about doing so for the first time before Piers. Her fingers were strangely clumsy on the buttons that fastened her chemise down the front; she gave an impatient, frustrated laugh and moved toward Piers, dimly visible as a white-clad form in the shadows.

"I can't get this . . . this thing off. Help me?"

Piers's indrawn breath as she guided his fingers to the front of the chemise gave her deep satisfaction. To think that she, awkward Meg Beaumont from Yorkshire, could affect a man so! She felt his hands trembling as they closed over her breasts, and the knowledge of her power over him added to the sweet intoxication she was feeling. No, she wasn't that gawky shy girl anymore. She was . . . What had that Frenchman called her? She was "beautiful Marguerite," who could do anything, who was desired by Piers and who must therefore be desirable and worthy.

"You're very uninhibited tonight," Piers murmured as he covered her laughing lips with his own. "Where has this girl been hiding? What happened to that shy lady in the layers of unnecessary clothes?"

"I drowned her in the river." The buttons on the front of her chemise fell away and Meg moved away from Piers in a fluid, confident dancing motion, shrugging off the lacy folds and stepping out of her petticoats. She raised her arms to the roof and twirled around lazily, leaning backward into Piers's embrace. "Piers, today I've been drowned, knocked on the head, lost in the jungle, deflowered, engaged, jilted, reengaged, and almost served up as the main course at dinner. At some point," she told him seriously, arching back to make sure he met her wide gray eyes, "one has to stop worrying about the details. Life is too lovely to waste."

Piers caught his breath with renewed desire as Meg moved the palm of her hand slowly downward, gliding along the flat hard planes of his body while she nestled her head against his shoulder. His head felt thick as a morning river fog; all he knew clearly was that he had to have this woman, now, that he needed her more than he had ever needed anything or anyone in his life. She had touched right through all the armor of laughter and indifference with which he shielded himself against a world in which he had always been something of a misfit and a loner. His new vulnerability should have frightened him, but there was no room for fear with the magical, enchanting presence of Meg so close to him, so tempting and lissome and suddenly wanton in his arms.

Somehow he managed to tear off his clothes without ever letting go of her. Then he took the initiative from her, pressing his chest against the soft curves offered to him, showering kisses over her bared shoulders, and knotting his fingers in the silken masses of fair hair that cloaked her in mystery. She was Meg, his beloved girl, the comrade of his travels, and now she was so much more: slow and languorous and unashamed in this shadowy hut, she was all the mystery and delight of womanhood incarnate. Piers felt a driving urge to possess her, to make her his with fierce relentless thrusts, but his body would not obey the desires he felt. He too was moving slowly, caressing her at agonizing length until he felt her shudders reflecting the tension that built within him.

"Please," she breathed in his ear when he finally knelt with her upon the plaited grass mat. "Please, Piers, don't make me wait any longer. I need you so!"

Naked and shameless and vital in his arms, she seemed all fire and silver and moonlight. Piers did not know whether he was making love or worshiping; both acts blended together in the slow controlled force with which he entered her body and made her his once again.

Even then, some power stronger than his own selfish desires made him move slowly, holding still to savor the sweetness of her trembling body enclosing him. She sighed in his arms and clasped him to her, wordlessly begging for release of the sweet frustrating tension that held them both in its grip. "Meg, Meg," he murmured, lifting the weight of her hair to kiss the soft curve of her neck. His mouth blazed a trail of fire along her shoulder and down to the swelling peak of her breast, fastening over the aching tip in a tantalizing kiss that sent new bursts of hot desire coursing through her body.

"You're mine now," he told her. He thought of Harry, but would not say the name; he didn't want any ghosts of old dreams sharing the mat with them. He would have given all he had to know that Harry was finally driven from her heart, but he dared not ask. Instead he thrust deep into her, feeling the power that had been gathering within him until it exploded in a dark magical force that had to make her his entirely, wiping out all her old dreams of Harry, all his old jealousy of his brother.

When Piers murmured endearments against her throat, Meg felt as though she just might die from pleasure and frustration together if he didn't complete the act he had so lovingly begun. The tense, leashed strength of his muscular body, holding back for she knew not what, made her long unbearably for the moment when that power would be freed within her. The minute vibrations of his throat and lips against her skin made her purr with pleasure. She stretched languorously under him, open to him in every way, surrendered and conquering at once, her heart pounding with anticipation.

"Mine," Piers repeated. "My love, my goddess, my—"

Meg put her hand over his lips. "No. Only Meg."

"Everything!" he cried out as he took her, strength and desire freed now in a whirlwind that carried her away from herself, aware of nothing but their striving to come ever closer. Meg felt herself buffeted by the winds and the waves, as helpless now as when she'd been swept away by the rapids, and at the same time she knew that she was one with the fierce current that tossed the two of them together in mutual desire. She laughed aloud and rode the current strongly, clasping Piers with arms and legs and knowing nothing but the powerful rhythmic thrusts of his body. With each movement she felt an unbearably sweet, deep pleasure stroking upward from her center. When the final surge of delight came, she was no longer Meg; she was herself and Piers and the river current and the jungle outside—all joined together in a primeval explosion. At the last she cried out and fell slowly back into herself, felt the power leave her until she was no more than a leaf tossed on the foam of the rapids, blown on the wind from the mountains, and finally coming to rest on the grassy mat where they had begun. Piers's head was resting heavily on her breast, and his hands, limp and relaxed, still held her with the memory of passion. The hut was silent but for the pounding of her heart and his ragged breathing.

It might have been hours later, or only minutes, when Piers stirred lazily and looked up at her. "Meg. Do you think there was something in the food?"

"I know there was something in the cassava," Meg said. "Fish guts and mud. Need we discuss it?"

"I didn't mean that." Piers levered himself to a sitting position and slumped back against one of the supporting posts that ran down the center of the palaver hut. He took one of Meg's hands in his and caressed it absently as he talked, running his fingers up and down the palm and the inside of her wrist in a way that made her limp with the memory of their shared ecstasy. "I meant . . . Meg, I love you. You're special. But I never experienced anything like this before. Have you?"

Meg's low, husky laugh startled him. "You're forgetting that I haven't much to compare it with." But for all her evasions, she knew what Piers meant. Even before they made love, she had felt as though she were being lifted out of herself by some invisible agency. M'bo would probably have said she was possessed by the spirits of the jungle. Piers's suggestion of a drug in their dinner made more sense to her.

"But why would they want to drug us?" she wondered out loud.

Piers shook his head. "I don't know, but has it struck you that the closer we get to the Crocodile Society, the more trouble we run into?"

"You can't blame the Crocodile Society for everything that's happened on this trip," Meg protested. Her own voice sounded rather tinny and faraway in her ears, and some part of her wondered what this silly woman meant by rattling on about issues of no importance. The important thing was Piers, herself, the magic that had sprung to life between them, and the soft drifting afterglow of pleasure that still radiated through her body. Still, the other Meg, the silly logical one, wouldn't shut up. "How could they possibly have engineered M'nika's bad-wife palaver, and the underwater rocks in the rapids, and Kema's debt palaver?"

"Mmm." Piers was infuriatingly noncommittal. "I don't know . . . It doesn't matter. If we have the Crocodile Society to thank for this night, then maybe they're not so bad after all. In fact," he teased, drawing Meg into his arms, "I might make a deal for some more of whatever they slipped into the food."

Piers caressed Meg's hair almost absentmindedly. She stretched and purred under his hand, but felt no inclination to resume the wild lovemaking that had possessed them both earlier. It was too much trouble to make love, too much trouble to stretch out on the sleeping mats; nothing mattered anyway except this drowsy, happy, floating sensation that she felt, leaning against Piers's shoulder. All she wanted was to stay just like this forever.

So deep was her peaceful contentment that even the scratching, rustling sounds at the side of the hut did not disturb her. The Fan village was so filthy, one had to expect insect and scavengers of all sorts. Probably someone had left a half-gnawed bone or some other appetizing relic just outside the hut, and some little animal had slunk out of the forest to drag the trophy away.

"Sah! Sah!" came a thread of a whisper following the scratching noise.

"That," murmured Meg dreamily, "probably was not an animal."

"Probably not," Piers agreed, wrapping his arms around her.

"Sah! Kema here, sah!"

The bark covering one side of the hut crumpled and a dark figure slid inside.

Meg supposed she ought to cover herself. It was a nuisance, but she reached lazily for her petticoats and dragged one of the white circles of muslin over her body. Piers fumbled for his pants, also without any sense of urgency.

"Sah, you must listen!" Kema insisted. "Danger here—very bad palaver!"

Kema reported that he had found himself unable to sleep for fear the village elder to whom he was in debt might come after his head, having decided on reflection that Meg's boots were not adequate recompense for a large and almost perfect ivory tooth. He had wandered around the outskirts of the village and was just about to make himself comfortable in the bush outside the village walls when a party of masked men carrying torches approached. Kema hurled himself flat in the bush at once, fearing that he had accidentally stumbled upon a meeting of a secret society. The usual penalty for men who were not members observing these processions was a severe whipping, only women being punished with death; but Kema feared that in his case the elders might make an exception, as one of them already wanted his head.

To his horror, the procession halted only a few feet from his hiding place, and he overheard all their discussion while crouched in the bush and praying to his particular spirits that they would not raise their torches in his direction. As he had surmised, the men were returning from a secret-society meeting; but to his surprise, all the members except one were relatively young men. One of them was the young tough who'd behaved threateningly to Meg and Piers when he thought they were connected with Hatton and Cookson.

The one exception was an old man who was stark naked except for the carved head of a crocodile covering his face. His body glowed in the dark, and this, Kema explained, proved that he was no ordinary witch but a devil.

The men were arguing about what was to be done with the foreigners who had come to the village. One party was for rushing into the palaver hut and beating them to death on the spot, but the glowing crocodile-devil opposed this plan.

"Good for him," Piers approved.

Kema explained that the devil wanted the strangers given to the crocodiles at first light. He had pointed out that there was no need of a guard around their hut, since the drugs he had introduced into their food guaranteed that they would be unable to think of anything but their desire for each other until the morning. When one of the young men asked what was to be done about Kema and the other Fans, the crocodile-devil said that Kema would have to be killed; he had already been slated for sacrifice once, and for him to be still alive and walking around was a gross impiety that would rouse the wrath of the crocodiles on the entire village. The other two Fans in the party could be allowed to live on condition they were immediately initiated into the Crocodile Society.

As soon as the secret society members returned to the village, Kema had slithered through the bush to find the Mpongwe rowers who had camped below the cliffs. He had meant to tell them to be ready to row away as soon as he returned with Piers and Meg. Unfortunately, it seemed that the Mpongwes had anticipated his orders. They were gone, and so were both canoes.

Meg looked instinctively toward Piers as she heard this last crushing bit of information. She could not see him in the darkness of the palaver hut, but she knew he was there beside her. Her hand stole out and found his, warm and strong and comforting and alive. It didn't seem possible that they were trapped here, to die at the hands of some savage cult.

It wasn't possible.

Piers shook himself all over, like a dog coming out of the water—she felt the vibrations pass through his body—and when he spoke, his firm confident voice reassured her immediately. "Well, then, there's only one thing to do, isn't there?" he said. "We'll have to steal a canoe."

Seventeen

It didn't seem like a very good idea to try to leave the village by the path they'd taken to enter it; that path was likely to be guarded tonight. Piers and Kema conferred in whispers and decided that their best chance was to sneak out of the palaver hut and work their way around to the far side of the village, away from the river. Once they were out of the village, they could slither through the bush until they reached the cliffs bordering the river; then they'd have only to make their way down to the water, swim noiselessly upstream to the landing place where the Fans kept their canoes, and steal one.

Piers presented this plan to Meg without mentioning such minor difficulties as impenetrable bush, sheer cliffs, and the strong possibility of crocodiles in the river. Meg thought it over and decided there was no point in her pestering the men with trivial details. It wasn't as if she had any better ideas.

The moon was down when they crawled under the back mats of the palaver hut, emerging onto a muddy side "street" that snaked between Fan huts with occasional detours to avoid putrid-smelling mounds of offal. Meg hitched her petticoats up above her knees, picked her way carefully after Piers, and wished devoutly that English fashions called for underclothing of some less revealing color than pure white. Black, for instance. Black petticoats would be very practical for the traveler trying to sneak unobserved out of an African village; why hadn't she thought of that when she was packing for this trip? Of course, she hadn't exactly anticipated showing her lingerie to the world.

Meg felt hysterical giggles rising inside her. The situation was too insane; she couldn't believe it was real. She, plain Meg Beaumont of Yorkshire, tiptoeing around piles of monkey offal and expecting to be sacrificed to a crocodile! It was like one of the fantastic games of pirates and Indians and white hunters that she and Piers and Harry used to play as children.

Her foot slipped into a puddle and splashed muddy water up onto her bare legs. The minute sound of the splash sounded as loud as a tidal wave in the quiet of the sleeping village.

"Mm-mm?" A sleepy grunt came out of the shadowed veranda of the nearest hut. Piers raised his hand to check her and they all three stood like statues in the darkness, scarcely daring to breathe. After an enternity of silence the disturbed sleeper rolled over on his back and began snoring, and Meg let a trickle of air into her aching lungs.

This adventure was real. The icy fear that had spread down her spine left no more room for pretending that they were all just playing a game. She moved on with twice the caution she'd used before, so intent on creeping noiselessly through the shadows that she fell behind Piers and Kema and they had to wait for her at the edge of the village. They lifted her over the spiked palisade, here sagging low from years of heavy rains and tropical winds that tugged it loose from the earth. A trailing frill of white lace caught on one of the sharp branches and Meg snatched at it in an agony of fear lest the sound of ripping cloth waken someone else. Then she was down, stumbling ungracefully on the hard-packed mud strip between the palisade and the bush, and before she'd recovered her balance, Piers and Kema had swung themselves silently over the barrier to join her.

Half-crouching, Kema glided before them toward the dense fringe of small trees and bushes which bordered the tall, silent forest. Meg followed as closely as she could; it was hard to keep his dark figure in view against the even darker background of the bush, and she kept bruising her bare feet against unseen obstacles. He kept disappearing from view, then reappearing to beckon her onward. Behind her she heard Piers crunching over small bushes and vines with the confidence of a man who has not lost his boots.

Suddenly Kema disappeared behind a tall fringed fern so suddenly and completely that he seemed to have melted into the shadowy air. Meg hurried forward, eyes fixed on the spot where she'd last glimpsed Kema, and felt a sickening hollowness in her heart as her foot came down on nothing. She pitched forward, her other ankle caught in a thorny loop of vine, and her groping hands brushed through a light barrier of bracken and half-dead vines. It seemed to take forever, that headlong fall into darkness, and then she hit the ground with a thump that knocked the breath out of her. Something warm and rustling moved beside her; Meg shivered away from its touch and then recognized Kema's hand.

His hand was sticky, and there was an agonized catch to his breathing that hadn't been there before. "Kema, are you hurt?"

He grunted under his breath; Meg couldn't understand what he was saying. She began to take stock of her own condition. Something was pinning her in place like a long spike through her skirts. Meg rose to her knees, feeling upward along the thing, and found that it was a long spike—a tall wooden stake fixed in the bottom of the pit with its sharpened point upward. When she stood to tug her petticoats free, she kicked another such stake, and tardily recognized what had happened to them. They had fallen into an elephant trap—one of the great deep pits studded with pointed stakes that Kema had pointed out to her long ago in the bush around Talagouga. She had been incredibly lucky to come down between two stakes, suffering no worse damage than a torn skirt and a bruising fall. And Kema apparently hadn't been so lucky. Meg wished with all her heart for a light. Without knowing the extent of his injuries, she couldn't guess whether they dared haul him out of the pit.

"Piers?" she called upward, pitching her voice low to blend in with the small sounds of the bush at night.

"Shut up, woman," Piers hissed back. "Do you want to invite the entire village to come and see what they've caught?"

Meg felt a flooding relief that weakened her knees. Until she heard Piers's voice, she hadn't let herself speculate on what had happened to him. Now a loop of a fat vine came slowly down from the top of the pit and hit her in the face, providing its one answer. While she had been floundering about on her hands and knees in the bottom of the pit, Piers had gone into the bush and, with his customary efficiency, had cut some lengths of bush rope to haul her and Kema out with.

She interrupted his whispered instructions on how to use the loop of vine. "Kema's hurt. I don't know if he can get himself out. I don't know if we dare try. What if we hurt him worse?"

"We won't hurt him any worse than the crocodiles will," Piers said grimly. "Look, you fasten this loop around under his arms, then lift him up as much as you can. I can't take his full weight for long."

Crouching in the muddy bottom of the pit, Meg felt around Kema's body with shaking hands and tried to tie the vines as tightly as she could in the darkness. His skin was damp with a cold sweat and his body was limp in her arms. He must have fainted from the pain of his injuries, whatever they were. Meg felt over the limp naked body lightly and found no blood apart from the long scratch on the palm of his hand. Perhaps, she thought optimistically, he'd merely been knocked out by the fall, and there was nothing more wrong with him than a sore head and a scratched hand.

Kneeling under the limp, musky-smelling weight of Kema's body, Meg braced her back against the wall of the pit and raised him until she felt Piers take some of the weight on his length of the bush rope. As he lifted, the loop around Kema's chest tightened and his body fell a few inches, brought up short with a jerk that wrenched a grunt out of Piers and an agonized scream from Kema.

"Keep him quiet, for God's sake, can't you?" Piers hissed down.

But it was already too late. The slack limpness of Kema's dangling limbs told Meg that he had fainted again; but that one cry of pain had already brought shouts from the village. Before Piers had hauled Kema's unconscious body to the top of the pit, the glow of bobbing bush lights surrounded them. Meg heard a confused babble of African voices, then the solid smack of fists landing on flesh; then there was silence again, and as the torches approached the edge of the pit she could hear only the sizzle of the resinous gum that they burned.

First she saw a circle of flames, then a circle of black faces looking down at her. Meg stood up straight with her arms folded, trying to show no fear as she awaited their judgment. What had happened to Piers and Kema? What were they going to do with her? Whatever came next, she felt sure that she would do herself and Piers no good by cringing before their captors. She thought briefly of the unspeakable stories half-hinted at by traders and missionaries, of cannibalism and worse, and hoped that she would be able to continue not cringing until the end.

Two men came down on lengths of bush rope, sliding into the pit with practiced ease. They tied her wrists and ankles; she offered no resistance, and they moved carefully, as if they had been ordered not to hurt her. When they were done, a net was dropped into the pit and Meg was gently wrapped in it and raised like a parcel being swung out of a ship's hold. The entire operation was carried out in an eerie silence that frightened her more than anything they actually did to her. It seemed her fate had already been decided, and that it was too serious to talk about.

When she was lifted up to ground level, the bright flare of torches thrust forward into her face blinded her for a moment, and the heat of the flames frightened her. She jerked her head away involuntarily, smelling the burning gum and something acrid that after a moment she identified as her own singed hair. There was a single harsh command from somewhere in the darkness behind the dazzling lights, and the men holding the bush lights retreated to stand around her in a circle.

As Meg's eyes adjusted she made out two other forms trussed in nets like the one that had been used to lift her out of the pit. Piers moved slightly as she looked at him, the bright hair stirring in the torchlight, and her heart leapt with relief. If Piers was still alive, there was a chance. A chance for what, she couldn't say. But she began illogically to hope for another miracle. They had escaped so much already!

At another word of command, the torches were reversed and extinguished in the soft, moist earth. What on earth was going on? Meg strained her eyes in the darkness. Men were shuffling and whispering around her, but she could see nothing save a vague glowing patch, some afterimage of the bright flames burned on her retina. She blinked, shook her head, and peered through the meshes of the net. No, the patch of light was getting bigger and stronger instead of fading away as it ought. What on earth. . . ?

A skeletal figure, ten feet tall, with the grotesque head of a crocodile over a man's chest and an androgynous long grass skirt, stalked slowly forward out of the bush. The Fans around them parted to let the thing through. Meg could see it clearly; its head and body glimmered with a sickly dead-white light that outlined the monstrous features all too well. She gave an involuntary gasp and closed her eyes for a moment, willing the monster out of existence. A thing like that, straight out of the darkest superstitions of this black continent, couldn't be real. She wouldn't believe it.

When she opened her eyes it was still there, bending over the net that held Piers's body and chuckling softly to itself. It reached toward him with impossibly long arms whose ends were tipped with glowing claws.

The scream that tore from Meg's throat had nothing to do with her. It was an involuntary denial of everything she saw. But it startled the monster. It pitched forward, almost falling over Piers's body, and Piers wriggled and kicked out strongly with his bound legs. His feet swept under the grass skirt and the glowing thing fell sideways. One of its long arms flew off and landed near Meg; the crocodile head bounced and rolled the other way. She curled herself in a ball, willing to do anything to keep that long sticklike arm with its glowing claw from touching her; and through her terror she heard a sound that paralyzed her with its total incongruity.

Piers was laughing.

His deep, full-throated laughter seemed to fill the night, bouncing off tall straight trees, echoing off the shocked and immobile tribesmen, setting the stars overhead to dancing. With her eyes closed Meg could imagine him standing, miraculously freed of the net, his head thrown back as he laughed the way he must have done over one of his college pranks.

"Some Crocodile God!" he exclaimed in English.

Meg opened her eyes. As far as she could tell in the darkness, Piers was still lying on the ground, still swathed in the net. But now she could see that the impossibly long, sticklike "arm" which had so horrified her was in fact only a long crooked stick with something that looked like a crab's claw tied onto the end. The crocodile head was a carved mask, and the ten-foot-high monster had diminished into a scrawny old man whose stilts, concealed by the grass skirt, had been knocked from under him by Piers's lucky kick.

Turning his head, Piers addressed Meg. "It's only old JuJu Jake, that old drunk who used to hang around the factories at Lambarene, cadging drinks off me and any other trader who was fool enough to let him in the door."

While Piers spoke, the old man scrambled nimbly to his feet and retrieved his crocodile mask. The other paraphernalia, the glowing claws and the stilts and the grass skirt, he left scattered on the ground where they had fallen. He should have been a ludicrous figure, top-heavy in the enormous wooden mask, but with the mask he seemed to put on once again a menacing dignity that commanded the respectful attention of the tribesmen. He spoke in a low voice, jabbing one hand toward the captives and shaking the long snout of his mask toward the river side of the village.

"I wonder what he's using to shine himself up like that," Piers speculated. "Do you suppose he's found some phosphorus locally? No one's ever studied the mining potential of this area."

"Your detached scientific interest amazes me," Meg whispered back. How could Piers take the situation so coolly? She was scared out of her wits, and what difference did it make whether she died at the hands of a crocodile monster or a drunken old derelict Fan? "I'd rather know what they're going to do to us."

Her question was partially answered when the Fans slipped long poles through the upper meshes of the nets and marched their captives around the village palisade, two men holding the ends of each pole. Meg found herself next to Piers for part of this bobbing, uncomfortable journey, and took an illogical comfort in being able to glimpse his bright head in the starlit night. When the path narrowed and they had to go single file, she felt horribly lonely and scared; when Piers was beside her, she still hoped for a miracle.

"At least they're not sacrificing us on the spot," she whispered once when they were together. Perhaps they were only being deported from the village? She didn't mind a bit if JuJu Jake declared her *persona non grata*. To hell with solving the mystery of who had burned down Piers's factories and framed him! All she wanted was to get out of here.

Piers dashed this incipient hope when the next bend in the path brought them in talking distance. "No crocodiles in the bush," he whispered. "They're taking us to the river."

Meg remembered the half-eaten corpse she had seen tied to a stake in the Ogowe. Was that to be their fate? For once in her life she wished that she could be one of those fragile, delicate girls who fainted at every crisis. If she was going to be tied up for the crocodiles, she would just as soon not be conscious while it was happening.

Eighteen

It had taken Harry several days to arrange for a canoe and rowers to take him up the river from Talagouga. He encountered much the same problem Meg and Piers had met: Fans didn't hire out as rowers, and Mpongwes didn't care to row into Fan territory. However, he had two advantages over his younger brother. The rowers he wanted to hire did not know—because Harry himself did not know—that he wanted to go up the Spirit River. And Harry had been pursuing a successful career in the diplomatic service for six years. After dealing with the whims of a minor European royal personage and his three mistresses, Harry found a group of African natives comparatively easy to handle. A judicious bribe to the headman's number-two wife, a hint that the easy wages and easy pickings offered by the mission might come to an end—the combination of greed and pressure worked for Harry, where Piers had failed with money and Meg had succeeded with friendship.

The only problem was that, as usual, it took several days for Harry to figure out exactly where to apply the recommended dosage of greed here and threats there. And in that interval, he encountered another problem that had not seriously troubled Piers. Madame Hélène Fanchot was by no means eager to see her second big blond, handsome Englishman go out of her ken.

Harry thought Hélène a pretty little thing, and he quite enjoyed the subtle net of flattery and attention to his wishes that she wove around him during his stay at the mission. He felt she behaved quite properly in placing the correct ordering of his dinner and airing of his sheets ahead of her responsibilities in the mission store and primary school. Wasn't that what a woman was for—to make a man comfortable and to decorate his home? If she wanted to play at saving souls in her spare time, Harry had no objection, but he saw no reason for a woman to let herself go the way Madame Molinier, for instance, had done—thin, almost gaunt, with lines of worry etched into her forehead, and her hair carelessly strained back into a severe bun.

No, these dedicated sorts were all very well in their way, but Harry much preferred a pretty little girl like Hélène, who knew the worth of a real man and who wasn't averse to showing it in a discreet cuddle or so after dinner, when the shadows gathering around the deep veranda concealed a multitude of sins. Indeed, he quite regretted the necessity of quitting this comfortable haven for the desperate trip upriver, with what could only be a tragic confrontation at the end of it.

"Me, I do not at all see the necessity for you to follow this black-sheep brother of yours, 'Arry!" Hélène protested on the very eve of his departure. They were sitting on the veranda as usual, Harry in a native-made chair of cane and rocker and Hélène kneeling on a big cushion at his feet, with her skirts spread out about her like some soft, black-petaled, scented flower.

Harry set his jaw and gazed out over the bronze sheet of water that flowed under the Moliniers' veranda, absentmindedly stroking Hélène's smooth black tresses with one hand. "It's an affair of honor. You wouldn't understand."

He could scarcely mention the matter of this hussy who had run off with Piers or been abducted, not to a decent woman like Hélène; it was bad enough that she'd been exposed to the girl's influence for the short time that Piers and this Marguerite had stayed at the mission. He'd noticed that Hélène didn't like to hear the girl's name mentioned, and one had to respect a virtuous woman's purity of mind; so it wouldn't do to reiterate that there was another party in the case besides Piers, perhaps not a blameless one, but still a white woman who could hardly be abandoned to the jungle in Piers's feckless care.

"No, I would not!" She pouted most prettily; the effect was lost on Harry, who was still watching images of his own making in the smooth reflections of the river. "If he does not come back, there is no problem. And if he does come back, you can talk to him here. He must pass the mission; there is no other way. Why do you not wait here? Do we not make you comfortable?" It might be weeks, perhaps months, before that Piers returned—if he ever came back at all.

And in the interim . . . Hélène smiled to herself and leaned her head on Harry's knee. This big Englishman was even bigger and handsomer than his brother, and far more receptive to her attentions. If they married, would he want her to live in London? A dreary place, with its damp fogs and boiled mutton—but nothing, *nothing* could be as dreary as this backwater of Africa to which Fanchot had dragged her in his missionary enthusiasm! Yes, Hélène decided, she would marry the Englishman. He needed a woman to take care of him, and he wanted her; given just a few more days, she felt sure that she could fan that want into a fever of longing that he could not resist.

"Aren't you 'appy?" she prodded softly when Harry did not reply.

"With you?" Harry smiled down at Hélène. Yes, she was everything he wanted in a woman—sweet, softly rounded, and completely removed from that other, harder world of honor and tragedy where his meeting with his brother must be played out. "If I were free, Hélène, there is nowhere I'd rather be than with you." And for the moment, he really meant it.

" 'I could not love thee, dear, so much, loved I not honor more,' " he quoted, feeling a sharp, poignant satisfaction in the thought that he was giving up this sweet loving woman to go off into the trackless bush after his worthless brother. He had set himself two tasks that must be performed before he was free to enjoy the sweet temptations offered by women like Hélène: to rescue the woman Piers had abducted, and to make his brother see that he must not come back to disgrace the family by trial and imprisonment in a French penal colony. He would have to give Piers a choice—disappearance into the jungle, or to be left alone with Harry's loaded pistol—and he had to hope, for the family's sake, that the boy would take the clean way out.

And when he came back after that, Hélène would scarcely want to marry him—the man who'd forced his own brother to commit suicide! Her sweet, womanly soul would be revolted at the thought, and she'd never understand an Englishman's stern code of honor. Harry stroked Hélène's hair again, rather absently, as he might have petted a favorite spaniel; and his eyes as he stared across the broad expanse of the river were so grim and bleak that Hélène forbore to interrupt him again.

In the morning, he started off with all the provisions the mission store could supply, and with a full complement of healthy, able, slightly sullen Mpongwe rowers.

Meg felt slightly sick by the time the Fans had carried their three prisoners, bobbing and swaying in the nets of tough plaited vines, to the cliffs overlooking the Spirit River. Here they were unceremoniously dumped on the ground and rolled out of the entangling nets. Two men took Meg and cut the bonds on her wrists and ankles, while two more held her firmly by the arms to discourage any notions of escape. Looking around, she saw that Piers and Kema were undergoing the same treatment. Kema was standing, swaying slightly, but conscious again. His face was a mask over the pain he must be feeling; Meg guessed that he had broken several ribs in his fall, and the subsequent trip in a net must not have been the best possible treatment.

But how did it happen that she could see them? Meg looked up and realized that dawn had come while they were being carried through the bush. A high cloud cover kept the light dim, but at least she could see where they were going now.

A glance downward made her regret this last

fact. They were standing at the very edge of the precipice, near the cleft in the rocks through which they had ascended—was it only yesterday? Meg shook her head, bemused. So much had happened, so quickly. She needed to sit down and sort it all out.

The two men holding her by the arms pushed her closer to the edge of the rock, gesturing toward the broad rope of knotted vines. Meg looked down past uncounted feet of sheer gray rock, to the foaming current at the bottom, and her knees gave way of their own accord. She sat down ungracefully at the very edge of the rock, feeling her head whirl with something more than the aftereffects of the drug. The men who'd been holding her stood back, arguing among themselves. After a moment they shoved Piers forward and he sat down beside her. Kema leaned against a tree, unbound and unheld; evidently they'd decided that he was in no state to try escaping. Besides, there was nowhere to go. The cliffs were before them, a semicircle of armed Fan warriors behind them.

"They want us to climb down," Piers muttered.

"I guessed that." Meg swallowed and forced herself to look away from the hypnotic, dizzying fall of the cliff. "I can't do it."

"Good," said Piers. "I don't think we should cooperate anymore. Best thing is to jump for it. We might land in the water—it's pretty deep here, as I recall."

"What if we land on the rocks?" Meg whispered. Her throat was achingly dry and stiff at the very thought of that fall.

Piers shrugged. "Beats being taken down and staked out for the crocodiles. Quicker." His eyes changed and he reached for Meg's hand, but one of the warriors guarding them grunted and thrust the end of his spear between them. "Megsie, I'm sorry I got you into this. If we get out alive . . ."

"I got myself into it," Meg contradicted him. Her voice sounded thin and unnatural against the roar of the water so far below them, echoing up the sheer cliff walls. "You tried to stop me. Anyway, we are getting out. When you say the word, I'll just . . ."

Her throat contracted as she looked over the edge of the precipice, and she knew she could never force her nerveless feet to carry her over that sheer drop. "You go first," she whispered, trying to make a joke out of it. When Piers found out she hadn't followed him, it would be too late for him to do anything about it. She bowed her head and stared at her linked fingers, trying not to show the fear she felt, and worse, the utter desolation brought by the thought of being left alone with the Fans after Piers made his escape. Just because she lacked the nerve to jump didn't mean they should both go tamely to the slaughter.

When she raised her head, Piers was still seated beside her, looking at her with a mixture of tenderness and amusement that brought a lump to her throat. "You're not going to jump," he said. "You're afraid of heights. Why didn't you ever tell me?"

"Thought you'd send me back," Meg whispered. "You were always trying to anyway. If you'd known how scared I was . . . Anyway, I thought we might not have to come back this way."

"Yes. Well. Our friends don't seem to have left us much other option, do they?" Piers's eyes softened. "Don't worry, Meg. If you want to know the truth, I'm relieved to find there's something you are afraid of. After all, I've seen you put up with snakes, explosions, and cannibals without blinking an eyelash. You take some living up to, my love. Never mind. We'll work out some other way to escape. The jump wouldn't be too good for Kema anyway, in his condition."

"You said . . . better than crocodiles?"

"Oh, there won't be any crocodiles below." Piers dismissed that possibility with an airy wave of his hand. "Water's too deep and swift to appeal to them—they like a nice sandy bank where they can sun themselves and wait for their prey."

Meg gulped at the mention of prey. In a few minutes, because of her cowardice, they would be that prey—tied to stakes and waiting for a crocodile or some other predator to give them a quick death. Wouldn't it be better to jump, even at the risk of being smashed on the rocks?

"Piers, you *must* go," she whispered. "Quickly . . . now, before they do anything. Please!"

Piers shook his head and she felt shamed at her relief that he refused to desert her. She tried to force out another plea, but there was no more time. At a word from JuJu Jake, the Fan warriors prodded them with the broad leaf-shaped blades of their spears until they were standing at the edge of the "ladder" down to the river. Meg looked down, trying to gauge the first foothold she would need, while two warriors climbed nimbly down. The Fans were taking no chances on letting their captives reach the river first and unguarded.

The dizzying sight made her head swim and her knees buckle. The harsh commands of the warrior behind her came dimly through the roaring in her ears. A spear point pricked her in the back, piercing the embroidered lace of her chemise. It wasn't as frightening as what lay before her. Meg's knees gave way and she sank down in a tumbled heap, waiting numbly for a foot or hand to shove her off the cliff and down to certain death.

Instead, there was more agitated discussion, and when a hand grabbed her arm, it was to yank her back several yards to the relative safety of the tree where Kema leaned. In an undertone he translated the argument for Piers and Meg. It seemed the Fans placed great importance on taking victims alive to the crocodile god. A dead body wouldn't appease the offended spirit of the god. Two men were being sent back to the village to bring a magic charm to take away Meg's fear.

The "charm," when it appeared, turned out to be a polished cow horn, closed at the thick end with a wooden plug, and banded with copper wire. A wooden stem stuck out from one side of the horn to support a small clay bowl in which a live coal glowed, pulsing with an ominous reddish light. Meg shrank away as they brought the strange contraption toward her face. What savage torture was this?

"Don't *worry*," Piers muttered. "It's just hemp." He seized the cow horn by the narrow end and, setting it to his lips, drew in a deep breath to demonstrate. Now Meg saw that there was a handful of dried leaves under the burning coal, smoldering quietly away and releasing a thin spiral of blue smoke into the air. When Piers breathed in, the smoke disappeared.

He coughed once or twice and handed the contraption to Meg. "Native pipe," he wheezed, coughing out a little blue smoke. "Water in the cow horn—cools the smoke. Helps you relax, so you won't be so scared of the heights."

Meg took a cautious puff and bent over double, coughing. Piers barely rescued the pipe before she dropped it. He handed the cow horn up to Kema, who took several puffs with a grateful smile while Meg was still recovering from the first onslaught of the acrid fumes on her throat. A drink of water, thoughtfully provided in a dirty calabash with a crust of dried agouma clinging to its lip, soothed her throat so that she was able to go on smoking when the pipe returned to her.

After a few puffs she found that the bitter fumes no longer bothered her. The smoke still tasted terrible, but she didn't mind so much, and her muscles were relaxed so that she could breathe more easily. When the smoldering herbs in the bottom of the clay bowl were almost burned up, the old man in the crocodile mask lifted up the coal between two twigs and added another handful of his herbal mixture. Meg watched him without fear, now able to see his dual identity perfectly. He was an old drunken derelict who used to cadge drinks off the traders at Lambarene; he was also a god and the incarnation of the spirit of the crocodile. They were all gods. It made perfect sense. Perhaps if she smoked a little more she would be able to explain it to Piers.

Her head whirled and the ground underneath her seemed pleasantly soft. All around her, bathed in the milky light that came through a cloud-covered sky, the natural world and the men in it took on a new radiant glory. How beautiful life was! Trees, sky, ground—Meg threw her arms wide to embrace the universe, and the empty pipe fell unnoticed to the ground beside her. This was something like what she had felt for Piers the night before, but multiplied a thousandfold. Piers was a young god this morning, all gold and bronze and white against the ebony darkness of the half-naked warriors behind him; he was a god, and she his consort. She looked down over the edge of the precipice and knew no more fear.

"Feeling better?" Piers murmured in her ear. "Not so afraid of the climb down?"

She gave him a lazy, relaxed smile. "Of course I'm not afraid." They were gods. How could they die? The concept was ridi . . . redi . . . Oh, the word floated away from her, but no matter. Piers would understand without her saying it. "But it's silly to climb down," she said. "Why don't we fly?"

"My sentiments exactly." Piers helped her up with one hand solicitously under her elbow. Meg wanted to tell him she didn't need any help, she was perfectly capable of spreading her wings and flying by herself. But standing did seem to be a more difficult proposition. Her legs were ridiculously unsteady and the ground underneath her feet was tilting and swooping from side to side like the deck of the small coast steamer on which she'd come out to Africa. Really inexcusable of the crew to just stand there in an expectant semicircle, doing nothing about the instability of the deck!

"Tell them to stop that," she said severely to Piers. "It's not as if there was a storm or something."

Piers turned toward the circle of warriors, but

instead of speaking he snatched a spear from the nearest man and swung it in a wide circle about them, barking shins and knocking men off their feet. In the moment of shock after his sudden move he grabbed Kema's hand and hit Meg in the side with the spear butt. She saw it swinging toward her with mild interest, growing larger and larger until it hit her with a thud that knocked the breath out of her and threw her off balance. She started to speak harshly to Piers about his carelessness, but was distracted by the novel sensation of nothingness under her. Her full white petticoats swirled up about her face and hands, blinding and binding her. Or were they clouds? She had dreamed of flying like this, free and weightless and happy, and . . .

"Ow!"

The cold water hit Meg like a mighty dash of sobriety. She opened her mouth to shout another protest and got a drink of cold river water for her pains. The petticoats buoyed her up and caught on branches that trailed into the river, holding her against the fierce tug of the current. As she bobbed on the surface of the water, she heard three more splashes in quick succession. That would be Piers and Kema.

Three? Some confusion stirred in Meg's swimming, sodden brain. She pushed the hair out of her eyes and looked upstream to see three forms, two black and one white, floundering in the deep center of the stream. A moment later Piers was beside her, swept down by the current. He grabbed at the branch that was holding her. "Get onto the rocks, Meg! You'll be safe there!" He tore her petticoat free of the branch and gave her a firm shove into midstream, a push that sent her face underwater and filled her mouth and nose with stinging wetness. A moment later she bumped into a large, smoothly rounded black boulder and crawled atop that refuge, choking and spitting out water.

Piers was swimming toward her, striking out firmly with one arm while the other dragged a half-conscious Kema along. Behind them, the skeletal body of the Crocodile God pulled itself up onto a mass of twigs and branches and dead logs that some trick of the current had trapped against a bend in the Spirit River. The crocodile mask had been knocked awry, so that the old man seemed to have his head twisted around backward, and he clearly could not see where he was going. As he reached the top of the pile of dead branches, Meg saw the highest log give a mighty yawn that exposed an orange throat rimmed by yellowish teeth. She screamed in warning, but the slight sound was drowned out by a much louder scream as the real crocodile closed its mouth on JuJu Jake's body. Meg got a confused impression of glistening brown coils spilling out of the old man's midsection, of a red cloud staining the rushing green waters of the river; then Piers was beside her, holding her face against his wet shoulder and enclosing her with strong arms.

"Don't look . . . don't look," he repeated, rocking her back and forth like a child. And then, in a different tone he said, "Will you be all right here for a moment? With Kema? Good girl. I'll be right back."

He slid into the water and was gone before she could protest, striking out underwater for the curtain of green vines that covered the Fans' secret landing place. Meg held her breath, expecting at any minute to see another trail of red blood staining the water, oblivious of Kema moaning beside her. The vines rippled slightly; she had no other clue as to what had happened to Piers. Moments later, the sharp nose of a Fan canoe slid out through the green curtain. Meg tensed, ready to throw herself into the water rather than risk recapture; then, as she saw that Piers was the only occupant of the canoe, she relaxed again.

Piers steered up to the central boulder with a neat flourish of his paddle. "Spirit River transport for Talagouga, Lambarene, and points west, now departing," he announced. "All aboard, please. And look snappy. Those two Fans who were supposed to guard the canoes are busy trying to rescue Jake, but they may be a mite annoyed when they look around and notice that we're leaving so unceremoniously."

As he spoke, he helped Meg steady the canoe and lift Kema in. She scrambled in after Kema and seized a broken paddle that was lying on the floor of the canoe. "Oh, quit being funny and get us out of this!" she cried, and Piers pushed off until the full force of the Spirit River caught the canoe and swept them downstream at a breakneck pace.

Nineteen

"I hope you're sober now," Piers called over his shoulder after the first dangerously fast stretch of current was past.

"Why?" Meg wasn't sure if she was or not. The floating, dreamy sensation induced by the drugged smoke had vanished when the cold waters of the Spirit River closed over her head, but she still wasn't scared, and she had a vague feeling that wasn't natural. Shouldn't she be worrying about crocodiles, cannibals, and rapids, instead of thoroughly enjoying this mad dash down a stream that could smash their canoe like a matchstick?

"Because we're about to hit the Ogowe, and I don't want to stop to portage around the rapids. I'll need you to help steer."

Meg lifted one hand in salute. The current snatched at her paddle and tried to whirl it out of her grasp, and she hastily grabbed the handle firmly again. What was Piers worried about? At least they were going downstream this time. They'd never have made it upstream through three sets of rapids with only two able-bodied rowers, but going this way, the current would help. The sun was breaking through the clouds ahead of them, setting dancing rainbows alight in the spray where the two rivers rushed together, and Meg felt as though the light canoe was also dancing and swooping over the water.

The shock of the opposing currents meeting knocked the canoe sideways, and Meg put her knee on Kema when she was trying to lean over him to balance them again, and then she almost lost her paddle again. By the time they were straightened out again, they were bearing straight down on the ominous stretch where surface ripples marked the hidden rocks, and she found out just what was different about going downstream through rapids.

On the way up, they'd had some control over the canoe as long as the rowers kept a steady stroke and the steersman guided them away from the rocks. This was different. The long, light canoe was designed to carry a party of twelve rowers and all their supplies. Even in calm water it bobbed on the surface rather than splitting the stream with its pointed prow; in the grip of the rapids it was as uncontrollable as a cork in a fountain. Tossed this way and that, Meg braced both knees against the sides of the canoe to keep from being thrown out and used her paddle like a punting pole to push them off from one rock after another.

Would it never end? Meg's world narrowed to a pitiless stream of danger: rocks lunging at them from all sides, the ominous scraping as the canoe slid over other rocks, the spray in her face and the roaring water that almost drowned out Kema's moans. Her wet hair hung in her face, and she couldn't spare a hand to push it away; she shook her head like a dog coming out of the water and gripped the shattered remnants of the paddle, looking bemusedly around for the next rock to fend off.

There were no more rocks. The bronze stream of the Ogowe glided on, smooth and deceptively peaceful. In the sudden cessation of sound, Kema's moans of pain were loud in her ears. Meg looked at the paddle in her hands and discovered that she was holding only a splintered stick, and not a very long stick at that. Her hands stung as though they'd been blistered by the last few minutes of desperate work, and the palms felt sticky. She didn't really want to inspect that damage just yet, though, and there were more urgent matters awaiting her attention.

"Piers!" she screamed, without meaning to, her voice pitched to carry over the deafening roar of the rapids that had surrounded them a few moments ago. "Piers," she repeated in a quieter voice, "we have to stop."

"No time. They'll be following." Piers's broad shoulders moved from side to side with practiced ease, his paddle guiding rather than propelling the canoe as they headed downstream along the strong central current of the river. Meg looked at his back with a trace of envy. Didn't he ever get tired? And how had he managed to come through the rapids with his paddle intact, when hers was only a splintered wreck?

"Just long enough for me to bandage Kema's ribs," she pleaded. "And I need a new paddle—or a long stick, anyway—you can cut one in the bush, can't you? This isn't going to help us through any more rapids." She held up her broken stick to make the point clear.

"Don't need to," Piers mumbled, without even turning around to glance at her evidence. "I'll take care of the rapids. Have to keep going—"

A sharp crack rang out over the sound of the river, and something whistled by them. Piers stopped in mid-sentence and began back-paddling. Two more shots followed in quick succession, both passing well in front of the canoe.

"Stop where you are!" called an English voice. Meg almost dropped her paddle in surprise.

"What the devil does he mean, stop where we are?" Piers muttered in an undertone. "How the hell can I stop in the middle of the river? Meg, if you don't help me hold this damn canoe steady, we'll be swept right down into that bastard's line of fire."

"Piers, that sounded like—"

"Yes, I know he's speaking English. And whoever he is, he's armed. Now, will you help, or . . . For God's sake! Get down before you have us over!"

Meg got up on one knee, shading her eyes with the palm of her hand and searching the green wall of the forest to their left. She could almost swear she had seen a telltale flash of a golden head among the trees, but the river current carried them past the point where she could see between trees. "Piers, you're not going to believe this, but I think—"

Another shot interrupted her, this time passing perilously close to the bow of the canoe. "Piers Damery!" came the voice again, this time with a hollow booming sound as though the speaker were shouting through his cupped hands. "Bring the canoe in to shore and surrender yourself."

"He's crazy," Piers muttered under his breath. "We'll have to slip by when he's not expecting it. All right," he shouted loudly over the water, "I'm coming in." He turned the canoe slightly toward shore. "Lie down, Meg. There's no point in both of us presenting a target."

Instead, Meg took up the remains of her own paddle and began pushing toward the bank with long, sweeping strokes. Where she hit water the stick was useless, but here and there was a submerged rock on which she could punt the canoe toward shore. "Piers, we have to stop. Didn't you recognize that voice? That's Harry."

Piers paused openmouthed with his paddle raised out of the water. "You're hallucinating. Harry is in South America. Don't you think I'd know my own brother's voice?"

"Not as well as I would. You haven't seen him lately. And anyway, whether it's Harry or not, he's an Englishman and we can't just leave him here with the Fans about to attack."

"Want to bet we can't? The bastard just tried to kill us."

"He shot to stop us, not to kill."

The swift mid-channel current released the canoe at last and they spun into the slack water under the bank. Piers thrust his paddle at the tangle of roots above them to shove the canoe out into deep water again, but before he could find a firm place to push against the squishy tangle, a hand reached out through the vines and grasped the end of the paddle—a broad, long-fingered hand with reddish skin and a sprinkling of gold hairs on the knuckles.

"My God," said Piers, sitting back rather suddenly on his heels, "it really is Harry."

Harry Damery's face, red from sun and gilt with the prickles of an incipient beard, appeared between the vines. He was still holding on to the end of the paddle. "Will you come ashore peacefully, Piers, or do I have to hold a pistol on you?"

"Oh, coming, coming, certainly." Piers planted one foot on a submerged root, the other on the canoe, and reached a hand to Meg. "Although you'd be better advised to come with us. We can discuss what the hell you're doing here on the way down. Meg, can you make it from here, or do you want me to wade through the shallows and carry you?"

"*Meg*?" Harry's jaw dropped and his eyes bulged slightly as he stared at the slim, golden girl who leapt lightly from canoe to tree roots to semisolid land with the support of Piers's hand. "Meg," he repeated, shaking his head in disbelief.

Yes, he knew those wide gray eyes and that generous mouth, but never had he seen them set in a face so glowing with life. The African sun had gilded her skin to a shade like the bloom on a ripening peach, while the pale fine hair that had always been braided tightly at home now floated around her face like a halo. The scraps of garments she wore, with their rents that showed too much golden shoulder and thigh, and their soft white fabric that clung to her body like a second skin, showed off the full womanly curves that had always been hidden by Meg Beaumont's sensible English dresses.

"But, Meg, you're . . . you're beautiful!" Harry stammered. "Here, let me help you. You shouldn't have to scramble over these roots and things."

Meg was stunned by the look in Harry's eyes. Was this the moment she had dreamed of for so long? She'd almost forgotten her wish to have Harry look at her, just once, as though he loved and desired her. And now it wasn't quite what she had imagined. Well, one couldn't expect to feel transports of ecstasy when there were other things going on in the background, like mud and mosquitoes and a whole war party of Fans coming after them.

When Harry offered to help her over the tangle of roots that covered the bank, she lifted her arms slightly, ready for him to pick her up in his arms and carry her over the obstacles. His hands closed about her waist, but he was leaning forward and couldn't quite lift her high enough. Her feet caught in a trail of thorny vine and she heard another rip from her much-abused petticoats.

"Put me down, I can make it." It was easier to find her own way through the vines than to be half-carried, half-dragged by Harry. Meg heard a subdued chuckle in the background from Piers. Chin high, she hiked her torn petticoats to her knees and clambered over the vines with as much dignity as possible under the circumstances. Beyond the barrier of roots and vines was a cleared space where several Mpongwe rowers squatted around a campfire, while a hammock slung between two trees held Harry's camping gear. The ashes of two abandoned cooking fires off to one side helped Meg to identify the place. Wasn't this where she and Piers had rested after the accident on the way upriver?

Yes, and there were even some abandoned paddles lying on the ground, tokens of the haste with which they'd departed the campsite. Meg picked up two of the longest and strongest of the smooth wooden paddles and balanced them on her sore palms, trying to judge which might be more useful. It occurred to her that she was certainly developing some new skills on this trip. She'd never expected to become a connoisseur of Mpongwe river paddles.

"Now, Piers. You too. Come up to the campground where I can keep an eye on you." To Meg's astonishment, Harry actually drew a pistol from his pocket and pointed it at Piers.

"Listen, Harry," Piers began, "I don't know what game you're playing at, but we don't have time for this sort of nonsense. We're about to be attacked by some very angry Fans."

"What are fans?"

Rather than explain, Piers repeated his statement in Mpongwe. Behind Harry, Meg saw one of the Mpongwes turning grayish-blue as he whispered to the rest. A low-voiced babble broke out and was hushed instantly by the leader. One by one, the Mpongwe rowers began inching away from the campfire.

"Harry, your rowers are leaving."

"Don't try to distract me by such puerile tricks, Meg!" Harry's eyes never wavered from Piers and the gleaming blue-black barrel of the pistol pointed straight at his brother's midsection. Meg hefted her chosen paddle wistfully. Dared she swing it into the back of Harry's head? Only if he moved. Now there was too much risk that the shock would cause his finger to twitch on the trigger . . . and he was not more than four feet from Piers.

"Piers, I've heard all about the mess you left behind in Lambarene. Arson, abusing the natives, theft of the company's goods. If you went back, you'd have to stand trial, and the family would never recover from the disgrace. I came to offer you another way out."

"Very generous of you, old man," drawled Piers. His hands hung loosely at his sides and his whole body appeared relaxed—to anyone who didn't know him well. Meg tensed, recognizing the signs that he was about to spring forward.

So did Harry. He took a step backward. "Don't even think about it," he warned Piers. "Do you think I can't tell when you're planning to jump? You never could beat me wrestling—the way you telegraph your moves."

"Telegraph my moves! I like that!" Piers exclaimed. "You were three years bigger and older, that's all. Want to try a couple of falls now? I've been working for a living while you lived soft in the diplomatic corps. It'd be a different story now."

"Ha! I could take you with one hand tied behind my . . ." With a visible effort, Harry resumed his adult manner. "That won't work either, Piers," he said. "We have to discuss this thing like adults. You've got two choices. Either consider yourself my prisoner and return to Lambarene to give yourself up, or agree to take the decent way out now."

"Meaning?"

"On your word as a gentleman," Harry said, "I'd agree to leave you alone with the pistol for fifteen minutes. There's writing paper and ink in my gear, so you could write a letter first if there's anyone you want to say good-bye to. But first, you'd better tell me what happened to the girl you abducted."

"*Meg*?" Piers gave a short laugh. "Abducted? Somebody's been feeding you a pack of horse droppings, old fellow. I didn't abduct Meg, I merely failed to detach myself from her when she insisted on following me. And if you think you could have done any better," he added with feeling, "I'd . . . I'd just like to see you try, that's all!"

"Meg? Meg is the girl you abducted? But François Chaillot told me that girl was . . ." Harry stopped for a moment and tried to rearrange his features. "But then," he said slowly, "she *is* beautiful. Can't think how I failed to notice it before. But . . . no. François wouldn't have thought you abducted your own cousin. There was some other girl; something happened to her, and you're using Meg to cover it up."

Piers threw up both hands in disgust. "There is no other girl. Meg is the only one I've got. If she doesn't suit, I'm afraid you'll have to go back to England and pick out your own. In fact," Piers added thoughtfully, "you'd better do that anyway, for I've no intention of giving her up. Nor of taking what you describe as the 'gentleman's way out.' I'm not about to kill myself in remorse for crimes I never committed, Harry."

Harry sighed and nodded. "I suppose it's too much to expect you to take a decent attitude. But it's certainly too much to expect me to . . . What do you mean, crimes you never committed?"

"He means somebody is trying to ruin him," Meg burst in, "and we've been up the river trying to find out why. Harry, you can't really believe Piers did all those things? It's all as much a pack of lies as this latest story. Saying he abducted me! How could you take that seriously?"

"Wouldn't have," Harry admitted, "if I'd known it was you." His eyes slid over her figure and Meg suddenly felt naked. "At least, not before I'd seen you again . . ." To her relief, he turned back to Piers. "Well then, old fellow. If you're innocent, it certainly puts a different complexion on things. *If*," he emphasized grimly.

"What do you mean, *if*?" Meg demanded indignantly.

"Well," said Harry slowly, "it would certainly be the first time Piers was innocent of the charges against him."

"Those other times were different! Pranks! You can't hold that against him. Besides," Meg added triumphantly, "you can't tell me Piers has ever lied to you!"

"No. That would be a first time too." Slowly, almost reluctantly, Harry slid the pistol down into the waistband of his trousers. One hand hovered near the butt, as though he was still not totally convinced. "Look here, Piers. I think you'd better consider yourself my prisoner for the moment. If you are innocent, we've got to go down to Lambarene and get all this officially straightened out. You can't go on skulking in the bush like this."

"Nothing I'd like better," said Piers, "but if we don't get moving, we're all going to be officially dead." In a few terse sentences he explained about the war party of angry Fans that they could expect to catch up with them at any minute.

Harry shook his head in disbelief. "Do you really expect me to take a story like that seriously? It's like something out of the *Boys' Own Adventure Magazine*."

"Your rowers took it seriously," Meg said. "They've left."

Harry spun around and looked at the deserted campground. Then he ran down to the landing place where his canoe had been tied up. Piers leaned back against a tree and laughed immoderately.

"Come on, Harry," he called, "you're going to have to use your prisoner's canoe for transport back. We'd better get going." Grabbing Meg's arm, he towed her ruthlessly through the thorny vines and over the roots half-submerged in mud.

"Wait a minute!" Harry came breathless through the bushes, making heavy going of it. He jumped into the middle of the canoe and landed on Kema's feet. Kema yelped in protest and Harry shifted his bulk, nearly capsizing the canoe while Meg scrambled into the stern. "What's this? A prisoner?"

"A friend." Piers took his paddle and shoved off from shore.

"Wait! I hear my fellows coming back!"

The splash of paddles upstream was just audible over the sound of the river current.

"Those aren't," said Piers between his teeth, "your fellows. And believe me, you don't want to stick around and meet this lot."

With a last dexterous twist of his paddle he guided the canoe into the swift water in mid-channel. Meg bent to her own paddle in the stern and they swept around the bend in the river just ahead of the pursuing Fans. The roar of the rapids ahead of them drowned out Harry's demands that they stop a moment and talk this over.

Twenty

After that supremely nasty stretch of submerged rocks and rapids that they had just passed, this second set of rapids held no fears for Meg. Well, almost none, she amended as the black cliffs rose high on each side and she saw the high black rock sticking out of the center of the river with its foaming torrent of white water on either side. But there wasn't time to be properly frightened; they were past the rock before she'd begun to imagine what could happen if the canoe overturned, sliding down the wall of white water with a sickening swoop that left her stomach somewhere near the top of her head.

Harry turned halfway around and Meg saw the blue-black gleam of his pistol. "Get down!" he yelled. Before she could respond he raised his pistol and let a shot fly to one side. Meg ducked her head to give him a clearer field of fire. His shout of triumph rang out over the rushing water, and Meg thought she heard a scream and a splash behind them.

"That'll slow them!" Harry shouted. "Shot the steersman. Canoe capsized." Meg grinned and nodded at him and bent her attention to steering through the last of the rapids. It really was a pity they hadn't remembered to grab a paddle for

Harry, Meg thought; she hated to see all that muscle going to waste while her own arms and shoulders ached abominably from the effort of steering and fending off rocks. But she wouldn't trust Harry with her own paddle. He probably had no idea what to do with it. No, better to leave him managing the shooting gallery—she'd have even less idea what to do with a gun.

Harry blew on the barrel of his pistol and put it away with a satisfied expression. Meg risked a glance behind her as the current slowed. She saw nothing at first but the rocks through which they'd steered; then one of the rocks bobbed in the current, turned slowly, and became the outline of an overturned canoe with two men clinging to it. Even as she watched, the canoe wedged itself between two rocks in midstream and the current carried them on, out of sight of the Fans.

As they went on downstream, the river broadened again, and the sharp cliffs became lower, smoothing out to hills covered with the usual tangled mass of green vegetation. If they'd had time to slow down and enjoy the trip downriver, it would have been pleasant to drift with the current, watching the brilliantly colored flowers and birds that dotted the walls of green on either side, fishing over the side of the canoe and holding hands with . . .

Meg frowned in an effort to resolve the blurred image of the man she held hands with in her fantasy. Tall he was, certainly, broad-shouldered, with piercing blue eyes and hair that gleamed like gold in the African sunshine. All that was clear enough. It was just the name that was giving her some trouble. The sight of Harry had shaken her. The way he looked at her had been still more troubling. No woman with any sense, given the choice between solid sensible Harry and scapegrace Piers, would choose the remittance man over the diplomat. And it seemed that Meg had the choice, or might have. . . .

No, not if Harry knew what had happened between her and Piers. He might think he wanted her now, but no man would take his little brother's leavings. Meg thought she ought to feel humiliated at that, but all she felt was a sense of relief that the decision was out of her power. She took up the paddle and pulled forward with long, steady sweeps that, added to Piers's paddling and the thrust of the current, sent the canoe shooting forward so rapidly that the green banks of vegetation on either side were no more than blurs dotted with flashes of red and yellow flowers.

One more set of rapids to get through, and then they'd have a clear journey down to Talagouga and the safety of the mission—for surely the Fans, even if they picked themselves up out of the river and followed on, would hardly dare attack the mission? Hot baths, Meg thought. A decent dress, for I'm sure Madame Molinier will lend me something. Cooked food. Civilization. Safety!

And failure, for they'd never discovered why the Crocodile Society was so set against Piers and his trading firm, or how that grudge could have inspired someone to frame him with brandy and hired witnesses. What would happen when they returned to civilization? Trial . . . arrest . . . the penal colony Harry had hinted at?

Impossible! Meg paddled furiously, pushing against the river water as though it were a palpable enemy that she could defeat by sheer force of will. She would not permit that to happen to Piers. It was inconceivable, anyway, that a man could be sentenced to a penal colony because of rumors and a bad reputation and a bunch of obviously perjured African witnesses. And where had all this talk of arrest come from, anyway? Before they left Lambarene, the French authorities had seemed content to let Piers drink himself to death in the top half of his abandoned factory. The only new charges against him could be of burning down the factory with François Chaillot's goods in it, and of abducting Meg herself. Meg could disprove the abduction charge, and surely François Chaillot would not prosecute Piers, especially when Meg could testify that Piers had almost lost his own life in the explosion that destroyed the factory.

Ridiculous, that Harry should think Piers was in any danger from the law! But Meg was uneasily aware that she knew very little of French law. Such blatant injustice couldn't happen in England, of that she felt sure. But in French territory—with no powerful friends to stand by Piers, and with even his own brother no more than uneasily half-convinced of his innocence—who knew what might be the outcome?

Meg was so busy devising a plan to smuggle Piers out of French territory and into the nearest British crown colony that she completely missed his low call of warning. A moment later, before she had time to react, the long pointed bow of the canoe was entangled in a net of fine twisted hairs, daubed all over with some sticky resin and hung from one end to the other with little jingling brass bells. Meg didn't need Piers's instructions to start back-paddling while he hacked at the net with his belt knife, trying desperately to free the canoe. Before more than half a dozen strands had parted, another net dropped over their heads, and Meg put up her hands to keep the disgusting sticky stuff away from her face.

"What the hell is this about?" roared Harry, struggling in vain to reach his pistol. The entangling meshes of the net clung to his arms and shoulders and kept him from moving more than a few inches.

Meg peered through the net and realized that they had floated straight into a natural trap. At this point the deepest channel of the river, where the current was swift and strong, ran close to a small island. The net that had entrapped them had been strung just underwater, from this island to the left bank of the river, where it would catch anything coming downstream. A canoe heading upstream, on the other hand, would naturally pass between the island and the right bank, where a broad stretch of shallow water gave easy passage.

Harry was still reaching for the pistol in his waistband, fingers straining white through the meshes of the net. It had been less than a minute since the first bells sounded as they ran into the trapline. Now splashing sounds behind her alerted Meg that canoes were being slid into the water. She twisted her head, at the cost of an agonizing pull on her hair where the sticky net had wrapped around the short fine strands at the back of her neck, and saw two canoes full of painted Mpongwe warriors pulling for them.

"Thank God," she sighed, "it's only Mpongwes, not Fans."

"Damned if I know how you can tell. And what difference does it make anyway? They're all a bunch of damned savages and they need to be taught a lesson if they think they can treat Englishmen this way." Harry's straining fingers had reached the butt of the pistol. He drew it out of his waistband and pointed it somewhat unsteadily at the lead canoe.

"Don't be a fool, man!" Piers had been patiently working, all this time, to free himself by sawing through one fine strand after another with his belt knife. Now, with one arm free to the elbow, he swung his whole body forward against the net and chopped down hard on Harry's wrist with the edge of his hand. The pistol bounced down into the bottom of the canoe and hit Kema on the side. Kema yelped and Harry called Piers a traitor.

"There's obviously some mistake," Piers said. "You shoot one of these gentlemen, we'll have a blood feud on our hands, and then they'll be sure to kill us. Now, will you shut up and let me handle this?"

As the leading canoe approached them, Meg thought she saw expressions of disappointment on the faces of the warriors in front. "Only white men and a Fan!" exclaimed one of them. He turned to Piers and asked in halting pidgin what had happened to the Mpongwe rowers who had taken the white people upstream.

"I assume the one you're really interested in is M'nika," Piers drawled.

The spokesman for the group nodded his head vigorously at the mention of the young Mpongwe's name.

"Bad-wife palaver, hey? Well, I'm afraid he's—"

"Harry," Meg whispered, "kick Piers."

"Huh?"

"*Make him shut up*!"

The urgency in her tone communicated itself to Harry. Without another question, he kicked Piers on the ankle hard enough to make him gasp and break off.

"What did you do that for?"

Harry shrugged and looked at Meg.

Leaning as far as she could toward the Mpongwe canoe, Meg summoned up her halting reserves of Pidgin English and proposed that if the warriors would let them go, she would tell them where they could find M'nika. At once both canoes full of men glided up to the net and they carefully lifted it free of the white party, inch by inch. There was some growling and complaint when they saw how many strands Piers had sawed through, but Meg quickly pointed out that nets could be mended, whereas the honor of the Mpongwe village could be retrieved only with her help.

When they were free at last, she told their captors that M'nika had stayed behind in a Fan village on the Spirit River, where he had been initiated into the Crocodile Society together with the other rowers. Now that M'nika had all the bloodthirsty Fans of the Spirit River as his society brothers, he proposed to come back down the Ogowe, raid this village, and steal the headman's wife, selling the rest of the villagers to the rubber plantations in the Belgian Congo. She, Piers, and Kema had overheard these plans and sneaked out of the Fan village at dead of night, just so they could come downriver and warn their good Mpongwe friends of the horrid fate awaiting them.

Piers's mouth fell slightly open as he heard this story, but he didn't interrupt her. Harry was more of a problem. He hadn't been in Africa long enough to become familiar with Pidgin English, and he kept muttering, "What? I don't understand . . . But that's not what you told . . . Slow down, will you?" until Piers kicked him on the ankle to shut him up.

The Mpongwes fell into vigorous debate after hearing Meg's story. "What are they saying?" Meg demanded. Her few words of Mpongwe were totally inadequate to follow the many voices all talking at once.

"One party wants to run away into deep bush," Piers said. "The other wants to stay and fight it out."

"Tell them," Meg suggested, "that they don't have time to run away, because the Fans are right behind us. If they made it through the rapids, that is."

"Oh, they've picked themselves up by now," said Piers. "Can you paddle the canoe past this damned net if I hold it up for you?"

The bells tinkled again when Piers lifted the net to let their canoe pass under, but the Mpongwes made no move to stop their departure. Once they were safely on the other side, Piers called back the information that the Fans were heading downstream at this very moment.

"Now," he said, "paddle like hell!"

"I had a feeling you were going to say something like that," Meg sighed, taking up her paddle with blistered hands and aching shoulders. Piers was right, of course. The best thing they could do was to get well out of sight before the fight they had tried to foment got started. Still, she couldn't resist pausing for one glance back at the island. Two young Mpongwes were in the water, working furiously to restring the net, while the rest of the men concealed themselves on the island.

"I don't think the Fans will get past this so easily," she said with satisfaction, thrusting her paddle into the water and pushing with all her might.

"You're all totally irresponsible," said Harry. "Fomenting tribal war! I should report this to the authorities."

They were past all but the easiest rapids by now, and Meg's hands were terribly sore. She lifted her paddle and shoved it at Harry. "Here. Row like hell, as Piers suggested, and maybe you'll live to report us officially."

Behind them, the explosions of rusty flintlocks loaded with iron shards signaled the official beginning of hostilities.

They made it through the last rapids without incident, unless one counted Harry's turning pale green and vomiting over the side of the canoe an incident. On the far side, Meg finally persuaded Piers to halt and let her bandage Kema's ribs with strips torn from her last petticoat. They grounded the canoe on a long golden sandbank that rose gently out of the shallow water, shaded by the tall trees of the forest and cooled by a gentle breeze from the Sierra del Cristal behind them. It might, under other circumstances, have been an idyllic resting place, were not the tempers of all the party too jangled to permit them to enjoy it.

Piers was on edge; he would much have preferred to go straight on down to Talagouga, without counting on the Mpongwe villagers to hold off the remnants of the Fan war party. All the time they were halted, he prowled back and forth at the water's edge, looking upstream and fiddling with Harry's pistol. Meg understood his feelings and worked as quickly as she could to make Kema comfortable, but she snapped at him when he asked her for the third time to hurry up.

"I'm not a battlefield surgeon, Piers. I don't even know what I'm doing. Give me your knife." She had washed Kema's cuts and felt as gently as she could along his side, trying to verify her guess that a couple of ribs were broken. Now she hacked off her last whole petticoat at the knee and rinsed off the muddy, lace-fringed frill in the river water. "All I can do is wrap this around and hope it holds him together till we reach the mission."

"If we reach the mission." Piers resumed his moody pacing.

"We'll get there. Don't get any ideas about disappearing into the bush, little brother. For once in your life you're going to face the music like a man. And until we get to civilization, I'll just take charge of that." Harry retrieved his pistol from Piers's grasp.

"Oh, certainly, certainly, just do me a favor and shoot the Fans first," Piers requested. "Dammit, man, where do you think I'm going?"

"To Lambarene. To answer the charges against you."

Piers stopped pacing and stared at his brother. "I thought you'd decided that I should die in the jungle rather than disgrace the family by standing trial. Why don't you shoot me now and save time?"

"Harry, *no*!" Meg rocketed to her feet and plunged between the brothers, trailing scraps of white lace and muddy muslin. "Piers, stop aggravating him. You're both acting like fools. Why can't you be reasonable?"

Harry's gaze dropped from Piers's face to Meg's wide gray eyes. "Why not, indeed?" he said softly. His hand went out to caress her shoulder, then drew back as if her bare skin had burned him. "Don't worry, little Meg. Piers has been aggravating me for upwards of twenty years. If I haven't killed him yet, he'll not goad me into it at this late date. But for once in his life he's going to do the right thing, if I have to march him into Lambarene at pistol-point. Even a formal trial is better than having a Damery run fugitive in the jungle, to be brought in at last by some native police."

"I'm not running away!" Piers exploded between clenched teeth. "I'm doing my damnedest to get you back to civilization in one piece, though God knows why I try."

"God knows why you do anything, from dancing naked in a fountain to starting a tribal war. *I* gave up trying to understand you long ago."

"It was the ladies," Meg interrupted.

"What?"

"It was the girls who were naked in the fountain, not Piers. And I'm the one who tried to start a tribal war just now, and you'd better hope I succeeded, or we'll all be dead before we get to the mission. Can't you get anything straight, Harry?"

Tucking the pistol in the waistband of his trousers, Harry slowly unbuttoned his coat. "Poor Meg," he said, "you're confused, and no wonder. After being at Piers's mercy all these days in the wilderness, you must feel you have to defend him. But don't worry now. Your ordeal is over. From now on, I'll take care of you." He took off his jacket and laid it over Meg's shoulders. "You must be cold," he said gently.

"Cold? Why, no, I'm . . ." Meg broke off, her cheeks flaming. Of course, Harry was too much a gentleman to say what he meant, that she was indecently exposed in nothing but her chemise and the tattered remains of a single petticoat. But somehow, his reluctance to say it made her feel more naked than Piers's matter-of-fact acceptance of the situation. "Thank you, Harry," she murmured, looking down at the sand and trying to choke back the unreasonable resentment she felt. He was trying to take care of her. It was what she'd always wanted. Piers never took care of her—he expected her to take care of herself, and in sheer surprise and vexation she'd found herself doing more than she ever thought she could. Why did she find Harry's tender care so much more irritating than Piers's cheerful teasing? It was all too confusing—she would do better to concentrate on the simple tasks in front of her. "I'd better get back to Kema."

"You had indeed," Piers concurred. He was scowling angrily at her, though she couldn't think what she'd done to offend him.

While Meg knelt and finished the task of wrapping Kema's ribs securely, the two men paced on opposite ends of the sandbank, Piers watching upstream for the appearance of their pursuers and Harry watching Piers as though he might dart into the jungle at any moment. Men! Meg gave the bandages an unnecessary twist and apologized when Kema groaned. Why did Piers have to tease Harry every time he opened his mouth? Why did Harry have to be so wrapped up in the tragic nobility of surrendering his own brother to the authorities that he couldn't see the plain fact of Piers's total innocence?

Piers was incorrigible, but Meg had one more try at talking sense into Harry when they lifted Kema into the canoe prepratory to shoving off. "I'll be back in a minute," Piers said when Kema was lifted in. He turned and took a few paces toward the bushes that clustered along the southern tip of the sandbank.

"Halt!" Harry's voice rang out like a military command, and the pistol was in his hand before Piers could turn.

"For God's sake, man," Piers said irritably without turning his head, "I have to answer a call of nature. You've got Meg and the canoe. Do you really think I'm going to disappear into the bush and leave you alone with her?"

Harry's face turned red and he shoved the pistol back. "All right. But don't be long."

"Harry, I wish you'd stop treating Piers like a fugitive from justice," Meg pleaded in an undertone as soon as Piers was out of earshot. "You must see how ridiculous all these stories about him are, and you're just irritating him. You don't really think Piers would commit arson, do you? Abuse the natives? Steal from his trading firm?"

"I long ago lost count of the things Piers has done that I couldn't really believe," Harry said. "Even if half the charges against him are lies, there's enough in the other half to stain the honor of a Damery."

"They're *all* lies!" Meg cried.

"One thing I can see for my own eyes, for which I'll never forgive him. And that's what he's done to you. To drag an innocent English girl through the bush, bleeding, half-naked, subject to the torments of black savages! And possibly worse, for all I know." He lifted one of Meg's hands and pressed a reverent kiss on the blistered palm.

"Oh, stop making a mountain out of a mole-hill!" Meg snapped. "I insisted on going along with Piers—he couldn't have stopped me. And your hands will be bleeding too by the time we get to Talagouga, if you take your turn with the paddle. We're not hardened to the bush life the way Piers is, that's all."

"I should be sorry to see a lovely Englishwoman become 'hardened,' as you put it, Meg," said Harry. He turned her hand over and over, stroking her long sun-browned fingers and staring downward at the sand. "Meg, I swear it will make no difference between us—you know I'll always take care of you, whatever the answer. But I must know the truth. Did Piers . . . take advantage of you?"

Meg's face burned with more than sunburn and she snatched her hand free of Harry's grip. "No!" she snapped, knowing her denial for the truth, knowing Harry would think it was a lie. The nights of love she and Piers had shared were above that sort of coarse interpretation. Only Harry, who'd never understood Piers, would think that he had just taken advantage of her unprotected state to enjoy a few nights' pleasure.

"I wish I could believe that," said Harry. "But it's hardly credible—alone together in the jungle for so long, unchaperoned. Can't you bring yourself to tell me the truth, Meg? Remember," he warned her, "I know what sort of man my brother is."

"And I know what sort of man you are," Meg said. "A stuffed shirt!"

Harry's face reddened again at the childish insult. "Oh, yeah? And you're a hussy! You didn't even think to cover yourself decently until I begged you to!"

Piers emerged from the clump of bushes, and with unspoken agreement Meg and Harry dropped their quarrel at once. They were standing perfectly quiet, gazing out over the river, when he came up and proposed that they get going at once. He was grinning, Meg noticed, and when they were pushing the canoe into the water he gave her a friendly pat on the rear, which she didn't even resent, so glad was she to find that his ill temper had blown over.

There were some reeds clustering around the edge of the sandbank, and as Meg waded into the shallow water to get into the canoe she found the perfect reply to Harry's stuffy closed mind in the reeds. By some miracle the pocket hanging from the waist of her petticoat was still whole and untorn; she put her revenge in there.

She waited till they were well out in midstream, where Harry needed both hands to manage the paddle, before she put the frog down his back.

By the time they reached Talagouga in late afternoon, hot, thirsty, and tired, conversation in the canoe had degenerated to a series of teasing jabs reminiscent of their squabbles in the schoolroom. Meg was annoyed with Harry for his oft-expressed intention of taking care of her and with Piers for making her look like a bedraggled mess that somebody needed to take care of. Harry was thoroughly irritated with the irresponsible attitude shown by both Piers and Meg, but still determined to save Meg from herself and to bring his erring brother to justice. And Piers preserved an attitude of ironic detachment that both Meg and Harry found unspeakably annoying.

"Just tell me this, Piers," said Harry for perhaps the fortieth time as they glided downstream. "If you were framed, who did it? Huh? Don't try to blame this misguided bunch of natives. They'd have no reason to attack a white man, and if they did so, they'd be much more straightforward about it."

"They would," Piers agreed. "They were . . . on the Spirit River . . . quite straightforward, I'd say. I don't know why they didn't simply feed me to the crocodiles when I interrupted their burning of the factory at Talagouga."

"Neither do I," said Harry with satisfaction, "*if* it happened as you say."

"You don't know your nether parts from a hole in the ground," Piers retorted, paddling forward with short vicious strokes.

"And you don't know of any white man who'd want to frame you in this manner?" Harry persisted.

"I already told you. The missionaries wouldn't interfere. Cavanaugh and Walters may be my trade rivals, but they're English gentlemen. And François Chaillot stood my friend through the whole stinking mess. No, there has to be some other explanation."

"Then," said Harry, "I hope you can find it before I deliver you to the French authorities. You'll have one more chance to take the gentlemanly way out tonight, Piers. If you don't take it—if you don't care enough for your family to spare them the disgrace of a trial—we'll have to go on to Lambarene in the morning. For I cannot and will not countenance your continued flight from justice."

"For God's sake," Meg exploded, "you sound as if it would give you pleasure to see Piers shoot himself!"

Harry turned to look back at her. His lips were compressed to a taut line, and the pain in his eyes shocked her. "Don't take the Lord's name in vain, Meg. It's unbecoming in a woman. And stay out of this. It's between Piers and myself. A man must do what a man must do."

"At least we're agreed on one thing," said Piers. "It's nothing to do with Meg."

"Of course not," Harry agreed. "Have to keep a lady's name out of it, what?"

They nodded at each other and resumed rowing. Meg sank back against the stern of the canoe and wished she had another frog.

Better yet, two frogs.

Twenty-One

There was an unfamiliar boat anchored in the river at Talagouga: an ungainly, snub-nosed craft with a French tricolor fluttering above a plain gray-painted deck. The sight of it depressed Meg even before she knew what it was.

"A French gunboat," said Harry. "Well, well . . . it looks as if my responsibility ends here."

"It does indeed," said Piers. "Does this mean you'll stop nattering on about leaving me in an empty room with a loaded pistol?"

"Shouldn't think I'll be given the opportunity." Harry weighed the smoothly balanced dueling pistol in his palm. "You could, of course, be shot while trying to escape . . ."

"I wouldn't dream of trying to escape, old man," said Piers with his blandest smile.

"And you couldn't shoot Piers!" put in Meg, indignantly to cover her fear. "Your own brother!"

Harry glanced up and down her bedraggled, sunburned figure. "After what he's done to you, I'd be a cad if I didn't want to." He sighed deeply and pocketed the pistol. "But I'm afraid you're right. Doubt I could bring myself to do it, even if honor demands."

They tied up the canoe and made their way up the steep path to the mission station in an apprehensive silence. Meg wondered when Piers would be arrested, and who had been sent to do the task. If only it was a reasonable man, someone she could talk to! She could see from Harry's reactions that the rumors about Piers must have been blown all out of proportion while they had been exploring upriver. She pictured the tubby little official who had tried so earnestly to dissuade her from going inland in the first place, and her heart sank. A man like that, wedded to his bureaucratic rules and regulations, would hardly listen to reason.

As they rounded the last curve in the path, Meg heard a muffled exclamation burst from Piers's lips. She stopped, massaging her aching side, and looked up to the broad veranda of the mission house, where a familiar slim, dark figure lounged on one of the missionaries' native-built chairs.

"François!" Meg felt as though her sore feet had been given wings. She fairly danced up the path ahead of Piers and Harry, elated at discovering a friend where she'd feared to meet some stuffy old French government official. François Chaillot had always taken Piers's side, even when things were blackest against him; surely he could persuade this man with the gunboat not to arrest Piers until he'd heard both sides of the story!

"François, how absolutely marvelous to find you here! Tell me, who brought that gunboat up the river? Is it true they've come to arrest Piers? You won't let them, will you?" Meg fell into the chair beside François, mopping her brow and breathing hard from the last dash up the path. She noticed that François was looking at her rather oddly, but she didn't have time to explain what had happened to her clothes—and it was too long a story, in any case. First they must get this matter of Piers's arrest out of the way.

"How do you happen to be at Talagouga just now when we need you? Oh, of course, you must have come to tell them what nonsense all these stories are. *You* know I wanted to go with Piers, he didn't abduct me, and of course you don't blame him for the explosion that destroyed your goods. I bet you were wonderfully relieved to hear that he was still alive, weren't you?"

"Wonderfully," François Chaillot agreed, his lips curling in a smile that somehow did not convey any warmth to his glistening black eyes. "And you, *ma chère* Marguerite? You seem to have been through a considerable ordeal."

"Oh, nothing to signify," Meg assured him, but somehow his penetrating glance made her glad of Harry's jacket over her shoulders. "I'll tell you about it later, but first we've got to settle about Piers. You know, Harry seems to have got the ridiculous notion that all these things that have happened are Piers's fault. His own brother! I'm *ashamed* of him. But you can talk some sense into him, can't you?"

"I look forward to meeting Mr. Harry Damery again," François agreed.

Just then, as Piers and Harry were about to reach the veranda, Madame Molinier and Hélène Fanchot swooped down on Meg with little cries of protest and alarm. "*Ah, la pauvre petite*! How she must have suffered. *Toute nue*! It is a scandal!"

"I'm not totally naked," Meg said with hauteur. She glanced down at the remains of her petticoat, ripped off at the knee and torn from there to mid-thigh. "Just *almost* naked. It's quite different."

All her dignity did not save her from being carried off into the mission house, where the good ladies fussed over her with hot baths and combs for her hair and clean clothing and all the little luxuries that Meg had been dreaming of on the way back down the river. Now they meant less than nothing to her; she was in a fever of impatience to get back to the veranda, to hear what Piers and Harry and François had decided to do about this new complication of the French gunboat.

In the end she flatly refused to sit still in a spare bedroom while her newly washed hair dried and had the tangles combed out of it. Dressed in a black dress of Hélène's, a dress that was too large almost everywhere and several inches too short, with her ankles showing scandalously beneath the skirt hem and her damp hair clustering in tangled ringlets about her brow, she marched out onto the veranda and demanded flatly to know what the men intended to do next.

François Chaillot raised one dark, silky eyebrow and somehow made Meg feel that she had been both rude and childish. "We were just discussing that very point, *ma chère* Marguerite. There are certain complications . . . Pray join us." He indicated the broad hammock that swung invitingly from the porch beams.

Meg didn't want to lounge in a hammock while Piers's fate was being discussed, but still less did she want to disrupt the conversation any more by having one of the men jump up to fetch her a chair. She compromised by sitting primly in the exact center of the hammock, ankles together and hands folded.

"*Une jeune fille bien élevée,*" muttered François under his breath. "One would scarcely credit the adventures she has been through. I am afraid, my dear Piers, that your forcing the lady to accompany you will cause the authorities to look even less favorably upon your case."

Piers was lounging on a long cane-covered chaise, white-clad legs crossed at the ankles and hands relaxed at his sides. He seemed to have fared better than Meg in the matter of clothes; at least his shirt and trousers fit him reasonably well. Meg thought he seemed almost indecently calm in the face of François's preposterous accusation. "He didn't force me. I forced him to take me."

Piers opened one eye and surveyed Meg's bedraggled figure with a lazy smile. The curve of his lips made Meg long to bridge the space between them. She needed to feel his mouth on hers again, to feel him holding her close and molding her body against his as though he couldn't bear to let her go. Ever since Harry had appeared on the scene, Piers had been oddly detached. Did he regret the passionate commitment he'd made in the jungle? But he didn't seem like a man who regretted anything—only like one who no longer cared very much about anything, including whether French soldiers took him away to a rigged trial and a penal colony. His pose of indifference hurt Meg like a physical wound. If only she could lie in his arms again, she would know whether he still cared—about her, anyway—and then she might have the strength to fight for him.

But why wasn't he fighting for himself?

Both of François's eyebrows shot up at Meg's assertion. "You . . . forced M'sieu Piers to take you with him? At spear-point? Or did you hold a gun to his back? Forgive me, Marguerite, but I find it difficult to believe that a young lady could force Piers into doing anything he did not wish to do."

Piers's laugh cracked in the middle, betraying the strain he must be feeling under his pose of relaxation. "Do you? Then you're not so well acquainted with Meg as you claim, Chaillot.'"

"In any case," Meg insisted, "I went with him willingly. He can't be prosecuted on that charge."

François gave her a pitying glance. "But of course, you must say so, Marguerite. As you must say that he has done you no harm. Rest assured, the courts will accept your statement for exactly what it is worth. We have no wish to blemish the honor of a lady." He turned to Harry.

"All things considered, a quick marriage might be best, don't you think? In case," he elaborated delicately, "there should be any unfortunate consequences of this escapade. I would offer for the lady myself, but I understand you have a prior claim."

"I certainly do," said Harry, speaking rather thickly. He set down a half-empty glass and rose to his feet. Crossing the veranda, he patted Meg's shoulder. "Always liked you, Megsie. Practically one of the family. Family owes you something now . . . make it up . . . not the way I would have wished it, but . . . mean to say, you'll do me the honor?"

"Of becoming your wife?" Meg inquired. She

wished Harry would take his hand off her shoulder. The afternoon was hot and sticky enough already without his hot, sticky hand on her. Of course she admired Harry tremendously, she always had, but this wasn't the way she had dreamed that he would propose to her. "To remove the stain on my virtue? How noble of you, Harry. What a sacrifice it must be for you to accept spoiled goods."

In a kind of frozen horror she listened to the shrewish words spilling out of her mouth. Harry had made a generous offer and she was carping at him because he couldn't add to his generosity any pretense of loving her. The least she could do was turn him down politely.

"No sacrifice," Harry insisted. The weight of his hand on her shoulder grew heavier. One finger touched her bare neck, entangling itself in the damp curls that tumbled down her back. "You'll forget this . . . unfortunate interlude. Sure we'll be very happy together."

While Piers rots in a French penal colony? No, she mustn't say that. Mustn't lose her temper. Let a woman raise her voice, and men decreed her "hysterical" and used that as an excuse to ignore her entirely. Besides, Harry was trying to do his best, in his bumbling, good-hearted way. How strange that his vaunted diplomatic skills should desert him so completely where she was concerned!

This time Meg collected her thoughts before she spoke. "Harry, I'm honored and flattered by your offer, but I cannot accept it. You don't love me, you know that. And—"

"Actually, Meg, I do." Harry flushed and ran

one finger around the inside of his shirt collar. "Never loved anybody else, anyway."

"Oh, yes?" Secure in her newfound emotional distance, Meg laughed up at Harry and leaned back in the hammock so that he would have to let go of her shoulder. One end of the hammock sagged down a couple of inches with a protesting squeak as she shifted her weight. "What about Claire, and Isabel, and Clementine, and—"

"Different," said Harry. "Not serious." He took Meg by surprise by dropping to one knee before her. It was unkind of her, she thought contritely, to notice that his joints creaked slightly as he did so. After all, a life of diplomatic offices was poor preparation for a wild canoe ride down the upper reaches of the Ogowe River.

"You forget about those girls," he said. "I'll forget about . . . whatever happened up the river. We'll start fresh. Mean it, Meg. All right . . . I admit I never noticed you at home. You've changed in Africa. Grown up, or something. You're a damn fine woman, and I can't think of anybody I'd rather have for my wife."

"Don't you mean," Piers insinuated, "that you can't resist the urge to take a woman away from your little brother?"

"You keep out of this, or I'll make such a mess out of your face the French judges won't know which end of you to question!" Harry swiveled to face Piers, still on one knee, and raised his fist.

Piers crossed his legs and leaned back in his chair. "You and what army? Go on, try it. I've been longing to knock you down ever since you ran your lascivious eyes over Meg."

"Gentlemen! Gentlemen!"

Both brothers ignored François's low-keyed protest. As Harry stood up and advanced on Piers, Meg thought it was high time someone created an effective diversion. Hélène Fanchot would have screamed and fainted. Meg didn't feel able to do that. Her fingers twitched at the knots supporting the hammock as she watched the brothers.

Harry swung first, while Piers was still seated. As he swung, Piers caught his wrist with a motion too quick to follow, and forced his arm down inch by inch with agonizing slowness. "Told you . . . I could take you now . . . big brother!" he grunted between breaths. "Want to come outside and finish this thing properly?"

The hammock's supporting rope came loose and Meg crashed to the floor with an undignified bump. Piers let go of Harry and both brothers plunged to her rescue. Somehow Harry's feet got entangled in a cane footstool and Piers got there first. He picked Meg up bodily while François tsked and fretted over the remains of the hammock.

"Are you hurt, Meg?"

"*Imbéciles*! These natives can't even tie a knot that will hold unless some white man stands over them!" François picked up the hammock and deftly knotted the supporting rope back onto the ring with a quick series of over-and-under turns.

"I'm fine," said Meg reluctantly. Piers didn't put her down, though, but that was perfectly all right with her. As long as he was holding her, he and Harry weren't fighting—and she felt more secure about her decision. Yes, she knew which brother she wanted. How could there have been any doubt? She leaned her head comfortably against Piers's broad chest and watched François's white fingers finishing off the complicated lashing with which he secured the hammock. His hands moved quickly, as if he had tied that complex knot so often that he didn't have to watch what he was doing.

Meg's eyes widened and she pushed against Piers's arms. "Put me down! I have to . . . have to . . ."

Piers let her go without a word of protest. He stepped back with his arms folded while Harry chuckled in the background. For once Meg paid no attention to the byplay between the two of them. All her interest was on the loops of the knot François had just tied so easily, the complex series of turns and twists that she had seen so often in the past few days. On rubber vines cut by disciples of the Crocodile Society . . . on a fetish bag containing parts of a human body . . . on the nets that bound them for ceremonial sacrifice in the Fan village.

And now, the same knot took shape under the fingers of a Frenchman who had been ideally placed, under the guise of friendship with Piers, to fan the sparks of rumor that blackened his reputation.

Too late she saw François watching her, and remembered to disguise her interest in what he was doing. Before she could back away, he had moved between her and Piers. "You recognize that, don't you?"

Meg nodded, her mouth dry. What kind of story would François come up with to explain the coincidence? She thought she knew him well enough to predict that it would be a good story, good enough to fool Harry.

"Where did you see it before?" He still spoke casually, in an undertone, as though the matter could be of interest to no one but the two of them.

Meg shook her head. "Enough places to know what it means. What's your connection with the Crocodile Society? Do they initiate white men?"

She'd hoped, by firing the questions rapidly, to startle François into a revealing answer. She succeeded better than she had intended. One arm flashed out and caught her around the neck, drawing her back against his body while a small snub-nosed pistol appeared in his free hand. Piers and Harry were as taken by surprise as Meg.

"If you value the young lady, don't move." François's voice was as suave as ever, but Meg could feel his hand shaking against her side. The hand that held the pistol. A flash of heat began there, against her lower ribs, and slowly spread upward. For a moment she thought he'd shot her, but there was no pain, no noise. It was only her nerves, exquisitely aware of the threat in François's trembling hand.

"Damery! Back against the porch railing!"

Piers and Harry looked at each other, miming confusion. "Which of us?" As they spoke, Piers moved to his left, Harry to his right.

"Both. Don't try to distract me with these childish games."

"What's the matter with the Frog?" Harry asked, as though the answer were of no great moment.

"Fetish knot," Meg croaked through lips gone suddenly dry. "He tied—"

The tightening of the arm about her neck cut off her breath and speech alike. The world went black around the edges; her chest hurt. When he released her, just enough to let a tiny thread of air through, she was too grateful to do anything but breathe.

Piers looked at her with dawning comprehension. "The hammock? The rubber plants! The Crocodile Society fetish!"

Meg nodded weakly and was punished by an immediate tightening of François's arm. She could still breathe, but just barely.

"I don't understand," Harry complained.

"You never did," Piers told him. "Do you understand that François is going to hurt Meg? It's time to decide which side you're on, big brother."

"The lady will not be hurt if you do exactly as I say," François told them. "You must remain on the veranda, giving your word of honor not to raise the alarm, while Marguerite and I take a little stroll down to the river. I shall inform the captain of the gunboat that the dangerous criminal we are seeking has slipped by us in the night and is making his way to the coast, having abandoned this unfortunate girl to the mercy of the missionaries. We have both something to gain from this bargain, Piers. I shall reach the coast unhindered by your puerile efforts at detection, and you will be allowed to make your escape from French justice in any direction you choose."

"François, you're mad," Meg protested. "You can't possibly drag me onto the boat at gunpoint. Even a French ship's captain would be bound to notice something wrong."

"I don't need to," François told her. "You will have been overcome by your sufferings and will be carried unconscious onto the boat. During the journey downriver, you will regretfully remain in a delirious fever. I have the means to make sure of that."

"A little present from JuJu Jake's collection of native drugs," Piers guessed. "Chaillot, you're stupid as well as mad. If you hadn't threatened Meg, I would never have suspected you of being mixed up with the Crocodile Society."

"No, you probably would not," agreed François. "But she would. The young lady is too clever an antagonist for me to risk letting her go free—until, of course, I have reached freedom myself. There are places outside the jurisdiction of France where a man with sufficient savings may live quite comfortably. Who knows? Perhaps by the time we reach our destination, Mademoiselle Marguerite will feel friendlier toward me."

Harry had been looking back and forth between Piers and François during this exchange. "What do you suspect him of, Piers?"

"I'm not quite sure yet," Piers admitted, "but it must be bad, or he wouldn't be taking this desperate way out just because a girl noticed something funny about the way he ties knots. And once we get Meg free of him, I guarantee you I'll find out the rest of the story."

"Ah, but you won't free the charming mademoiselle," François said softly. "In fact, I think it is time for you to make your farewells to her. Make no disturbance, please. It is so easy for people to be accidentally hurt in such a melee." The barrel of his pistol, pressed against Meg's side, underlined his threat.

Harry looked at Piers and nodded slightly. "The man's right. We can't risk Meg getting hurt in some kind of *Red Indian fracas*."

The last words were spoken with a peculiar emphasis that brought Meg's head up sharply, her heart thumping with excitement. A blue spark lit in the depths of Piers's eyes. "Apache captive, eh? Yes, but wait a moment . . ."

François backed up, edging along the veranda railing and dragging Meg with him. When they reached the steps, Piers nodded at Meg. Her knees buckled under her and she went down as a deadweight, dragging François's arm down with her chin. He cursed, tried to lift her, and was bowled down the steps by a concerted rush from Piers and Harry. The pistol went skidding harmlessly into the red dust in the center of the path.

Meg slumped on the bottom step and stared at the gleaming barrel, winking with the last rays of the setting sun. From the corner of her eye she could just see three bodies rolling over and over on the dusty path, grunting and thumping energetically. She wondered vaguely why it was taking Piers and Harry so long to subdue François. Should she do something to help them? After thinking it over for a while, she ambled over to pick up François's pistol.

When she turned to use the pistol, she found it was no longer necessary. The struggling knot of three bodies had frozen like a complicated set of statuary. François was stretched out on the ground, breathing hard as a trickle of blood ran from his nose. Piers sat on his chest and Harry on his ankles, grinning at each other. Their yellow hair hung down over their foreheads, and they had impressive matching black eyes.

"I'm disappointed in you two," Meg said. "Two Englishmen ought to be able to sit on one Frenchman without getting punched in the face."

"Chaillot didn't do that," Piers exclaimed indignantly. "Harry hit me."

"Accident, old chap." Harry grinned. "Just as I'm sure it was entirely accidental when your elbow collided with my face."

"Entirely."

Meg smiled to herself. So that explained why it had taken them so long to get François under control. Piers and Harry had used the occasion to work off their own bad feelings. "If you're quite through squabbling," she said, "I'd like to hear François's explanation for all this."

François glared up at her. "Why should I tell you anything?" he mumbled through a rapidly swelling split lip.

"Because I'm going to twist your dirty French head off if you don't talk." Piers seized François by the ears and gave a preparatory twist as he spoke.

"Because we might make a deal," Harry proposed more temperately. "We don't have you arrested if you drop the charges against Piers. Assuming, of course, that you don't tell us you've done anything a gentleman can't countenance."

François nodded. "I think I understand. Rest assured that I won't tell you anything that would make it impossible for you to release me honorably."

"You shouldn't use words like that," Piers growled. "You don't know what they mean. And I thought you were my friend!"

"I was," François protested. "Am. Why do you think you weren't killed when you interrupted the first factory burning? I have protected you to the limits of my power, *mon cher* Piers, and is this the gratitude you show me?"

"Suppose you tell us exactly what you've been up to," Piers suggested, "and I'll decide just how grateful I feel."

François's dark eyes blinked rapidly and Meg

had the impression of wheels whirring around in his head. No doubt he was trying to decide how to suppress the most damning parts of his story.

"Well?" Harry shifted his weight slightly so as not to break François's ankles while he was thinking.

"If you'd let me sit up," François suggested in his turn, "I could think better."

"Piers?"

"I don't care if he thinks," Piers grumbled, "and I don't see why the slimy bastard can't talk lying down."

François regarded him through slitted dark eyes. "You really don't approve of anybody's threatening Marguerite, do you? I see that was a mistake. Strange, I should have thought your brother the one to object more strongly. After all, he has been trying to protect the lady, while all you have done, as far as I can tell, is to drag her through the bush backwards."

An inarticulate growl came from Piers's throat and his big hands fastened around the Frenchman's neck.

"Piers! Stop it this minute!" Meg prodded him in the ribs with the pointed toe of the too-small shoes lent to her by Madame Molinier. "Can't you see he's only trying to get you to assault him?"

"Wouldn't have to try very hard," Piers complained, but he released the Frenchman's neck before he turned positively blue. "Be a pleasure."

"It would also," said Meg sharply, "complicate matters immeasurably. If you three start brawling again, François might escape and we'd never find out what's been going on here!"

Piers inspected his bruised knuckles with a

slight smile. "Oh, no. He wouldn't escape. But you may have a point, Meg. I suppose he can talk better before I mash him to a pulp."

"No mashing," croaked François, "or I don't talk."

"Oh, for heaven's sake, get off the man's chest!" Meg snapped. "Can't you see he can hardly breathe? And I want to find out what he's been up to, even if you don't care."

With some grumbling from Piers, they worked out an arrangement whereby François was allowed to sit up in the chair he had originally occupied on the veranda, his ankles lashed to the chair legs by Harry's belt and the chair itself tied to the veranda railing by a length of bush rope.

"Much pleasanter," said François. "If I could trouble you to refill my glass, Damery?"

The brothers looked at one another with slightly nonplussed expressions.

"Either one of you can do it," François added. "It really doesn't matter to me."

"You've got a damned cheek," Harry informed him. "Straight brandy, or do you want it with soda?"

Meg's impatience grew while Harry solemnly mixed drinks and handed them all around.

"Ah, this is better!" sighed François. Despite the rapidly darkening bruises on his face and the belt lashing his ankles to the chair, he seemed to have recovered all his civilized manners intact. They might, Meg thought, have been four friends sitting out on the porch chatting about the perils of upriver travel and the difficulty of training the Africans to be good servants. "I begin to feel like myself again. If only one of you gentlemen had some decent cigars, we should be quite comfortable. There is just one small point I should like to clear up. How did the three of you know exactly what to do when Piers gave the signal to attack me? I thought my English was quite good, but I did not hear you making any arrangements."

Harry chuckled. "These two brats used to play at Red Indians as children," he told François. "We—they, rather—had one favorite game in which Meg was an Apache captive and Piers rescued her. Er . . . they occasionally talked me into playing with them."

"Harry was, of course, much older and wiser and not very interested in our childish games," Piers corroborated with a wicked glance at his older brother. "Besides, he was angry with me that summer because he thought I'd broken his new velocipede."

Harry's fists doubled up. "You did, you little sneak, and don't attempt to deny it!"

Piers waved one hand airily. "It was a cheap toy at best. How was I to know it would fall apart in my hands the first time I took it out?"

"You could at least have asked my permission!"

"*Will* you two stop letting François distract you? By the time you've finished squabbling about your childhood quarrels, he'll have had time to make up an entire three-volume novel!"

Piers and Harry glanced sheepishly at Meg and then down at the floor.

"I don't think it is really a childhood rivalry that animates the gentlemen," said François with a smile. "You must be prepared to take some of the blame yourself, my lovely Marguerite."

Meg felt the heat rising to her cheeks at François's insinuations. It was true, she hadn't quite settled the matter of Harry's proposal when all this other trouble started. But couldn't that wait? "Never mind about us. We want to hear what you've been doing with the Crocodile Society."

François sighed, attempted to cross his legs, and gave up when the creaking leather of Harry's belt impeded the movement. "Oh, nothing so very much. I only created it."

Twenty-Two

All three of his listeners jerked upright, and half the brandy and soda in Piers's hand splashed over his knees. "You did *what*?"

"It seemed like a good idea at the time," said François, raising one hand as if to ward off attack. "*Mon Dieu*! It *was* a good idea. It's just that things have gotten a little out of hand since then. To tell the truth, I am not entirely unhappy to enlist your help in stopping the menace that the Crocodile Society has become. Somebody must discredit that old man—JuJu Jake, you English call him—before he perverts my entire society into a fetish and murder organization."

"Oh, you don't need to worry—" Piers began. Meg joggled his elbow and made him spill his remaining brandy.

"No, you certainly don't need to worry about that, François," she interrupted before Piers could finish his sentence. She made her eyes wide and innocent. "My goodness, we'll certainly do everything we can to help you get him under control! Do you think you can tell us how it all came about, though? I mean, it sounds so strange—for a white man to gain the trust of the natives and even start a new secret society!"

"I think I can make a guess as to *how*, anyway," said Piers. He had taken Harry's handkerchief and was mopping at the brandy stains on his trousers. "I was wondering how the old witch doctor got hold of phosphorus. You wouldn't have been supplying him, by any chance?"

François nodded. "It fitted so neatly with their legends about a spirit who walked in the night and glowed with an unearthly light," he explained. "That was what gave me the idea originally, hearing the legends. At first I thought I would do it myself, but you are right. A white man could never have pulled it off. I needed a tool, and that old drunk with his spirit tales and his drunken hallucinations seemed like the ideal one. He had the knowledge of the people, and I had the phosphorus to give him credibility." He gave a regretful sigh and sipped at his brandy. "Too much credibility, as it turned out. . . ."

"But *why*?" Meg burst out.

"It seemed like a good idea at the time," François repeated with a defensive shrug. "You should understand, *ma belle*. Do you remember the day you arrived in Lambarene, when I escorted you to see Piers? We walked through desolate patches of bush that had been thriving with rubber vines a few years earlier. Remember my telling you that the stupid natives were killing off their own source of livelihood?"

Meg nodded. "Yes. The way they tap the rubber vines kills them, and so the bush is depleted and they have to go farther and farther back to collect rubber, and then it passes through more and more middlemen on the way to the trader, and the price becomes higher. You said that soon it would not be profitable for any traders on the Ogowe to buy rubber at all, unless someone could teach the natives to tap the rubber vines without killing them."

François nodded. "And as for teaching them. . . !" He lifted one hand and let it fall back down onto his lap, palm open. "Have you ever tried to change one minute detail of native life? No, you've not been here long enough, any of you." His bright black glance flickered over the three of them, imperceptibly shutting them out. "Eugène Molinier would understand the difficulty of what I attempted, and why I turned to . . . other means of persuasion."

"The difficulty, perhaps, but not the means," said Piers. "But thank you for mentioning him, François. I think perhaps Monsieur Molinier should hear this little story."

He disappeared through the open door that led to the long hallway running through the mission, and came back a few minutes later with the missionary and another man whom Meg did not recognize. The stranger was dressed in a French Army uniform.

François paled at the sight of the new arrival and licked his lips nervously. "I did not bargain for talking before officials."

"You are in no position to bargain at all," Piers reminded him. "If you want us to help you put down the Crocodile Society, and if you don't want us to bring charges concerning certain incidents which occurred a few minutes ago—"

The uniformed man stirred. "Incidents?" he asked in a softly accented voice.

"Of no concern, Colonel. Or rather, of far less concern than Monsieur Chaillot's story."

The colonel's gaze glanced over the disheveled men, Meg with her damp hair flying loose about her shoulders, and the trampled leaves and scattered dust in the path below the veranda. "*Peut-être*. Pray continue, Monsieur Chaillot."

François shrugged his shoulders. "Why not? It's all over anyway. If I hadn't lost my head just now—if you weren't so cursed sharp-eyed, Marguerite . . ." He broke off his half-conscious lamentations and shrugged again. "No matter. It was over in any case. This matter of the Crocodile Society had gotten out of my control. Believe me, I had agonized over whether or not to alert the authorities. It is almost a relief," he said with a crooked smile, "to have the decision taken out of my hands."

The colonel and Monsieur Molinier had leaned forward at the mention of the Crocodile Society, but neither of them interrupted François.

He went on to explain what Piers and Meg had already half-guessed: that when his attempts at educating the natives failed, he had enlisted the help of JuJu Jake to start a new secret society which might control them by fear. First the old witch doctor made a number of appearances in his guise as the glowing spirit, using the phosphorus supplied by François; then, after he had the requisite number of converts, he taught the proper method of harvesting rubber as a fetish matter, hedged about with fetish bags and invocations to the spirits and always performed with the special knot which was one of the trademarks of the Crocodile Society.

"It wasn't just teaching, was it?" Piers remarked at this point. "There've been a lot of sacrifices to the Crocodile God this year. Ask Eugène Molinier how many half-eaten bodies he's untied from stakes in the river since this Crocodile Society began. Were they all people who wouldn't learn the new way of harvesting rubber? Or were some of them just stupid Mpongwe tribesmen who wanted to stay loyal to their old gods?"

François's eyelids drooped slightly, giving his face a shuttered look. "I know nothing of any sacrifices. I never instructed the witch doctor to murder anyone. My only aim was to educate the natives and to help preserve the economy of the region."

"Mmm. Of course," Piers agreed. "After all, if you'd incited old Jake to murder, you might be liable with him before the courts of France. Well, we won't press that point. I'd be more interested in hearing just how this laudable interest in agricultural economics led to the burning down of my factory."

François swallowed hard, asked for some more brandy, and talked around that issue for some time. For some reason, he said, the Crocodile Society had decided not to allow any traders other than Chaillot Père et Fils to operate on the Ogowe.

"Some reason," Piers drawled. "Your idea?"

"Perhaps Jake started this crusade against the English traders out of loyalty to me, as the co-founder of the society," François said smoothly. "I regret that I cannot tell you his precise motives. You had better ask him yourself."

He stuck to this remarkably thin story, refusing to acknowledge that in his greed he had used the Crocodile Society to put the other traders out of business. However, as he went on explaining the details of the operation, none of François

Chaillot's audience doubted that the inspiration had been his from start to finish.

"I sincerely wish you had not been such a fool as to come up to Talagouga to defend your factory, Piers. But what could I do? I followed you to save your life, but I was afraid that you had seen me. How could I explain my presence at such a time, when you had been warned most secretly? You will understand that it was absolutely necessary to discredit any evidence you might give."

Under pressure from Piers, François admitted that he had arranged for Piers to be found reeking with brandy on the morning after the burning of the factory. He had also used the power of the Crocodile Society to produce witnesses who would swear that Piers had burned down the factory himself and that he had been abusing his native laborers for some time.

"You casually ruined his life just to protect yourself!" Meg could hardly credit it. And what was worse, François didn't look the least bit ashamed.

"His testimony would have ruined my life. At that time I still felt I could control the Crocodile Society."

"And now?"

François put on a mournful expression. "Alas, subsequent incidents have shown me how wrong I was. I was shocked and horrified when I learned about the explosion which destroyed Piers's other factory at Lambarene. That, too, must have been the work of the Crocodile Society, though I doubt anything can ever be proved in the matter."

He brought out this last sentence with a smug little smile that convinced Meg of only one thing:

François was sure no one could prove any connection between him and the man who'd set the factory afire. Doubtless that had been another Crocodile Society member, now vanished forever into the bush. There would be no way to prove that François had known of the gunpowder stored under the factory, or that he had timed the fire to blow up Piers along with the rest of the contents of the building.

The unnamed colonel who had come up the river with the gunboat had a face as gray and hard as stone. "I think we have heard enough," he said. He stood and bowed formally first to Meg, then to Monsieur Molinier. "I will not trouble your hospitality further, *monsieur.* My soldiers will remove this miserable specimen and place him where he belongs—in the prison at the coast."

"Wait a minute!" François yelped. He turned to Piers and Harry. "That's not fair! You said you wouldn't press charges if I cleared you, Damery!"

"I," said the colonel with sublime simplicity, "made no such promise. Will you untie your prisoner, Monsieur Damery? I have no wish to take the chair." Stepping to the edge of the veranda, he gave a shrill whistle. At once a file of French soldiers came hurrying up the path from the river.

"I've confessed to nothing," François insisted. "You can prove nothing. I acted for the best. It's not my fault things got a little out of hand!"

As the soldiers called by the colonel took him away, his last words were, "You'll be sorry! It was a *good* idea! Just wait till you try to teach the damned natives anything. . . ."

"Monsieur Damery," said the colonel, bowing to Piers, "I must apologize for my countryman. Pray rest assured that, whatever the outcome of the case against him, there will be no charges against you on any account whatsoever."

Piers bowed and made an appropriately grateful reply in fluent French.

" 'Fraid there won't be much of a case, though," Harry put in, frowning. "He's too slippery to admit to anything you can try him for. And we didn't tell him, but old JuJu Jake is dead."

"And the other Crocodile Society members," Piers put in, "always kill themselves when captured."

The colonel smiled blandly. "If they can get at their poison in time. The man who set your factory on fire at Lambarene," he said, "was not so fortunate. We have him in custody now. It should be illuminating to put him in a cell together with Monsieur Chaillot, do you not agree?"

"My God," said Piers. "Illuminating, yes, but possibly fatal."

"Have no fear," said the colonel with a benign smile. "My men and I shall be observing the meeting closely. As we observed your meeting with Monsieur Chaillot this afternoon. You were never in any danger of arrest, Monsieur Damery, and this charming young lady," he added with a slight bow toward Meg, "was in no danger of the coercion which Monsieur Chaillot threatened. You were all under close observation the entire time."

With a military click of his heels, he straightened and marched down the path in the wake of his prisoner, leaving a stunned silence on the veranda behind him.

Meg took a long shaky breath and felt the tight

seams of her borrowed dress creaking under the strain. "Efficient, the French," she said, looking up at the ceiling.

"Not honorable, though, what?" Harry put in. "Listening behind doors. Not the way an English officer would behave."

"Thank God," said Piers with a smile, "we're not in an English crown colony."

"Can't trust these damned Frogs. Oh, sorry, Molinier . . ."

But Monsieur Molinier had tactfully slipped away, leaving the three English to resolve their personal relationships by themselves. Meg glanced from Harry's blunt, confident features to Piers's strained face, pale under his tan, and wished there were some way to get the two of them apart. What she had to say to Harry should not be heard by Piers, and vice versa. Perhaps she could stave off the coming confrontation by continuing to dissect what she had begun to think of as *l'affaire Chaillot*.

"I rather suspect that's the end of the Crocodile Society, don't you?" she said, slipping into the nearest chair. She stretched her legs out in a most unladylike manner and kicked off her borrowed slippers. "With no phosphorus and no leader, the thing should fall apart quickly enough."

"Mmm." Harry stroked his chin. "A little encouragement might be in order. This Frog missionary, Molinier, seems to be pretty strong in preaching against the cult societies. I think I'll make a contribution to his mission."

Meg had her doubts about the effectiveness of missionary persuasion on African customs. However, she thought, there was more than one way to skin a cat. "I may make a small contribution myself."

"I don't think—" Piers began.

"Not directly to the mission," Meg interrupted him. "I thought I'd ask you to order a box of fireworks from England. Isn't there a legitimate tribal society that upholds tribal law?"

"Ikuku. Yes." Piers began to laugh. "I should imagine they've been having a hard time maintaining prestige against the competition of old JuJu Jake and his glowing spirits. Yes, a box of fireworks should do a lot to restore their image. You're a damned clever girl, Megsie! But you'll allow me to pay for the fireworks."

Bending over Meg's chair, he put one arm around her waist and pulled her halfway up into his arms, at the same time kissing her in a manner that left her both breathless and badly scratched by his unshaven chin.

"Just a minute, Piers." Harry tapped him on the shoulder and Piers broke off the kiss to glance around at his brother with an irritated look.

"This ain't a dance, big brother. You can't cut in."

"I'm not playing," said Harry. "I'm telling you to put down the woman I intend to marry."

Piers released Meg so suddenly that she fell back into her chair with a jarring thump. Standing to face Harry, he balanced lightly on half-bent knees and inspected the knuckles of his right hand. "You might have a little trouble proving your claim. I was there first."

"I'm willing to overlook that," said Harry. Nonetheless, he prudently backed off a few paces before continuing. "What's more, I'm willing to admit that in certain matters I may have been overly hasty in coming to a conclusion."

"Hasty?" Piers's laugh had an undertone of

bitterness that hurt Meg. "You snapped up Chaillot's bait faster than a hungry alligator takes a woman carrying water. You jumped to your conclusions like a startled frog on a lily pad. You—"

"All right, all *right.*" Harry held up both hands, palms out. "I get the general idea. And I admit it seems that you are, after all, innocent of the worst charges that François Chaillot raised against you. But the evidence seemed strong enough at the time, particularly in view of your past exploits. I don't think you can blame me for assuming that you were simply continuing your career of disgracing the family in any manner possible."

"Oh, can't I?" murmured Piers. He blew on his knuckles and took a step toward Harry.

"Particularly since you have done your damnedest to disgrace Meg as well as yourself," Harry went on.

Meg rose from her chair and threw her full weight on Piers's forearm. She could feel her nails digging into his tensed muscles; she didn't think he felt anything except the weight that held him back from hitting his brother.

"It's all right, Meg," said Harry. "You don't need to defend me. I'm rather looking forward to this fight. And when it's over, my love, you will come away with me. We can be quietly married as soon as I can find an English minister, and this entire unfortunate affair will be forgotten."

Still clinging to Piers's arm, Meg took a deep breath. "But, Harry, I don't—"

"I know," Harry interrupted. "You don't believe I love you. I can't blame you. Took me long enough to realize it. But believe me, Meg—and nothing was ever more true—I do love you. I need you. I can't let you go out of my life again. I didn't know how much you meant to me until I saw you here in Africa, sunburned, half-naked, in danger, needing *me*. You always seemed so cool and self-sufficient at home. Now I see that you need me to protect you—and I will, Meg. All my life. So that's settled." He reached one hand confidently toward her.

For just one second Meg was torn. Here was all she'd ever dreamed of, the golden god of her childhood fantasies offering to cherish and protect her, offering her the love she'd ached for. How could she be turning him down?

She shook her head. "No." The word was out before she was consciously aware of her decision.

Harry gave a slightly embarrassed laugh, his face reddening above his tight high shirt collar. "Come, come, Meg. You can't expect a man to come up with a poetic proposal in front of his little brother. Get rid of Piers, and then I'll go down on my knees and repeat the thing formally if you like. But don't play games with me. You know there's nothing you want more than to marry me. Now I want it too. Besides," he added with the air of one clinching an irrefutable argument, "what else is there for you to do? After the way you spent the last few days, no man in the world would believe you're still innocent."

"They might," said Piers, "refrain from saying so. If they didn't want their teeth knocked down their throats."

"Oh? And are you always going to be there to defend Meg's dubious honor?"

"Starting with you—"

"Piers, *no*!" Just in time, Meg held down his right arm again. He looked down at her in some surprise.

"I do," he told her mildly, "have another hand." His left fist shot out and knocked Harry over the veranda railing to land with a crash in some pink flowering bush below them. From Harry's anguished yelps, Meg concluded that the bush had thorns. Long ones.

"That won't solve anything, Piers!" Harry struggled out of the bush and vaulted up over the splintered railing. Meg thrust herself between the brothers.

"Harry, cut it out. Piers, if you hit Harry again I shall be seriously annoyed with you. Now, sit down. Both of you. I'm not going to be an excuse for you two to fight it out. Harry, I'm not going to marry you." Meg felt her hands twisting together in the old nervous gesture. She forced them apart and raised her eyes to meet Harry's puzzled blue gaze.

"I don't love you, Harry, and I don't want to live with you. I may have thought I did at one time, but now I know better."

"Don't be shy, Meg," said Harry, reaching for her with a smile. "What do you know about love? I'll teach you to love me—and you can forget all about whatever bad experiences you had in the jungle," he added with a venomous glance at Piers. "Besides, what else—"

"What else am I going to do?" Meg sighed. She looked at Piers, who had obeyed her command to sit down. A muscle was throbbing in his jaw, and he looked sick under his tan and the golden prickles of his beard, but he said nothing.

A week earlier Meg would have been unable to go on without a word from Piers. She would have stood there torturing herself with self-doubt. What if he regretted his words of love to her?

What if all he really wanted was to be free of her? What if she was nothing more than an unwelcome obligation to him?

Now, she prayed, she understood him and herself better. Within the limits of his patience, he was trying to stay out of the way until she decided whether or not she really wanted to go with Harry, her childhood idol. He might break his self-imposed boundaries to the extent of knocking Harry down, but he wouldn't try to charm her out of her decision.

Trembling inwardly, praying that she understood Piers as well as she thought she did, Meg took three long steps over to him and sat down in his lap. His arms went about her with a convulsive grip, as a drowning man might clutch a floating spar, and she leaned her head down into the curve between his neck and shoulder with a great sense of relief and homecoming.

Harry's shocked gasp was echoed by a French exclamation from the door. Meg recognized Hélène Fanchot's voice. She also understood the words.

"It doesn't matter," she told Piers, feeling him tense beneath her. "It's true. I always wanted to be a forward hussy."

He relaxed slightly, but not enough to let her go. "And I always wanted to marry one." But there was a trailing doubt in his voice. "Meg . . . you're sure? Harry's got a great future ahead of him. And I . . . well, you've seen what I am. I'd rather risk my neck exploring the Ogowe than sit on my butt and make a fortune trading with the natives. But for you," he said with determination, "for you I can do it."

"Become a sober settled citizen? Open the factory six days a week, go to church on Sunday, and wait for other men to bring back tales of what's in the interior?" Meg kissed his bristly cheek.

Piers gulped. "Yes. If that's what you want."

"And what," Meg asked him, "if I'd rather be dumped out of a canoe in the middle of the rapids than lead that sort of life? What if I say I won't marry you unless you promise to take me back up the river as soon as we've finished off the Crocodile Society?"

Piers's arms tightened around her until she thought a rib would crack under the strain. "I daresay something could be arranged. How about after dinner?"

"Leave after dark?" Meg was taken aback. But perhaps Piers was testing her desire to go exploring with him. "All right, if that's what you want."

"No, stupid. Get married after dinner. Molinier can do it. I'm not waiting around till we scare up an English minister."

"Mmm." Meg burrowed into the comfortable solidity of Piers's body, feeling his six feet of bone and muscle tense and responsive under her. "What shall we do until dinner?"

"I daresay," Piers repeated softly into the fine masses of her hair, "something can be arranged."

PASSION RIDES THE PAST

- ☐ **TO LOVE A ROGUE by Valerie Sherwood.** Raile Cameron, a renegade gunrunner, lovingly rescues the sensuous and charming Lorraine London from indentured servitude in Revolutionary America. Lorraine fights his wild and teasing embraces, as they sail the stormy Caribbean seas, until finally she surrenders to fiery passion. (400518—$4.50)
- ☐ **WINDS OF BETRAYAL by June Lund Shiplett.** She was caught between two passionate men—and her own wild desire. Beautiful Lizette Kolter deeply loves her husband Bain Kolter, but the strong and virile free-booter, Sancho de Cordoba, seeks revenge on Bain by making her his prisoner of love. She was one man's lawful wife, but another's lawless desire. (150376—$3.95)
- ☐ **HIGHLAND SUNSET by Joan Wolf.** She surrendered to the power of his passion . . . and her own undeniable desire. When beautiful, dark-haired Vanessa Maclan met Edward Romney, Earl of Linton, she told herself she should hate this strong and handsome English lord. But it was not hate but hunger that this man of so much power and passion woke within the Highland beauty. (400488—$3.95)

Buy them at your local bookstore or use this convenient coupon for ordering.

NEW AMERICAN LIBRARY,
P.O. Box 999, Bergenfield, New Jersey 07621

Please send me the books I have checked above. I am enclosing $_________ (please add $1.00 to this order to cover postage and handling). Send check or money order—no cash or C.O.D.'s. Prices and numbers subject to change without notice.

Name ____

Address ______________________________________

City ____________ State ____________ Zip Code _________

Allow 4-6 weeks for delivery.
This offer is subject to withdrawal without notice.